THE DAWN OF MERCY

A NOVEL

MICHAEL R. JOENS

MOODY PRESS

CHICAGO

ISBN: 0-8024-1711-6

1 3 5 7 9 10 8 6 4 2

Printed in the United States of America

To my dad,
who at times was hard as steel, at times playful.
Who always loved me, I see now through the years.
I love you, Papa.

1

My father never seemed to have the right tools for the job: whether to fix the old Fordson tractor, or to mend any one of the innumerable ailments of the ranch house, or to raise each of his four children, of whom I was the eldest and, it seemed from my father's perspective, most in need of repair.

He was a big man, my father, carved out of a granite monolith of soul and will and fire, a rock that rose better than six feet off the ground, weighing a good two hundred pounds or more, of which there was no equal upon the earth. He was larger than life—like a Greek champion or a giant. At least he seemed so to Billy and me, and we were like grasshoppers in our sight. There were times, as a young boy, when I thought sure that the sun rose and set upon his broad shoulders, when the moon and planets orbited about his windswept brow. Indeed, sometimes I still think that they do.

But that's the grasshopper in me talking.

From Billy's and my bedroom window on the second floor of the white frame house in which three generations of Hochreiters were born, I watched him pacing before the old Fordson next to the windmill, some fifty yards away, pausing only to fiddle with something, to jiggle or pull on a portion of the tractor's entrails; watched the Montana sun, in the season of its strength, rising over the hills in the east like a great brazen hammer, all shiny and terrible and determined to beat upon that rock.

Papa pushed back his brown fedora—black with sweat around the band—and was scratching his head as he surveyed the Fordson, and every so often his head jerked to one side and a stream of brown juice spattered into the dirt. Then he took hold of the back of his neck and held it, while he continued to stare hard at the tractor, no doubt thinking how he might beat it. There was a rugged serenity that enveloped the man that, in spite of his many contradictions, moved me to a kind of awe.

Behind him the barn was standing on its last legs and looking over the steading solemnly, eyeing the house with its single eye, which stared unblinking from over the bay. Bleached now to a pinkish gray by the sun, the remnant of its paint peeling, its roof sagging from sixty Montana winters and groaning every now and then when a breeze picked up, it looked as though it might give up the ghost any moment.

In the distance, beyond the rise where my ancestors were gathered beneath some live oaks, I could just see the silver gleam of the Yellowstone as it snaked its way through the ancient buttes across the prairie to the foothills of the Beartooths rearing in the west. And rushing to meet it was the Stillwater, with its cool banks of aspens that lined the edge of the ranch, their silver-dollar leaves glittering in the river breezes.

I lost sight of Papa for a minute or so as a plume of gray dust, coming up the road in the distance, caught my attention. I knew it to be Sy and Jimbo, our two ranch hands, who were full-blooded Crow Indians.

Papa exited the barn through a ground cover of chickens, looked up the road, and shook his head. He was carrying a set of plugs to replace the four that were always fouling, and a handful of screwdrivers, all of which I knew the Fordson would reject. There was no appeasing it. Papa had fought with it since the day we bought it from the Widow Seagram back in '28, like Jacob and the Angel, though it seemed unlikely that he would prevail.

A curse jumped into the air, causing a jolt in the barometric pressure. I returned my gaze to the tractor as the screwdrivers were flung one at a time to the ground in quick succession, each followed by another curse, until Papa was out of screwdrivers. However, there was no end to the expletives as he stormed back to the barn.

An ache sounded in my chest. I sighed deeply. *O God, what am I going to do? He's gonna kill me.*

We'd been on a collision course for five months now, ever since I got the letter. Papa knew nothing of the letter, since I hadn't told him about it yet. Still, he knew something was amiss. He had a way of knowing things, as a prophet knows things, his prophet's eye ranging about, looking for the cause and every so often lighting upon mine, holding, then peering intently before moving on.

The signs had been clear, every morning a reddening band flushing the horizon, heralding an approaching storm, and there was no way for me to clear out of its path. The storm would take me, I was certain, but what I couldn't know then was that, before the end of summer, it would also take nearly every one of us in Stillwater County.

I looked down at the letter in my hands, the edges smooth from my oft handling.

Shaking my head, I folded it carefully and put it away in the top drawer of my dresser. I would tell him today, I determined. Yes, today.

I looked over at Kate. She smiled encouragingly at me from her silver frame that sat upon the dresser, the frame angled in such a way that I could see her face from my bed, that pretty smile of hers wrapped in a red bow that tasted of wild strawberries and those pretty hazel eyes that followed me around the room. The horses in the stables whickered. I glanced out the window as Sy and Jimbo swung the pickup wide of the tractor, scattering chickens, and backfired to a stop next to the barn. They climbed out, and Sy called, "Hello, Mr. Henry . . . it is good day, no?" as Papa came out of the barn with another selection of tools.

He towered over the two hands. From a distance they seemed like children next to him, though they were full-grown men, and I listened as Papa talked with them. They were late back from some errand, it appeared, and he redressed them—Indians weren't known for their clock-watching—but they nodded and smiled amiably.

And then Sy said, "It's all right, Mr. Henry, it won't happen again," and Jimbo agreed. "Yes, Mr. Henry, that's right."

Now Papa knew better, and Sy and Jimbo knew better, but every day their presence seemed to take the edge off Papa's foul humor and got him off on a better foot. And so a daily truce was drawn, the hatchet buried. Then he would brief them on the remainder of the day's chores, and Sy and Jimbo would leave for the stables to saddle their horses and head out to the stock, and Papa would pick up where he left off, pacing or scratching or spitting. There was a certain comfort in the regularity of the event, like the rhythmic progressions of a grandfather clock or the turning of seasons, but that's my German half telling.

I fiddled aimlessly with the seam of my trousers for another five minutes, watching my father wrestle the Angel. A cool, rich aroma of dawn wafted into my bedroom through the window, like the breath of God off the river. I breathed it in deeply, held onto it for a moment, then blew it out hard. A train whistled in the distance, calling me from my reverie. I still had another harvest to put up, I thought, watching Papa. Just a few more weeks. Come September I would be set free. Smiling, I turned and left the room, with Kate's twinkling eyes following me to the door.

As I came downstairs, the wooden treads groaned under my weight, and the staring eyes of dead Hochreiters, frozen in sepia, followed my descent from their oval perches on the right-hand wall, as they glared at me with German austerity, each visage, particularly around the eyes, bearing a haunting familiarity to the one preceding it.

Descending the other wall were the McInnises, Mama's family, every one of them smiling his Irish blessings upon me. I often thought of the left wall as Mount Gerizim and the right as Mount Ebal—the walls of the blessings and curses—and the stairwell running through them was the valley of decision. But that was my theological bent showing.

As I drew alongside Bapa Otto, my great-grandfather on Papa's side, I paused, drawn to the fierce look in his eyes. He was sitting ramrod straight in a ladder-back chair, wearing a black suit and a white shirt buttoned to a collar that was pinching his neck, and behind him was Nana Gertie, her hair pulled violently back off her forehead and her left hand gripping a King James Bible with ecclesiastical fervor. Otto was holding a wide-brimmed black hat across one knee, and clutched proudly against the other was his rifle. Their combined glare convicted me of myriad sins.

My eyes crept to the rifle, drawn to it by some morbid fascination, like a child peering into a casket at a dead face—horrified, yet at the same time compelled to look at it. It was a Winchester Model '95, a lever-action, chambered in .45- 70—Teddy Roosevelt's favorite model, Papa once told me. However, the sight of the rifle never ceased to send a shiver of dread up my spine, with its history and all. I took the remaining steps two at a time.

As I entered the kitchen, the smells were warm and friendly: pancakes, bacon and sausages sizzling, and coffee aroma, all mixed together by a morning breeze sifting through the back screen door. Jenny and Trout were manning their battle stations like veterans and seemed unaware that I had arrived.

I walked over to the stove where Mama was ladling some batter onto the skillet. She was humming "When the Roll Is Called Up Yonder"—which was the featured hymn Sunday—and as she angled her cheek to me, I leaned over and kissed it.

"Mornin', Mama."

"Good morning, Tyler, honey—I see you've washed the creek mud off your face." She smiled at me generously. "You and Billy get that calf out of the bog all right?"

"For the third time this week," I replied. "I got no use for a calf that don't have a lick of sense."

"She's just trying her legs out on the world," Mama said. "Some just don't fancy the ways of the herd."

"Well, the mountain lions can take her for all I care," I grunted.

"Bet Old Lucifer'll get her!" Trout chimed in.

Mama ignored the comment. "You hungry?"

"You bet."

"Have some coffee while these cakes fluff up. They'll just be a minute."

"They smell good," I said, bending over the skillet and watching the bubbles form little craters.

Mama looked at me and smiled, but I could see that the corners of her mouth had tightened.

"Are you going to tell him after breakfast, Tyler?" she asked.

I reached over the skillet and grabbed the pot off the back burner and poured a cup of coffee. It was black and hot and steamed up into my face as I took a sip. I could feel Mama's eyes on me. "I thought I might wait until Billy and I got back from town."

"You've been putting it off."

"I'll tell him when I get back from town, Mama."

"You can't put it off anymore, Tyler. You just can't. If you don't tell him today, I will. I can see how it's tearing you up inside." She gazed at me for a moment longer, then looked away, shaking her head. "It's a strain on me as well, I confess. You know I can't keep things from your father."

Though she tried to hide it, I knew she was churning inside. Her eyes had glistened and were red around the edges, and that added to the ache in my chest. "I'll tell him, Mama. I promise."

Presently the screen door banged open, and my brother Billy blew into the kitchen. "I'm so hungry I could eat hog slop!" he roared as he grabbed his chair and jerked it under him. The legs scraped against the linoleum. "Those for me, Mama?"

"These are for Tyler," Mama replied, composing herself. "You can have the next stack."

Billy let out a melodramatic groan, as if he had just been sentenced to death.

"Let him have them, Mama," I said. "I'll just finish my coffee first."

Mama shook her head as she scraped each pancake onto a plate next to a half-dozen sausages. Then she carried them over to the ravenous seventeen year old.

"Is Papa coming in for breakfast, Billy?" she asked, shooting a look out the screen door.

"Doubt it." Billy knifed a chunk of butter with one hand, grabbed the maple syrup with the other, and proceeded to baptize the pancakes.

I looked over the rim of my coffee cup at a familiar scene. Billy now had a mouthful of sausages in various stages of ingestion; he was chewing them wildly and making strange noises, and their ends were sticking out of his mouth, wiggling. Mama crooked an eyebrow at him, clucked her tongue, then ladled out six more batter coins. Billy stabbed at a wedge of pancakes.

Jenny looked over at him and made a face.

"That's disgusting, Billy." She scowled, screwing her upper lip. "It looks like you got worms eating your face."

"Mmph-mmph, no fooling?" Billy replied around the worms. "Hmm-mmm!"

Jenny shuddered, then averted her eyes to Trout, who, catching her reaction to Billy, took a swallow of milk and opened his mouth as she turned his way. She stared coldly at him for a moment, then gave him a kick under the table, causing him to choke, and the milk came out through his nose.

Mama looked over from the stove, but Jenny was looking innocently at something on the ceiling.

"Don't eat so fast now, Joseph—you'll get a turn in your stomach. You don't want to end up like Malachi, do you?"

Trout's face blanched, and he got rigid in his chair.

Malachi was a big Doberman who had a bad habit of inhaling his meals. The poor creature had died from a kinked bowel, and Mama had used his failings ever since to correct certain animal-like traits that were known to descend upon the Hochreiter children at mealtimes. However, the only one the threats still worked on was Trout, Trout being a lad of eight years and prone to nightmares. For a solid month after Malachi's horrible demise his dreams troubled him, descending upon him with visions of the Dobe lying in the weeds by the well all wretched and grisly looking.

"Answer me, young man!" Mama said. "You don't want to end up like poor old Malachi, do you?"

"No, ma'am," Trout coughed, meaning it. Then he sneered at Jenny.

Billy crammed what was left of his stack into his mouth and chased it with coffee. Since he was now seventeen and weaned off milk, he was allowed to drink coffee like an adult, and Jenny was green with envy.

"Hmm-mmm! Now, that's a good cup of coffee!" he gloated. "Mama, have I ever told you what a good cup of coffee you make?"

"Not since yesterday, Billy," she replied.

"I hear it stunts your growth," Jenny barbed.

"You would know, runt," Billy countered in an aside. "You must've drunk a truckload behind Mama's back."

"Very funny."

Snickering, Billy grabbed the paper off the chair next to him and leafed through to the sports section.

Mama flipped pancakes as I sat down at the table next to Billy.

He looked over the paper. "Hey, Tyler," he said affably. "What'ya say we shoot that calf when we get back from town? I'm getting tired of her waking me up with her bawling. Even Sylvester's getting bent out of shape. He gets his feathers all ruffled if he ain't the first one to crow in the morning." He wiped up the syrup around the edge of his plate with his finger. Licking it, he looked around me and asked, "Any more pancakes, Mama?"

"I just gave you a stack!" she said, looking over at his empty plate incredulously. "What you do—give them to Mutt and Jeff?"

The black Labs, who both had been asleep under the table, looked up sleepily at the mention of their names. But since neither of them saw any hands with food in them, they groaned and went back to their rabbits, somewhat annoyed at the interruption.

"You just wait till your older brother has some—I swear, William, all I do it seems is shovel food down your gullet." Mama came to the table and scooped a stack onto my plate. I set into them at once, lifting each cake gingerly and spreading lumps of butter over it, then drowning each layer in maple syrup. I could feel Billy eyeing them greedily.

"But I'm still a growing boy, Mama," he moaned.

"If you grow any more, we're going to have to put you out with the cattle," she said, as she ladled more batter onto the skillet.

"We'd lose half our stock, Mama," Jenny put in. "Why, they'd have to leave the county, I expect, looking for food."

"You're in over your head, little sister," Billy sneered, then disappeared into the baseball stats.

Trout chuckled with the superior air of the last child in the litter.

Jenny leaned over and whispered in his ear. "Shut up, squirt, or I'll give you a knuckle sandwich."

"Mama, Jenny said the 'S' word."

Billy rolled his eyes.

"Are you being vulgar again, Jennifer?" Mama asked in a voice that could strip paint.

"No, Mama. All I said was squirt."

"Well, you just hush, or I'll wash your mouth out with soap."

"Mama, I'm not a little kid anymore—I'm sixteen years old."

"Not for another six months, you ain't," Billy corrected from behind the paper. "You're still a runt."

"Shut up, Billy!"

"Jennifer! You go upstairs right this minute and ask Jesus to forgive you! I'll tolerate no such language in this house."

"Daddy cusses all the time," Jenny protested.

That was a mistake. There was a moment of silence during which we all knew she was dead.

Mama's cheeks flushed. "Don't you get smart with me, young lady!" she scolded as she wagged the spatula at her. "I won't tolerate your sass! Now get upstairs, before I lose my temper!"

Jenny muttered something under her breath as she pushed away from the table. Trout smiled broadly, having clearly won the round.

Jenny leaned over and whispered in his ear. "You just wait till later, you little punk."

"Your father's going to hear about this, young lady," Mama said, following her to the foot of the stairs. "You're always sassin' lately! You might think you're the Queen of Sheba around here, but you're not! Do you hear me?"

A door slammed upstairs. It had the effect of a cannon report. Fort Sumter had been fired upon, and the three of us boys looked at one another, wondering what manner of war might develop.

Mama entered the kitchen, fixing a strand of red hair that had blown loose in the exchange. "I don't know what's gotten into her lately," she said, as she began to clear away the dishes. "I swear, I don't know."

"It's puberty, Mama," Billy offered.

"You hush, William. Joseph's not old enough to hear that word."

"Why not, Mama?" Trout whined.

"You just aren't, that's why. Now finish your breakfast and get back to your chores."

"Why do I have to be the youngest?" he complained. "It's not fair! I never get to know anything fun. It's not—"

Mama shot him her pulpit look.

Trout ducked to his breakfast.

However, Billy, sniffing, looked up in panic. "Mama, are my pancakes burning?"

2

After breakfast, Mama handed me a grocery list, then followed me out onto the front porch as Billy pulled up in the Ford, his elbow bent out the window. He grinned and gave me a "let's get a move on" look.

"You'll tell him as soon as you get back?"

A frown furrowed across my brow. "You're gonna wear me out, Mama!"

"I'll say a prayer for you," she said, smiling, and stopped me cold. Though Mama was a dyed-in-the-wool Irish Protestant, she was as holy-minded as the pope, and there was no defense against her when she had taken to the high ground.

I looked at her, shaking my head, softening under her maternal gaze. The sun reached the porch with its fingers and combed through her hair, lit the red hues, made the green in her eyes sparkle like emeralds, like the green hills of Ireland in spring. She glowed radiantly in the reaching light. Her floral-print dress swayed softly as a breeze collected around her feet, and she looked like a bouquet. I surrendered quietly.

The terror of the Depression years had been merciful to Beulah May McInnis, passing over her red crown like the death angel of the Exodus passing over the blood, ravaging others and blessing her with a plunder taken from the pride of other women her age and younger. Only a few strands of silver ran through her hair, and there were only a few lines etched along her upper lip and radiating from the corners of her mouth that betrayed her age.

But her hands, her hands were the ready chroniclers of her toil, her pain, revealing every sacrifice of womanhood. For there isn't enough grace under heaven to cover a woman's hands that have pulled calves and fence wire, and scrubbed clothes and floors and pots and dishes, and reared children, bound their wounds, stitched their clothes, mended their souls, held the wolves at bay, ruled a desperate kingdom through the extremes of the Depression. No, her hands could not hide these, but though they were red and chafed at times, sometimes raw and sometimes hard with callus, still they were hands swift to knead, to pull and stitch, to sacrifice their beauty on the altar of Motherhood, to lightly touch and heal.

Mama reached up and placed the cool of her palm against my cheek and smiled. "I will say a prayer for you, Tyler," she repeated. "God is merciful, you will see."

"I hope so, Mama," I said, hiding my doubt as I glanced at the truck. "I hope so."

"Let's go," Billy called, tooting the horn.

I climbed into the passenger side, he put the truck into gear, and it coughed forward.

Papa signaled us over to him, and the transmission whined in submission. He had asked us the night before to run into town and pick up a radiator hose for the tractor, a case of oil, several bags of feed for the chickens, and an assortment of screwdrivers, small gauge. It was always a relief to get away, even if it was only for a few hours.

"I want you boys back before noon," he said, grabbing hold of my door. He raised one foot onto the running board and leaned forward, lowering into the shadows of the cab. And though his face was lined and dark, his pale blue eyes sparkled. I could smell the tobacco on his breath mingled with the sweat of his toil, the bittersweet smells that were my father's own, that were both a comfort and a terror.

"Hear that, Tyler?" he said, "No horsing around in town, now. Just collect the things and get on back, hear?"

He was smiling when he said it, but I could see that the smile was uncomfortable on his face, that it was struggling to make peace with the words as they passed through his lips.

"Don't worry, Papa," I said, a little uncomfortable at the proximity of his eyes.

"Papa nothing. We got lots of work to do," he added. "Big day tomorrow."

"We'll be back before noon," I replied, gathering back the discomfiture.

"No later."

Billy leaned across me and asked, "How many hands do you think we'll need, Pa?"

"Six ought to do it, with Sy and Jimbo. We'll see how it goes—depends on the tractor. We don't get it running today, we'll pay the devil putting up hay with just the teams."

"That's for sure!" Billy grinned. "Them new plugs gonna work?"

"I expect so. Now get along."

Papa slapped me on the arm and smiled, then headed back to the tractor. He stopped suddenly and spun around as though struck by a thought. He peered at me with those prophet's eyes of his until I had to look away. I swear, he knew about the letter.

"Let's go," I said, feeling unnerved.

Billy said OK, then jerked the gear stick into place, and the truck lurched forward. Trout looked up from throwing cobs at the pigs and waved as the Ford parted a sea of chickens, and then we turned north toward the highway, and Mutt and Jeff ran howling after us in the kicked-up dust.

I watched the hood of the truck swallowing the brown weeds between the strips of dirt that guided our tires, watched the fields on our left slipping by, rolling green with windrows of drying alfalfa, some of which grew through the fence and along the road. On either side of the road there were cottonwood trees, equidistant from one another, like Grecian columns in a perfect line.

Grandpa Otto had planted them as a windbreak, and they were tall now, and their branches stretched over the road and touched those on the other side, and they dominated the final approach to the ranch. The sun shone through the leaves, dappling the dirt road with cool shadow patterns, and through the shaded boles off to the left I could see the small rise of land, crowned with the live oaks, beneath which the bones of dead Hochreiters lay brittle and quiet.

Bits of flung gravel and dirt peppered the underside of our fenders and running board, making a plinking noise, and then the fourth cylinder missed, and then it missed and missed and missed again as it settled into its characteristic broken rhythm, and the left wheel bearing stuttered plaintively. Four mulies grazing midfield looked up at our approach, wide-eyed, then bounded away, easily clearing the cross-fencing. The dogs caught wind of them and took off, howling.

Billy saw them also and pointed his finger at them like a gun. *"Pow! Pow!"* he said, dropping the buck easily. "Can't wait till hunting season opens. What'ya say, Ty? Get that bull this year, maybe?"

"Hm?" I wasn't listening.

"Gonna get that bull elk this year," he repeated. He slapped the wheel. "You bet!"

Then he frowned and began working his scalp with his free hand, his eyes busy working the road and the fields and the trees behind the fields. "Wish I had something bigger than a .30-.30—might as well throw BBs at him. I hope Nils Johansson's got the new Winchester Model 70 in—said he'd have it in by July. Now with a rifle like that—a .30- 06—why, I could drop him from four maybe five hundred yards, easy!"

He frowned again and switched hands on his scalp. "I wonder how much it'd cost. Got any idea, Ty? How much do you think I could get one for?" He looked over at me.

"You listening?"

"Hm?"

"You ain't heard a word I've said," Billy lamented as he fished a little round tin can out of his shirt pocket.

"What're you talking about?" I asked, stirring out of my thoughts. I watched him fumble with the lid of the tin as he eyed the road, his left palm draped over the steering wheel. He pinched a little wad of tobacco and stuck it into his lip well and tamped it in place with his tongue.

Billy shook his head and grunted. "It's Pa, ain't it?"

I didn't answer, and after a time he let it drop.

I looked out my window at some Herefords scattered over the low hills, the rising heat driving them toward the cool cottonwoods and willows that grew along one of the creeks running through our property. The spring calves were beginning to wander from their mothers' teats now, romping to and fro, butting heads. By the end of the month they would be fully weaned and ready for branding and dehorning and castrating. Some would be driven up to the railhead in Columbus, where they would be loaded into stock cars, then sold at auction in Billings, forty miles east, to thin out the herd over winter.

We shadowed the creek for a while before it passed under the road through a culvert, where it then meandered drunkenly through cottonwoods and aspens and huge elms before finally spilling into the Stillwater River. An almost sheer wall of bluffs formed our western boundary; our eastern boundary lay beyond the highway somewhere in the forested hills.

A wall of Brahma/Shorthorn cows were grazing along the fence and looked up curiously at us as we passed. A calf bawled for its mother. Papa had bought five Brahma bulls and ten Shorthorn cows after the foot-and-mouth epidemic of '29 swept across the nation and took a quarter of our herd.

Papa had managed to keep us afloat through the Depression years, kept us growing without the government subsidies. He said he wouldn't take a nickel from the government, not as long as he had one good hand and an acre of land to plow. He was a good rancher, he

17

knew his business, knew the land, knew the sky, knew how to get the land to produce under the sky, knew how to get his livestock to produce over the land. At a profit. A small profit, but a profit nonetheless.

It was a remarkable thing to make a profit during the twenties and thirties. The ranchers recognized the gift in Papa and respected him for it. The gift reached back through three generations of Hochreiters, through Honus and Otto and Ulrick, each of whom improved upon the gift before passing it along. Some of the ranchers despised the gift in Papa, for such a thing was a mystery to them and, because of it, was dangerous. However, most revered the gift and came to him for advice, for little kernels of wisdom that they might take and plant and grow a profit. A small profit, perhaps, but a profit nonetheless.

But Papa didn't ranch in order to make a profit; he made a profit in order to ranch. That was the mystery of it. For to Henry Hochreiter the ranch was a living thing, it breathed, it laughed, it cried, it reproduced, it was a giver of life, it had a soul, a living soul. And if it had a soul the husk could get sick, the body could die, the soul could fly. And so Papa nursed the soul of the ranch with his gift, fathered and mothered and tended the soul like his very own. Strike the soul, and you struck Papa; cut the soul and you cut Papa; desert the soul, and in Papa's eyes you were a vile thing, an infidel, a traitor. And Papa loathed a traitor.

Billy looked out his window over the even, rolling windrows that seemed to stretch forever, took a deep breath of air. "Smell that, Tyler! It's something, don't you think?"

"What's that?" I asked.

"The ranch. Smell that sweet alfalfa! There ain't nothing like it!" His eyes flashed as he talked, and there glowed on his face a kind of radiance. "No, there's nothing like it this side of heaven!"

I shook my head in amazement. "I don't see how anybody can look at a field of cut hay, knowing that come first light he's gonna be breaking his back baling, and still smile about it."

Billy grinned broadly at me. "Think I'm nuts, big brother?"

I looked at him for a moment, making an appraisal. But for the red in his hair and the leanness of his youth, he was a young Henry Hochreiter. His shoulders were broad and his waist narrow, and his tanned arms showing below the rolls of his sleeves were muscled from putting up tons of hay, snapping like springs when in use, though mostly he moved with the easygoing languor of youth. His eyes had the same shape and pale blue color as Papa's, thinking, calculating

18

eyes but without the crow's-feet, and they were intelligent and quick with impish humor.

I, on the other hand, was a mite stockier, taking after the McInnises, and it was an even bet who could whip the other. I knew, and Billy knew, but neither of us wanted to chance it again. Like Mama, my eyes were green, though my hair was the same color as Billy's. For that matter, every one of us Hochreiter children was a strawberry blond; with Papa's German blond and Mama's Irish red, the angel standing guard over the gene pool, not able to make up his mind, had compromised with a little of each.

Billy had the gift. I knew it, and Papa knew it. Papa tried to bestow the gift on me, my birthright, but his efforts were in vain. For whatever reasons, the dead Hochreiters had waved me aside and placed their hands on Billy. He was the heir apparent. He had received the blessing of the firstborn. He was the keeper of the soul. Billy breathed in the soul of the ranch with his first breath, and the land and the sky moved before him, growing, producing, yielding its fruits. Billy would turn a profit when the ranch fell into his hands, and the bestowers of the gift knew it.

"You ain't answered my question," Billy said.

"No, I don't think you're nuts."

"Really?"

"A little crazy, maybe. A quarter-bubble off plumb, definitely. But nuts? Shoot . . ."

Billy took in an exaggerated breath of air and blew it out hard. "I love it, Ty! I surely do!" He looked at me and winked. "You know, sometimes I think I love it more than girls."

I shook my head. "I take it back—you *are* nuts."

Billy threw his head back and laughed. He began to sing a few spirited bars of "Buffalo Gal," his right hand slapping out the lively tempo on the steering wheel.

I glanced at him from time to time but let him alone, and it wasn't long before the song lost its fervor and trailed off into an atonal humming. Then even that died, and we drove along in silence for a while. The Ford rattled and bumped over the washboard road and liked to jar out our teeth, and the flung gravel plinked the fenders and running boards. The sun beat against the side of my face.

"You gonna tell him today?" Billy asked, breaking into my thoughts. "I heard you talking to Mama at breakfast."

My countenance fell. *"You* gonna start on me now?"

19

"Just let me know when you do, so I can get out of earshot. Mama may've raised a coward, but she didn't raise no fool."

I smiled at him wryly. "Thanks a lot."

Billy offered me the tin as a truce.

"No, thanks."

"It ain't a sin, Tyler. I asked Reverend Jacks."

"I never said it was a sin. I just don't want to get started whittling my teeth down to nubs is all."

"He said it was OK to chew as long as you didn't make a habit of it. I don't chew but a couple three times a day, so I figure it ain't a habit just yet."

I rolled my eyes.

Billy offered the tin again. "Sure you don't want a pinch?"

"You put that in my face again, and it's going out the window."

He put it back in his pocket.

"You're sure in a sour mood today."

We came to the edge of our property. A twenty-foot-high portal made of lodgepole pine framed the gateway; bluebunch wheatgrass grew wild around the supports.

Four or five ruffed grouse jumped up from the grass with a violent rush of wings as Billy downshifted through the gears. They flew outward in a scattergun spread, alighting in the alfalfa along a cross-fence where the mowers missed, and immediately they began sounding the recall.

I climbed out of the truck and swung the gate open to let Billy pass. As he did, I looked up at our brand, the Flying Bar H, scrolled in rope across the transom. A bald hornet drove past my face in search of meat. I swiped at it, missed, then swung the gate closed and climbed back into the pickup.

We turned onto the highway, and the ranch gates began to fall steadily behind us. A flash of light caught my eye, and I turned and saw Sy and Jimbo in the northeast corner of the ranch, stretching barbed wire across a pasture.

They looked up and waved, and Billy honked twice and pulled over.

"Hey, Tyler—Billy!" Sy called out, tossing his wire wrench to the ground.

The two of them walked over to us, and Sy leaned against a fence post. They were both wearing beat-up straw Stetsons that had little shocks of straw sticking up around the torn crowns. Light filtered through the torn brims and dappled their faces, and their shiny black

20

hair glistened with gray highlights. Each wore a pair of denim overalls, faded and worn and loose-fitting, with thin print shirts that were faded to near white by the sun. Their near whiskerless skin, by contrast, was leathery and tawny and lined with a network of wrinkles that were as tough as cowhide and stretched tortoiselike over high, rugged cheekbones and low, sloping brows. And when the sun shone under the brims on their Indian features, in the rich red hues of dusk, they took on a burnished copper color that was beautiful.

Since before I was born, Sy and Jimbo had worked the ranch; since before Papa was born, Sy and Jimbo were there, working the ranch. Besides Mama and Papa, my earliest memories were of Sy and Jimbo. Without them it would not be the Flying Bar H, for they were connected to the land like a tree or a stream is connected to the land. Take away the trees and rivers, and a part of its soul would cease to be.

They were both old men, but we didn't know how old. Ever since Billy and I were kids, we had a running debate as to their ages. We used to lie awake at night wondering about it. Billy guessed Sy at around eighty or so—I thought older—but it is impossible to tell how old an Indian is, for an Indian's face is as ageless as the land. Pick up a handful of dirt and guess how old it is, and that's how old an Indian is. He might be fifty or a hundred for all you could tell. And we never dared to ask them either—you didn't ask an Indian such things.

"You take me and Jimbo into town with you?" Sy said, smiling over the fence at us, with his back to the sun. "It's too hot workin' out here, and we're just getting started. Say, why don't Mister Henry hire a coupla colored boys and let us go into town with you?"

Billy leaned past me and called out the window, "Pa's got too much respect for colored folks—that's why he's kept you two on. He told me so this very morning."

Sy ignored the remark. He pulled out his cigarette papers and a worn leather pouch. Then, very slow and deliberate, he sprinkled tobacco into a little trough he made in the paper with his calloused index finger, careful not to spill any, and put the pouch back in his pocket.

"This ain't no work for Crow Indian braves," he said, dabbing the edge of the paper with his thick white tongue. He rolled the ends, then twisted it in and out of his lips, moistening it. "Why, a Crow brave was born to hunt buffalo, to take scalps from his enemies the Dakotas, the Siksikas . . . from white boys with too much sass and no respect for their elders."

He struck a match along the fence post and lighted the end. "Ain't that right, Jimbo?"

Jimbo, the larger of the two, slipped his hands into his pockets and grinned broadly. He was also the younger of the two. We knew that because he was Sy's son. However, they looked about the same age. One of his front teeth was silver-plated, and it flashed when the sun hit it right. He was proud of his teeth and showed them frequently.

"You wouldn't know a buffalo if you tripped over one," Billy said, grinning.

"Then maybe we come into town with you and get some cold beers together," Jimbo suggested. "Get drunk, maybe!"

"We do and Pa'll skin us alive!" I countered. "Make seat pillows out of us for that old tractor of his!"

Sy shrugged his shoulders, then blew a cloud of smoke into the air. "Why, he's been riding us hard now for over thirty years. And his papa before that. We wouldn't know the difference, would we, Jimbo?"

Jimbo nodded and grinned, and his tooth flashed under his brim. "Maybe we scalp these two colts right now—take the truck and get drunk without 'em."

"Sounds good to me," Sy said, pulling hard on the cigarette so that his cheeks hollowed into his face.

A flatbed roared past, sucking the air, showering us with little bits of hay. We all turned and watched it grow small on the road.

Sy flicked an ash as he studied the sky. "Maybe if you bring us each a cold beer, we won't lift your scalps."

"It'll be warm by the time we get back," I said. "If you don't mind warm beer."

"Warm beer's OK—what you think, Jimbo?"

Jimbo nodded and grinned. "Warm beer get you plenty drunk. Bring two each."

"We'll bring two Coca-Colas. Pa's expecting to have that pasture cross-fenced sometime today."

"We work plenty fast with a buzz on," Jimbo reasoned.

"Yeah, but Pa don't want no drunk Indian fences zigzagging across his field. He wants good German fences, nice and straight. Fences that would make a randy bull fall down and cry."

"Then you boys take over, and we'll go to town and bring you back warm beers."

We all laughed and waved, then Billy and I took off down the road, Sy and Jimbo looking after us.

3

The Stillwater rushed alongside us, blue and shimmering with a million lights, as it raced us to the Yellowstone. Sometimes it drew up close to the road, and we could see tall green reeds along the banks and white egrets standing still like little porcelain figurines, hunting fish with their stiletto beaks. And sometimes the river swung wide of the road and hid below a line of bluffs, allowing fields in between, and we could catch only glimpses of it as it wound around them.

We drove along in silence for a few miles, the tires singing beneath the firewall. The wind rushing past the windows drew air into the cab, hot air, doused with moisture from the river, and the sweet, cut smells of harvest clinging to the moisture.

I stared out the window away from the morning sun that burned through the windshield, letting my eyes have their will along the trees and hills to my right, and to the left I watched the road following the river and the trees following the river. The sun struck fields of green alfalfa and golden wheat and lighted their heads, ripening them, and the morning breezes bent them gently.

It was summer, mid-July, when great grottoes of bird's-foot trefoil covered the hills everywhere, giving meaning to the color yellow. It was the month before the skies would turn black as sin over Stillwater County, bringing with them the early August snow.

Ranchers were in the fields, men and boys, obedient to the ancient dictates of the land, to the perfect color of the grain, to the perfect smells, to the sky, to the stirrings of their blood that drove them forth into the fields. Some were on old tractors that coughed plumes of bluish smoke. Most were behind teams of horses or mules that strained against worn harnesses, their great hammering necks and flanks flecked with foam as they cut wide, even swaths through the ripened grain with mowers, leaving cuttings of grain that followed the ess contours of the land, and the cuttings were raked into windrows and left to dry in the sun, and the morning breezes swept over the fields and perfumed the air.

Billy was muttering to himself, which was his way of letting you know he wanted to tell you something without coming right out and saying it. But I guessed what it was by the pantomime working through his features—the new Model 70.

Then I could feel him looking at me out of the corner of his eye.

He cleared his throat. "I expect you'll be wanting to stop off at the drugstore first—maybe see Kate," he said. "You can go in and see her while I take care of Mama's groceries at Johansson's—give you two a chance to—you know . . ."

"You heard what Pa said—we have to be back by noon," I said. "Now if I go in and see Kate, there's no telling when I'll get out. No. I figure we'd stop by the feed store first, get that out of the way, then pick up the hose, then hit Johansson's on the way out. If I happen to see Kate—why, I'll give her a little wave."

"It's up to you. Fine by me either way," Billy said unconvincingly. He waited a minute, and I could hear his mind working. "You don't want to maybe go to Johansson's first? You know—get Ma's groceries filled? Shoot, I don't care. Whatever you want to do's fine by me."

He waited another minute, his fingers drumming the cadences of his thinking on the wheel. "Why not just go to Johansson's first, then pick up the feed on the way back? I mean, what difference does it make? None, that I can see."

"None. None whatsoever," I agreed. "You're driving—do what you want."

Billy's fingers continued to drum. "Sure, that's what we'll do. Why not?"

I smiled, then looked out at the rolling-by fields of hay and wheat, gazed aimlessly at them until they were a blur of yellows and greens.

We passed some little ranch houses: the Keillors', the Joneses', the Brodericks'—their brands once proudly displayed over their transoms like coats of arms—now barely hanging on through the extremes of Montana or bent low and sagging and vacant, their fields fallow and overrun with weeds.

These were little ranches, too small to qualify for the government subsidies—forty-, sixty-, and eighty-acre ranches that had been worked by tenants mostly, men and women too stubborn or foolish to know they had been licked by the Depression until the banks called in their paper, forced them to vacate or sell out. The big ranches took them, swooped in on the carrion steadings like vultures, bought them out at

24

depressed prices and became rich. Josiah Fisk had amassed great wealth and become a powerful voice in the state capital on the bones of other men's failures.

We passed a barn that had broken under last winter's snow. One end of it was collapsed to the ground, the other end high and trembling, and light shone through the gaps in its walls. It looked like an old buffalo crumpled on its forelegs, too tired to get up another time, waiting stoically for the scavengers to come and pick it clean.

I waved at Carl Peterson, who was mowing along the fence. He was a small, sinewy man in his early fifties and wore a long-billed cap to fight off the sun. One of his hands was on the wheel of his Massey-Harris and one on the back of his seat. He cast up a quick look, and his face was grim as he nodded to me, then he looked back on his even rows, and the blades of the gangs were cutting a wide swath, dusting the air with sweetness.

Here and there we passed some rickety stands set up along the highway with wheat, corn, apples, and pears for sale, and signs, crudely painted, indicating the price: two bits a bushel, nickel a dozen, penny an ear, dime a dozen. And there were bales of hay stacked twenty feet high along the road, priced low, cheaper than in town, but you had to load them yourself.

Sometimes we saw a car or a tractor or other farming equipment, whole or in part, priced to sell, and we knew what that meant. Another ranch shutting down. Another family quitting, abandoning their dream, cashing in what little they had in hopes of starting over somewhere else. The vultures would come.

Women and children manned the rickety stands, no men. They were stunned at the turn of events that took them from the fields of work and play and thrust them along the road to sell the contents of their lives, and their faces all bore the same drawn and wide-eyed look of incredulity. The older children wore fierce expressions and shuffled in the dirt, and they looked away as the cars passed, like their mothers, whose backs straightened with a dignity born of generations of independent men and women. And when the cars passed, they looked down at their hands and smoothed them and reviewed the passage of time in their hands and remembered dreams.

The men, too proud to show their faces along the road, were in the fields working the land and stock, sweating out their shame. Like a snake writhing in the dirt with its head cut off, the thick muscles along its spine still obeying the last impulses from its brain, so the ranchers went through the motions of their lives by rote, stoically obeying the ancient dictates of land and blood that drummed in their breasts, knowing full well that their efforts were futile. But what else was there for them to do? They couldn't just sit along the road and watch the passing of cars while there was a crop in the field, or a calf to be branded, or an engine to be tuned. There had to be some means by which they measured themselves, some tangible scales by which they weighed the sum of their manhood, and so they worked in the fields and writhed in their souls until the drumming ceased.

Suddenly the Ford slowed down.

"What's wrong?" I asked, looking ahead for some obstruction.

But Billy was glancing over his shoulder out the back window. "Looks like the Gibsons are packing it in," he said.

"What?" I jerked my head out the window, and for an instant I caught Ellie Gibson's eyes before she looked away. "Yeah, looks like it," I said, then Billy and I exchanged looks, for we knew. My heart sank.

"Think we should stop?" he asked. "Maybe we might be able to help or something."

"You want to make it harder on them?" I replied. "Ellie couldn't even look at me. C'mon, let's go."

"You sure?"

"Let's go!" I snapped.

The truck sped forward, and we both stared out at the road moving swiftly below us.

"Should we tell Pa?" Billy asked, breaking a long silence. "We should tell Pa, don't you think?"

I made no reply. I had grown sullen.

"Tyler, I think we should tell him."

"You tell him."

"Why me? You're older."

"I've got enough on my mind without adding someone else's grief to it. If anybody's gonna tell him, you are. I sure ain't."

"All right," Billy conceded. "He's gonna take it hard though." He glanced into the rearview mirror. "All them kids—eight of 'em. That's a real shame. Just couldn't hold on, I guess."

"I don't know how anybody does anymore." I leaned my head against the door and let out a sigh. "Wait till tomorrow to tell him, Billy. Better yet, wait a couple of days."

"You sure?"

"Just wait a couple of days, or don't tell him at all."

26

"He's gonna take it hard."

"I expect so. He takes everything hard, doesn't he?"

Whenever a rancher went under, it was like a little piece of Papa's soul had been chipped away and he was diminished because of it. For days following, Papa would storm around the ranch to see if there were any cracks in its walls, to see if there was a betraying fissure that might break through the banks and threaten the soul. He would watch us closely. We felt his eyes at the table, out in the fields, everywhere his eyes were on us—the glaring Hochreiter hawk's eyes—piercing the veneer of our expressions for weakness, studying the light in our faces for uncertain shadows. We shuddered under his gaze and hid within ourselves.

As Papa paced over the steading, scratching his head, spitting brown arcs into the dirt and roaring commands like a general, we watched him too, watched from the corners of our eyes, with furtive glances stolen across his face as we moved quietly about our chores, waiting, praying for the release of his shoulders, the ease of his brow, a humor to return to his eyes.

I looked outside the truck window at the speeding blur of yellows and greens, and the wind rushed past my face and dried my eyes. I closed them, and a cool darkness filled in the colors, and I could feel the healing moisture of my tear ducts washing over the wind burns. I began to look inward, thinking of the Gibsons, the eight bewildered-looking children fidgeting in the dirt, their eyes fierce, and Ellie turning away and looking at her hands, and immediately a melancholy air descended on me again. It must have slipped around Mama's prayers. And then there was Papa in my sight, a little oval of light glowing in the darkness behind my eyes, and I was telling him that I had to leave the ranch in September—that I'd been awarded a full scholarship to the Chicago Divinity School to study for the ministry.

His eyes—the cold Hochreiter eyes that stared at everything from their sepia perches, perceiving nothing—were set and flashing with anger. And I could see three generations of soul-tenders glaring at me through the oval of light, and their accusations were working Papa's hard jaw and snapping through his teeth, denouncing me for my treason.

I cringed guiltily, and my chest began to ache. I sat up straight in my seat and jerked my head away from the fields, shaking the images from my mind. Fear lingered, and I fought the fear with anger. Fought the anger with anger, for anger was my ready weapon, and it lay buried just beneath the skin where it could be quickly summoned. Adjusting my head against the door, I blinked heavily and sighed, listening to the irregular rhythm of the engine, and soon darkness filled in the oval of light, and I slept.

4

Billy nudged me awake, and I looked out, and we were in front of Chuck's Automotive. I shot Billy a curious look. His brow was set now with the humorless cast of the Hochreiters, and Papa's look burned through his eyes. I don't know if it was a look of compassion or dismay, but I knew what had caused it. Without a word he jumped out of the truck and headed into the store. I followed.

Minutes later we were rolling down Pike Avenue to the Grain and Feed on the other end of town, radiator hose and case of oil on the seat between us.

On our left were the tracks and behind them the granaries, looming four stories tall with their walls of rusted corrugated iron shining dully, and beyond them a stone's throw the Yellowstone coursed easily along its bed. On our right, the red brick storefronts, of nineteenth century vintage, with their wooden, painted facades, faced the street stolidly, and merchants and patrons rustled about under their scrutiny in the casual, early morning intercourse of commerce. Old ladies were bent over display windows, jabbering and pointing, and old men were clumped on stoops and benches, smoking and quibbling over the state of the union or the state of the herds or crops. Mostly, however, they talked about the weather and fly-fishing.

Columbus was an old town—always had been. It was the county seat, a ranching and a sometimes mining town. With Billings only forty-odd miles to the east, though, the young were quickly snatched away to higher paying jobs, to jobs with futures, government jobs, New Deal jobs, so that the promise of growth was in perpetual still-birth. Ranching kept the town alive, and interstate commerce along Highway 10—the old Yellowstone Trail—pumped the local economy with a blood-trickle of dollars and ideas. The merchants smiled upon the dollars, but the ideas took away the youth, so they were frowned upon.

After loading the bed with sacks of feed, we retraced our route and turned left on Cooper Street, which took us into the center of town toward the county courthouse, and the courthouse had the word

29

Stillwater chiseled in big Romanesque letters across its face, reminding everyone not to take life too seriously. There were still plenty of rainbows in the river, and you could always get after them when things got too tough.

Johansson's General Store was on the right, about two blocks up the street, and, seeing it, Billy's eyes lit up. For the time being, the orbiting Soul was eclipsed by a greater light.

You could buy just about anything you needed at Johansson's: beans and bacon, dry goods, canned goods and fresh vegetables and blankets and clothing, candy and guns and ammunition, fishing tackle and six dozen other sundry items of needs and wants. In front of the store stood two ancient Mobiloil pumps on a little island that appeared to predate automobiles. A bell dinged as we pulled up to the island, and Billy shut off the engine.

A hush settled into the quiet for just a moment as we both looked at the screen door.

Moments later, Took, the only son of Nils Johansson, burst out of the store and tipped his cap. His stride was broken and exaggerated, some steps long and others short; it had the effect of an ape loping. He was a sloping-shouldered boy of fifteen with a head too large for his frame, the back of which was flattened like a skillet. His face bore an inscrutable expression, guileless and wide-eyed, and, though it deflected inquiry, it seemed to project the quiet blaze of an inner fury. He wore a pair of quarter-inch thick glasses, and his pale blue eyes seemed to spread across his face behind the lenses, giving him a comic, almost monstrous look. Sandy hair that was close-cropped around the ears stuck out beneath his cap in little thatches, and there were welts over his eyes and neck. There was a welt on the corner of his upper lip that made it swell out queerly over the other.

"Morning, Took," Billy said. "Fill 'er up with the cheap stuff and check the oil, could you?"

"OK, Billy," Took said, smiling. Only one side of his mouth turned up, while the other hung down under the weight of the swelling. Took liked Billy, but of course everyone did. Suddenly his eyes widened like little pale blue pies. "Hey! I didn't tell you that Pa's gonna let me get after the honey today."

"Ain't that somethin'," Billy replied, looking over at me. "Hear that, Tyler?"

"Can't be," I said.

Took looked at me, frowning fiercely. He didn't like me. Never did. "It's true, Tyler!" He scowled. "He told me this morning!"

30

"Well, I'll be," I said, as amicably as I could. "You must be doing a real fine job, Took. I hear your Pa's pretty peculiar about letting anyone near his bees. Why, them bees of his are world famous —make the best honey I ever tasted."

Took nodded furiously as he twisted off the gas cap, then he peered intently to one side of the hole as he placed the nozzle into it. A lumpy contortion of a smile spread over his face as he considered my words. "Won a ribbon at the fair last year," he said to Billy. "A blue one. Got it next to my bed." He chuckled, then squeezed the lever on the handle, and a little bell sounded each gallon.

"You think them bees are ready to put out?" I asked him.

"I was checkin' yesterday," Took replied. "There's a whole mess of honey in the combs—sides of the hives 'bout to bust." His eyes lit up. "I took me a little piece of comb."

"Don't look like them bees were too friendly about letting go of it," I said, eyeing the lumps on his head. "Looks like they tore into you plenty good."

Took nodded his head again, slowly. "Yes, they did," he said deliberately, still looking intently to one side of the nozzle as though there was something of singular interest in the paint. "But I ain't gonna let no bees sting me today." His eyes broke free and shifted conspiratorially to the door handle. "No, sir. Gonna smoke 'em. Pa says they get real sleepy if they get smoked, and then they got no mind to sting."

His shoulders began to bounce and roll, and he covered his mouth with his free hand as he giggled. The air hissed through his fingers. "When them bees wake up—why, they'll wonder who stung *them!*"

Billy grinned at him and turned to leave. "Smoked bees, huh? What'ya know? Next thing you know we'll be barbecuing 'em."

Took looked at him blankly, missing the joke, as he picked at a bee welt over his eye with his free hand. "Pa sent for a smoker in the Sears and Roebuck—we got it yesterday. It's just a little can you put some kindling in and light—" He broke off, and his eyes glared intensely. "But Pa says he's got to light it. And then I get to put some wet moss or grass or something on top till it starts to smoking."

The boy paused for a moment, and the little bell sounded another gallon. His eyes cooled during the interlude. "You just put the can next to the hive and pump the smoke into a little hole in the top."

"How do you pump the smoke out of the can?" Billy asked.

"Why, it's got a trigger that you pull on, just like this here," Took replied, indicating the gas pump handle. "And the smoke comes out t'other end."

"Maybe the trigger works a little bellows inside," Billy suggested.

"Bellows?"

"Yeah, like the kind you blow over a fire."

"We got one of them, but we don't use it on bees," Took said. "We got a smoker now that we put kindling in and wet grass, and we smoke 'em with that."

Billy looked at him for a moment. "Take care you don't spill now, Took," he said, glancing at me. Then he headed into the store, and I followed.

"Don't be worried," Took replied, and as I passed he frowned at me and said, "Pa says the smoke don't hurt the bees none—it just makes 'em sleepy. Why, bees don't live but a coupla months, anyhow. Bet you didn't know that either."

"No, I didn't, Took," I replied. "You learn something new every day."

Took stared at me as the little bell sounded.

Just before I entered the store, I paused, looked up, and saw an Indian youth heading down the street, staggering and angling back and forth over the sidewalk. It was a familiar gait, and I knew him at once to be Sammy Two Feathers. He was drunk by all appearances, but then I never knew him to be sober. Strangely, a shiver trundled up my spine as I watched him.

I started to wave, but the sight of a dirty brown truck turning into the street beyond him caught my eye. My first impression of the vehicle was that of an ugly dark smudge spreading against the red of the brick walls; the second impression reminded me that the truck belonged to the Fisk ranch. My heart skipped a beat as I beheld the three silhouettes inside the cab, bent in various attitudes of malevolence.

I watched the truck for a moment, waited for it to pass Sammy; and as it did, Booster Fisk yelled something out his window at him.

Then the truck continued down the street toward me, and as it crawled slowly past the store like a predator stalking game, Booster's face flashed suddenly out of the dark cab, and I caught the glint of hatred in his eyes. A thin, cruel smile curled across his face as he looked me over, and inside the cab the other two shapes bent around him, and I could hear them laughing throatily. It was malicious, devilish laughter.

Then the truck lurched suddenly forward and sped away, belching plumes of blue smoke, and I watched until the morning sounds of wind brushing over the buildings swept everything quiet. And then a prescient dread began to claw at my mind.

In every community of man, it seems, there is some villainy—small or great, real or imagined—against which righteousness or justice or love must prevail. Some have contended against the corruption of a Boss Tweed, others against the bullying of a tyrant or the Brownshirts of Nazi Germany. Stillwater County had to reckon with the Fisks.

I took a breath and looked up the sidewalk, at which moment Sammy reeled off the curb, stumbled into the street, and, swaying and looking after the truck, he shook a menacing fist. No doubt his mind was culling a raft of indignations from the angry swirls in his brain and pummeling the haze with the savage pride of his fathers, who were Crow. Sammy yawed and pitched back over the great wall of the curb and, steadying himself, resumed his meandering course.

Quickly I slipped into the store.

5

Inside Johansson's a couple of old men were playing checkers over a cracker barrel; a third was sitting in an overstuffed easy chair, reading a newspaper. A trapezoidal pool of warm light, swimming with dust particles, spilled in through the storefront window over a curled black-and-white cat. Behind the men, stretching lengthwise into the store, were four rows of shelves stacked high with canned and dry goods, breads and sundry staples, and beyond these were the white-enameled refrigerators that hummed and kept the dairy products and meats cold.

To the far right an elderly woman named Mrs. Stivers was ferreting through a rack of clothes, while Nils Johansson filled her order. I say "ferreting" because her mannerisms resembled those of a small carnivore, quick, purposeful, attacking, always attacking. She was chittering to herself, while her narrow-set eyes peered over a small, rodentlike nose. She wore a pained expression, as if her constitution had backed up on her. Toward the rear of the store was an Indian woman sifting through some wool blankets, whom I recognized as Sammy's mother; and as Mrs. Stivers clawed a dress off the rack, she paused and eyed the Crow woman coldly for a moment. Her little nose twitched, and she shook her head with a grunt.

Billy was leaning against the counter—a glass one displaying an array of handguns, hunting knives, barlow and many-bladed knives, fishing reels, and a thousand wet and dry flies—and he was fidgeting, waiting impatiently, while Mr. Johansson ambled through the aisles with a bewildered look on his face.

Behind the counter against the wall was a long rack of rifles and shotguns: bolt-actions, lever-actions, breechloaders, and semiautomatics, four deep. Billy's eyes caressed their stocks and shiny blue barrels and calculated their velocities and foot-pounds of killing energy by their calibers, their availability by the bright orange tags dangling from trigger guards.

A magnificent bull elk gazed dully from over the lintel of the door leading into the storeroom, its six-tined antlers—like two great tree limbs—sweeping back and away toward the ceiling, its mouth opened slightly before the swollen arched neck, bugling silent contempt. Its head beetled out and inclined a little to one side, allowing it to eye the cash register.

There was a dry smell of cardboard boxes and printed labels and groceries in the store, and the sweet smell of fresh vegetables and fruit, of gun oil and tobacco and brewed coffee, and when I'd opened the door and entered I brought in the cool morning smells of the town—the old brick and cement and gas pump smells—and the men playing checkers looked up as I did.

The one was a heavy-set balding man, wide of girth and chest, with a bull neck that sat down into a nest of curly white hair sticking out from his collar. He wore a faded pair of bib overalls and a flannel work shirt with the sleeves rolled up over his big forearms, brown arms thick with working muscle. And on the right arm there was a faded tattoo of a woman, naked but for a doughboy helmet and a Springfield rifle, and on the left arm the United States Marine Corps globe and anchor was just visible through the curly hair.

The other man was small and wiry, muscled, and built hard and compact like a terrier, with salty black hair and white stubble glistening over a lean, hatchet face. He wore a plaid flannel shirt and faded blue jeans, with cuffs rolled up over a muddy pair of worn, thick-soled brogans that crimped up at the toes.

"Well, what do you know," the heavy-set man boomed, glancing at me. "For a moment there, I'd've sworn it was Sean McInnis coming through the door! What do you think, Enos? Doesn't Tyler here look like a young Sean?"

Enos Stubbins looked up from the checkerboard and gave me the once-over. He took a sip of coffee from his mug and said, "Naw, if he ain't a dead ringer for old Honus Hochreiter. A dead ringer." Enos chuckled as though he had made a clever joke, then he set his mug down in a little space beside the checkerboard and added, "Now there was a mean one."

Charley Reese started. "Now what do you want to go and say that for?"

"Hey, Charley—Enos," I said, chuckling a little embarrassedly. "How are you fellas doing?"

"Just fine, son," Charley said. "Don't you mind Enos, now. Your grandfather was a real fine gentleman. Always had a kind word."

Enos turned sharply to Charley and eyed the worn edges of his bib overalls. "And what do you know about gentlemen?" he asked. "I suppose you're an authority on the subject?"

Charley raised his head a little indignantly. "You'd be surprised what I know. Why, I'll have you know that it was my pleasure to meet some of the finest gentlemen you'll ever hope to know during the war—men who were honorable and decent-educated men—who knew more about the world than the rear end of a mule team."

"There's more wisdom in the rear end of a mule than in most educated men I've known," Enos retorted. "But then I wasn't an officer and a gentleman like you was. I was just an ordinary leatherneck—trained to kill Germans and raise a ripping good time."

"A little attention to culture never hurt anyone," Charley said.

"I expect you'll be wanting tea and crumpets served around here now," Enos gibed.

Charley narrowed his eye on the smaller man. "I like a good cup of tea now and then."

Enos looked around the store for Nils Johansson and found him rounding an aisle. "Say, Nils? How about stocking some tea and crumpets in your store for Charley here—might give the place a real touch of class. Why, people would drive in from miles around just to breathe in a little culture. Ain't that so, Charley?"

"We've got tea," Nils said proudly, with his thick Scandinavian accent. "But what is crumpets?"

"Tell him, Charley," Enos said. "Tell Swedish Nils here how you and all them limey officers used to sit around in Paris, drinking tea and eating crumpets, while the rest of us unrefined leathernecks was off killing Germans at Belleau Wood."

A rush of scarlet colored Charley's thick neck. "I was at the Wood," he growled through his teeth. "I lost a lot of good men there too, and I don't appreciate you making light of it, Enos. It's a flaw in your character to always be making light of things that are honorable."

"Ain't nothing honorable about getting your head blowed off so's a bunch a dandified limeys and frogs can sit around in the afternoon and swap recipes. Why, even you—"

Charley's glare cut him off. "I won't allow it in my presence, Enos. I won't."

"Take it easy, Charley, take it easy." Enos grinned. "It was over twenty years ago."

"It isn't funny."

Charley Reese had been an adjutant on Brigadier General James Harbord's staff but was given a field command and the rank of captain after devastating losses to the Fourth Marine Brigade in June 1918. Charley was a brawler and a lousy adjutant, but he distinguished himself on the field of battle. He was a good Marine. However, when he took shrapnel in his legs from a trench mortar, he was returned to Paris to the naval hospital to convalesce, after which he returned home with a chestful of medals, a steel pin in his left knee, and a marked limp.

Still fuming, Charley cleared his throat, then thrust a checker forward.

Enos looked down at the board and shook his head pathetically. "That your move?"

"What of it?"

"Well, there you have it now . . . leave it to the mud leathernecks to show the gentlemen tea-totalers the finer points of battle tactics." Enos hopped two of Charley's checkers and landed in his corner. "Crown me, your lordship."

"Crown you?" Charley grunted sourly at the board. He smoothed a big calloused hand over his balding pate, burned to a deep, shiny rust red, then took hold of his lower lip between his thumb and forefinger.

The man reading the newspaper had never looked up once during this exchange but merely leafed through his paper idly, apparently numb to such barrages.

I walked through the trapezoidal shape of sunlight that had edged some toward the window, avoiding the black-and-white cat, and headed to the counter where Billy drummed his fingers quietly on the glass, oblivious to the goings-on.

He greeted me with a jerk of his eyebrows.

Enos Stubbins looked over at us and grinned. His teeth were brown, and there were holes between the lower ones where the tobacco had eaten at the enamel. He angled his head to one side and a stream of brown juice slung from his lip into a coffee can. "How're your folks, boys?" he asked, wiping his chin. "I ain't seen your ma since the Fourth."

"Fine," I said.

"And them other young'uns?"

An image of Jenny tromping upstairs with Mama on her tail flashed into my mind. I shrugged. "OK, I suppose. Nobody's shot anybody yet," I added with a chuckle.

Charley looked over at me sharply, then returned to his dilemma on the checkerboard.

Now Enos Stubbins was a talker. He lived alone on a small spread west of town where the Stillwater spilled into the Yellowstone, and the few beeves and chickens he raised didn't afford him much in the way of conversation. Consequently he spent most of his time in town pulling ears. I could tell by the gleam in his eye that he was about to unload a wagonload of talk, and I wanted to keep my end of it light if we were going to get back to the ranch by noon.

Enos stared at me, sizing up a new crate of thought. "Your pa put up his hay yet?"

"Tomorrow."

"Tomorrow, huh? Gonna hire a bunch of them Injuns again?"

"Why not? They're good workers."

"Good workers? That's a joke." Enos laughed. "Why, I used 'em once—*once*, mind you. Know what happened? Half them bucks ran off before noon. The other half scratched around, not doin' a lick till right before I threw 'em off my property Wanted a day's pay too, the lazy good-for-nothings."

"That doesn't sound right," I said. "They're all we've ever used." Enos shook his head. "Now there's a trusting soul, your pa. I swear, he must be part Injun himself to get any work out of 'em. It's truly an enigma. Wouldn't you say it was an enigma, Charley?"

Charley rolled his eyes.

"Don't know what it means, do you?"

Charley ignored him.

"Indians aren't any different than most folks," I said, a little cocky. "You just got to know their ways. Sometimes they're just like little children, I admit. But they work hard if they know you're gonna give 'em a piece of candy."

"You mean a bottle of corn." Enos laughed again.

I had begun to laugh too when suddenly I felt a rise of heat around my collar and ears. Instinctively I looked across the store and found Sammy's mother staring at me, her round face shining like a caramel-colored moon.

I smiled at her, ashamedly, my ears still burning, and she looked away, making like she didn't hear me. But I knew. She lay a blanket back on the table and smoothed her hand over it, then slowly moved around the shelves out of sight.

"Know their ways?" Enos rejoined, half-mockingly. "Ain't no

way a white man can ever know the ways of an Injun, lessen he's part Injun himself."

My hands crawled into my pockets as I stared at him. "Like I said, they're good workers. We never had any trouble with 'em."

Enos grunted, then he eyed Charley, who was still pinching his lower lip and staring down at the board. "You gonna move, or should we send for the coroner?"

"Shut up! I'm thinking."

Enos took a sip of his coffee and grinned at the large man. "They let you say things like that at your tea parties?"

Presently Took threw open the door and loped into the store. Seeing Billy and me, he headed over to the counter. "Didn't spill a drop, Billy!" he said, with his lumpy half smile. "Washed your windows too!"

"Good. How's the oil?"

Took drew up sharply and his expression jerked into a rigid stare. "Th-the oil?" he stuttered, as the terror of some imagined crime drew across his face. His wide eyes shifted warily to the aisle where his father was and blinked nervously.

But Nils's back was turned.

"You—you gonna tell on me?" Took bleated, stepping closer to us. It seemed he was about ready to burst into tears. "If you tell on me, Pa maybe won't let me smoke the bees today. I ain't messed up nothing lately—honest, Billy. I swear I ain't. This is the first time. Wait!" he said, brightening. "What if I go check it now? Why, that's what I'll do, all right—hey, then it wouldn't be like I forgot!"

But as the boy turned to leave, Billy caught him by the sleeve. "That's OK, Took," he said, absolving him, "we'll check the oil on the way out."

Nils Johansson glanced over at us. He was a big man, a first generation Swede who had emigrated to the United States after the war, stayed a few years farming corn in Minnesota, then moved West gradually until he finally settled in Columbus. His wife, Ilse, was small and sickly, and it was rumored among the quilting bees of Stillwater County that he had hit her while she was pregnant with Took and ruined him.

All big men with foreign accents hit their wives, didn't they? Mrs. Stivers had no doubt of it. She was sure that he was fleeing his country because of some heinous offense he had committed, some dark sin for which he was fleeing the face of God. There was no mark on his forehead like Cain's, but he had his mark. Surely, in the skillet-headed Took, his sins had found him out.

"Where haff you painted the peas today, Took?" Nils, with his thick accent, asked.

Took reeled about and faced his father. "What, Pa?" he cried, nearly shouting.

"The peas—I can't seem to find them," Nils replied. "They're the ones wit' the bright green labels, son. Be a good boy and find two cans for Mrs. Stivers—the big ones."

For a moment Took's brow furrowed darkly, his eyes shifting sideways and brooding on the edge of the counter. It was his responsibility to stock the shelves every morning, and he did so by arranging the cans and boxes, not necessarily according to their kind or size, but according to their labels, using the various colors as a kind of palette from which to make shelf paintings.

Each day the shelves presented a new canvas; each day a new painting was created as Took rearranged them, creating order out of the chaos in his mind. To the fettered brain of Took, yellow cans of corn became the warming sun or a field of grain gently swaying. Bright blue bleach boxes became the sky and lakes and rivers coursing through brown hills of potato sacks, and green peas and beans were brush strokes of bushes and grass and trees, and orange carrots became cows or cats. Bright red catsup bottles were to the boy a sunset or a blazing hearth, and it excited him to add fire to his paintings.

Suddenly Took's eyes lit up, and he glanced over at the shelves. Forgetting Billy and the oil, he loped away and in less than thirty seconds produced two cans of peas with green labels from different parts of the store.

"Good boy, Took," his father said, clapping him on the shoulder. "Now go and find a box to put Mrs. Stivers's groceries in."

Mrs. Stivers came scurrying toward the counter, avoiding Enos and Charley and the man reading the newspaper in the center of the room. And Nils, lowering a pair of half-glass spectacles onto the bridge of his nose, began to ring up her items.

"Why do you allow them to come in here?" She scowled as she reached the counter.

"I beg your pardon, ma'am?"

"Why do you allow those kind onto your premises?" she clarified, casting a censorious look across the store.

Nils Johansson looked over the rim of his glasses and chuckled. "Why, Charley and Enos are just playing checkers, Mrs. Stivers," he said as he hefted a can from the counter to check its price. "And Stu—why, he's just reading the newspaper. They don't mean any harm."

"I'm referring to those Indian women you let shop in here, of course," Mrs. Stivers snapped. "Always coming into town and parading their ways in front of decent white folks. Don't they have their own stores on the reservation?"

The big Swede was silent.

"Well, you just know she's back there robbing you blind," Mrs. Stivers went on. "They all do, you know."

Nils peered at her for several moments over the glass rims. "That'll be four dollars and fifty-seven cents," he said flatly, holding out his hand.

Mrs. Stivers regarded him with her narrow-set eyes until her rodentlike nose began to twitch. Then she stabbed into her handbag and retrieved a little beaded coin purse and produced a five dollar bill. She snapped it under Johansson's nose.

Nils quickly made change for her and placed several coins on the glass counter.

Mrs. Stivers sorted them briskly with her forefinger, then, satisfied with the count, she squirreled them away into her purse and snapped it shut.

"Honestly, I don't know what good it is talking to foreigners," she said, returning the purse to her handbag. "And why I continue to shop here, I'll never know."

Johansson turned to his son, who, still beaming with the satisfaction of finding the peas, had just finished boxing the grocery items. "Took, could you help Mrs. Stivers outside wit' her groceries?" he said, forcing a smile. "She was just leaving."

Took nodded furiously as he grabbed the box, and everyone's eyes followed Mrs. Stivers as she stormed out of the store—the boy loping behind with his head full of smoked bees.

"Got her corset pinched a might too tight," Enos remarked, as she cleared the threshold. "You hear that, you old goat?" he yelled. Then he slung another lipful of tobacco at the coffee can.

Nils Johansson took a deep breath as he turned to face Billy and me. He smiled broadly at us as he always did. "Now, what can I do for you boys?"

Billy handed him the list. "The new Winchester come in yet, Nils?"

The smile disintegrated. "What new Winchester?" Nils said, dead serious. But being the good-natured man that he was, apparently

41

he couldn't bear the sight of Billy's face collapsing, and he quickly added, "They come in just yesterday, Billy. Haven't even pulled them out of the crate yet."

"Hot diggedy!" Billy hooted. "Mind if I take a look at one while you're filling Ma's order?"

The smile was back. "Sure t'ing, son. You just hold on a minute while I go and unpack one for you."

Billy looked at me and made a goofy face, one of those ear-to-ear grins that could be made by any imbecile. Then he jerked his eyes back to the storeroom door and drummed his fingers excitedly on the glass countertop.

I glanced back over the store.

The man reading the paper grunted bemusedly. He was wearing a starched cotton shirt, buttoned to the top, and a clean pair of pressed woolen trousers with red suspenders strung so tight they kept his cuffs at the high-water mark, revealing white ankles above his thin black socks. He was a homely sort of man, neat as a pin though, with a lean, horse face that was cleanly shaven, except for an impeccably groomed little mustache that traced his thin upper lip. His thinning white hair was short-cropped around the ears and slicked down with grease and combed neatly down the center, and his ears stuck out like little fans. He smelled of barbershop tonic. Since he was a barber, it was his duty to smell like one, he often reasoned with Enos.

Enos, on the other hand, saw it as his born duty to correct Stu concerning his "womanly ways" and told him on more than one occasion that he smelled prettier than any one of Miss Abbie's girls.

"'Hitler Takes Paris,'" Stu Dunnegan said, breaking into a lull that had descended momentarily. "Shows them German fellas marching through the Arc de Triomphe." He clucked his tongue. "What next?"

No one paid any attention to him. Stu was prone to such unprecipitated outbursts but was generally considered harmless.

Another lull descended, during which Billy's finger drumming, Stu's paper turning, Enos's hitting the side of the coffee can, and Charley's grunting fought for supremacy. The barber won out.

"'Brits in a Scramble at Dunkirk,'" he read. Then he added, "'Over 300,000 Men Stranded in Port.'" He looked over his newspaper. "Say, where is Dunkirk anyways?"

"Who cares?" Enos snarled.

"Dunkirk?" Charley Reese repeated, distracted from his game.

"One of them frog towns," Enos interposed with a surly edge. "On the coast—near Belgium, as I recall. Still your move, Charley. I swear, you play checkers like an old lady."

"France, huh?" Stu mused. He let out a short whistle, then said, "Them oom-pah-pahs sure are the warringest bunch of fellows, aren't they? I guess they figured that them Frenchmen were so easy to whoop, they might as well oblige 'em. Ain't nobody been whooped more'n a Frenchman, I suppose."

"Excluding Charley here, you mean?" Enos grinned. "I'm thinkin' it's pretty much neck and neck between Charley and the frogs. And by the look of things here, I'd say Charley is nosing into the lead."

Charley ignored the remark.

Enos fished the lump of tobacco out of his lip and flung it into the can.

Charley cleared his throat, then slid a checker forward.

Enos peered down at the checker. "That your move?"

Charley crooked an eyebrow at him. "What of it?"

Enos leered at him. "Then take your finger off it."

Charley slid the checker back out of reflex and scowled down at the board.

Just then Nils came out of the storeroom holding a long, narrow cardboard box and set it on the glass counter. As he opened it Billy's eyes widened with the joy of anticipation.

Nils began to take the rifle out of the box, and Billy's eyes were on his hands as he unwrapped the brown waxed paper, hurrying them with his eyes as a child might help another to tear away the wrapping of a gift.

Nils held out the rifle to him. "It's quite nice, isn't it?" he said, smiling.

Quite nice? Billy was speechless. For several moments he just stared at the rifle, the *rifle*, the "rifleman's rifle," as it was dubbed. "It's—it's swell!" he exclaimed.

"Go on, take it," Nils smiled. "It won't bite."

Billy looked at Nils to see if he meant it, then he took the rifle and hefted its solid weight. He turned the length of it in his hands, feeling the thing becoming one with his arms as he scrutinized the workmanship, admired the neat wood-to-metal fit, the satin sheen of a hand-rubbed wood finish, the impeccable bluing, the flats, the curves, the five-point checkering on the forestock and pistol grip.

"What you t'ink?" Nils asked. "She's a dandy, isn't she?"

"Real swell," Billy said worshipfully.

He snapped the butt of the stock to his shoulder and sighted along the barrel. Then sweeping the barrel over the store, he shot everything in his sights, the Q on the Quaker Oats box, the O on the Ovaltine, Aunt Jemima's nose, and, seemingly remembering the elk, he swept the barrel upwards and slowed as its head filled the sights.

"Pow!" he exclaimed under his breath. Then he pulled the rifle from his shoulder and inspected the action, the straight walnut grain in the stock, the long, shiny blue of the barrel, the checkering again, feeling, always feeling, his hands moving over its length, the wood, the metal.

"Boy, is she a beaut! What's it chambered in?" he asked, angling the rifle.

".30-06," Nils answered. "That little honey can drop an elk from as far away as you can see it. Furt'er even, if you mount a four power Weaver on it." Billy snapped the rifle back to his shoulder and sighted at the elk again. "No fooling? A four power, huh? *Pow!"*

"Be careful not to drool on it, Billy," I put in wryly. "You're liable to gum up the action."

Nils chuckled.

"Can I open the bolt?" Billy asked the big Swede, ignoring my comment.

"Sure."

He drew the bolt up and back, then chambered an imaginary round. "How much?" he asked, sighting on the gas pump outside.

Nils told him, and Billy's exuberance immediately fell. He looked at the thing with greater awe now, the kind of awe that accompanies all things forbidden to the touch of mortals. "She sure is a beaut," he repeated, smoothing his hand over the stock one last time before handing it back to Nils. "She surely is."

"We haff a layaway program," Nils offered hopefully.

"Yeah . . . well . . . I'd have to layaway for a hundred years on what I make," Billy said despairingly.

Suddenly Took threw open the door and ran into the store. He was wild-eyed and gasping for breath. "Th-th-they're beatin' him up!" he stuttered as he jerked his head back and forth between his father and the screen door. "They're g-gonna kill him sure!"

Nils rushed out from behind the counter and took hold of his son's shoulders. "Calm down, Took," he said. "Now just tell me, who's beating who up?"

"S-Sammy," Took replied. "They're beatin' Sammy up! They're gonna kill him!"

Billy and I exchanged glances. I knew at once, and I ran out of the store.

6

I rushed out of the store in time to see Booster's boot strike Sammy's flank and the latter go down with the yelp of a wounded animal. The Crow boy rolled onto his right side, curled his knees to his chin fetus-like, and moaned unintelligible words. It seemed he was railing at the universe for having begotten him.

Booster Fisk sneered at him, laughed at someone behind him, then made ready to kick him again.

"That's enough, Booster!" I yelled.

Seeing me, he pointed his finger and threatened, "Stay out of it, Hochreiter! This ain't none of your concern!"

I looked from Sammy to Booster, saw the big fist pointing at me, then I looked down at Sammy again. Sammy continued to mutter incoherently as he raised himself up onto his hands. There was blood on the side of his face and streaming from his nose and a bloody slaver slinging from his mouth. That he was drunk was obvious; that he had vomited whatever he had recently eaten was also obvious, and his left hand slopped around in it as he struggled to his knees.

Booster shoved him over with his boot again, and Sammy landed hard against the pavement. "Stay down, Injun." Booster scowled at him.

But Sammy began to struggle to his knees again, not comprehending the violence that had befallen him. A string of profanity and curses gushed from his throat.

I started forward. "Leave him alone, Booster."

"Or you'll do what?"

I felt a jolt of adrenaline, tasted the bile collecting in the pit of my stomach and mouth, twisting my gut into knots.

Then Arly, Booster's younger brother, stepped out of the shadows and threw his hands truculently onto his hips. "You hear that, Boos?" he chortled. "He wants us to leave the Injun alone. Maybe he's gonna preach us a sermon."

Booster stared at me with his deadly eyes. "That what you're

46

gonna do, preacher boy?" he sneered. "You gonna beat us up with your Bible?"

"I'd like to see him try it," Arly added, doubling his fists.

It is common knowledge that redheads like to fight, and both Fisk brothers had fiery red hair. They were also fair-skinned and freckled, the kind of complexion that seems always on fire from sunburn, always peeling on the nose and never tanning. Each wore faded dungarees with suspenders and a plaid work shirt—sleeves rolled up to the elbows—and a beat-up straw Stetson with the brim crimped down in front to give him a tough look.

Both Fisks were big boys, easily over six feet in their worn cowboy boots; large-boned and heavy-set boys, not fat but thick-muscled, thick-necked, thick-shouldered, with sloping foreheads. Dumb Montana plowboys with red hair and freckles, and they liked to fight.

Booster was my age, maybe a little older. His nose had been broken several times playing high school football, though most of the breakings occurred after the games in the locker room with players on the opposing team. But these did little to mar his looks, for he was already ugly to the bone from birth. Natural selection had seen to that. When he was twelve years old his father had knocked out a front tooth, adding to the effect, and he constantly shot streams of tobacco juice through the gap to impress the girls at school.

Booster was mean, all mean, mean and surly like a beaten dog, mean like his father, Josiah Fisk, was mean, mean from birth, mean with no apparent purpose for his meanness other than to vent some festering gene that he'd inherited from his mean ancestors.

Arly, a year his junior, was just like him, just as mean, just as ugly.

The two of them stood scowling at me in the sum of their meanness and ugliness, their arms now hanging loosely to their sides with fists clenched.

My eyes shifted warily from them and, in a moment of time, made a wider sweep of the area. There had been a third one in the truck. I had seen three shapes. Where was the youngest?

There, leaning against the dirty brown pickup, with his arms folded and his legs crossed nonchalantly at the ankles, looking at me from beneath dark brooding brows, was Nate, a thin, devil smile twisting over his mouth in mockery.

Nate was a throwback to some other limb in the Fisk family tree. He was handsome, strikingly so. His was a mystical kind of handsomeness that girls were unable to resist—a dangerous and reckless kind—the kind of handsome dangerousness that drew girls—like moths —irresistibly to the flame, that made mothers of daughters immediately wary and fathers of daughters at once suspect the worst.

He was slender and muscular like an athlete and darker complexioned than his brothers, with jet black hair and piercing eyes like twin blue lasers, boring out fiercely from their dark tunnels, revealing nothing incriminating. You couldn't tell by looking at Nate what he was thinking, but you would immediately suspect that his mind was calculating innumerable ways behind the dark tunnels to draw the hapless moths closer.

"Lookit him shaking," Arly chortled.

I *was* shaking, it's true, shaking with rage. Something in me wanted to leap into savagery, and something in me was fighting desperately to hold it back.

Booster laughed and gave Sammy another kick, and the boy went down with a cry of pain.

And then Sammy's mother ran out of the store screaming, seeing Sammy on the ground, throwing her hands into the air as she ran over to him and shielded him from Booster's pointed boots.

Sammy blurted out something incoherent and began to curse and resist her, swinging wildly at her and at the universe, but she prevailed with maternal strength and pulled him to the side.

Then the old men inside the store spilled out of the doorway (I could hear Enos chuckling. "There's gonna be a fight!"), and Billy quickly drew alongside me.

"You OK, Ty?" he asked.

I sensed in his voice that he was ready for a fight, maybe even looking forward to it. He had a bit of red in his hair too. I did too, for that matter.

"Yeah, I'm fine," I said.

"All of a sudden the air's kinda foul around here, don't you think, big brother?"

"What've you fellas got against Sammy here, anyhow?" I said to Booster, suddenly feeling a tad more confident. "He hasn't done anything. Now why don't you just get back in your truck and go on about your business, and we'll leave it at that?"

Booster took a step forward and shook his fist in my face. "I say it ain't any of your business if I want to kick the teeth out of every stinkin' Injun in town."

Arly cast a smirk at Booster. "He sure does sound like a chicken clucking, don't he, Boos?"

48

Booster grinned wickedly, revealing the gap in his front teeth, and shot a stream of juice onto the tarmac.

Billy stepped forward. "You want to fight, smart mouth? Let's do it."

"This is between Ty and me," Booster snarled. "It's none of your concern."

"I guess I don't see it that way," Billy said. "There's three of you and two of us. Even odds if you ask me. Right, Ty?"

Yeah, right, Billy.

Booster chortled, but I could see his mind working. Billy had a reputation. He was a known fighter. He had the kind of reputation in school that, once it gets hung around your neck, goes a long way in keeping you out of fights.

Me? I had a reputation for being a straight A student, a lover of American literature and theology. A winner of full scholarships to divinity schools. I never really considered myself a fighter, and right now I doubted very seriously that Booster Fisk did either.

It was then that I remembered Papa's words of wisdom that had been impressed upon us Hochreiter boys since we were weaned. They amounted to: "It isn't who's the biggest or who's the strongest that necessarily wins a fight, or even who's the best fighter, but it's the one who's most willing to lose everything that usually wins."

Comforting.

"You boys take this somewhere else," I heard Nils Johansson call out from the doorway of the general store. "If you don't, I go and call the sheriff. I go call the sheriff anyway."

Arly nudged his brother with his elbow. "What're we gonna do, Boos? We ain't gonna just leave, are we? We can take 'em."

"Shut up," Booster snapped, his thumbs rubbing the inside of his forefingers.

By the way the sun struck his red hair, igniting it with a furious glow, I knew that it was time, that the gods of war had descended. A lump swelled in my throat.

Suddenly Booster stepped to one side and swung wide at me, telegraphing the swing a country mile. I ducked, and he missed, and when I came up my right fist landed a lucky punch on his face. I heard the sickening crunch, saw his face kind of close in on itself, and I knew at once that I had rebroken his nose.

Blood gushed onto his shirt, and when he clasped his face it came through his fingers. Looking down at the blood in his hands, he wiped his nose with his sleeve and glared at me with pure hatred. As he lunged, I could see Billy out of the corner of my eye, springing catlike at Arly, knocking him down, then grabbing him by an arm and putting him into a half nelson. I couldn't see Nate, so I knew it was just between Booster and me.

What happened over the next few moments was a mystery, and later I would need Billy to fill me in on the blow-by-blow details. All I remember was a blur of fists and colors, shadowy shapes swiping by, gruntings and coughings that sounded like animal noises. Booster was making them, and I was making them, and in the muted, surreal crawl of time I heard between the animal noises someone shouting, "That's it! That's it! Hit him! Watch your guard—there! That's it!" I felt the gravel grating under my feet. *Watch the feet. Weight forward. There. Watch the lead. There. Shoulders down, swing up now—there. There!*

And then the face of Nate Fisk leaped out of the blur with his piercing blue eyes and froze with pristine clarity like a photograph. He was perched on the hood of the truck now, his crooked smile locked in place, and the thought flashed through my mind that he was a devil, that he really *was* a devil, that Booster and Arly were merely his subordinates.

Then the image was gone, and Booster was there, and the last thing I remember I was leading with my right (something Papa had taught me might lead to dire consequences), and there followed a blinding flash of light in my head, like a Roman candle going off, and then there was blackness.

And absolute silence.

The first sensation I recalled was the smell of hot tarmac, soaked in gasoline, burning the inside of my nostrils; the second was the heat of the tarmac against the palms of my hands and the back of my head. I felt as though I might vomit.

"What happened?" I heard someone ask.

Then I heard a groan, and I realized it was my own voice. Light began to filter through the darkness in my brain, found and wakened my consciousness, coaxed me into awareness. Colors swirled, light found objects, defined them, brought them into focus. Almost.

"Looks like you ran into a truck, Tyler," a girl's—or was it a woman's?—voice said.

Whose voice? No matter, I liked it.

"You're going to have a real nice shiner, Tyler. Big as a moon pie."

I groaned as a sharp pain stabbed my head. Wincing, I shut my eyes, and opening them I saw Kate, blurry at first, then she came into focus—sharp, beautiful focus. Of course—Kate.

She was smiling down at me and was dabbing a cool rag around my eye.

"Ouch!" I winced.

"Big baby," she said and smoothed the hair from my eyes with the cool of her fingers. "No need to be bawling like a spring calf."

"It hurts." I touched the corner of my mouth with my tongue and tasted the metallic saltiness of blood. "Here, give me that," I said, taking the rag and wiping it.

Billy grinned at me. "You led with your right, Tyler."

"You're telling me?" I said and groaned some more for effect.

"He gonna be OK?" a voice asked. It was Nils Johansson.

I could see him behind Kate, and behind him there was a pair of pale blue pie eyes, looking at me astonished.

"You best let Doc Turner haff a look at that eye," Nils said.

"No, I'm all right," I protested. "I just need a little air." I sat upright, groaned, and waited for my head to clear. "How long I been out?"

"Coupla minutes," Billy said. He was on my left. "You should see Booster, Tyler," he added. "He looks a whole lot worse than you."

"Did I knock *him* out?" I asked sarcastically.

"Well, no. But I could tell he didn't want any more part of it."

"That makes two of us." I looked around the gas pumps and up and down the street. There was no sign of the Fisks, no sign of anyone but Billy, Kate, Nils, and Took.

Took was picking at a welt on his neck as he peered around his father at me. His cap was slightly askew, as if he had knocked the bill and hadn't thought to straighten it. "Did you ever sock 'im good, Ty," he said. "You socked him real good." He liked me now, I suppose.

When no one responded, Took seized the floor.

"There was blood all over," he said, stepping in front of his father. "I ain't never seen nothing like it. Blood was gushin' out his nose . . . and on his shirt . . . and he looked madder'n hornets. He was cryin', too, I bet, wasn't he, Pa? Sure looked like he was."

"That's enough, son," Nils said, reeling him back. "We go inside now and finish stocking the shelves. OK?" He led Took away by his arm, but the boy was blinking over his shoulder at me with that same look of astonishment as before. "Maybe we'll close early for lunch—what do you say to that?" Nils added, and the way he bent over and said it into Took's ear got his immediate attention.

Took's eyes lit up, and he appeared to forget in an instant that there was ever a fight. He began to jump up and down like a happy chimpanzee, whirling and hopping and tugging affectionately on his father's sleeve. "If we go home for lunch, m-m-maybe we can smoke the bees, huh, Pa?"

Nils straightened the boy's cap. *"Ja, ja,* sure." He chuckled as they entered the store. "We'll go home and smoke the bees."

Took let out a squeal and trailed it with a laugh that had a raspy, seal-barking sound to it.

I struggled to my feet and tried to dust the smell of gasoline off my shirt. "How's Sammy?" I asked.

"He's OK," Billy said. "Enos and Charley have him next door at Stu's shop, cleaning him up. Sheriff Bonner's over there too. I think he's gonna keep Sammy in a cell till he sobers up."

"That could be a life sentence," I said, then looked up and down the street again.

Two boys around eleven or twelve were walking down the sidewalk toward us, apparently heading for the river, for each was carrying a fishing pole and an old wicker creel slung over his shoulder. They looked at us queerly as they passed, as though they knew instinctively that some kind of aberration in the cosmos was unfolding. As our eyes met, one of them averted his gaze, the other studied my black eye intently, then let out a long shrill whistle.

"What happened to the Fisks?" I asked Billy.

He was picking up some coins that must have spilled from someone's pockets during the fight. "They lit out as soon as they caught sight of the sheriff," he replied, struggling to get a fingernail under a dime.

"Well, that's a good riddance, I say," Kate added with a scowl. "As far as I'm concerned, they can keep on driving till they fall off the planet."

"Sammy's mama told me to thank you for what you done, Tyler," Billy said. "She said there ain't too many white folks that'd stick up for an Indian." He handed me the change.

I grunted.

"You feel well enough to drive over to the drugstore?" Kate asked. "I want to get some iodine on your eye before that puffy old thing swallows up the rest of your pretty face."

"I'm OK, really." I started walking to the truck, but my toe caught a tuft of grass that had pushed through the asphalt, and I nearly tripped.

"Nonsense," Kate said. "You just come along now. Billy, give me a hand with this hero, won't you?"

7

Now this might sting a little," Kate said as she applied the tincture of
iodine.

"Ow!"

"You really are a baby, you know," she teased. She screwed the
applicator back into the little vial, then scooped some ice out of a bowl
and folded it into a towel. "Here, hold this against your eye. It should
help take the swelling down."

Billy laughed as he turned away. "Well, I'll leave him in your
hands, Kate. Don't forget to burp him."

I glowered at him. "Don't you have something better to do?"

"I'll be back in a few minutes." Billy chuckled. "I'll just get the
groceries and maybe have another look at that rifle."

"Well, don't be long."

"We got plenty of time. You two lovebirds just roost here awhile
and play kootchie-coo while I attend to business." Then Billy walked
out of the store, wearing a little smirk as though he was in possession
of some well-kept secret.

We were sitting on swivel stools at the counter of the fountain
and watched him through the window until he disappeared.

"I like Billy," Kate said. "He's a real nice boy—and handsome
too. Every girl in Columbus would give their eyeteeth to be his girl."

"He tell you that too?"

"Not a word of it, Tyler Hochreiter. I've got eyes, you know."

"I suppose you think he's more handsome than me."

"Right now King Kong is more handsome than you."

"You're so kind." I looked at my reflection in the large mirror
behind the counter. I eased the ice pack from my eye. My left eye was
dark and purplish and nearly swollen shut, and the skin was red
where the ice had drawn the blood to the surface. There was a slight
swelling at the corner of my mouth where I must have bit my lip
during the fight, my jaw ached, and my hair was disheveled. In short,
I looked beat-up. "But you love me, right?"

"I always was attracted to big apes with black eyes," she said. "Looks aren't everything."

"Hmm." I returned the ice pack to my eye, then put on my best wounded face. "Well, I'm sure there will be lots of girls in Chicago who will think I'm quite handsome," I said. "Pretty girls, mind you. There are lots of them there, you know."

"And what do you know of Chicago girls?" she asked. "You've never been east of Billings."

"I've seen pictures. The magazines are loaded with them. Yes, sir. Why, I'll bet Chicago has the prettiest girls in the country . . . maybe even the world."

"Is that so?" Kate frowned. "Will you find it in your heart to write and tell me that they don't mean a thing to you? That your only real love is back in Stillwater County, pining over the counter of a drugstore till you get back?"

"With all those pretty girls in Chicago to chase? Well, I don't know," I said, daring another look into the mirror. "I doubt if I'll have the time."

"It's just as well," she said dryly. "I would be too busy chasing Billy to read them."

"I'll write."

She giggled, then kissed me, and her lips tasted of wild strawberries.

I pulled away suddenly, remembering where we were. I looked over at the druggist's window, peering at us from the rear of the store.

Kate smiled. "Don't worry, lover boy. There's no one in here but us. The blue-haired brigade's already been and gone—already gotten their daily doses of placebos and ointments. Things won't pick up again till after lunch."

"You sure? What about Mr. Turnbull?"

"He's gone to take a prescription over to Mrs. Ebers."

"Don't you have a boy comes round to do that?"

Kate cast me a knowing wink. "Mr. Turnbull sees to her deliveries personally."

Mrs. Ebers was wealthy Coon Ebers's young and pretty new wife he'd found on a business trip to San Francisco last spring. She created quite a sensation with the folks along the Yellowstone when she arrived, wearing her glossy lipstick and short skirts and red pumps with the racy open toes.

The Eberses' marriage had been one of those queer aberrations in life, like a cannon shot over the prow of social mores. However, she apparently proved to be too much for the old boy in the end, and she was now the single most eligible widow in Stillwater County.

Kate was craning her neck to see down one of the aisles. "Hmm."

"What is it?" I asked.

"Well, you know, Mrs. Stivers did come in here just before the ruckus started outside." She looked down another aisle. "Now to tell you the truth," she continued, "I never did see her leave the store. She might be watching us this very minute."

"Really?" The thought was chilling.

I looked around; however, there was no sign of Old Ferret Nose. There was nothing but rows and rows of over-the-counter drugs, tonics and salts, and other medicinal items designed to aid and comfort the failing human body before the inevitable.

In the storefront window there was a prominent display of Dr. Scholl's items to entice the sore-footed passersby, sure cures for corns and bunions and fallen arches. Dominating one corner of the window was a life-size cutout of a beautiful girl in a bathing suit, tossing a beach ball to a handsome boy. They were both laughing and having a grand time, demonstrating the kind of life one might expect if he took good care of his feet.

A middle-aged man limped along outside and paused to look in, looked at the girl in the bathing suit, never looked at her feet though. Then, checking his watch, he hobbled away.

Against the right wall of the store were four red vinyl-covered booths with Formica tabletops and rimmed with chrome bumpers. A Wurlitzer was in the corner, its wood and glass and chrome gleaming, looking like some blinking mechanical monster. After hours Kate and I would select swing music by Tommy Dorsey, Benny Goodman, and Artie Shaw and dance across the red-and-white tiles.

Kate could jitterbug with abandon, but I was lousy at it—irreparably wooden was more like it—and felt as if the whole world was watching me. But of course there was only Kate in the store.

Still, I preferred the slower songs, the big band stuff by Glenn Miller or the jazzy rhythms of Count Basie and Billie Holiday, where the tempo would allow me to hold her close and move gracefully across the floor, smelling her hair against my face as I sang the words into her ear.

Later we would drive down to the old Iris theater in Red Lodge for a movie—or drive over to Itch-kep-pe Park outside Columbus. There we would sit on a bench and watch the moon spangle the surface of the Yellowstone and count rainbow trout rising for midges, all the while listening attentively to the lap of water on the rocks and the wind through the pines—the ghosts of medicine men whispering to us stories of the Indians who had once lived along these banks.

And afterward when we talked, when the words of our hearts had ceased, and the drum in our temples stilled to a quiet reflectiveness, we talked of anything that came to mind: the state of the economy, the war in Europe, but mostly we talked of literature.

Books were my passion—fiction, non-fiction, theological commentaries—I devoured one after the other. I found in books a quiet sanctuary wherein I could reflect upon the universal nature of man, his glorious triumphs, his feet of clay, find my place in the ranks, so to speak, breathe through the collective lungs of the race. It was that love of books that drew me beyond the ardor of my youth to love Kate, to love her not just as a woman of superior beauty and intellect but as a fellow pilgrim through time and space.

Kate preferred the witty, socially minded English authors such as Dickens and Hardy, or the melancholy novels of the Brontë sisters, while I tended toward the American symbolists such as Hawthorne and Melville and the realists such as Hemingway and Steinbeck. But we found a common ground in the plays of Shakespeare and the verse of Tennyson.

We spent hours sitting on the banks of Itch-kep-pe, leaning over the Formica planes in the drugstore, and walking along the quiet recesses of the mountains that were worn down by the travail of rivers and the soles of restless men, trading lines, discussing the finds in each verse, wondering of their relevance to people who lived in Stillwater County, Montana, in July 1940.

"She came in here to complain that the laxative we gave her didn't work," Kate said, breaking into my quiet reverie. "Even demanded her money back. Can you believe that woman?"

"Huh? What woman?"

"Mrs. Stivers. Now how am I supposed to know if she's telling the truth or not? So I said to her, 'It would work well enough if you'd go easy on the cheese and peanut butter for a while, Mrs. Stivers—eat more cereals and vegetables and such.' Know what she did? She just gave me a sour look. I swear. One of these days they're going to find that old biddy doubled over in a ditch or something, you mark my words."

"Consider them duly marked. How 'bout a kiss?"

"Not now," Kate scolded, holding her fingers to my mouth. She glanced over at the doorway as a pregnant woman, carrying a baby in her arms, waddled into the store. There was a string of children with her, and she made them wait at the door.

"Hello, Mrs. Ruiz," Kate said.

"Buenos dias," the woman returned. She nodded her head and, chucking the baby in her arms, smiled an exasperated smile. She had to be at least seven months along.

"How are you feeling?" Kate asked.

"Que? Oh, bien, gracias!"

"Is there anything I can help you with?"

"No, no. I have come to buy some bottles for the bambina. Esteban does not remember what he did with the others." The woman shot a scowl at one of the boys standing in a knot just inside the doorway, every one of them gaping at the jar of red licorice ropes on the counter. "I think he uses them for throwing rocks."

"Not Esteban!" Kate said, loud enough for the six-year-old boy to hear. "Why, I've always known Esteban to be a little angel."

The little boy's chest swelled just noticeably.

"Si, si, Esteban," Mrs. Ruiz assured her earnestly. *"Esteban ven es de niño!* A bad boy—*el Diablo!"*

Esteban's chest deflated just noticeably.

Kate giggled. "Aren't they all?" she said, shooting me a wry look.

"Si, I pray to the Blessed Virgin that this one"—she patted her stomach—"is bambina. No more boys. Is very bad."

"I know what you mean," Kate said, nodding sympathetically.

I grunted.

"The bottles are on the third aisle, second shelf," Kate added, pointing Mrs. Ruiz in the right direction.

"Gracias, thank you," Mrs. Ruiz said and waddled away down the aisle.

Kate smiled as the brown-faced baby looked back at her with his large black eyes.

I felt around my own large black eye gingerly, for one corner had begun to twitch.

"Tyler, look at your hands!" Kate said, taking hold of them in hers. "I was so busy taking care of your eye that I didn't even notice them."

I looked down. My knuckles were bleeding and had begun to swell. "It's nothing." I shrugged. "They'll be OK."

"If I don't take care of them this minute, they'll swell up to the size of footballs."

She went to the sink behind the counter and filled a bowl with hot water, mixed disinfectant into it, then returned and cleansed each knuckle with a towel, daubing gently to wash away the dried blood and ooze. She repeated this several times until the wounds were cleansed to her satisfaction.

I watched attentively as her long, slender fingers gently worked the towel over my hands. "You make a lovely nurse," I said, smiling.

"I wanted to be one, you know."

"You never told me."

"It's true." She paused wistfully. "But you have to go to college to become a nurse. There's no way that my father could afford the tuition." She looked at me and added, "And they don't give scholarships for nurses, either, like they do divinity students."

I shrugged.

"I thought if I worked in a drugstore," Kate said, "I would at least be around medicine a little bit, help some of the old ladies find things for their little aches and pains—pat their hands and comfort them. You know, things like that. It's not nursing, but it's something."

"Well, I still say you make a lovely nurse." Looking down at my wounded hands, I asked, "Will I live?"

Kate suddenly put on a very officious bedside manner. "The human mouth is the filthiest place on earth," she said, as she applied iodine to the cuts and abrasions. "Teeming with nasty little germs that can cause infection." Frowning, she added, "Especially the nasty little germs in Booster Fisk's mouth."

"Where'd you hear that?" I asked.

"Mr. Turnbull. He may be a stodgy old bird, but he knows his germs."

I thought about it for a moment. "Then why don't our lips swell up like footballs when we kiss?"

She thought about it for a moment too, then arched an eyebrow. "That's different. Lips are designed to take the punishment." She giggled. "I guess the nasty little germs from one mouth size up the nasty little germs in the other mouth and decide to call for a truce."

"All's fair in love and war, is that it?"

"Something like that."

"Then I'm all for making peace," I said. Then I puckered my lips for effect and said dramatically, "'Come on, and kiss me, Kate.'"

She smiled as she replied, "'Twill be a pleasure, my Petruchio.'" She peeked to see where Mrs. Ruiz was, then leaned forward and kissed me, and I didn't care who might come into the store.

"Ouch!"

Pulling away, Kate smiled. "You really are a baby, you know."

The knot of boys in the doorway giggled. I had forgotten about them.

Kate smoothed her hand over my cheek, looking at me intently, then her smile relaxed into a look of concern. "Have you told your father your decision yet?"

I looked at her sharply. "No, and I wish people would stop bothering me about it."

"Bothering you?"

"My mother put you up to this?"

"Put me up to what?"

"Talking to my father about me going to college."

"Don't be silly."

Just then Mrs. Ruiz brought her bottles and a few other baby things to the cash register, and Kate rang up the items.

I turned back to the counter and stared at a saltshaker.

"Thank you, Mrs. Ruiz." Kate smiled, putting the items into a paper bag, then she grabbed a handful of red licorice ropes and put them in also.

I could see the knot of boys in the mirror light up.

"No, no, no," Mrs. Ruiz protested, removing them, and I heard a collective groan from the doorway.

"Perhaps if they have licorice they will be extra good." Kate smiled, putting the candy back in the bag. "Perhaps even Esteban will be mindful where he throws his rocks. Isn't that right, Esteban?"

The little boy nodded vigorously.

Mrs. Ruiz scowled at the boy, then she shook her head resignedly. "Such a boy. Oh, that the good God would give me a little girl."

But she relented, and I heard a collective "Ahh!" from the doorway.

Kate patted her hand. "Now remember, Mrs. Ruiz, if there's anything I can do for you, please don't hesitate to call."

"*Si, si.* You are good woman." Mrs. Ruiz smiled. Then she turned and lumbered out of the store, and the knot of boys followed after her, squealing for the licorice.

"You never give *me* any licorice," I objected.

"There's still hope for them," Kate said. "You, on the other hand, are incorrigible." Then she frowned at me and, picking up our earlier conversation, added, "And I'll have you know that your mother did nothing of the sort."

"Did nothing of what sort?"

"You know—put me up to prodding you. I just assumed you'd already talked to your father, the way you were talking so gaily about Chicago and all. I don't know why it's such a big deal anyway. He's your father. He's not going to shoot you, is he?"

"He just might."

"Nonsense. Fathers don't shoot their sons for going off to college and bettering themselves."

"You don't understand, Kate. Henry Hochreiter looks at things a little differently than the rest of us. Going off to college would be like an act of treason to him—desertion in the face of duty. He might just put me against a wall and have done with it."

"I think you're being a little hard on him."

"Hard on him?" I grunted. "That would take an act of God." A trickle of water rolled down my sleeve. "I think I need some more ice—" I groaned "—this is melting all over the place."

"Here, let me take that." She walked behind the counter and opened the ice bin and dipped a scoopful of ice into the cloth with a pewter trowel. Looking up, she caught her reflection in the mirror, studied it for a moment, then straightened a wisp of hair. She was wearing a perplexed expression and seemed to drift away to some distant place where thoughts go to graze.

Looking at her now, I felt as though I was some kind of a voyeur, invading her privacy.

She had a lovely figure and a pretty face, with dark hazel eyes that sparkled like gemstones in their high, well-formed cheekbone settings, and thick auburn tresses that fell well below her shoulders. In my mind she rivaled any of the starlets that adorned the silver screen, and she awakened in me the quiet benedictions of manhood.

Perhaps sensing my thoughts, she turned to me, and there it was! Her smile. I loved the way her full lips wrapped a red bow around a mouthful of gleaming white teeth. A smile to die for. It came easily for her, and she was generous with it.

"You're beautiful, Kate."

"What?" she said, reeling a little. "Oh, nonsense."

"Yes, you are, Kate. You're beautiful."

She rolled her eyes. "Patients are always falling in love with their nurses," she said. "It's because the painkillers have dulled their senses, you know." She walked around the counter to me and placed the fresh ice pack on my eye and held it there. "There. How's that?"

"My senses are just fine." I took her hand and squeezed it. "I think you're the prettiest girl in Stillwater County."

"You do? But what about Laura Miller? I thought all the boys in these parts worshiped her as the reigning beauty."

"Laura Miller? . . . Laura Miller? Let me see now . . . I know a Laura Halpern—waitress down at the Dewdrop Inn—arm-wrestles the drivers. Beats most of 'em too! But that can't be her, can it? You said Laura Miller . . ."

Kate sat down on the stool and crooked an eyebrow at me. "You know—Laura Miller—nice pair of gams—looks great in a sweater . . ."

"Oh, that Laura Miller!" I grunted. "Why, she can't hold a candle to you. Not even in the same league. No, sir."

I fibbed. OK, I lied. Laura Miller was indeed the prettiest girl in Stillwater County, but she knew it and tortured any boy who was gullible enough to fall for her wiles. She was the resident Scarlett O'Hara but without the Southern charm—a black widow spider, who'd chew any hapless fool to pieces, then spit him out as a blithering little puddle of sap.

"Nice try," Kate said, smiling. "There's an animated movie playing down at the Iris, about a little wooden boy whose nose would grow an inch every time he'd tell a whopper." She pinched my nose and said, "How's your nose, my little block of wood?"

"My nose is just fine. It's my eye that's growing."

"And I think you'll have a nice shiner too." Then she combed her fingers through my ruffled hair; there were bits of gravel still caught in it, and they sprinkled onto my lap. She kissed me gently around the eye and said, "I love a man with a nice shiner, you know. It makes him look so . . . so . . ."

"Beat up?"

"No. So manly."

"Manly?" It was the most ridiculous thing I'd ever heard her say. "Manly?" How in the world can a black, puffy eye make someone look manly? A tattoo of a bulldog on my arm or a battleship on my chest might make me look manly, but a black eye?

I shook my head and chuckled, then I stood up and took her in my arms. "I love you, Kate. Why don't you come with me to Chicago!"

"What?"

"I mean, will you marry me, Katherine?"

"Marry you? But—"

"But what? Why not?"

"Don't you think that we should wait until you're out of school? Get settled into something?"

"But that won't be for another four years—more if I go on to grad school!"

She looked at me for a moment, then lay her head against my chest and sighed. We held each other for a while, neither of us speaking, just listening. Finally I took a step back, still holding her, and looked at her thoughtfully. The sun, streaming through the storefront window, played over her face, catching the auburn highlights in her hair, catching the tentative upturns at the corners of her mouth as she struggled to smile. Suddenly she was the most beautiful woman in the world, more beautiful than Laura Miller could ever hope to be, and I leaned over and kissed her.

"Why don't I just stay here then? Forget about Chicago. Who needs it anyway?"

She looked up at me with her lovely hazel eyes. "Is that what you want, Tyler?" she asked. "What you really want? What about the ministry?"

I shrugged. "I don't know." I waited a moment, glancing away from those lovely penetrating eyes. "Sometimes I don't think I'm fit to be a minister," I said. "Lately, mostly." I grunted. "Sometimes I feel like if you just pricked the surface of my skin all the devils in hell would come spewing out."

"You think you have to be able to walk on water before you can make the cut?" she asked. "Is that it? As I recall, there was only one Man who ever did that, and He died on a cross for murderers and thieves."

I didn't answer; I just looked at her, thinking. "Ministers are broke mostly, you know. They don't make anything."

"Some do."

"Most don't make beans."

"But you have such broad shoulders," she said, smoothing her hands over them.

"What's that got to do with anything?"

She got a funny look in her eyes. "It makes up for a lot of beans."

"And my eye?"

"Especially your eye. There's a bean field in your eye. Your eye makes you look so—"

"Manly, I know." I looked at her and shook my head. "You're crazy."

"Yes, and I think you'll make a fine minister, Tyler," she said, smoothing my hair now. "You're kind and sensitive, and you've got such a fine mind. The world is sick and needs people like you to touch it with kindness."

"Like I touched Booster's nose, you mean?"

"He deserved that."

"I don't recall anywhere in the Bible where the apostles Sunday-punched their enemies."

"Well, I'm sure they would have if they had met Booster Fisk!" Kate said, then she laughed and stepped up onto her toes and kissed me again and left me with the taste of strawberries.

"I like it when you laugh, Kate," I said. "It makes me feel clean and strong inside—strong enough to take on any amount of devils. Maybe even my father too."

"You don't really think he's a devil, do you, Tyler?"

I let out a sigh. "No. No, that wouldn't do, would it?"

"No, Tyler."

We held each other for a while longer, and soon we began to dance, slowly at first, swaying to the gentle rhythms in the air, and then as the tempo quickened I twirled Kate across the floor, and she began to jitterbug with abandon. There was no music coming from the Wurlitzer, but there was music.

We both heard it.

8

Ichabod!" Papa had said in a grange meeting three years ago. "Ranching ain't nothing anymore but Ichabod!"

Everyone in the hall agreed wholeheartedly with him, but no one had a clue what he meant.

Long before the stock market crash of 1929, farmers and ranchers were well into the slump of economic decline. Most of them were paying out more than they were taking in and consequently going broke.

It was a case of simple economics, of supply and demand: the supply was greater than the demand, and the prices plummeted below the profit margins. And then the droughts of the early thirties came and razed the land of its fruit, turned millions of square miles of once fertile soil into worthless dust. Mortgages on farms and ranches were foreclosed, and there began a desperate exodus of migrants westward to the promised land of California.

Roosevelt's "New Deal" was supposed to stem the tide. Through the Agricultural Adjustment Acts of 1933 and 1938 the government paid farmers and ranchers not to grow certain crops but to grow others, paid them to cut back on cattle production—"subsidies," they were called—the idea being that this would create a demand in the marketplace, drive prices up, kick-start the agricultural economy.

The AAA helped some by stabilizing wages and fixing prices, but it hurt others. Small tenant farmers and ranchers suffered because they couldn't qualify for the subsidies and were forced to liquidate.

The larger ranchers bought up the little ones at depressed prices, merged with others and became conglomerates that were then run like big corporations by men like Josiah Fisk—men who took subsidies not to grow, charged more for what they did, made greater profits, but at the cost of allowing the government into their businesses and homes, into their stalls and cribs and time-honored way of life. They were men who looked upon the land now with soulless eyes that measured land and rivers and sky with ledger columns; men who withheld the rolling, fruited womb from bearing fruit, treated the land as if it was an impersonal, nonliving thing, and the soul of ranching departed —departed like the Glory from Israel—and ranching in Papa's mind became an Ichabod.

We loaned Rube Gibson a young Brahma bull that night three years ago, since his had died, and gave him a small breeding stock of heifers to go along with the bull, good sturdy Shorthorns that would augment his flagging herd. He was going through some pretty tough times. Ellie had taken sick, the bank wanted to call in his mortgage, and Rube about gave up in despair.

Sid Doyle stood up in the meeting and loaned him hay through the winter, since Rube had waited too long to bale and the rains came and leached out the bulk of his crop.

Then the menfolk along the Stillwater came with their teams and tractors, hammers and saws, lumber and beer, and shored up the sagging bulwarks of the Gibson ranch. And the womenfolk descended like so many she-wolves and worked in shifts around the clock, nursing Ellie back to health with fierce devotion, as well as feeding and washing and taking care of her eight scrawny kids.

Never was such unity of souls displayed in recent memory, such an outpouring of mercy and kindness and the grit of human fortitude, all working together like a great symphony. Rube and Ellie Gibson pulled through a most difficult time without a nickel from the government, and we all agreed in retrospect that it was our finest hour in Stillwater County.

I was thinking about that hour as we passed the Gibson ranch going home. Ellie and the children had gone into their house, their possessions gone down the road, it appeared, but their haunting eyes would not give me rest. I tried to shake my head free of them and forced my mind to other things.

A few miles farther along, as the road made a broad sweep to the left around a pine-covered table of rock, our fields came into view, and suddenly I felt a jolt in my chest, like a kick. I felt the jolt up in my throat too, felt it all the way down in the pit of my stomach. No longer was I thinking about the Gibsons.

I had been rehearsing several conversations with my father, like an actor rehearsing his lines before going on stage, and the terror of the audience began to grip me. I peeled away from the seat where my shirt had stuck, and I felt a trickle of sweat ease down my right flank until it was absorbed into my trousers.

Then the road dipped down and spanned a dry creek, and as we climbed the rise where the road pulled out of the dip, our gate came into view. My pulse was rapid now. I could feel it at my temples and around my swollen eye, and I was fighting against a general queasiness that was due in part to the heat and in part to the adrenaline that had worked through my system from the fight with Booster, sickening me now as I anticipated the confrontation with my father.

Billy turned off the highway. As I opened the gate to let him through, I scanned the fields that were ripening sweetly in the sun, looking for Sy and Jimbo to give them each a Coca-Cola, but neither they nor their horses were in sight. A few cows moved stolidly along the repaired fence, some examining it, some scratching their heads over the taut barbs; others were in the field grazing and not a bit aware that they were newly enclosed.

The white sun blazed over the soundless drum of the earth and cast little shadow, only heat, a sweltering, humid kind of heat that lay heavily over the ground and smothered the lazy drone of insects caught in the fragrant draft of flower lanes. A red-tailed hawk circled lazily against the endless sky as it drilled the earth for rodents.

I climbed into the cab and grabbed one of the Coca-Cola bottles out of the sack of ice and held it against my eye, and when we entered the curtained shadows of cottonwoods that lined the road, there was a sudden relief from the heat. Like an exhale.

"There they are," Billy said, pointing through the trees.

I glanced to my left and saw Sy and Jimbo in the round pen, working one of the spring colts.

"Want to stop?"

"No," I said.

Billy glanced at me.

I looked out my window in time to see the stand of oaks, hovering over the remains of my ancestors. And I blew out a sigh.

As we cleared the last little rise before the trees opened up into the steading proper, I was surprised to see Rube Gibson's truck parked in front of the house. We looked off to our left and saw Rube talking with Papa over by the tractor, and behind them was the barn, looking on with its single, merciless unblinking eye.

Billy and I looked at one another and knew what lay ahead.

"Pa's gonna take this hard," Billy said.

"Yeah, but he takes everything hard, doesn't he?"

I ran my tongue over my lips, for there was a taste of strawberries lingering on them, and a smile forced its way inward, into the pit where the jolt had sounded, giving me a little courage.

Billy pulled the truck next to the barn under a great oak, and we got out and stood in the shade, looking on.

Mutt and Jeff, seeing us, slipped out from under the porch and padded over to us happily, greeting us with wagging tails and wet noses. We patted their heads as they looked up at us admiringly, their eyes bright and liquid and their thick black tails thumping fiercely on the ground. But our eyes were fixed on the two men by the tractor, so they padded back to the cool dirt beneath the porch.

By all appearances Rube Gibson was a broken man. He was looking at the ground out of the dark hollows of his eyes, looking haggard and beat down. The bill of his cap shaded his gaunt face, and his eyes were watery and large—like a hound's—and were sunk in resignation as they swept the area at his feet. His neck was lined and leathery from the sun and burned red, and his small head sat back on it like a chick bird's, giving him away; for it is there, in the sunken area of the nape, that a man first shows his weakness.

He was a small, lean man, wearing a dirty white shirt, sleeves rolled up, a hat that was dark and frayed, and a pair of faded dungarees that were worn through at the knees. He stood rigidly with his thick thumbs hooked in his pockets, knees locked, and looking awkward, as if he were trying out a new pair of trousers and didn't want to break the crease in them. Every so often he would look up to test the reaction in Papa's eyes, and every so often he would draw his coarse fingers over the stubble on his face and make a scratching sound.

"I'm sorry, Hank," he said, pulling on his lower lip, "I had to do it—couldn't hold it together. I should've gotten out years ago. But I thought . . . well, shoot, I don't know what I think anymore. Things were changing so fast that I just couldn't hold it together no more. Bank called in my paper—said Fisk could take the whole lot, since he had offered them a price, so they forced me to sell."

"Fisk?" Papa's face drew taut. "You sold it to *Fisk?*"

"That's right. I sold it to Josiah. Everything. The ranch, the big equipment, the herd—what was left of it, anyways. Sold it at a loss, Hank . . . I had no choice." Rube shook his head sadly. "You can send the boys over for the bull. The bank knows it's yours."

While Rube waited for Papa to say something, he shoveled the dirt around with the worn toe of his boot, as though trying to uncover words to speak, but Papa only looked at him, his mind obviously still reeling from the news.

Rube pulled off his cap, a shapeless canvas thing that was sweat-ringed around the band, and he raked back the wet and matted tangles of brown hair that had crept over his brow.

Then he slapped the cap over his head and said, "They ain't men, Hank. They ain't ranching men—not like you'n me—yet they were telling me how I was s'posed to ranch. Said I wasn't keeping up with the times. 'What times?' I wanted to know. 'What in thunder times are you talking about? Shoot, I'm just startin' to pull out of this long slump of bad times like everybody else.' I asked them to give me another season—that's all I'd need to pull some things together—but they wouldn't listen, Hank. Fisk was there, grinning like a devil, and they were itching to get his money." Rube looked up at Papa, keeping his eyes just inside the shade of his bill.

"You sold it to Fisk," Papa said, still incredulous.

"Yes."

"Everything?"

"That's right, Hank," Rube said, eyeing him skeptically.

Papa pulled on the back of his neck and cursed.

Rube let out a sigh. "I know, Hank, I know. It's a terrible thing, a man selling off his life. I don't know what I'm going to do. Ranching's all I know." He surveyed the little swirls he'd made with his boot, then made swirls going the other way. "I guess we'll stay with Ellie's folks up in Fort Peck for a while, till I can get back on my feet. Maybe get a job workin' on the dam. The pay's pretty good and steady, I hear. Maybe put away enough to buy a little spread. Shoot . . . I might even be able to afford shoes for my kids. Can't keep them in 'em—their feet grow so fast."

He looked up at Papa and chuckled woodenly, but Papa was looking away into the distance.

Then Rube straightened his back, ramrod straight, and pulled his shoulders back so that his arms swung free of his sides, and his tone changed as pride edged into it. He looked at Papa with his watery hound's eyes. "I'm sorry, Hank. I know I let you down, but they gave me no choice. Can you argue me that?"

"No. No, I don't suppose I can, Rube," Papa said, his eyes working steadily over the horizon. "But why Fisk? My word, Rube, anybody but Fisk!"

"He was right there. The bank called me in, and I thought they were going to give me another season, but there was Josiah, grinning at me. They had it all set up. I didn't know what else I could do."

"You could've called me!" Papa snapped. "I'd've come right over and helped you out, you know that. We'd have thought of something—anything to stall them vultures. We'd have kept your place out of Fisk's hands."

Then something dark came over Papa. I could see it in the way he threw his hands onto his hips, in the bull arch of his back and neck. And as he spoke, a hardness came over his face. His features grew sharp and cold. "Confound it, Rube, didn't we all help you three years back when Ellie took sick?" he snarled. "Didn't we look after you?"

Rube looked over at the ranch house and studied it for a long while as if he hadn't heard the question. Then he looked straight at Papa and said quietly, "Yes, you did, Hank, yes, you did. And the Lord knows Ellie and me were grateful for it. But a man can only take so much charity 'fore he stops being a man."

Then he looked up and away from Papa, and the sun caught his eyes under the bill, revealing that the wetness had begun to bead around the edges. "Couldn't look my sons in the eyes no more, Hank," he said sadly, his voice cracking. "Just couldn't look 'em in the eyes no more. Do you know what it's like to look across the table at your sons with them knowing you're a failure? That they've only got half a man for a pa?"

Papa scratched the back of his neck, then looked over at us for the first time, and I could tell by his look that he was finished with the conversation, finished with talk of failure.

Rube knew it too. "No, I don't suppose you have. You've got something, Hank. I don't know what it is, but the good Lord smiles on you." He chuckled. "I trust you're aware of it."

Papa grunted and spat a stream of tobacco.

"You've done right by me, Hank. I'm sorry it had to end like this—I'll always consider you a friend." He stuck out his hand, but Papa hesitated taking it, and Rube pulled it back sharply.

I could see that it was an awkward moment between them as both men looked into the other's eyes, knowing that it would never be the same.

Then Rube's shoulders straightened, and pride came back into his voice. He looked every bit as hard as Papa now. "They gave me no choice, Hank. Got my family to think of," he said bitterly. "You can't fault me there. No man can fault me there."

Papa didn't say a word; he just looked at Rube, and I could see the wound working its way into him. I knew that the heat would cause the wound to fester, and by night it would come to a head and need lancing.

Rube straightened his cap, then turned away, his shoulders slumping forward a little, as though he were carrying a sack of grain. He took hold of the door handle of his truck and started as he caught sight of Billy and me. "Why—hello, boys," he said embarrassedly. "Didn't see you standing there. Ellie saw you heading into town earlier."

We both nodded, and as I looked into his watery eyes I could see a great sadness, and I felt the sadness move into my chest and settle there. For the man standing before us was not the spry, robust man who used to come over and play touch football with us after roundup, who could run circles around us kids and pass a ball like nobody I'd ever seen. This was not the man who, afterwards, would sit by the radio with Papa, hooting and hollering and drinking beer as Red Grange and Bronko Nagurski would lead the Chicago Bears to another victory.

No, the man before us was an old man, old and haggard-looking, with the fire gone out of his spirit and eyes. He looked as worn out as his dungarees. It was hard for me to believe that Rube Gibson was only forty-one years old.

Billy said, "Sorry about your place, Rube. If there's anything—"

"That's all right, son," Rube said, grinning quickly. "I'm free of her now." He clapped Billy on the shoulder. "You learn all you can from your pa, you hear? If anybody can beat them bankers and keep a ranch afloat, your pa can."

"I will," Billy said.

"I mean it, listen to your pa. He's a fine man."

Billy and I just nodded our heads.

Rube looked at me and noticed my face for the first time. "Say, what happened to your eye? Got a mean-lookin' shiner there." He chuckled a hollow, forced-sounding chuckle. "I hope the other fella looks worse."

I grinned, but Billy said proudly, "He does."

"Anybody I know?"

"Booster Fisk," I said.

Rube's head perked up. "Is that so? Well, that's something." He climbed into his truck, pushed the starter button, and the engine coughed to life. "You tell your pa to come and get his bull, hear?"

"We will," I said.

Billy leaned his elbow on the window of the cab. "You know, the Giants are playing the Cards later, Rube. Maybe you could come by after supper and listen to the game. Have a beer or two."

Rube nodded and smiled, but his mind seemed elsewhere as he drove away.

We watched him until the colonnade of trees swallowed him, staring long after the place where the trees took him, saying nothing, just thinking about the better times, mourning them. I looked back at Papa, and he had a distant expression on his face, as though his spirit had taken leave of his body and was out wandering.

"Is Rube going to be OK?" I asked as I carried the box of hoses and tools over to the tractor.

Papa didn't answer at first; his expression remained distant and unattached. Then as I set the box on the ground next to the steel treads of the wheel, the contents rattling and clinking, I could see his mind collecting itself behind his eyes.

"What's this about you fighting with Booster Fisk?" he asked, as though suddenly aware of my presence.

I turned to him, and he eyed my beat-up face.

Then he grunted. "Haven't I told you boys to stay clear of them Fisks?"

Looking into his eyes, eyes that were as blue and pale as the August sky but without the August warmth in them, I said, "I had no choice, Papa. They were beating up on Sammy. I had to do something."

"Sammy?"

"Sammy Two Feathers—the Crow boy."

"The drunk?"

"You should have seen Tyler, Pa," Billy said as he approached, carrying the groceries. "Booster looked a sight. Tyler really got in some good licks."

"Rube really sell his place to Josiah Fisk?" I asked, changing the subject.

Papa ignored my question and headed toward the truck. "You boys get them hoses on the tractor. I'll be along later."

"Sure, Papa," I said. "Where are you going?"

"Just get them hoses hooked up and the tractor running, you hear?"

"Yes, sir."

Billy and I looked at each other as Papa sped away, a great plume of dust kicking up behind him. I looked over at the porch, and Mama was there, looking down the road after Papa and wiping her hands on a towel.

Then the screen door slammed as Trout blew past her and ran

over to Billy and me, shouting, "Where's Papa goin'? Where's Papa goin'? Why'n't somebody tell me he was goin' somewhere?"

"Here, take these to Mama," Billy said, handing the box of groceries to him. "Tyler and I gotta fix the tractor."

"I'm not taking them," Trout protested. "Who died and put you in charge?"

"You either take these to Mama, you little runt, or I'll make you eat a road apple."

Trout snarled, "It ain't fair. I never get to go anywhere. Why do I always got to do everything?" And as he slunk away, carrying the box, he grumbled, "When do I get to be in charge? It ain't fair, everybody always telling me what to do."

9

It was the kind of day in the middle of summer when the sun ascends its fiery throne and judges the earth without mercy. It bleached the sky of its blue and left nothing but a burning, moistureless whiteness that scorched the ground to a dirty crust. A thin film of dust settled on the crops and roofs and in the leaves of trees and shrubs, settled in the hides of animals and in our hair. Swarms of no-see-ums gathered in frenetic clouds and strove furiously over the wavering ground. Cattle and horses sought the haven of shade trees, pigs burrowed into mud, and surly dogs and cats crawled to the musky dampness under porches until a happy indolence consumed their fevers.

The chickens alone were left in the open to battle the heat, and they stabbed the ground defiantly and scratched little puffs of dust into the air with their claws.

Billy and I worked on the tractor all afternoon in the merciless sun, putting it in holds, jiggling wires and hoses, loosening clamps, tightening clamps, filing points, poking and stabbing and wrestling with the thing, getting it ready for tomorrow.

Billy got it going for a few seconds before it quit. He stepped back from it and cursed, all the while scratching the back of his neck.

Every so often Mama would walk out onto the porch, look down the road for a while, then look over at us, wiping her brow with the back of her hand. Our eyes met once, and I shrugged my shoulders, for I knew what she was asking me with her eyes.

The heat was unbearable and made Billy and me irritable. And Billy made me irritable, for that matter. Everything about him seemed to get under my skin—the way he kept whistling "My Darling Clementine" over and over until it became a kind of monotonous torture. And the way he cleared his throat every five minutes was irritating, and the manner in which he shuffled from side to side in the dirt as though he had to go to the bathroom.

But I knew the latter was just his way of expressing something he didn't understand and that he was working it out through his feet.

Papa paced and spit tobacco when he was confused over a matter; Billy cleared his throat and shuffled.

And furthermore, as we labored over the tractor, the no-see-ums found our ears and tortured us. And the ground was as hard as flint, and I could feel the heat rising through the soles of my boots, and my toes burned and itched. I tried to wiggle them to scratch them against each other, but they had swollen and wouldn't budge. Dust hovered over the ground, mingled with our sweat, and formed a thin, grimy paste on the back of our necks, got in our eyes and mouth, and rimmed our nostrils with a gritty crust. Even so, I found myself dozing.

"Ty!"

"Huh?"

"You gonna hand me the spanner, or what?" Billy growled.

"The half-inch?" I asked, digging a wet gnat out of my ear.

"No, the five-eighths, like I said." And I handed him the five-eighths, but it was the wrong size, of course, and he cursed and flung it across the yard as Papa would have.

"Should've used the half-incher," I said, feeling a tinge of surliness come over me. I tossed it to him this time, and it landed in the dirt just out of his reach.

"Try handing it to me next time," he snarled, as he snatched it up from the ground.

And it fit, of course. But he tore it off the nut and rapped his knuckles, cursed, and flung it across the yard too.

"Temper, temper," I said, fully surly now.

Then he told me to retrieve it, and I told him to get it himself, and we almost got into it.

Mama came out then with a pitcher of lemonade and made us cool ourselves on the porch for a while, which we did, sipping the drink and lazing about in a heat-sapped and sullen manner on the top steps just inside the shade that was edging over them.

Mama went inside the house for a minute and brought out an ice pack for my eye. Then she sat down in the swing behind us and began shucking corn.

I shucked my boots and wiggled my toes. They felt better but not that much better. I scraped the sand out from between them, then lowered my head between my legs and groaned. In time I began to rock back and forth to some listless tempo, moaning a kind of death chant, occasionally dropping spit bombs on hapless ants that skittered between my feet.

Mama tossed an ear of corn into a pan, then she began to fend off the heat with an Oriental paper fan that Papa had bought her at the county fair last Fourth of July.

"Tell me now, Tyler, if you can last the minute," she said. "What happened this morning between you and that Fisk boy? You know I don't approve of fighting."

"Couldn't be helped, Ma," Billy said, rallying suddenly. "Why, we had to fight."

"I asked Tyler."

"Yes, ma'am."

"Tyler?"

But as I retold the fight I could see that her mind was clearly on the road that led through the trees, for she would respond, "Mm-hmm," or, "Isn't that terrible?" at inappropriate moments in the story.

Billy, perhaps feeling that my rendition was a little lackluster, added embellishments that I don't recall happening, so I'm sure they were fabrications, but even these had little effect on her. She just pushed the swing easily with her feet, snapping her fan, and every so often she would look across the yard, her eyes and mouth taut with concern, and sigh.

Jenny came outside with a bucket of sweet peas and sat next to her in the swing—a kind of mother/daughter truce between them in place. And as she began to snap the peas she hummed "Ain't Mis-behavin'," which she'd been playing on the radio earlier while listening in secretly as Billy and I described the fight.

Then she wanted to know if all three of the Fisk boys had gotten into the fight, and when I told her that only Booster and Arly had, she said, "I think it's gal*lant* of Nate to have stayed out, even if it meant you two whipping his brothers."

Billy and I looked at each other curiously, more for the way she said "gal-lant," with the accent on the last syllable, than for defending the character of Nate Fisk.

"There's nothing gal*lant* about it," Billy said, mimicking her. "Nate Fisk's nothing but a yellow coward."

"He is not," Jenny protested, throwing a pod at him. "Not all the Fisk boys are mean like their daddy." She looked down at her bare feet and admired her freshly painted red toenails. Then, twirling a pea pod between her fingers, she smiled demurely and said, "I might even go out with him sometime, if he were to ask me."

Mama shot her a fierce look.

But Billy stepped in and said, "Don't you ever let me catch you near that Nate character, or I'll box his ears in."

Jenny grunted. "Isn't that just like you, Billy. Don't understand somebody, and you want to box his ears in."

Billy glared at her incredulously. "You just stay clear of him, or I'll box his fool ears in! You hear me?"

"It's a free country," she sneered. "I'll see him if I like."

"No, you won't," Mama said, bristling. "You'll stay clear of him like your brother says. Nothing good ever came out of that family." Then, tearing at the husk of an ear, she added, "I swear, every one of them's the devil's own kin, clean through!"

"Doesn't the Bible tell us to love our enemies, Mama?" Jenny said slyly.

Mama glared at her. "Don't start with me again, little lady. Just don't start. I'm not in the mood for it."

Jenny lowered her eyes with just a trace of a smile lingering in them and returned to her bucket of peas, snapping them recklessly. Then the phone rang and Mama started, but Jenny jumped up to answer it, surreptitiously sticking her tongue out at Billy as she passed in front of him.

Billy swung at her legs, but she hopped out of his reach and giggled her way into the house.

Then we all listened as she picked up the receiver and her voice filtered through the screen door, thinking it might be Papa, but we could tell at once it was one of her girlfriends.

Mama stiffened.

"Don't tie up the phone, Jenny," she called out. "Papa may be trying to get through."

"I won't," Jenny said sweetly, then proceeded to tie up the phone.

Presently Trout swaggered up to the porch with Mutt and Jeff trailing him, their tongues lolling. The boy was holding an old milking pail, and in it he had placed mud and leaves and such. He was shirtless, and his shoulders and nose were freckled and bright red from the sun, and flakes of skin were peeling off, giving him the look of a lizard shedding its hide. His strawberry blond hair stuck out in thatches at odd angles where he'd run his muddy fingers through it, leaving bits of dried mud behind in the tangles. There were also mud splotches here and there on his belly and arms. His dungarees, slung low over his hips, were rolled up to his knees, and his bare feet were covered with dried chalky mud up to the muddy cuffs.

Both dogs were caked with mud from muzzle to tail, and mud hung from their bellies in long thick knots like stalactites. Seeing Mama's scowl, they slunk away under the porch to seek the cool dampness of the ground.

"Boy! It's sure hot, ain't it?" Trout said to all of us, grinning broadly and showing off his front teeth, which seemed too big for his face.

"*Isn't* it," Mama corrected him.

"It sure is." Trout whistled. "Even the fish are sweatin'." He chuckled at his little joke and wiped a big brown smear over his brow with the back of his hand.

"You're filthy," Mama said.

"Ain't nothin'." Trout grinned, scuffing one foot over the other and wiggling his toes. "Shoot, it'll wash right off."

"Then just you get over to the pump and wash it off." Mama glowered, and she grabbed hold of another ear of corn and began ripping the husk off it.

"Yes, ma'am."

But Billy turned a belligerent eye on him and said, "Where've you been, anyway?"

"Catchin' newts," Trout said just as belligerently, indicating his pail. "Got four of 'em." Suddenly his face broke into a big-toothed grin, and he said proudly, "Two of them was easy 'cause they was copalatin'."

Mama's eyes shot open in horror. "Joseph Otto! Where'd you hear that word?"

"What word?" Trout asked innocently. But he knew what word. The one he'd never used before; the one up until now he had doubts about. It was one of those words that carried with it a certain suspiciousness just in the way it sounded, the way it rolled off the tongue, sounding scientific and grown-up yet sneaky and wonderful all at the same time.

Trout no doubt had treasured the word from the moment he got wind of it and waited a whole month to try it out. "Oh, you mean copalatin'?" he said sheepishly.

"Don't say it!" Mama snapped. "Now where'd you hear it?"

The boy fidgeted embarrassedly with his toes in the dirt, eyeing the still-dark mud between them. "Uh . . . I heard Papa say it to Jimbo once," he said, head down but eyes now looking up at Mama. "They was in the barn, and I was in the loft catchin' mice, though I don't think they knew I was."

"Well, you just forget it, you hear me?"

"Yes, ma'am."

"And don't you be sneaking around listening in on folks' conversations."

"I wasn't sneakin', I was—"

"Joseph!"

"Yes, ma'am." And his eyes lowered to his toes.

Then Billy's still-belligerent eyes narrowed on the small boy. "You do your chores?"

"Sure."

"All of them?"

"You ain't Papa," Trout retorted, stiffening with indignation.

"Well, Papa ain't here," Jenny sniped as she came back out onto the porch. The screen door slammed behind her and startled Mama.

"Jennifer!" she snapped.

"Sorry." Jenny shrugged as she returned to her bucket of peas.

Trout stood at the foot of the steps, frowning at all of us. "What's everybody so mad about, anyways?" he groused. "I ain't showing my newts to nobody again." And with that he tromped off in the direction of the well. One of the Labs under the porch let out a loud, disgruntled moan.

It was then I realized that the sun had played only a minor role in our collective irritability, that perhaps the major player was the wound Papa had suffered earlier. It seemed it had begun to fester a little in each of us.

"Sy and Jimbo take off?" I asked Mama, hoping to lighten the conversation. "Haven't seen 'em all afternoon."

"They went to collect some men at the reservation," she said. "They should be back before nightfall."

"I like it with the hands here," I said. "Makes the place seem more lively."

"Well, the place is gonna be plenty lively come sunup," Billy said. "There might even be a band." Having said this, he kind of poured himself down the stairs and fell over the edge into the dirt and lay there as though he were dead.

Mama shook her head.

I watched an ant skitter up to my last spit crater and rise up onto its hind legs with its tiny antennae wiggling, before it headed off in another direction. I laid my big toe lightly on it, then smashed it into the plank.

The porch swing made a creaking noise behind me as Mama groaned. "You boys gonna lay around all afternoon and kill ants?"

"Yes, Mama," I said.

"What about the tractor?"

"Too hot, Mama," Billy whined. "We'll tend to it after supper."

"Yeah, we'll tend to it after supper, Mama," I concurred, then blew a big spit bubble.

"You'd best. Papa's counting on you boys getting it running before he gets home."

"Don't worry, Mama."

"Well, then you'd best get along to the river." She smiled, unbuttoning the top buttons of her dress and snapping the fan over herself. "No point in all of us roasting in this infernal heat."

Billy and I looked at each other as though the Red Sea had just parted. *Why didn't we think of that?* Then we jumped to our feet with a hoot, grabbed our fly rods from inside the house, and took off with Mutt and Jeff.

The Stillwater River sprang pure from the Absaroka Beartooth Range thirty miles beyond Nye, where the bugling challenges of bull elks echoed through the pines and bald eagles circled high overhead in air so clear and clean it must have been God-breathed. The river fell in a rush from its headwaters, a wild thing of grace and beauty (Stillwater was certainly a misnomer, for it was rarely still), and then it was fed by the Rosebud just beyond Absarokee as it crossed through the back of several large ranches (ours being one of them), then spilled into the Yellowstone about a mile west of Columbus.

During the autumn, Yellowstone trout traced silvery courses up the Stillwater to spawn, driven by a fierce appetite to reproduce their kind. And now, driven by a fierce appetite to eat them, I pulled out my fly rod and, since it was nearly August and every field in Montana crackled with grasshoppers, attached a yellow-belly hopper to my tippet and began working upstream along the cool and shaded banks.

I knew where they were, where they lay in wait, flicking their tails to stay their positions, in the cool quiet eddies behind large stones—the stones breaking the river, drawing the current around them with an offering of fallen insects. But nothing happened. I couldn't lure a trout up so that he might give it a sneer.

I selected another fly—an olive woolly worm this time—then set it lightly down above a likely looking stone with a supple cast of the tapered line, let the current carry it downstream and pull it into the eddy, then waited for the violent hit. Nothing.

I tried again. Nothing. I did so, time and again, changing flies, nymphs, and worms, dry and wet, casting the line over the river, adjusting it, stripping it back, mending the line, then letting the current carry the fly to the place where I knew the trout to be. But time and again the trout weren't there.

But that was all right. Billy and I knew that trout wouldn't surface for a fly in this heat if they wanted to. So, thinking that since Mr. Trout wasn't going to join us, we might as well join him, we tossed our rods, stripped off our clothes, and jumped into a clear inlet off the river, and paddled around like a couple of pink otters. Never was the Stillwater so refreshing.

I swam down to the river bottom and grabbed onto a boulder and let the pulling current stretch my body out behind me, listening to the cool rush of water flow past my head, watching bits of debris sail past like tiny birds. I let go of the boulder and floated downstream a few yards and grabbed hold of another one, intermittently surfacing to breathe, then crawled my way back upstream like a giant crawdad, using the bottom rocks like ladder rungs. We did this until we were waterlogged and turning blue, then we lay under a big shady cottonwood and dozed peacefully amid the cool river grasses and smells.

The first shotgun blast woke us up with a start. Billy and I looked at each other wide-eyed, wondering if we had each dreamed it. But then there were two more booms, a pause, followed by another two. By the time the last two sounded, we had triangulated their direction, and we knew at once that the sun had loosed some malevolence upon us. We ran home, but long before we got there we could hear the pigs squealing and our two mules, Moses and Elijah, braying.

When we arrived at the steading, our eyes met a grisly spectacle. Mama was hobbling back to the house from the chicken coop, breathing heavily and using the pump gun as a crutch. She looked wild-eyed and fierce, like a she-bear, and her mouth was drawn into a grim scar.

"What happened, Mama?" I asked.

But she didn't look at us, didn't even seem to be aware of us. She just stared intently at the porch as she limped past us, a bloody skinned spot on her right knee.

Looking down at my feet I noticed several shotgun shells scattered about; Billy had one in his hands already, examining it. Then immediately I surveyed the grounds. There were two dead dogs in the yard—some kind of spaniel and a rat terrier—their heads nearly blown off, and I knew at once they were two of the strays we had chased off the week before.

The third was lying in a ditch about fifty feet away, with a mass of red along its left flank. Then, everywhere we looked, there were little lumps of white and rust-colored feathers, some panting away the heat, some flapping pathetically in place, others lying quiet and still in death.

I had never seen such a slaughter, by rough count an even dozen. Chicken parts were strewn everywhere, feathers were floating along on the thermals and lighting in the shrubbery and sticking to the sides of outbuildings, and what chickens were still alive were running and flapping every which way, raising a squall.

I handed Billy my rod, then caught up to Mama and helped her up the stairs and into the porch swing. She laid the shotgun against the wall and just sat there looking out over the yard, panting and shaking her head slowly as she snapped her Oriental fan with one hand and picked feathers off herself with the other. Her face was flushed, there were filigree patterns of matted hair on her cheeks, and she looked any moment as though she might expire.

"Lord, have mercy," was all she said, rocking back and forth on the swing. After supper (we had a chicken casserole) Billy and I got the tractor running as best we could, then we all gathered on the porch again in the waning heat of early evening (since the porch was the coolest place in the house besides the root cellar), finding our favorite worn-smooth places to settle and relax in sated indolence and to pick out the corn bits that had gotten stuck in our teeth.

A small wind stirred and kicked up little dust devils that swirled here and there across the yard, and every so often a chicken feather or two would sail past and catch on something, but the wind was still warm, and Mama snapped it away with her Oriental fan.

While Trout threw sticks for Mutt and Jeff over by the barn, we busied ourselves, watching the surviving chickens scratch around in the dirt, watching Sylvester chase after the hens, with his wings high and his spurs clicking rooster-ly.

Off to one side of the porch, one of the innumerable cats on the ranch was stalking a rat. Others were sitting on fence rails and on bales of hay, and two were on the tractor seat, watching and curling their tails contentedly, for there were plenty of rats and mice to go around, and they all looked as if they'd had their fill.

Mama, wearing a plaster on her skinned knee, sprinkled water on her bosom and fanned herself while she watched the road. "Jenny, dear?"

"Yes, Mama?"

"Be a sweet and bring me a glass of lemonade, won't you?"

"All right, Mama." Jenny left and minutes later returned and handed Mama a glass.

"Thank you, honey."

Jenny smiled sweetly and sat down on the swing next to her.

"Where's mine?" Billy wondered out loud.

"You got a broke leg or something?" Jenny sneered.

Billy grunted.

It seemed there was still some residual surliness sneaking about on the porch.

Later we heard the trucks rattling through the colonnade of trees, and Mama perked up.

But it was only Sy and Jimbo, in Sy's dilapidated pickup, followed by another truck full of Indians. They waved and smiled—the red sun glinting off Jimbo's silver tooth—and some hooted as they drove their trucks over to the bunkhouse behind the barn.

We didn't see them again that night; we only heard their laughter rising occasionally as they were settling in, and later when one of them brought out a guitar and strummed it quietly.

The summer twilights in Montana last forever, it seemed, rivaled only by those of the great white north. When at last the long, thin shadows of the day were spirited away into the darkening boles of cottonwoods, and the dusk gathered light and drew a bright band of scarlet over the broken hills to the west, bats came out of their haunts into the bright gloaming and swooped over the ranch in frenetic arcs against the clean, purpling sky, and a white barn owl hooted from its perch above the barn as it scanned the earth for mice.

We could hear the lowing of cattle along the river, moving closer and closer to the steading, pigs rooting amid the corn husks, and the keening of nighthawks circling overhead. Still there was no sign of Papa, and every so often Mama would look through the door into the hallway to see if Jenny was on the phone.

The night came stealthily, filling in the umbrage of the trees and around the barn with darkness, cloaking everything in stark silhouettes against the blood-red sunset, and gradually, in twos and threes, the stars winked on and spangled the sky. Moths beat furiously against the screens, and occasionally we heard the wing-drummings of ruffed grouse in their tree roosts and mice scurrying under the porch as cats got wind of them.

Mama sent Trout to bed first, and he protested the injustice of it, and then Jenny followed a half hour later, the recklessness in her having subsided to an introspective aloofness. Then Billy went inside and brought out his harmonica and accompanied the distant guitar—together blessing the night and the creatures of the night with a soulful melody.

In time, the softly strumming guitar gave way to a strafing chorus of crickets that had crept tenuously from their blades of grass to try their legs, and then a little thundering of frogs drummed over by the well, filling in the timpani section, and the barn owl hooted in concert. And the Stillwater rustled peacefully in its course, and every now and then sent a cool air hovering low over the ground that was refreshing. And the sweet cut-smells of alfalfa, perfect to a turn under the sun, drifted over the steading, reminding us of tomorrow's labor.

The swing creaked a languid summer tempo as Mama pushed gently away, gently away on the floorboards, her Irish green eyes on the dark colonnade of trees. And she let out a heavy sigh.

"Best turn in," Billy said, slapping his harp against his palm to clear it. "I hope that calf don't get stuck in the bog tomorrow. We won't have time for it. Hope that tractor fires up." Stretching, he yawned, "You coming, Tyler? Got an early start."

"I'll just stay awhile."

"Hush, now. You get along, Tyler," Mama said, knowing why I'd said it. "Your father will be along presently, and he'll expect you in bed."

"I'll be up in a minute," I said to Billy and waited until he went upstairs. I listened to the night symphony for a while as the crickets and frogs competed for the ears of God, and then I asked, "Where do you suppose he is?"

Mama's features were rim-lit from the inside hall light that shone through the window and spilled an aureole of yellow light onto the porch, and as she turned to me her eyes glistened like the emeralds they were. "I don't know, son. I don't know," she said quietly. "Fighting off the torment somewhere, I expect."

We sat for a time in silence, listening to the night music and thinking. The porch swing rocked gently.

"I was going to tell him," I said.

"I know you were, son. But there's a time for everything under the sun, isn't there?" I caught a hint of smile in the shadows of her face as she looked away and peered into the darkness. "Best let it alone for a while. God will show you."

I got up from the steps and kissed her on the cheek and went upstairs to our room. An hour later as I lay on my bed in my undershorts, sheets cast off because of the heat, I could still hear the sound of the porch swing gently creaking back and forth, and I felt the ache in my chest. A lone coyote cried a soulful lament to the moon. But there was no answer.

Billy stirred in his bed. "Tyler, you asleep?" he whispered.

"No."

"You thinkin' about Pa?"

No response.

"You thinkin' about Pa, Ty?"

"Yes."

"What about?"

"I'm wondering if he'll blame us about them chickens."

"Course he will. But who cares?"

I groaned.

"You worry too much, Ty. You're liable to have a heart attack." He chuckled. "Mama sure made a mess of them dogs, didn't she?"

A half hour later we heard the truck rumbling toward the house like the front of a storm. It was probably a good half mile up the road yet, but the night stillness carried its peculiar engine sounds, dipping in and out with the terrain.

The swing stopped abruptly as Mama rose to her feet and walked across the porch, and everything was quiet on the ranch except the sound of the truck drawing closer. And then there was a hush.

Presently the truck door slammed shut, and then there was a curious shuffle of gravel underfoot as Papa made his way to the house. Billy and I listened as Mama went to him; and as their voices met, hers was edged with relief and protest. His had a recklessness to it that we both knew.

"He's drunk," Billy whispered.

I agreed. Papa always had a certain gait when he had been drinking, and we could tell now he'd stepped into it. It wasn't the slow-footed, weight forward, slovenly gait that accompanies most drunks but one that was surprisingly spry and wing-footed, a gait such as might attend a man escaping a prison. Papa was a happy drunk. It was when he was drinking that we caught glimpses of his unfettered soul, the skipping youth that had foundered somewhere along the way.

"Henry, there's blood on your lip," we heard Mama say, as she pulled him into the light at the foot of the porch. The relief in her voice was being edged out now by the protest.

We heard them climbing the steps as Papa said, "It's nothing."

"What happened? You've been fighting."

He chuckled. "Met up with Jim Fergussen, then ran into some of Fisk's men at the Dewdrop." He let out a whistle. "Whooie, did Jim and me give 'em a shellacking! Them Fisk hands is the sorriest buncha women I ever did see. I expect they'll tell Josiah twenty Indians whooped 'em."

"First Tyler and Billy and now you," Mama scolded.

"It's truly a day for the Hochreiter men, ain't it!" Papa howled. Then he must have caught his toe on the top step for we heard him go down hard on the porch.

"You're drunk!"

Papa chuckled. "Just a little. Say! Them boys get the tractor runnin'?"

"Yes, no thanks to you."

"Blasted tractor. I'm gonna get rid of that old thing. Right after baling, it's gone!"

"You do that. Now let's get you in bed."

The screen door banged softly, and the downstairs hall light went out. Moments later there was a shuffle of feet on the stairs.

"We got some fine boys, don't we, Beulah, honey?" Papa bragged. "Yessir, some fine boys! You hear how they whooped them Fisk boys? Whooie! There's talk of it all over town. I hear Booster's got another gap in his teeth."

Mama suddenly shrieked. "I swear, Henry, not here."

"Gimme a kiss."

"I don't kiss drunks."

"Aw, come on, Beulah May. Just a little peck on the lips, maybe."

"Quiet! You want the children to hear?"

"What, they think we're too old to horse around? Come on, gimme a kiss. We'll show 'em who's old."

"Stop it, Henry." Mama giggled. "You'll wake the children."

"You think so? I think they're listening right now—every one of 'em listening at their doors. Hey, Tyler—Billy! You listening?"

"Henry!"

Papa stumbled at the head of the stairs and, from the sound of it, took Mama down with him a tread or two. And then the two of them began to laugh hushedly, like a couple of school kids stealing away

86

from class. There was a lot of whispering and giggling and knocking against the walls, and we could tell Mama had him on his feet again. Then we could hear her scolding him as they bumped along the wall in the darkness to their room, and then, once inside, she closed the door.

Billy and I heard muffled voices for about five minutes, and then there was nothing, and stealthily the night sounds crept back through the window and droned furiously. Minutes later I could hear Billy slipping into the heavy cadences of sleep, and once again, however fleeting, there was peace on the ranch. The wound had been lanced.

But the ache remained.

10

Over the next few days the ranch was a whirl of activity as the business of baling got under way. It was not a chaotic disorder such as a swarm of mosquitoes might suggest but an orchestrated order, deliberate, well-oiled and flawless. Indeed, Papa was the sun—absolute in its sovereign rule, fiercely enforcing the dictates of natural law—about whom the planets turned obediently in their courses with the precision and beauty of a fine watch.

And the watch got quickly into a steady rhythm, the gears turning and beating out the eternal pulse of the land, with the sky and the rivers working together, with everything clicking and humming in its time and course, and the whole of it breathing like some giant machine beast as it worked. And Papa had his finger on the pulse of the beast, testing it against his own, and the two beat as one for he had the gift.

And the caramel-colored men from the reservation laughed and sang the sad ancient songs of their forefathers as they moved along in the rhythm of the machine beast, raking and bucking and pitching hay as easily as brownies slip along in the Yellowstone. But time and again as I watched them toil, my heart ached. For I knew that in each heart there drummed the distant and fierce echoes of the Crow, who were once the proudest and most beautiful warriors of the Plains Indians, and never did an Indian sit a better horse.

Today they were ranch hands, horseless and featherless, wearing beaten Stetsons and faded blue jeans and scuffed boots as they toiled under the sun, and happy for the work; though every once in a while I caught a glimpse of the feathered ghost riders that once thundered proud over the plains flitting around the edges of their eyes.

Papa drove the round baler over the windrows behind the Fordson, and Billy and I took turns pitching hay into the compressor hopper and threading and tying the wires on the bales. There was a stir of cool breeze from the north for which we were glad, but the air was choked with bits of chaff, and we wore burlap over our faces and heads. Still the chaff got in our ears and down our backs and up our legs, scratching them, and every so often hornets would tear out of the hay coming up the loader and dive for us, and we were always mindful of snakes.

Working another field, Sy drove Moses and Elijah before the flatbed wagon, and several of the hands bucked the square bales onto it with their hooks and stacked them out in the fields, sometimes twenty-five feet high, to be rolled out in winter to feed the stock.

Jimbo and the rest of the hands drove wagonloads of loose hay to the barn, where they were winched up to the loft with the Jackson fork, swung in through the bay, and stacked until the rafters groaned and creaked and the barn seemed to shudder under the weight like an old bull elephant on his last legs.

Mama and Jenny kept a steady traffic of lemonade and sandwiches flowing, and Trout helped Sy and Jimbo drive the teams.

Kate came out on Tuesday, which was her day off, and helped Mama with the lemonade and sandwiches, and all day long I could feel her eyes on me. I'd look up from the baler, and there she'd be, looking at me from the corner of the barn with those rich hazel eyes. Or out in the fields as we made a big sweep, I'd feel those eyes, and there she was by the truck, or sitting on a fence post in the shade, or stripping a blade of grass, walking slowly, as a woman in love walks slowly, peering at me over the strewn bales, with bits of chaff alighting in her thick, pulled-back auburn hair and the smell and look of harvest all over her. And we would find times—make times—to steal away or rendezvous in the secret clefts of the place that I might taste the taste of strawberries.

And the baler swallowed the vast acres of windrows and made pretty round bales, scattering them over the soft, feminine contours of the land to be lifted on the fork hoist by Sy and his brown men and their teams, time and again, over and back. The stacks rose against the sky, and the watch ticked and turned, and Papa kept his fingers on the pulse of the great machine beast. And it seemed the land gave a great shout.

In the evenings we'd gather around on the porch, all washed up and aching good in the muscles, watching the big ball of gold, and then red, fire drop over the western bluffs beyond the Stillwater. We'd exchange stories and experiences of the day, while Papa worked the thick steaks and big potatoes over the outdoor grill, and the smoke rose from them like an offering.

All we Hochreiter children watched him as he glowed in some secret knowledge, and Mama watched him with a twinkle in her eyes.

After the meal, Earl Thomas would bring out his guitar for a while, and we would watch his hard brown fingers nimbly working over the strings, fascinated and contented as the men sang low and kind of mournfully.

Billy accompanied Earl every night with his harmonica, and the stars would gather low on the hills to listen as the giant beast machine quietly exhaled. Then the Indians would retire early to the bunkhouse, and we would hear them laughing, and the guitar would pick up faintly for a song or two, then finally fade. Watching the glow of their lantern against the field of stars, I was reminded of the prairie ghosts. I loved it when the hands were on the ranch; it made the place seem lively.

And I loved Tuesdays.

Then on the fourth day, which was Thursday, the tractor quit. The pulse stopped beating. The machine ground to a halt. The planets trembled in their orbits.

Papa got to wrestling with the Fordson right away, working it over as a doctor might a terminal patient. He poked and prodded and paced before it and spat curses into the dirt as he fumbled for the right tool in his box.

But there were no tools to stave off the inevitable. Two hours later he stepped back from the thing and grunted resignedly and scratched behind his ear, his fedora pushed back off the scowl of his brow, and he stared at it a long while as though the sheer force of his will might resuscitate it. But it had quit; it had given up the tractor ghost.

Then Papa looked over at Sy, who was studying something in the dirt, and said, "I think she's had it this time, Sy. Get out to the reservation and get me another crew."

Sy didn't even look at him. He just nodded and grunted and drove away in the pickup. It was fortunate that we were nearing day's end. We put up the teams and gave them some oats with their hay. However, each of us was feeling gut-punched as we headed to the porch, each of us looking askance at the dead thing as we passed by it. The guitar was silent that night. And so were the crickets, as I recall.

The following day at dawn, Sy showed up with four men, clearly second-stringers by their slovenly appearance, one of whom was Sammy Two Feathers, who obviously had made the cut by the skin of his teeth.

He was wearing a pair of ragged blue jeans and a faded cotton shirt, translucent with age, that was once red with some kind of floral print in it, and he wore a pair of leather moccasins with a beaded pattern on the toes. His eyes were black and watery, red-rimmed and rheumy eyes with the whites jaundiced from alcohol, and they seemed struggling to hold a focus.

He stood about five-eight, if he were standing erect, and would have been a handsome boy were it not for the gauntness of his features and the dark hollows of his eyes that betrayed the look of an alcoholic. Even so, he had a fine head of shiny black hair, was lean and square of shoulder. On his hip he now carried a large Bowie knife in a beaded leather sheath; it had elkhorn grips and a brass S-shaped hilt.

Papa took one look at him and said to Sy, "What's this?"

"It's Sammy Two Feathers, Mr. Henry," Sy said. "You know Sammy."

"I know who he is—he's a drunk. I want to know what he's doing here."

Sy looked from Papa to Sammy, then back to Papa. "He says he's willing to work hard, Mr. Henry," he said, a smile breaking through his old-as-dirt face, stretching the skin over the high cheekbones. "Him and his mama's poor."

Papa chuckled. "I expect so, with this young buck guzzling away every penny she earns. Show him the road," he said and started to turn away. "I got no use for drunks."

"He won't drink here," Sy assured Papa.

Papa pulled up short and glared at Sy. "He's a drunk," he growled. "What else would he do?"

"If he drinks, Mr. Henry, you take it out of my pay."

"I don't pay you enough. What happened to Bear Littlejohn?"

"He's up in Miles City."

"And Frankie? What about Frankie? He's a good hand."

"He's took sick. I tried."

Papa looked at the three slovenly looking men that Sy had brought. They were all three gazing in different directions and probably wondering when they'd have to start working. They were clearly second stringers. Then he looked over at the boy, and then at Sy, who was pinching his lower lip.

"What stake you got in this drunk, anyhow?" Papa asked him. "Shoot, Sy, ain't there nobody else?"

He was getting angry now, I could tell.

Sammy, who had been following the conversation without much interest, suddenly spat into the ground. "I don't need this—not from no white rancher." He scowled, then started to walk away.

91

Papa's face suddenly went dark. Quick as a rattlesnake he took hold of the boy's collar and yanked him back, tearing his shirt, and the boy stumbled to the ground and landed hard.

I felt the jolt all the way over by the tractor. I could see the holes in his moccasins as his legs flew up and his feet showed through them.

"You mind your manners, son," Papa said, looking down at him.

Sammy sat upright and grabbed the haft of his knife, his eyes lighted with hate. The three men who'd come with Sy were watching the proceedings with interest now.

Papa stared hard at Sammy, and Sy and the three men stared hard at the boy, at his hand on the knife, at his hateful eyes that had narrowed.

But Papa said, "You think you're man enough to use that thing, you little runt, you go right ahead and try."

Sammy reeled a bit as he sat there in the dirt. I could see the change coming over his face as he glowered at Papa, and he slid the knife back into its beaded sheath. Then he climbed to his feet, eyeing Papa fiercely as he dusted himself off with sloppy whacks against his legs. He was muttering obscenities under his breath. His shirt hung now in two pieces from his neck.

The dark bruises Booster's boot had made showed on his ribs and flanks through the tears, and Papa eyed them. He grunted as his eyes shifted over to Sy, who was studying him from under the torn brim of his Stetson.

"What you think, Mr. Henry?" Sy asked. "He'll buck pretty good, I think."

Papa grunted again. "He'll buck, all right. Shoot. I don't know what's come over us, Sy, but if we keep on like this I expect we'll have to take up missionary work."

"It pay any better than ranching?" Sy asked, showing his old white teeth.

"Probably."

With the excitement over, the three new men went back to looking in three different directions, one at a drifting cloud, one at a bird preening itself in the big oak by the barn, one at a stinkbug laboring over the dirt, each likely thinking again that the work would start soon. There was no getting around it.

The sun was just slanting across the yard when Papa turned to Sammy and said, "I don't allow drinking, son. You want to get tanked, you do it on your own time." Then he stepped forward and jabbed a big finger at the boy's chest, the anger rising again in his voice. "I catch you drinking and—I swear—I'll throw your tail outta here faster'n you can spit. You hear me?"

Sammy just looked at him for a moment, then shifted his rheumy eyes to Sy, who nodded. Looking back at Papa, the Crow boy asked, "What's it pay?"

"What's it pay?" Papa looked at him for a second, stunned, then threw his head back and laughed. "Did you hear that, Sy?" He laughed again. "Shoot, from what I hear about you, boy, I don't expect you'll be around here long enough to pinch a nickel. Now, do you want the job or don't you? My missionarylike qualities are wearing thin."

"Yeah."

"Yeah, what?"

Sy took a step closer to the boy and slapped a leathery hand on his shoulder. "Listen, buck," said the old Indian, "do not think you're on reservation here. You call the boss Mr. Hochreiter, or sir, or you'll feel the back of my hand. Savvy?"

Sammy looked at him, wincing beneath the old man's fingers, then he nodded with a grunt.

"Now what you got to say to the boss?" the old man said, still gripping the shoulder.

"Thanks," said Sammy. "Sir," he added.

"There's no need to thank me," Papa said brusquely. "I don't give charity. You're going to work your tail off for every dollar I give you." And then the anger cleared from his face as if it was never there. "Now, how's your mama doing?"

"Huh?"

"You deaf?"

"No . . . er . . . she's fine."

"That's good. Your mother's a fine woman. Your father wasn't worth a dead battery, as you well know—he was a drunk too. But your mother is a fine gal."

Papa looked over at Sy, who was eyeing the three others skeptically. "Sy, show them where to put up their totes, then meet me back here in five minutes. We've wasted enough daylight already."

"Will do, Mr. Henry."

"And, Sy . . ."

"Yes, Mr. Henry?"

"It'll come out of your pay."

The old Indian smiled. "Pay? What is pay?"

The four new hands slung their totes over their shoulders and followed Sy toward the bunkhouse. Papa had his hands on his hips, and he was shaking his head as he watched them. I knew what he was thinking. He was thinking we had a long day ahead of us and we were still short on hands.

I was giving the tractor one last going over. Papa thought I might try filtering the gasoline, thinking that it might have gotten dirty and was somehow clogging the carburetor. It was worth a try. Anything was worth a try, considering those second-stringers. I had siphoned the gas out with a rubber hose and strained it through an old linen cloth, but it looked clean to me.

I was just filling the primer tank when I heard the *slap, slap, slap* of Sammy's big knife hitting his thigh as Sy and the four new hands swung by on their approach to the bunkhouse. I gave the crank a turn, but nothing happened. Again I cranked it, and nothing happened.

Then I noticed that the slapping of the big knife had stopped, and I looked up, and Sammy was standing there, staring at me with his watery black eyes. I glanced over at Sy, who had passed by me and was walking away with the second-stringers behind him, every one of them but Sy looking at the dirt. They wouldn't last, I thought.

"Busted, huh?" Sammy grunted.

"Huh?"

"The tractor . . . busted."

"Yeah, you could say that."

"What's wrong with it?"

"Shoot if I know. It just quit on us."

He eyed the thing and shook his head. "Just quit on you?"

"Yeah."

"1919 Fordson?"

"Yep."

"I thought this was a class operation. Can't you afford nothing newer? The 9N's a honey. Cost you about five hundred and eighty. Course, if you ain't got the jack . . ."

I looked at him briefly, interpreting his tone, then reached for the crank and gave it another turn. Nothing. "If we could afford a new tractor," I replied flatly, "you wouldn't be here, would you?" I gave it another turn. Dead. I could feel him looking at my swollen eye.

A few moments later he said, "Why'd you do it? Ain't no white boy ever done that before."

"Do what?"

"Take on Booster Fisk like you did."

"It wasn't anything. I expect you'd have done the same."

"No, I wouldn't have," Sammy said, now with an edge of contempt. "No, I clearly wouldn't have. I'd've let 'im kick your brains in."

I looked at him again, hard this time, looked into the black, red-rimmed eyes that swam around in the dark pools. "I expect Sy's looking for you," I said, then I gave the crank another turn. Nothing. And another.

Dead.

Sammy didn't move. He just stood there watching me. "It ain't goin' to budge." He grinned. "You can crank 'er till doomsday, and she won't pop." Now he chuckled. "Course it's your arm. You can do anything you've a mind to with your arm."

He wasn't going to last the day, I was thinking.

He walked around the tractor, looking it over. "Trouble with old Fordsons is the points get fouled easy," he said. "This'n's a real clunker."

"Tell me something I don't know." I was really getting irritated with his smart mouth. I was thinking now he wouldn't make it till noon.

Sammy said, "If it was up to me, I'd get rid of them gummed up coils and put in an impulse magneto."

"A what?"

"They got 'em at Chuck's."

"How do you know about tractors?"

"You mean, how does a dumb Injun like me know anything about tractors?"

"I didn't say that."

"You meant to."

"You got a mighty big chip on your shoulder," I said.

But he was looking at the tractor as though he hadn't heard me.

I was beginning to wish I'd let Booster kick his teeth in. "OK, then, how does a dumb Injun like you know anything about tractors?"

Sammy looked at me and smiled. "My father—you know, the drunk—he used to salvage parts from scrap heaps, then clean 'em up and rebuild engines. Then he'd sell 'em to the people on the reservation to put in their rusted-out heaps—get paid in whiskey. With rotgut too. And there's plenty of rotgut on the reservation, isn't there?"

Then he got a mean look in his eyes, and I could see the liquid focus steadying in the pools a bit. "Yes, *sir*, rancher boy," he sneered, "my dumb drunken Indian father knew everything there was to know about engines, so he got paid all right. Didn't he? Yes, sir. Plenty, all right. And he taught me everything he knew."

I didn't want to touch that last line, but I asked, "Your wealth of education include old Fordsons?"

He grunted contemptuously. "I can get anything with a piston in it runnin', rancher boy. But this'n will just conk on you again with the coils all gummed. Hook up an impulse magneto, and it'll go to everlasting."

It was then that I noticed his hands. "You got the shakes," I said. "How long you been dry?"

"It ain't none of your concern, rancher boy."

No, he wouldn't last till noon.

Then Papa came over to us and looked hard at Sammy. "What's going on here? Why aren't you in the bunkhouse with Sy?"

I was looking at Sammy and wiping my hands with a rag. "Sammy here says he can get this cheap old tractor running, Papa. Says he knows everything there is to know about junk tractors—that the coils on ours are all gummed up. Says he wrote the manual Henry Ford uses to build 'em too." I was fed up with the guy, and I fought an urge to give him back my black eye.

I looked at Papa, who was staring intently at Sammy. "You say it's the coils gummed up?"

Sammy quickly took the cover off the coils and peered in at them. "Looks like it."

"I checked them," Papa said. "They look fine to me."

"They're gummed. Sir," he added, remembering. He stood there, having slipped his hands in his pockets.

Papa stared at him for a long moment, thinking. Hank Hochreiter knew ranching—it was second nature to him—but put a tool in his hands, and he was lost; put a machine before him, and he would pace and scratch his head and spit brown arcs into the dirt. He had an immense respect for anyone who knew the secret ways of machines and tools, even if the person was a known drunk.

He looked over at the tractor and then at me. "Get on to town and pick up one of them things, Tyler. What was it—an impulse magneto?"

"She'll purr like a kitten," Sammy said.

"You believe him?" I asked Papa.

"You ain't doing anything with it—not as I can see. Now get on to town, and no lollygagging."

"Yes, sir." I looked askance at Sammy as I headed for the truck but was glad for the trip. I needed to cool down some, to repair the rift that had let the devils out.

An hour later I was back with the magneto, and Sammy had already gone over the tractor and made it ready. I gave him the piece, and he slipped it in as if he knew what he was doing. His hands were shaking more noticeably as he worked the screwdriver. Then he gave the crank a turn, and the Fordson coughed to life.

"Well, that's something," Papa said, gazing intently at the Crow boy. And then to me, "Looks like we might make a day of it after all."

"Looks like it."

Sy came over to Papa then, holding his hat with a real hangdog expression on his face, and the three second-stringers were behind him, looking uncomfortable.

Sy stepped away from the three and said to Papa, "They say they don't want to buck no more hay, Mr. Henry—not for no two dollars a day. They said they ought to get two-fifty at least. Maybe three." He shot a look of disgust at the men, so that they recoiled from it and cast their eyes to the ground, each wearing a fitting look of self-deprecation.

Sy eyed their looks before he added with contempt, "They think maybe they can make more at the chromium mine. I tell them they are lazy fools. It's my fault for hiring these bums, so I gave 'em the sack. You can dock my pay."

"Forget it, Sy," Papa said. "Sammy here got the tractor going."

It was only then that Sy noticed it running, and his eyes lit up. "That's pretty good. Hey! How 'bout that kid! I'll show these three the road, Mr. Henry."

"How long did they work?" asked Papa.

Sy laughed. "Work? They didn't work a lick. They worked at not working." He looked crossly at them, and their heads sank further into their chests. "I think you pay Mr. Henry for wasting his time."

They shrugged and eyed one another.

But Papa dug into his pocket and pulled out three silver dollars, with the liberty head on them, each of which he placed in a man's hand for a half-day's wage. Then he told them to take off. Each man looked at the coin in his hand that shone as the sun struck it, smiled faintly, then thrust it quickly into his pocket and left without a word.

"It is too much," Sy said to Papa, then he called out something in the Crow tongue, and the second-stringers quickened their pace. Sy

97

watched them for a moment, the sun reaching now his chin and lighting the little stubble of whiskers. Then turning he asked, "What about this one? He's worth something, no?"

And Papa said, "I expect we'll find some use for him."

I looked at Sammy, and his eyes were seeping with discharge. His hands had edged contemptuously back into the pockets.

11

The great machine beast came to life with an angry snort, shuddered to its feet, and came roaring out of its crib to make up for lost time. And as the Fordson rolled again over the windrows, the caramel-colored men followed with their baling hooks and their easy smiles, and the rhythm of the machine got into its cadence, and the sad ancient songs kept time with it.

Sy had put Sammy to bucking with the others, but in the first few minutes of his labor it became obvious that he had never bucked hay before in his life. He'd miss with the hooks, stagger under the awkward weight of the bales, sometimes spilling them over the ground and breaking them. And when he did, his eyes would search for Papa's and, finding them peering at him, his own would grow fierce, and he would attack his work with renewed ferocity. But it wasn't long before he was again missing with the hooks and staggering under the bales. And as Papa kept an eye on the Crow boy, Billy and I kept an eye on Papa, watching him furtively from the baler. Throughout the morning we saw in his eyes the tenuous glints of tolerance, of mercy, that shone no doubt because of Sammy's skill with tools and perhaps because of something altogether unknown to us. But what we did know was that, as with everything under the sun, there is only a season to mercy—a season not determined by the position of the sun or moon or constellations but by the dictates of the soul, of the gift that pulsed in Papa's brain.

The morning had passed, and the sun was up now in its heat and drew the moisture from the air, drew the moisture through our shirts and hatbands as our bodies sacrificed their precious fluids to cool themselves. Mama and Jenny drove out to the fields in the pickup and brought us plenty of water and lemonade to replenish the fluids, for without them the sun would wither us to dust.

But Sammy didn't want water; he didn't want lemonade; he wanted alcohol. His brain was convinced of it and rebelled against his body. The rebellion was in his trembling hands, and it rose in a riot of sweat across his brow. Later, as we were ending a long sweep with the baler, we saw him ahead, kneeling on the ground with one arm draped over a bale, vomiting.

Papa leaned over the tractor as we passed him and called out, "I ain't payin' you to fertilize the weeds, son. Get up now and get to it, or you can draw your pay."

Sammy looked up. His face was drawn and pale, and his eyes were watery, but there was yet a spark of fierceness in them. He looked sick, real sick. "Yes, sir," he groaned and spat the bile from his mouth, too miserable to wipe it off his chin. Then the fierceness flickered in his eyes and was gone, and he vomited again.

"I think he needs help," I said. "Maybe a doctor."

Papa eyed him coldly, then looked back on the windrow. "Ain't no doctor can fix what's ailing him. His body's got to work it out," he said. "If he wants to quit, he's got two legs that can carry him to the road."

"But Papa, I think—"

"Leave him be," Papa said brusquely. "Now mind your work."

I looked back at Sammy, who stiffened and arched convulsively as the tremors wracked through his limbs. Then he began to dry heave with raspy guttural sounds. He sounded like an animal caught in the travail of birth or the throes of death. He struggled to his feet and looked around dazedly for his baling hooks, then he bobbled and sat down heavily on the bale, and his head sank between his knees.

I looked over at Billy, who was shaking his head.

The season of mercy had passed.

The bunkhouse had been recently painted white to match the ranch house. It was a long and low-slung building of wood siding and shake that sat on a little rise of dirt and wheatgrass behind the barn, with a good view of the house, the stables to the side of the barn, and the other outbuildings. There was a porch that extended its length, facing west for the sunsets, with some crates and old ladder-back chairs arranged in a semicircle on it, and there were a few cats that lazed about on them, enjoying the shade before their evening hunts.

A grove of ancient live oaks encircled the building that were probably acorns long before the Crow Indians migrated to these parts in the 1600s. These provided a decent windbreak from the winds that came ripping from Canada in the fall and winter, and a bit of shade to ease the summer.

Inside the building were ten bunks, five to a wall, and a small window between every second bunk, three facing the steading and the others looking out on the hills to the east, and the morning sun shone through them, making big trapezoids of light on the plank floor in which the dust particles wandered.

Dominating the center of the room was a large cast-iron cook stove. On it sat a chipped blue enamel coffeepot, and to one side of the stovepipe a wooden crate in which the coffee and cups and sugar were kept hung suspended from the ceiling on wires. There was a long table next to the stove, with benches on either side, where the men ate their meals and played cards and carved their initials.

The bunkhouse had been added on to an old soddy by Honus Hochreiter in 1905; he had done so when the hands complained about having to sleep in the barn night after night and threatened to quit.

The soddy had thick whitewashed walls of lime and rough-hewn floor planks that had been sanded smooth over the years by boots and moccasins; a small window; a large fireplace made of river rock; and its only door opened into the bunkhouse. Sy and Jimbo lived in the soddy because its thick walls better insulated them against the cold and heat; its Spartan furnishings (two beds, a small wash table, and lampstand) serviced their simple needs.

The soddy had been built by two gold miners during the 1850s, supposedly as a base of operations, and it was said that they murdered one another with pickaxes for their gold. It was a story that fascinated me as a boy. As youngsters Billy and I spent many macabre hours searching between the planks for traces of gold and blood that might have been missed, each of us swearing that every dark stain on the floor was a remnant of violence.

The sun was just touching the hills in the west now, and the glory of it lit a boil of mosquitoes that were dipping in and out of some shrubs. It seemed their tiny wings were on fire.

Jimbo was building a fire in the cook stove when Billy and I helped Sammy into one of the free bunks. Sy helped us lay him out and stripped off his shirt and moccasins and loosened his jeans.

The boy's face was pale and drawn with fatigue. Water rushed from his pores as fever raged on his brow, and he thrashed his head and threshed about with his arms. But there was no strength in his fight; it seemed his mind and his body were disconnected. His chest and belly heaved, pumping furiously for oxygen, then all at once, as the delirium took him, he began to shake with agues.

The hired men hurried in and took up positions of observation. Sy brought a basin of cool water and began to wipe the boy's head and chest with a wet towel. He worked quickly and efficiently as Billy and I held Sammy's arms.

"What do you think, Sy?" I asked.

"Much sun. Much whiskey. No good," he replied, wiping the boy's face with the towel and occasionally squeezing excess water into his parched mouth.

Billy was genuinely surprised. "Sun? I never knew an Indian could get too much sun," he said, apparently intrigued by the thought.

"Too much sun is no good for anybody," Sy said, then added with a little smile, "even for Indian boy."

Billy was stumped for a while and grew reflective.

I looked at the dark, purple-yellowish areas on Sammy's ribs and flanks where Booster had kicked him. I had no idea that he had been kicked so many times. I became indignant at the thought of Booster cruelly working his pointy boots over a boy who was too drunk to defend himself, all the while grinning like some chicken-killing dog.

And then I noticed other marks. There were several thin, pale ridges, raised from Sammy's skin, that crisscrossed his abdomen and chest. I was perplexed by them, thinking at first they were some kind of birthmarks, and I looked up at Sy.

He was looking at me and read my mind. "Knife," he said.

"Knife?" I wasn't sure I'd heard him correctly. And then I was stunned. "You mean—a knife made these? But—"

Sy smoothed the moist towel over Sammy's body, gently dabbing the bruised areas around his still-heaving ribs. "His father was bad man. He get plenty drunk too. Lotsa times. Many nights come home and carve on Sammy with knife. This knife here," he said, indicating the big Bowie at Sammy's hip. "Carve his mama too."

I looked at the knife and asked, "What happened?"

"Yeah, what happened?" Billy asked, suddenly into the conversation again. "She call the sheriff?"

"Sheriff?" Sy chuckled. "What's the big deal? The sheriff think Indians are all the time carving on each other. Just two less Indians to worry about, I think."

Sy dipped the towel into the bowl reflectively and wrung it, fanned it in the air to cool it, then he folded it neatly over Sammy's brow. He said, "No, she didn't call the sheriff. She took the boy and hid in the hills until she heard that Sammy's father got killed in knife fight."

I looked down at Sammy, at the thin, wicked-looking scars, at the knife again, stunned. "I never knew."

Billy just said, "Shoot!"

"What were they fighting about?" I asked.

"Sammy's father stab some minister. Some big buck down in Lodge Grass carve him up pretty good 'cause of it." Sy shrugged. "Liked that minister, I guess."

I gaped at him. "He stabbed a *minister?*"

"I guess Sammy's father did not like his words." Sy paused for a moment as he studied the Crow boy. The muscles on Sammy's face were twitching, and the veins in his neck and arms stood out. "The demons fight Sammy, and Sammy fights his father," Sy said. "I think that he will lose, though; he is too much like him." Sy looked at both of us and added, "It is why I brought him here to work. Mr. Henry will help him."

"What do the Fisk boys got against him?" I asked.

Sy shrugged his shoulders. "Who knows? Maybe they just don't like Indians. Maybe they don't like Sammy's face. Maybe there's no reason at all . . . just meanness."

Presently Mama came into the bunkhouse with a bowl of chicken broth, and the men drew away from the bunk to allow her through. One brought a chair in from the porch for her, and she thanked him for it and sat down.

The Indian, a tall, rangy-looking man named John Thorpe, nodded and smiled shyly as he backed away, his eyes lowering out of courtesy.

Mama took one look at the boy, at the scars and bruises across his chest and stomach, and gasped, "Dear Lord—what an affront to Your loveliness." Then she dipped the spoon into the broth and aimed it over the boy's lip. "Here you go, child. That's it. This will do you good. There now."

But tasting the broth, the boy began to roll his head and wouldn't let her near his mouth with the spoon. "We've got to get this down him, Sy. His body needs nourishment," Mama said. "Hold his head steady, will you?"

"Yes, Miss Beulah," Sy answered courteously. Seated at his head, he cradled Sammy's head between his arms and pried open his chin with his strong, leathery hands.

Mama spooned in some broth, but the boy choked on it and wrenched free of Sy's grip. The broth dribbled out of his mouth onto his chin and chest.

"Strong boy," Sy said, redoubling his efforts.

"Do you think we got any in?" Mama asked.

"I don't think so, Miss Beulah."

The old Indian was never completely comfortable talking with her, especially when Papa wasn't around. She was a beautiful lady. He had lost his own wife a few years before, and it might not look right being so familiar with her. After all, he was now an eligible bachelor, and so he tried to maintain a gentlemanly detachment.

After she had married Papa, she used to scold Sy for calling her Miss Beulah; it made her feel so old, she said. Sy was mortified and stopped calling her that at once. In fact, he stopped calling her anything at all. Then for the next several weeks he moved about the ranch in a quandary, fearful of running into her and not knowing how to address her. It consumed his waking hours and tormented his sleep. We discussed the subject at length once.

He told me that, on those occasions when his work demanded he speak to her, he'd stand around diffidently until she made eye contact with him, and then he would begin talking before her eyes would shift away. Or he'd grunt a few times to get her attention, if it seemed she wasn't going to look at him, or he'd start conversations with "Uh . . ." or "Excuse me . . ." and then wait awkwardly.

It was when he discovered the word *ma'am* that she put her foot down and told him, "Sy, you just call me anything you like, you hear? Just don't grunt at me anymore, all right? And never, never, *never* call me ma'am. You're old enough to be my—" But she caught herself.

Sy had smiled and nodded, and, according to Mama, he looked as though a great weight had been removed from his shoulders. She had been Miss Beulah ever since.

"Let's try it again, Sy," Mama said.

But Sammy was moaning deliriously, and Sy let him be. "It is best to wait until his spirit is quiet," Sy said.

"But he's dehydrated," Mama insisted. "If we don't get some fluids down him, he'll get the fits."

"We must wait," Sy said, adding a little force to his words. "Pull too tight on the reins, the horse bucks . . . especially one that is sick."

Mama looked into the old Indian's eyes, considered his words and the dark lines on his face that had written them. "Perhaps you are right," she said, easing back. She handed me the bowl of chicken broth, and I set it on the floor under the bed out of harm's way.

Sy took the towel from Sammy's brow, dipped it in the basin, and dabbed it over the boy's face, again squeezing drops of water into his mouth.

"Let me do that, Sy," Mama said. "I can at least do that, can't I?"

Sy smiled. "Yes, Miss Beulah."

He handed her the towel, then walked over to the stove and helped Jimbo with the dinner preparations. Some of the men took their cue from Sy and pulled back to a more respectable distance, busying themselves about the bunkhouse with pedestrian chores. Others sat down at the table and played cards, every so often darting furtive looks at the beautiful Miss Beulah.

Mama hummed softly as she continued to smooth the towel over the boy's face and limbs. Her voice seemed to have a taming effect on his spirit, for he grew quiet, as though he had fallen asleep.

Jenny came in with some clean hand towels and looked down at Sammy with pity. She blushed a little at seeing his trousers undone and was careful to avert her eyes. "Is he gonna die, Mama?" she asked, studying his placid face.

"No, but I bet he'll wish he could."

Jenny's eyes darkened. "Why'n't Papa let up on him some?"

Mama thought about it for a moment as she dipped the towel in the basin. "It isn't his way, Jenny," she said, wringing it free of water. "If your father let up on him, the men wouldn't respect him. They need him to be strong."

"I think he's cruel."

Mama's cheeks flushed, and I thought she was going to scold her, but the anger left her face as she dabbed the towel across Sammy's brow. Looking thoughtfully at him, she said, "He's your father, honey. I don't like to hear you talking about him that way."

Jenny's face worked through a range of expressions. "Couldn't he just once act like everybody else—like a human being? You know, I can't remember the last time I saw him smile."

"He's not like everybody else," Mama said. "If he was, I'm sure you'd find fault with that too. You'd say he was boring."

"I would not. I would say he was a fine human being and a wonderful father."

Billy looked at me and rolled his eyes.

"He *is* a wonderful father," Mama chided. "And he's a decent man too."

Jenny grunted. "He has a queer way of showing it, unless not showing it is wonderful."

"You just don't always see his qualities from your perspective. You would not believe the sacrifices he makes so that you children can have three squares in your bellies every day and a roof over your heads."

"You're right, I don't believe it," Jenny said sarcastically. "O me of little faith."

Mama glared at her. "I won't stand for your impudence, young lady! Nor your irreverence!"

Some of the men playing cards looked embarrassedly at one another, and a few of them got up and went outside.

Mama watched them leave, then she snapped her eyes back to Jenny. I saw her trying to control her temper. "Must you be so contrary all the time? Can't you see this just isn't the time or place? Try being a little more considerate of others beside yourself all the time." She shook her head, clearly exasperated to the point of tears. "I just don't understand where you got all of your selfishness, Jenny. I swear, I just don't understand it. Here, give me one of those towels." And she snatched one from Jenny's pile, dipped it into the basin, and exchanged it with the one over Sammy's brow.

Jenny scowled darkly at the side of Mama's face.

Sammy moaned and turned his head on the pillow, back and forth, until his eyes labored opened and fell on Jenny. He regarded her strangely for a moment with glassy, uncomprehending eyes, then suddenly his body shuddered violently, and he let out a scream.

Mama and Jenny reeled back, startled.

Sy rushed over to the bed and helped Billy and me to restrain him. Sammy flailed his arms, and it took all of our combined efforts to subdue him.

"We will take care of him now, Miss Beulah," Sy said. "The demons come to dance in the alcohol brain, but there is no alcohol there, and they are angry. They fight with Sammy. They tell him to find whiskey, but they know we will not let him, and they fight us with his fists." And then he became visibly uncomfortable, his features working through the tragic repertoire of a Greek actor. "Maybe is best you . . . uh . . . Miss Beulah, maybe if you and . . . Mr. Henry would not like for his woman to be beaten up by Indian boy."

Looking into Sy's struggling face, Mama smiled and stood to her feet. She knew that Sammy was in no condition to beat up anything, but she knew that the Indians would be pressed to the limits of their courtesies until she left.

"Let's go now," she said to the three of us. "Your father will be wanting supper."

Two of the men came over to the bunk and relieved Billy and me.

"I'll be back after supper," I said. Standing, I looked again at the pale, wicked-looking ridges that crisscrossed his body, and shook my head.

Jenny followed my eyes absently to his chest, and I saw her visibly shudder. "Come on, Jenny," I said, and I led her out onto the porch.

Mama and Billy were already headed to the house. The sun was dark in the west and bathed the porch in blood red hues, and, as I watched Mama and Billy walking away, the sun caught Mama's hair and lit it with the last glorious fire of the day. The trees quickly became dark silhouettes and crisp against the sky.

Jenny stood beside me, and I could tell that she was in a surly mood. "Don't you think Papa's cruel, Tyler?" she asked. "Or am I the only one around here that can see it?"

"Keep it to yourself, Jenny," I said, irritated with her. I stepped off the porch and headed to the house. "Just keep it to yourself. I swear, sometimes you ain't got the sense God gave a turnip."

Jenny scowled at me. "When was the last time you saw him smile, Superman? Not since the last time he whacked you on the head, I bet."

12

After supper I headed back to the bunkhouse. The moon had not yet risen. The stars were out, and ribbons of dark clouds floated overhead on a light, cool breeze. The frogs were in fine voice, and there was a heavy scent of hay in the air that cleared my head.

Rounding the barn, I could hear the men talking on the porch in hushed voices and the occasional dull slap on flesh as the mosquitoes found their arms and necks. From a distance I could make out the men's shapes and could see the glow of their cigarettes as they pulled hard on them, then watched the reddish lights fall like tiny shooting stars as they lowered their arms.

Several cat shapes curled back and forth in front of the lighted doorway, then Jimbo's silhouette filled the opening and lowered something into the shadows, and the cat shapes hurried to it. The men greeted me as the light from the kerosene lamps inside pulled my face out of the darkness.

I stepped up onto the porch and greeted them with a comment on the fine summer evening we were having. They all looked out over the steading and nodded respectfully. A few answered with affirmative grunts. Those who were smoking, which was all of them, held off smoking while I was there. John Thorpe cupped his hand under his ash. Then one of them made a remark about the work tomorrow.

I nodded respectfully back and made an attempt at humor. The men laughed politely. We'd all run out of things to say. I could see they were uncomfortable, so I let them be. The smoking resumed.

Sammy lay moaning on his bed when I stepped into the bunkhouse, but he had quieted some.

Sy was dabbing his head and bare chest with a cool rag and chanting to him quietly in the Crow language, of which I could make out only the occasional word or phrase. He looked up as I entered and smiled, as did Jimbo, who was over by the stove, cooking a stew.

Earl Thomas sat on his bunk tuning his guitar. He was a fat man with a round face that seemed always to have a smile on it, and the mattress bowed beneath his weight. He wore his hair in two long braids. He looked up and smiled, then down at his guitar, still smiling, his chubby brown fingers deftly tweaking the old ivory pegs.

"How is he?" I asked Sy.

"Jimbo got him to take broth," Sy replied. "The demons are quiet now."

"Is he better, then?"

"They will return, I am sure," he said, wiping the boy's hands and arms. "It will be a long night. But he is young and strong. We will make a sweat hut behind the bunkhouse to work the poison out of him. He will get well."

Jimbo called the men in off the porch, and they filed in orderly, squinting in the light and curling their upper lips as though that helped them to see better.

"Belii shik," Earl Thomas said, smiling happily as he rubbed his round belly.

Jimbo laughed. "You are always hungry. You eat like *iigiila.*"

The other men laughed as they crowded around the stove; however, Earl Thomas failed to see the humor.

Then each man collected his tin bowl, and Jimbo ladled stew into it. It was a thick beef stew with lots of vegetables and a few green jalapeño peppers, trucked up from Mexico, laced into it to give it spice. There was nothing like Jimbo's stew when the peppers were fresh, and even though I had eaten a full dinner, my saliva glands started up again. One of the men pulled a tray of biscuits from the oven, and another had the coffee going.

Then the men bowed their heads, and Sy said a blessing in the Crow tongue and ended it with the "Amen," and they ate their meal.

Looking at them talking and laughing easily, I envied their simplicity, their humility, their guileless smiles, their genuine friendliness. There were many times that I wished that I was one of them—a Crow Indian. And this was one of those times.

I tried to enter into their conversation, mingle with them, but they would grow shy, and the rhythm would break. I was Henry Hochreiter's son, the heir apparent. I knew that as close as I could come to them, there would always be a chasm between us. They had their world, and I had mine; I could never cross over into theirs, and neither could they cross over into mine. We saw this in each other's eyes.

After their meal, Earl Thomas, smiling satedly now, picked up his guitar and began to strum lightly and hum a sad song of his people. Sammy grew quiet on his bed, as though the music was a balm to his mind.

The men gathered around on the bunks, some on the bench, forming a circle. Then each in turn around the circle, with the kerosene light turned down low so that the room took on a reverent kind of glow and hush, they began to tell stories.

Some were humorous stories, mostly anecdotes relating to their work or their wives or families on the reservation, and the men laughed at them. Listening, I laughed too, for I understood their laughter and felt a part of their joy.

Other stories were not so humorous. These were born of the Indian's longing that reached back to a time when the plains once thundered with buffalo and antelope; to a time before gold was discovered and the Homestead Act enacted, which brought the white man in droves with his killing diseases and reckless pluralistic culture and his whiskey; to a time before the soldiers came with the long knives, and before the plows of pioneers furrowed the ground, pushing the elk and deer farther north, forcing the Indians to uproot their homes and follow them; to a time before the iron rails were laid and divided the land and killed the buffalo and brought more soldiers and settlers and plows and whiskey; to a time before they were forced to live on reservations with little game, before the government treaties that would be broken time and again, reinforcing their helplessness; to a time before the ghost dances of the Sioux, before Sand Creek and Wounded Knee. And as each story was told, it collected sadness with the telling, and all the while Earl Thomas was sadly playing his guitar.

As I listened to each man lend his voice to the collective lore of travail, I felt a great loneliness welling up inside me. These were stories I could not relate to, pain I could feel no part of, and they only served to illustrate how really wide the chasm was between us. I let out many sighs.

And then it was Sy's turn. He was the oldest, and so it was his honor to speak last.

"Tell us the story of when you met Crazy Horse, Sy," I said.

The men turned and stared at me, perhaps as stunned as I was that I had just blurted it out.

But Sy smiled. His eyes twinkled in the yellow light, and the ancient wrinkles of his face spread outward as he looked thoughtfully at me. I had heard the story a hundred times, but I wanted to hear it again.

"It is a good story," Sy said, and the men nodded and grunted approval.

Then the room grew quiet, and Sy's vision seemed to turn inward on some ancient place; his eyes were liquid and colorless with age and were focused on a point in the middle of the circle and just above it. Raising his hand prophetlike, he began.

"I will tell you the story of when the Akbadádéa—the Great Father —was watching over me. It is a good story with much honor in it."

His words fell quickly into a deliberate cadence. It was a tale that had been told and retold many times, and the words were old words and hewed to fit neatly into the story, and the lines of the story were as old and worn as those in the old Indian's face, radiating from his temples, which shone warmly in the yellow light.

"My father was Standing Elk." Sy spoke slowly and deliberately, and there was a measure of pride in his voice. "He was a great warrior of the Crow people. This is a true statement, and there is no one who can speak against it, unless he is a liar."

He paused, as though to allow a liar his objection. He glanced fiercely around the room, but there were no liars present.

"Standing Elk was also a wise man, who sat in many councils with the tribal chiefs. He hoped to bring peace to his people, but the Sioux did not want peace. They came into our hunting lands and took our elk and deer, so that the children hungered and looked into their parents' eyes with wonder. And there was no thunder of the buffalo."

The old Indian hesitated for a moment—a perfect moment—to let this sink into our minds. Then, as he continued, his hands moved along with the story, interpreting the words with a silent choreography. And I was mesmerized by it.

"The Sioux made war with the Crow, and they made war with the white man, and so the hills were lit with their campfires, and their tepees were as many as the stars. For many nights we heard their drums. The drums spoke of war, for there was anger in their voices. And every night more drums added their voices, more voices of anger, and our medicine men said it was the end of the world.

"And then the wise General Crook and his soldiers came to our village to speak with our tribal chiefs. He said that they had come to fight our enemies the Sioux and wondered if there was a Crow warrior who could read sign and scout for him. The chiefs said that there was no reader of sign like Standing Elk—that his eyes were keen like the hawk's and his nose like the wolf's, and they asked him if he would scout for the great general of the white soldiers. It was a great honor for Standing Elk.

"Before he led the soldiers away from our village, he kissed my mother, Fawn Woman, and gave me a little knife to protect her. I was proud that he asked me to protect her. Then he asked me if I was going to be a good brave, and I said that I would. He smiled at me, then laid his hand gently on my head and said, 'You will be a great warrior one day, Sycamore Stands Tall. I am proud of you,' but as I looked into his eyes I could see the spirit bird flying in them, and I knew that I would never see him again. And the pride in my breast became very heavy."

The old Indian's eyes glistened with sadness; and when he said the last line he raised his hand and patted the air as though touching the scene in his mind. "It was true that Standing Elk was a good scout and read sign like the wolf. For many days he followed the trail of Sioux warriors. Then he returned to the soldiers and told the wise general that there were many Sioux and Cheyenne waiting to kill him at the Rosebud Creek and that Iigiimaa Laxa—the one the white men call Crazy Horse—was the war chief of the Oglala and was like the fox. But the General Crook said that he had no fear of Iigiimaa Laxa and did not listen to his counsel; it was foolish of him because he had heard that the words of Standing Elk were good and never fell.

"It was said that Standing Elk fought fierce in battle and killed many Sioux braves, but it was his day to die. It was said that he died like a Crow warrior. Many arrows whispered through the battle like the snake and bit into his flesh. And many bullets found his breast and burrowed deep, seeking his spirit, but Standing Elk did not fall, because his spirit was great, and he killed many enemies before it flew from his body. Iigiimaa Laxa was much amazed at the spirit of Standing Elk and said to his braves that a great warrior had fallen and that the taking of his scalp had given them much power.

"Then the Sioux rode into our village to kill our braves. They were as many as the locust plague, and there were only few of us, for our braves had gone with Standing Elk to help the soldiers fight our enemies. Mostly there were old men and women and children left in the village, and many were killed as they hurried from their tepees to fight the bullets of the locusts with arrows and clubs. The slaughter was great, and the cries of death went up from our people and were heard for many miles. But there was no one to save us. Many ran away from the village and hid in the tall grasses of the Yellowstone, like the water snakes hiding from the heron."

Pointing to his temple, Sy said, "And then Fawn Woman was struck in the head with a bullet, and she fell at my side, and I could hear her spirit crying like the osprey as it flew over my head. But I did not run, for I remembered my oath to Standing Elk. I held my tears, and I stayed and guarded her body with the little knife that he gave to me, though I knew that the end of the world had come.

"Many Sioux and Cheyenne braves rode past me as they chased the women and children to make them squaws and slaves, and there was much screaming. It was a terrible day for my people. None of the braves even looked down at Sycamore Stands Tall, so I knew that the Akbadádéa had made me invisible. I was strong in this knowledge. I felt his power in me. And then the shadow of a terrible Sioux warrior fell upon me."

He paused. A fierce silence burned up the air in the room, and I found myself gulping for breath. I leaned forward with my hands on my knees, caught in the spell of the old Indian's tale.

"His head blotted out the sun, so that I could not see his face, though I could see the shape of his war bonnet, and there were many feathers in it. I could only see his eyes, for they were fierce—fierce like those of the eagle—and I was the chipmunk in his eyes. On his war lance there were many new scalps that he had taken in battle, but I was not afraid of their power, though my heart beat like the chick's in my breast." Sy struck his breast gently as he said this, and his hands slipped through the air effortlessly.

"The eagle looked at the body of Fawn Woman at my feet and the little knife in my hands, and he saw that I was not afraid. He laughed when I spit at the hooves of his horse. Then he took his knife and threw it between my legs to see if I would run.

"But I did not run. I did not even look to see where the knife had stuck. I looked into the eyes of the eagle and felt the power of the Akbadádéa upon me.

"Then the one whose war bonnet blotted out the sun said to me, 'You are a fierce warrior, little one. What is your name?' And I told him that I was Sycamore Stands Tall. The eagle laughed again and said, 'I shall call you Little Sparrow Bear,' and then he asked the name of my father. I told him that his name was Standing Elk, and that he was a great warrior. I said that if he were here now he would kill him and lift the scalp from his head—that he would hang it from our lodgepole, and I would poke at it with sticks to avenge the death of my mother.

"The Sioux warrior said that Standing Elk was truly a great warrior but that his spirit and the spirit of my mother had flown together and would not return. I fought hard to keep the tears from my eyes, but they came, and I was ashamed. The eagle could see the struggle on my face, and as he reined his horse he said, 'I will send my braves for you, Little Sparrow Bear, when you have become a great warrior like your father. We will meet in the spring, where the Bighorn and the Yellowstone become one, and then I will kill you as I killed Standing Elk.'

"I asked him his name that I might know it was he who had sent for me and not some other, and he said, 'My braves will tell you that Iigiimaa Laxa has sent for you.' He shook his lance at me and then rode away, shouting the war cry. I knew then that the Akbadádéa was truly watching over me. And I was afraid in this knowledge, and my knees trembled.

"Every spring I put on the war bonnet and paint, and I rode to the place where the Bighorn flows into the Yellowstone. There I waited, with my war lance at the ready and the sun to my back . . . I waited for Iigiimaa Laxa to send his braves for me that I might avenge the deaths of Standing Elk and Fawn Woman."

Sy paused and took a deep breath. Then shaking his head sadly, he said, "But they did not come. No, they did not come, and then I knew that the spirit of Iigiimaa Laxa had joined his fathers. And every spring since, as I ride from the Crow reservation to the place where the two rivers join, I can just hear his voice, like a whisper on the *huché,* and the spirit of Iigiimaa Laxa says he is sad that the great warriors are no more."

Then Sy grew quiet, and his eyes twinkled to life as they returned from their inward place. And his hands rested quietly on his lap.

"*Ichik, ichik.* It is good story," Earl Thomas said, and the others grunted and nodded their affirmation. Earl Thomas lay the guitar on the bunk.

"Maybe Tyler would tell us story," Sy said, looking at me.

"Me? I don't know any stories," I said, stunned that they should ask me.

"Yes, tell us a story," Jimbo agreed. He had walked to the stove to pour himself another cup of coffee and was smiling broadly at me.

I looked around the room as though for help, but all of the men were looking at me with the same entreating expressions. Suddenly I felt my ears burning. "But I don't know any stories," I said, gulping down my heart. "Honest!"

"There are many stories in you," Sy said, his eyes twinkling brightly at me. "They move like the *aáshe* through your spirit. You must not keep them in you."

I gaped dumbfounded at the floor as several scenes raced through my head, snatched from vignettes of my childhood, most involving reptiles of one kind or another or girls that I either liked too much or that liked me too much. None seemed appropriate to reproduce in front of a bunkhouseful of Crow Indians.

And then I heard the heavy tread of Papa's boots on the porch, and never was I so relieved for the sound. The screen opened, and he stepped just over the threshold and filled the doorway with his squared, muscled frame, and the yellow light struck the brim of his fedora, revealing in the lower shadows of his features hard, austere lines.

The room was immediately charged with his presence, and all of the Indians turned in unison to look at him. Papa was good with his entrances. He took in their faces with a commanding sweep of his steel blue eyes, much as a general surveying his troops might do, and he followed that with a grunt.

"Good evening, men," he said, pushing back the fedora to offset his austerity. The light bathed his face, at once leaching the hardness from the lines of his toil and revealing an amiable countenance. His voice was deep, ruggedly masculine, and resonated off the walls. It had a touch of the general in it, though friendly enough in tone—the kind of voice that could inspire men to charge into the rifles.

Papa was always friendly when he came into the bunkhouse, it seemed; it was as though he felt at liberty to remove his invisible armor, hang it on the wall, and take his ease among fellow warriors.

The Indians stood up respectfully from their bunks and chairs and returned his greeting, and Papa told them to sit down and not to trouble themselves. And they did so with humble reticence. They liked him—I could tell by the way they lit up whenever he came around. It was a genuine affection too, for the friendship between them had been seeded generations ago, then fertilized over the years by a common toil and watered through the seasons of the ranch. Some of their fathers had worked for Bapa Honus, and some of their grandfathers had worked for Bapa Otto; before that—who knows?—we were probably shooting at each other.

Papa walked over to where Sammy lay and looked him over.

115

"He gonna be fit for baling tomorrow, Sy?" he asked, throwing his big calloused hands on his hips.

The Indians studied his hands and the back of his neck.

Sy walked over to the bunk and looked down at the boy. Sammy shivered a little and moaned quietly, but it appeared the worst of his delirium had passed. Sy lay the back of his hand on his brow. "No. In two, maybe three days he will be fit. The poison must leave him."

Papa looked down at the boy and began to pull on his jaw. "How many days would you say we saved getting the tractor running, Sy?"

Sy thought about it for a moment, then said, "Two, maybe three days."

Papa arched a brow at him and grinned. "Somehow I knew you were going to say that. He's got till Monday, Sy. Then see to it that he's pulling his load. OK?"

"OK, Mr. Henry."

"I swear it's a conspiracy the way you Indians stick together."

Sy wore a wry smile and said, "If Indians had stuck together, as you say, maybe Mr. Roosevelt would be Crow chief, and you would be working for Sy."

Papa looked at him, nonplussed. "Who says I ain't already? Good night, men."

The men nodded respectfully and smiled. *"Dii wágowík,"* they returned.

As Papa went to the door, he turned to me. "We got another early one tomorrow, Tyler," he said, pulling the brim down over his brow. "You coming?"

Something inside me tightened at the prospect of being alone with him right now, even if only for the short walk back to the house. "In a minute, Papa," I said, avoiding his eyes. "I want to see that Sammy's all right."

"Suit yourself," Papa said, and, as he closed the screen behind him, the electrical charge in the room fizzled and dissipated as though a generator had been shut down. A quiet exhale rushed in to fill the void.

A minute later I walked out onto the porch and looked up at the starry host. They sparkled like little jewels against a field of jet, and a shard of moon was just poking over the hills. Some horses were whickering in the stables off to the right, and I could hear the pigs snorting happily across the yard in the pens. They'd probably gotten hold of a rat. I took a deep breath, and the air tasted good.

Sy came out and stood next to me, and for a few moments neither of us spoke. Then he said, "You are wearing a heavy skin, Tyler. I have seen it many days now in your eyes."

"What are you talking about?" I asked defensively.

The old Indian smiled, then looked up at the stars. "The elk will be coming down from the mountains soon," he said, as though reading this in the sky.

"Er . . . yes," I agreed, somewhat off balance. "Hunting season starts in another month."

"Billy will get his bull." The way he said it—like a divine fiat— the event had already taken place in his mind.

"I suppose. If he's lucky this year, that is," I said, looking at Sy out of the corner of my eye.

"I would like to see that," Sy said wistfully. A moment later he chuckled.

"What's so funny?"

"Do you remember when you were a little boy and you left the gate open and the Brahma bull got out and chased the Herefords?"

"Huh?" For a second I thought that Sy had lapsed into some form of Indian senility.

"Your father gave you a whipping. Remember?"

"How could I forget? So?" I failed to see the point.

"Do you remember how you frowned at me and pretended it did not hurt?"

I thought about it for a moment, then I, too, chuckled. "Yes. I used to think if I just frowned a lot, then nobody would know that I had been crying." I grunted at the thought. We were quiet for a while as my mind swept back over the years to the scene.

"And your mama came out and wiped your tears and helped you up with your britches."

I frowned a little. "Yeah. And you were there with Socks, all brushed and bridled and wearing a new Indian blanket. You asked me if I wanted to ride with you to Big Medicine, and I said I'd never heard of any Big Medicine before."

"That's right."

"Hmm. Mama hadn't heard of it either," I said, moving along with the recollection. "She just shrugged her shoulders when I asked her, but she said it was OK with her if I wanted to go. I figured it had to be better than moping around the ranch, frowning at everybody. I remember you winking at Mama, and her winking back, but at the time I didn't gather any significance from it. Then you helped me up onto old Socks, and you swung up behind me Indian-style."

"Yes, yes, I remember," Sy said reflectively. "I have to stand on a bale now. My legs do not have springs like they used to."

But Sy's comments were lost to my hearing, for the scene began to brighten in my mind now, as though a lamp had been lit in some dark receptacle of my past, and my eyes had tightened on a point somewhere beyond the roof of the barn. As I continued, my voice dipped and climbed clumsily, breaking occasionally as the image faltered or dimmed, then, picking it up again and moving steadily along as the vignettes were knit together like a luminescent string of pearls. Somewhere along the way Sy's presence slipped away altogether into the umbrage.

"I remember as we rode clear of the ranch I kept asking you where Big Medicine was, and finally you told me that a good Indian brave is as silent as the lizard when he rides and that his eyes are always looking for signs of game or his enemies." I chuckled. "That shut me up.

"And then I saw a tiny herd of elk moving along the ridge line. I pointed them out to you, and you said that I had eyes sharper than an Indian's and that I would make a good Crow scout. From that moment on, you and I were Indian scouts. I remember thinking that I was the chief scout because I was sitting in front of you, even though it was your horse we were riding. My horse had gotten shot in an ambush, as I recall, and we were hot on the trail of the desperadoes who had shot it. I was sure they were lurking behind every mesquite bush and rock, and my keen scout's eyes were quick to spot 'em.

"When you told me that Big Medicine was just ahead around the break in the river, I remember envisioning it to be a place with lots of tepees and Indians. I figured that, when you and I rode into the village, the chiefs would hold a big council, and we would tell them what we had just scouted. Because I was the chief scout, it was my job to do all the talking. I would speak slowly and with great wisdom, so that the chiefs would be so impressed that they would make me a tribal chief as well.

"But when we got to Big Medicine, I remember being disappointed, because it was nothing more than a narrow island in the middle of the Stillwater. It was a quiet place, with a low morning mist still hovering over the water and clinging to the trees, that looked undisturbed by the tread of man." *And why wouldn't it be?* I thought, then said, "I didn't know why anyone would go to the trouble of fording the river to get there; there was nothing there . . . nothing but a stand of aspens, a few cottonwoods, and a big old willow that arched over the water. There were no tepees. No Indians. Just a pair of great blue herons and some sandhill cranes that took off at our approach.

"We sat under the willow for an hour or so, doing nothing . . . neither of us talking . . . while Socks contented himself in the river grasses. I remember counting white egrets as they hunted fish in the reeds . . . watched water turtles and little snakes slip into the water and wriggle away . . . stripped a million blades of grass.

"Looking out on the river through the leaves I got the feeling I was in a little green fort. I felt secure, invisible to the outside world . . . no one could see me or get to me. I remember imagining that the world was going by in a parade, looking for me but not finding me, then I'd squeal with delight at the prospects of it. When I grew tired of the parade, I stared at the willow branches floating on the water for a while, dozing, daydreaming . . . stared as the light filtered in through the veil of leaves and made shadow patterns on the banks. It was a quiet, serene cloister of nature, and I got the strangest feeling that I was in a church during the hush of prayer.

"Hmm," I mused. "Then I got fidgety and began to squirm. So I started chucking stones into the river, skipping some, splashing the big ones—pretending they were bombs and I was a cannon. When the stones splashed, I made big explosion sounds. I let a truckload of 'em go in the river that day. I can't remember who the enemy was—maybe it was Confederates. Come to think of it, it was just people in general, but I remember wreaking havoc on them."

I paused to let the smoke clear. Some coyotes started yapping in the hills; it sounded like they were tearing something apart, but I knew they were just playing, and my mind let them play. And then Big Medicine swept me along again. "Then I remember you whittling a piece of driftwood as you told me a story about Papa when he was a boy. I think you were making a boat—yes, a canoe. You told me how Papa had let off a firecracker next to the outhouse when Bapa Honus was inside, and how he let out a holler and came roaring out . . . how he chased Papa around with a switch in one hand and his trousers in the other, tripping and swearing and yelling his head off."

I paused for a moment to take it in and shook my head. "You got me to laughing so hard with that story that I forgot all about my licking. I couldn't imagine Papa doing something like that, knowing that Bapa was inside. But you said that Papa was like Old Man Coyote, the trickster, as I recall."

I chuckled at the thought. "You said that he would've made a good Crow, a good *Apsaruke*. Then you finished whittling the little canoe, and we let it go down the river."

I chuckled a couple more times as the last glowing images slipped away downstream, faded, then were gathered into the night.

My eyes fluttered and came to, then a reverie of night sounds suddenly burst upon my ears. The coyotes had taken their violent play elsewhere, but the frogs and crickets were still at it and going strong. The moon was up and cast a little light on the hills.

"*Ichik, ichik,*" Sy said, clapping me on the shoulder. "It was a good story."

"Story?"

"It is good to let your stories out, don't you think? They are too heavy if you keep them inside."

I looked at Sy, realizing what he'd gotten me to do. I grunted. "Good night, Sy," I said, stepping off the porch with a grin. "See you in the morning, bright-eyed and bushy-tailed."

Sy smiled and said, "You will wear a lighter skin, maybe."

I quickly slipped into the darkness of the night and headed back to the house, my mind filled with the stories of the Indians and of my first visit to Big Medicine. It wasn't much of a story really, but that old Indian had tricked me into telling it, and, indeed, I was feeling a little lighter in my skin for it.

A cool breeze picked up, and I stopped to enjoy it. *It won't be long now until fall,* I thought, as I smelled the first hints of decay in the air.

Billy will get his elk.

13

It was Sunday morning, and the household was going through its usual pre-church drills: Papa was arguing with Mama about something she was wearing or something she wanted him to wear, Billy and Trout were fighting over the bathroom, Mutt and Jeff were uncharacteristically surly and were snipping at one another, the chickens were cackling up a storm outside, and I was doing battle with my tie in the bedroom mirror. Every Sunday morning it was the same.

Jenny came into my room as I gave up the third of my efforts to get the fat end of my tie reasonably near my belt buckle. The first attempt it had ended up just over my belly button, and the second fell somewhere below my fly. I never could figure out how I could start out at exactly the same place every time but end up in any number of finishes, no two alike. It was one of the great mysteries in the universe.

Jenny eyed me awhile, not saying a word. *What does she want?* I thought. *In here to cause trouble, no doubt.* I could feel her eyes burning holes in my fingers as they fiddled clumsily over the knots. I ignored her as long as I could, pretending that my several attempts at getting the tie tied just so were all planned and part of some arcane ritual of manhood. I even started humming a tune. A manly tune.

Finally she said, "Once you get it tied right, why don't you just slip it off your head when you're finished? That way you wouldn't have to keep redoing it every time."

Huh? My fingers froze at my neck for a moment as my brain reeled from the perfect logic of it. *What a novel idea,* I thought. But I knew there had to be a crack in it somewhere. Jenny wasn't normally given to novel ideas or logic. And so I haughtily said, "You wouldn't understand."

"Well, it seems kinda stupid to me."

I looked at her skeptically. "What do you want, Jenny? Are you in here to just torment me, or is there another reason why I shouldn't slug you?"

She had a funny look in her eyes, one of those female looks that she fastened onto me. "Do you think I'm pretty, Tyler?" she asked, looking away coyly.

"*What?*" I was thunderstruck.

"I said, do you think I'm pretty?"

"What kind of a question is that? You're my sister."

"Just answer me."

"No."

"No you don't think I'm pretty, or no you won't answer my question?"

I refused to acknowledge her. Giving my tie-tying another whirl, I threw the long fat end over the short skinny one and picked up my manly humming.

"C'mon, Tyler."

I grunted. "Well, you asked for it," I said. "I'm sorry to have to be the one to break your heart, Jenny, but I know you'd have to find out sooner or later. You see, I'm already spoken for: ten gorgeous blondes have asked for my hand in marriage, and I've accepted." I shot a dead-serious look at her in the mirror and added, "And I'm true-blue, so fooling around on the side is out of the question."

"I'm serious," Jenny said.

"Go ask Billy."

"I already did."

"What'd he say?"

"He said I was ugly."

"So why're you bugging me?"

"You mean you think I'm ugly too?"

"Look, Jenny, can't you see I'm trying to get ready for church?" I looked at her in the mirror, and I could see that she was about to burst into tears. Feeling suddenly contrite, I allowed the wellspring of my better nature to trickle forth. "Well, you're not ugly, so how's that?" I said. "That make you feel any better?"

"Loads. But you haven't answered my question."

"What the—I don't know. You don't ask your brothers questions like that."

"Why not?"

"You just don't, that's why. Why don't you ask Papa?"

"Are you kidding? Papa never even looks at me. I doubt if he even knows I got a bustline yet." Jenny folded her arms. "Well?"

"Well, what?"

"Do you think I'm pretty or not?"

"I think you're beautiful. There. I said it. Happy now?"

"You're just saying that to get rid of me."

"Right, Jenny. I'd tell you most anything if I thought it'd get rid of you."

Jenny scowled at me. "Thanks a lot, Tyler. And here I thought I could at least get a straight answer out of you." She stormed out of the room. "Sometimes you can be a real jerk."

"Is that right?" I chased her to the door and called down the hall after her. "Well, did anybody ever tell you that you had a pig face? No? Really? Well, I'm telling you, because I'm your brother. Only a brother would tell you that you had a pig face! Oink! Oink!"

Jenny went into her room and slammed the door.

Just then Mama, undoing a curl from her hair, stuck her head out of her bedroom door and said, "Who's saying that word?"

I was the only one left in the hallway, so I asked, "What word?"

"You know good and well what word—the 'P' word."

"The 'P' word? You mean pig face?"

"Shh! Don't say it, Tyler—it's Sunday," Mama said in a harsh whisper. "Besides, Joseph might hear you and think it's all right to use that kind of language."

"Isn't it?"

"Heavens, no. It's vulgar." Then she ducked back into her room.

"Hear what?" Trout said, stepping out of the bathroom with a toothbrush hanging out of his mouth. "What's vulgar?"

"Nothing." I walked back to the mirror, feeling pretty lowdown and mean and resumed my war with the tie, but I knew already that it was a lost cause. "This stupid tie," I snarled and tore it off my neck.

Our church was built near the center of town as a beacon of light on the Yellowstone Way and a bulwark of righteousness against whiskey, gambling, and the likes of Miss Abbie and her girls. It was a sturdy construction of red brick upon a cement foundation, with a clapboard steeple that was painted white. The latter had been a favorite roost of wayward birds since the bell rusted over solid after the winter of '21.

Papa wheeled the pickup into the yard and found our usual parking place, a hard pack of gravel and clay beneath a stand of big leafy sycamores, and ground the truck to a halt. Billy, Trout, and I hopped out of the bed, while the rest of the family climbed out of the cab. Knots of people wearing their Sunday smiles idled by on their way to the church steps, and we all smiled back as though we had been smiling all morning long.

Only Trout was true to his nature. His face was screwed into an intemperate scowl as he curled his index finger along the inside of his stiff collar and tugged at his trousers.

Mama licked her fingers and combed his windblown hair into place. She told him to quit fidgeting and to mend his countenance, a word she loved to use on Sundays since it had such a fine King James ring to it.

Trout had no pretensions about the word or his misery, and so he put on his best martyr face, then, with Mama's hand clasped firmly on his shoulder, he marched heavily toward the steps of the gallows.

"Will you be sitting with us, Tyler?" Mama asked me, as was her weekly custom; to which I weekly answered, "No, Mama, I'll just sit with Kate, if it's all right with you." She smiled maternally at me as we strolled along toward the church, no doubt imagining some future squall of babies tugging at her heels.

Then turning to Billy, she repeated the question, and Billy reproduced his weekly excuse for why he had to sit somewhere else— which meant, of course, that he would be sitting with the Baxter boys at the rear of the church, each of them studying the catechism of Laura Miller with devoted affection.

Mama smiled grimly at him. Jenny and Trout had plenty of excuses to sit elsewhere but had no grounds for them; such grounds were not even considered until each would turn the magic age of seventeen and could drink coffee.

Papa was waiting for us on the steps, as was his weekly custom, talking ranching, fishing, or hunting with Reverend Jacks, who, hailing recently from the East Coast, smiled and nodded ignorantly but appreciatively for any knowledge that might enable him to become "all things to all men."

He was a tall, youthful man with long, El Greco-like fingers and an aquiline nose, a beatific smile that blessed his flock no matter how surly and sheeplike they got, and his voice was a rich baritone, smooth as a finely tuned guitar. He was a kind man, well-versed in the dead languages, and I'd spent many a Sunday afternoon in his study with him discussing theology and his call to the ministry.

"I felt it burning in me, Tyler," he'd tell me time and again, as he raised his dark eyes to the ceiling. "Had to let it out lest it consume me to ashes." And then his eyes would brim over with tears as they did most every Sunday during the altar calls, and mine would glisten too.

For as he spoke I could feel it burning in me as well, the fiery voice of God, it seemed, thundering over the rim of my soul, calling me to the precipice of my worldly confines, then beseeching me to step out and fly. Time and again I would chuckle with excitement as I felt the dangerous updraft shooting through my being; it was all I could do to keep from bursting into tears.

Concerning the altar calls, no one had gone forward in recent history to get saved. I do remember one or two of Miss Abbie's girls going forward, but when their sins came to light at the altar it created such a furor that several pillars of the community had to suddenly leave town.

I'd responded when I was ten, after hearing a sermon on the imminence of the Second Coming, terrified that the Lord would descend and snatch away His children before I could get to the altar. Jenny went forward three or four times the summer she reached puberty, and Mama was presently working on Trout. Billy said he wouldn't for all the tea in China, mainly due to the ribbing I got in school the day after my conversion. I'd heard Mama praying for him at night, though, and I was sure Billy has heard her too.

We climbed the steps of the church, and Mama smiled warmly at the minister as she shook his hand. "Good morning, Reverend Jacks."

"Good morning, Mrs. Hochreiter," he returned warmly. "How are you this Lord's day?"

"Just fine. And how's your darling wife, Millie? I missed her last Sunday. I heard she was ill? With a touch of influenza or something?"

"No, no, nothing so dramatic as that. She was just under the weather. But she's all right now, back in the saddle, as they say."

"That's good." Mama took a deep breath of the morning air. "It's a fine day to give the devil a scare, don't you think?"

"We'll do our best," Reverend Jacks said. "Today's text is from the book of Revelation."

Mama lit up. "Ooh, my favorite."

I could tell from Papa's distant expression that he hadn't heard a word of the conversation. He kept glancing back on the road.

Mama exchanged a few more pleasantries with the minister concerning the spiritual well-being of our sovereign state, then gathered her chicks into the church. Papa, rousing suddenly, followed in after her, after making a comment concerning the weather.

The Reverend Jacks suddenly got a detached look in his eyes.

"Good morning, Reverend Jacks," I said, shaking his hand.

"Good morning, Tyler," he said. "Your father said it might snow soon."

I looked up at the sky. It was bright and clear and scented with the morning freshness: in Montana a clear sign that it could thunder and lightning and get as mean as a penned bull in the next ten minutes. "It's been known to snow in August," I said to him. "Papa'd know if anybody would. He's got a nose for weather."

"Imagine that," Reverend Jacks remarked, gazing dully up at the sky. He had a habit of pulling on his eyebrows whenever he was pulling on a thought, and his hand drifted absently to a wispy thatch over his right eye. I do believe that in that moment Reverend Jacks felt a draft of doubt concerning his call to our fair state.

"Have you seen Katherine Morgan?" I asked, breaking into his puzzlement.

"Pardon me? Katherine? Oh, yes—Kate. She's inside."

I thanked him and left him tugging bemusedly on his brows.

As I walked into the church, Kate turned in her seat and smiled at me. The sun was streaming through the stained-glass window and dappling her face and hair in a spectrum of bright color. She looked lovely as a flower in it. I sat down beside her in the pew and squeezed her hand, telling her so.

Then I looked ahead eight rows to where my family was sitting, firmly ensconced in their pew. Trout was pulling on various parts of his anatomy, as if ants had gotten loose under his shirt and in his hair. Jenny kept looking furtively over her shoulder for something, and Mama was chatting quietly with Mrs. Morgan, Kate's mother, on her right.

Papa was holding down the center aisle, as usual, so that he could nod at the preacher whenever he made a point he understood, but mainly so he wouldn't have to socialize with anyone at the other end of the pew. Every so often he would look across the aisle to where the Gibson family usually sat, but they hadn't come in yet. He glanced toward the door, his eyes betraying an anxiousness, then he looked ahead.

The family pew was four rows from the front on the right side, an inviolate tradition that reached back twenty years. Papa had picked out the spot immediately after he and Mama got married. "This is the place, Beulah May," he told her as though selecting a site to erect a barn. He told her that people who sit on the front row are trying to prove something, and that those who occupy the back row are trying to hide something, and so we had sat there ever since, uncontested. The smooth, Hochreiter-shaped hollows in the wood bore unimpeachable witness to our claim.

Since I was nineteen I could sit anywhere I pleased, so I carved a place for my posterity four rows from the back, where not so many people could stare at the back of my head.

Suddenly Mama and Mrs. Morgan broke from their conversation and glanced back at Kate and me. They smiled confidentially at us.

We smiled innocently back.

Mrs. Morgan touched Mama's hand and said something, giggled, then they both turned away and resumed their conspiracy.

Kate and I exchanged knowing looks.

"Mama's sick of us kids and wants grandbabies now," I said.

Kate got a funny look in her eyes, then leaned over and whispered into my ear, "We'll make beautiful babies, don't you think?"

I got a funny look myself. "Yes, dozens of them."

"Dozens?"

"Well, maybe we'll start with two or three, and if we get sick of them we'll sell 'em off and try for a new batch."

Kate crooked an eyebrow at me, then patted my hand. "Can we have lunch together?"

"Maybe. Papa may want to get at them bales some more."

"Even on Sunday?"

I sighed for effect. "There's no rest for the wicked . . ." then added, "or ranchers."

She frowned. Then, looking down at my hand, she stroked it affectionately and pulled on each of my fingers. "I'm happy you want to be a minister, Tyler. I don't think I could make it as a rancher's wife."

I smiled at her wryly. "Ministers work on Sundays too, you know."

She gave my hand a little slap.

Chuckling, I glanced around the sanctuary.

Mrs. Stivers was sitting in her usual perch, I noted—front row center—with her eyes narrowed on everyone as they filed into the church. The women were all in their Sunday dresses and hats, looking pretty and pink, with their babes in tow, all combed and scrubbed raw. The girls giggled at one another and at the boys, and the boys wrinkled their noses and scratched the newly shorn places around their ears. The men, looking gruff in their clean, if not starched, collars and brushed coats—if they owned them—nodded at one another with civil grunts. There were a few in the congregation whose faces beamed with an anticipatory glow, with their Bibles opened and turned to the appropriate Scripture texts indicated on the wall in front.

Miss Hymes labored to her feet and waddled heavily over to the piano, and we all knew it was time. She screwed herself down into the seat—all feminine and daintylike, despite her immense bulk. Then, touching a bright red curl of hair into place, she flipped through the hymnbook, found the selection, and flattened the page into place. She smiled benignly over the congregation, poised her fingers delicately over the keys, then began to hammer out "Nearer, My God, to Thee."

After the third or fourth hymn, I looked across the aisle two rows back from us, and there was Booster Fisk sitting with his family in the half light between the windows, every one of them peering at me from the sum of their meanness and ugliness. Booster's eyes were dark-circled from his broken nose, giving his face the appearance of a skull, and he was staring at me with a smile that gave me a start. I hid my reaction well, but I thought, *How did the devil get in here? He can't come in here, can he? This is church.*

I turned away, one part of me wincing back to the refrain that Miss Hymes was struggling with, and the other part of me giving thought to the nature of evil.

Then Reverend Jacks stood up and strode solemnly across the platform, nodded politely at Miss Hymes, who lifted her hands from the keys. Then, setting his Bible down on the podium, he smiled warmly at each of our faces.

I saw his arms moving occasionally, and his lips working, but nothing coming out of them. It was as if I had suddenly lost most of my senses. I did hear something like a continual droning over my head, though, but if pressed I would have to confess that the devil had worked effectively through Booster's smile that Sunday.

After the service we all collected outside in little clumps of interest. The men pulled out their pocket knives and shaved slices off their plugs. Others smoked pipes or cigarettes. The women chatted furiously about recipes and their children. And their children, released from the strictures of piety, ran squealing over the church grounds in hellish fury, making up for lost time.

I saw Trout and a few boys angling toward the creek behind the church, Trout leading the pack with a stick he kept swiping at flying bugs. Billy and the Baxter boys were in a huddle of boyish jocularity around Laura Miller, each of them striving to win her glance. I thought I noticed a flutter of her eyes in Billy's direction. I glanced back at her in passing and immediately felt a jab to my ribs.

"'I made a covenant with mine eyes; why then should I think upon a maid?'" Kate teased. "Job, chapter thirty-one, verse one."

I raised my eyes in monklike devotion to the clouds. "I might run into something this way," I remarked.

"At least it won't be Laura Miller."

"Spoilsport."

Kate and I walked under the shade of a stand of big elms at the far edge of the grounds. It was quiet and secret here, except for occasional squirrel chatter. No one could see us from the front of the church, for the northeast corner of the building shielded us. It was a refuge away from inquiring eyes, often visited by courting couples and scoundrels after church services or Sunday school.

Across the street we could see glimpses of the Yellowstone through a line of cottonwoods, bright and brown and smoothing along in its wide earthen sluice. White egrets lit up here and there, accenting the morning stillness with flashes of brilliant light. In contrast a red-tailed hawk sat motionless atop a telephone pole, peering down at the field below him for rodents. A cool breeze traced over the earth, carrying with it the tart river smells, the first leaf falls of the autumn prelude, and I felt it move around my ankles. A little shiver skittered up my trouser legs. *An early winter,* I thought. *Papa may be right about the snow.*

Kate and I glanced about the refuge and saw neither lover nor scoundrel. Then I looked down into her upturned face, her eyes sparkling in a dollop of meridian sun, and caught a glistening of moisture on her full red lips. I felt the season turn in my stomach, and I leaned over and kissed her.

Wild strawberries.

I held her for a while, savoring the taste on my lips, both of us listening to the hush of the river across the road. Neither of us had anything to say and were comfortable in the silence. During the interlude I imagined a little white frame house with Kate and I sitting on the front porch, night after night, rocking gently on the swing, doing nothing but holding each other as we watched the sun dip silently to become a fiery coronet over the western bluffs.

The glory of the image faded into a smile. I don't know what Kate's thoughts were, but I suspect they had babies in them.

Kate broke out of her reverie and straightened my tie. She glanced up with that funny look in her eyes again, then looked down at the tie and smoothed her fingers over it. "I don't know if I can wait four years, Tyler," she said. "It seems like an eternity, doesn't it?"

I groaned. "Longer."

"You're no help."

"We could ask Reverend Jacks to hitch us up this afternoon," I said. "Pack up and head for Chicago in the morning."

"Be serious."

"I am."

"What would we do there? Where would we live? How would we eat?"

"O ye of little faith. And here you told me that there was a bean field in my eyes. We'll eat beans."

"Now I know you're joking."

"You could get a job waitressing or something. Maybe even in a drugstore—or a Woolworths or something. You know they got Woolworths in Chicago. I could get a part-time job after school. People do it all the time. We'd be OK—we'll sur—"

"Tyler."

"What?" I looked into her eyes and knew. Then I smiled. "You're right. But it's fun to dream about it, isn't it?"

"Fun, but impractical."

"O ye of little daring."

She gave me that arched-brow look again.

"You're right, you're right," I groaned. Then I brightened. "I know! How about we see how the first semester goes. And if we can't stand it—"

"That sounds reasonable." Kate hugged me.

We kissed again, then ambled back toward the church, arm in arm, so as not to be conspicuous by our absence.

And then, rounding the corner of the building, I heard, "Well, if it ain't the Injun lover!"

I immediately recognized the voice and turned, feeling a rush of blood to my throat, and there was Booster Fisk striding toward us, looking mean as ever.

Josiah and Mrs. Fisk were beyond him, I saw, walking stiffly across the yard toward their truck in the distance, walking as if they'd been shooed off the grounds and were trying to keep hold of their dignity. There was no sign of Nate. Arly was with them, though, dragging behind a step, and they were both giving him the business—

130

his mother mostly, reaching back and cuffing his ears repeatedly for some transgression he had committed.

Booster, seeing Kate and me rounding the corner of the church, had obviously stripped himself away from the quiet of his family to work some devilry on me. "We have some unfinished business, Hochreiter," he said, reaching us.

In the light I could see that the dark circles under his eyes were edged with yellow brown and that one corner of his mouth was purple and swollen from where my knuckles had struck it against his teeth. A thin white bandage spanned his flat nose to hold it in place. He looked a sight. Billy was right about that.

"Is that so?" I retorted, admiring my handiwork.

"That's so."

"Get you over here, Booster," his mother called out, glancing at us. "Don't you be makin' trouble with them Hochreiters now."

Booster shot a look at her, then glowered back at me. "We ain't finished by a long shot, Hochreiter! And next time it'll just be you and me."

"Anytime's fine with me," I said, clenching my fists. "Fact, we can square accounts right now."

Kate grabbed my arm. "No, Tyler!"

Booster looked at my fists and chortled wickedly. He looked like the devil again. I could see something dark calculating behind his eyes. "Didn't happen to notice Rube Gibson in church, did you?" he said, baiting me.

I held my tongue.

"Me neither." He laughed. "Pa said that Rube was a fool. Said he was gonna take his spread, and he did. Said it won't be too long before we scrape that two-bit grub farm of yours off the earth, either."

He grinned, showing the black hole in his front teeth. "You know what I'm gonna do when that happens? First thing I'm gonna do is kick every stinking red belly in the teeth and send 'em packing. Then I'm gonna dig out them graves of your kinfolk—let the varmints carry off their bones."

I wanted more than anything to fly at him. He must have known it too, and he chuckled, probably hoping I'd lose my head, maybe lead with my right again. I felt Kate's arms tugging on mine.

"Leave him be, Tyler," she said, glaring at Booster. "He's not worth the trouble."

I thought for a moment *she* was going to fly at him.

Booster narrowed his eyes at her and grunted.

"Booster! Get you over here right now, you hear me!"

"Comin', Ma!" He looked at me and shook his finger. "Like I said, Hochreiter, we ain't finished this yet."

"You just get on back to your mama," I snarled. "I expect she wants a look at your nose."

A murderous flame jumped into his eyes and licked around the edges. "We ain't quit of this. No, sir, we ain't!" Then he turned and loped away.

I looked at his back for a moment, feeling anger raging through my body, then glanced down at my feet and kicked it into the ground.

"Come on, Tyler," Kate said. "Just forget it. Let's go and ask your papa if you can stay awhile. I'll fix you a nice tuna sandwich."

I glanced over my shoulder at the Fisks. They were loading into their truck; still no sign of Nate though.

It was then that a movement caught my eyes, and, turning, I saw Jenny hurrying out from behind the toolshed of the church, straightening herself. She stooped quickly to pick up a little mess of wild flowers. She glanced guiltily around, missed my eyes, then slowed into a normal gait as she swung around the back of the church.

A moment later Nate Fisk followed out from behind the shed, a cool, sated look in his eyes, and slunk off toward his family. Our eyes met and locked. He broke stride momentarily. I could see his face go through a quick range of expression, from something startled and criminal to something that narrowed into a defiant sneer. I heard him chuckle as he trotted off.

A sudden squall of rage arose in me. "Nothing good is gonna come of this," I thought aloud.

Kate pulled my arm, then smoothed her fingers over my cheek. "Let it go, Tyler. Let it go."

I looked at her and felt the hard burning lines of my face relaxing under the cool of her fingers. I smiled. "My, but you're beautiful when you worry about me."

She shook her fist under my nose. "Tell me how beautiful I am once I sock you one."

"What does one bring to a barbecue?" Millie Jacks was asking Mama as Kate and I walked up to the foursome. "We never had them back in Cambridge," she said. "Not unless they're anything like our coming-out parties, where they serve teas and such."

Papa grunted, casting a surly look at the Fisk truck speeding away from the church. "I doubt if the folks coming out to the ranch will be drinking much tea," he said, looking back at Mrs. Jacks. "Not unless it's laced with sour mash."

Millie's face drew a blank. Reverend Jacks smiled at everyone doubtfully, then gazed absently to the east.

Mama elbowed Papa in his ribs. "Henry's just pulling your leg, Millie. Aren't you, Henry?"

Millie chuckled embarrassedly. She was a plain and pretty woman, with a back-East look about her—"a handsome woman" would better describe her. She wore her brown hair pulled neatly back into a French roll, allowing a twist of curls at each of her temples and the white lace of her bodice and high collar to soften the angular lines of her jaw. She brightened when she saw me.

"Why, hello, Tyler." She beamed. "Ralston . . . er . . . Reverend Jacks and I were just talking about you last night."

I nodded amiably, then glanced at Jenny, who was sitting alone in the truck cab, smelling her flowers. Our eyes met briefly this time, and she looked away innocently.

"Must've been a slow night," I said to Mrs. Jacks, grinning. And then inexplicably I felt my scalp crawl as though I had suddenly stumbled into danger. A high-pitched whine sounded a warning in my ears, but I knew I was powerless to escape.

"Nonsense," Millie said, smiling handsomely. "Tyler, I think it's just wonderful you studying for the ministry—a full scholarship too! Aren't you proud?"

I blanched and felt something let go inside me, felt my insides sheeting off my bones. My eyes darted to Papa, then quickly looked away before his eyes could fix on mine. Danger crawled all over me.

"What are you talking about?" Papa asked her.

Millie smiled sweetly at him, a little surprised at the question. "Why, Tyler going off to Bible school this—" I saw the Reverend Jacks nudge her gently. She looked up at him with a quizzical expression. "What?"

Suddenly the air became very tense. Millie struggled to maintain her smile as she looked at her husband, then back at Papa; but seeing the look on his face, she could not hold the smile in place. Blushing, she giggled nervously as she looked first at me and then at Mama. "Did I say something wrong?"

I looked at Papa through a fog. I thought I might be sick. "I was going to tell you," I said, tugging at the seam of my trousers.

Papa's pale blue eyes drilled through the fog. "Tell me what?"

Words came to my mind but struggled to find my tongue.

Mama took his arm. "Henry, Tyler has decided to become a minister. Isn't that wonderful?"

Reverend Jacks tugged at his wife's waist. "Come along, Mildred. We mustn't keep these good folks."

Millie looked from Papa's eyes to mine, and I could see a shade of self-reproach drawing over her face.

Just then Billy and Trout sauntered toward us, both smiling from their individual conquests.

"Look what I caught down by the crick." Trout held up a frog. Then noticing everyone's face he said, "What's wrong? It's just a little ol' frog—see?" He chucked it under its rump, and the frog leaped into the air. Quick as a snake, Trout snagged a leg with his other hand.

"Get in the truck," Billy said, reading the tension.

"Papa didn't say to," Trout protested.

Then, without standing on ceremony, Billy grabbed him up by the waist with one arm and carried him to the truck bed and hauled him over the rail.

Trout flailed viciously.

In the distraction the frog saw its chance—now or never—and lit out of Trout's hand.

"Hey! My frog!"

14

That afternoon Papa brooded over Sunday supper as one stricken with an incurable disease. A sullenness filled in the lines of his brow, as his eyes turned inward on the wound. There was an economy of movement working through his limbs, a sick-like torpor curling stiffly through his fingers, hunching up his shoulders like a dog with rabies. Even the speed at which he chewed his food slowed to labored pumps that showed thickly along his jaws and throat. The stench of the wound pervaded the kitchen, infecting the air, and we all caught it, for there was no vaccine for the disease.

The sanctity of the ranch had been assailed, breached by one of Hochreiter's own, by the Judas son in the tribe, and the Soul demanded a sacrifice. Papa snapped at Trout for chewing loudly, snapped at Jenny for reaching across the table, snapped at Billy for eating too fast, and I could feel his eyes on me, stabbing in quick forays as they ranged predatorily back and forth over the table, looking for someone to breach some little law or etiquette that he might bring swift Hochreiter judgment to bear.

The tension grew with every passing moment. An oppressive vapor clung over the meal, swallowing every bit of cheer, choking everything but a fear of Papa's glowering eyes. My stomach skipped, then twisted into knots. Conversation was banished behind walls of introspection. Soon there wasn't a sound at the table but the occasional insurrections of a fork clinking against a plate, or a glass clunking a little too clumsily against the tabletop, or a tentative clearing of the throat—heinous crimes that were struck down with a scowl.

Eating ceased. Secretive eyes traced quick patterns in the tablecloth.

Mama cradled her head between her left thumb and forefinger and gazed across the infinite distance to her plate.

As I looked at her, anger rose in me. Then I looked at my father, and a terrific disgust gave it definition. Fear was abolished in a burst of disdain.

"Papa," I said with the authority of an Old Testament prophet. However, to my surprise, I realized that no sound had come out of my mouth. I tried again. *"Papa,"* I barked, overcompensating.

Everyone at the table jumped in their seats and turned to me. The thought entered my mind to ask him to pass the peas.

"Papa, will you please listen to me now?"

He reached for a piece of bread as if I didn't exist. Mama looked at me fearfully. Jenny and Trout sat rigidly in their chairs, looking at me out of the corner of their eyes. Billy took another hungry bite of food. Perhaps he alone was inoculated against the infection.

"It's what I want to do," I said. "I'm nineteen years old now. I waited a whole year since graduating from high school—it's time I decided a course for my life."

I waited a moment, eyed Mama, then said, "I feel that God has called me to be a minister, not a rancher. I've been accepted—full scholarship—at the Chicago Divinity School. It's a good school, and I would like to go."

"Hand me the butter," Papa said to Jenny, who was sitting immediately to his right.

Jenny had started to reach for the dish when Trout's hand stretched across the table and cut her off.

"Here you go, Papa!" he said.

Papa's eyes flared at him, and his butter knife rapped smartly over Trout's knuckles.

Trout dropped the butter dish with a clank.

"I asked Jenny."

We all looked at Trout's hand as he wrapped it in his fingers.

"Yes, sir," he said, sinking back into himself with a wounded look.

Papa carved a chunk of butter and spread it over his bread, then he fixed a malignant eye on Trout again. "Eat your peas."

Trout stared at his plate. "I'm not hungry, Papa."

Papa rapped the back of Trout's head with his knuckle. "You look at me when I'm talking to you. Mama took the time to fix this good meal, and you're going to eat it. Now get to your peas."

Trout rubbed the back of his head and looked sideways at Papa, tears spurting from his eyes. "Yes, Papa." He rolled a single pea sulkily onto his fork.

Something malignant and deadly took hold of Papa. He leaned forward, fixing on the weakness in Trout as a wolf might a sick member of its pack.

136

Mama got up quickly from her chair and interposed herself between Papa and Trout. "You do as your father says, Joseph," she said, shoveling her fork into his peas. Then she angled them into his mouth like a mother bird feeding her chick. Tears streamed from Trout's eyes as he coughed down the peas.

One of Papa's eyes narrowed on her. "You gonna make a sissy boy out of him too?"

I reeled from the verbal slap. Billy and I exchanged looks across the table. He shook his head and continued untroubled with his dinner. Jenny watched Mama feeding Trout.

"What're you lookin' at?" Papa said, turning his deadly gaze on her.

"Nothing, Papa."

"You just tend to your own business."

"Yes, Papa." Jenny took a quick bite of potatoes and chewed hastily. Her eyes worked nervously over her food, as Papa's intense stare bored through her. I could see the wound beading like a fever over his brow, sweeping him along into a rage, his feral eyes pouring over Jenny's feminine veneer for any chink of weakness. He found it and discharged a satisfied grunt. "What's this I hear you sneakin' around with that Fisk boy?" he snarled.

Jenny looked up at him, horrified. "I don't know what you mean, Papa."

"You know good and well what I mean, missy may. I ain't blind. D'you think I'm blind?"

"No, Papa."

Papa glanced sharply at Mama, who was holding a fork of peas suspended before Trout's quivering mouth. "What's the idea letting her run around with that filth?" But before she could answer, he turned his predator eyes back on Jenny. "I catch you anywhere near that boy and so help me I'll skin you to the bone, d'you hear me?"

Jenny looked away from him quickly and glared at her plate, fighting desperately to hold a crumbling defense. "I ain't been with him, Papa."

"You calling me a liar?"

I thought he was going to backhand her.

"No, Papa," Jenny said, flinching. She choked on her potatoes, then burst into tears. She reeled out of her chair and ran sobbing upstairs.

Papa glared at Mama, transferring his rage. "The thought of my daughter trampin' around with that filth. I won't tolerate it! I won't!"

He slammed his fist down on the table, and we all jumped along with the tableware.

I stared at Papa in disgust. "May I be excused?"

He looked hard at me. "I don't care what you do, sissy boy." He cut into his meat furiously and stabbed it with his fork. "You can go to the devil for all I care."

Mama dropped her fork on Trout's plate and looked at Papa astonished. "Henry!"

I pushed away from the table and banged the screen door angrily behind me. I heard the sharp scrape of his chair over the floor, and Papa was through the door before I had stepped off the porch.

"Come here, you!" he shouted. He caught up to me and stabbed his finger into my chest. "You think you can go around banging doors, Mr. High-and-mighty?"

"No, sir."

"You think you're too good for this house?"

"No, sir."

"Think you're better than everyone else around here?"

"No, sir."

"Think you're better than me?"

I held my tongue.

"Do you?"

I just stared at him, trembling involuntarily. I saw the violence burning in his eyes, the Hochreiter violence prowling like a pent beast, spent of grace, now clawing through the sepia vaults of dust and gathering itself for a leap. I saw the flash in his eyes.

"You answer me when I'm talking to you, you hear me!?" Then he shoved me in the chest, and I stumbled backward off the bottom step to the ground.

"Henry! I won't stand for this," Mama cried, hurrying out onto the porch.

Papa glowered at her. "Stay out of this!" he shouted.

Just then Billy came outside and stood beside her. Papa and he stared at one another for a tense moment, Billy's hands doubling into fists. I thought for a second that the two of us were actually going to have to fight Papa.

"It's all right, Mama," I said, climbing to my feet. "It's all right."

Papa looked at me. "Got your mama to do your fightin' for you, sissy boy?" I looked at the ground, fighting an intense desire to hit him. A shudder of spent fear wracked my body.

"Go on, get out of my sight," he yelled after me. "You make me sick."

"Henry!"

I strode quickly away. I didn't know in which direction—only that I had to get away from Papa. I couldn't think. My mind was in a whir. Thoughts were coming at me so fast it felt as though my brain was on fire—his words . . . Mama's words . . . my words . . . shooting at me like firebrands. The earth sped past in a dizzy retreat. At the same time a numbness chilled my limbs, slurring all sensation, weighting my steps.

When I came to an awareness of myself, I found that I was running swiftly through the colonnade of trees. I'd gotten about a half mile down the road when I heard the truck coming up fast behind me. I stepped into the weeds as Papa roared past in an angry plume of gravel and smoke and dust and watched as the pickup disappeared in a red cloud behind the trees, then waited several minutes until the trees became stark and lowering in the settled dust.

Then I sat down on a large flat stone poking through a thatch of wheatgrass and took several deep, cleansing breaths. And the revolutions of the earth slowed.

I shook my head plaintively at the ground between my feet. "Why, God . . . why?" I prayed. But the weight of shame upon me was too great for me to utter another thought or to hear an answer, so I just gazed at the earth until my vision blurred with tears. I looked off at the trees along the river. "Atta boy, Tyler. You sure showed him. Yes, sir, stood up to him real good." A curse jerked out of my throat. "Yeah, you sure got the makings of a fine minister."

Wiping my eyes, I plucked a piece of grass and stripped it. I chewed off the sweet white meat of the blade until it became bitter, then I speared it into the dirt.

A calf bawling for its mother penetrated my thoughts, and I looked up. It was the one Billy and I had been pulling out of the creek over the past week, now loping fresh mud-bellied across the field toward its mother. I snarled at it. "Stupid calf, ain't got a lick of sense. Some skinny lion's gonna come along and make you a nice meal. Maybe Lucifer himself."

I stood to my feet, glanced once more at the road bending around the trees, then slowly headed back toward the house. A dark gloom hung over me, fingering into my chest, and Papa's eyes hunted me in the gloom. I kicked a clod, and it shattered. A red racer slid across the road into the weeds, and a small cloud of no-see-ums boiled across the sky.

As I approached the steading proper, a sharp, animal-like howl, followed by a lugubrious moan, sounded off to my left, and I stopped to listen. There was another howl, and I smiled, knowing what it was, then struck out across the yard toward the bunkhouse. I passed the open bay of the barn, and Mutt and Jeff appeared from behind a squall of chickens and picked up happily alongside me. I reached down and scratched their heads.

"Hey, fellas. Don't you be chasing them chickens now, hear? Chicken-killing dogs is dead dogs on the Hochreiter spread."

The dogs panted up at me happily, and then at the sound of Trout's whistle calling them from the house they took off in a scramble.

Trout winged a stick across the yard, and the dogs tore after it, yapping furiously. Another howl. I looked toward the bunkhouse, allowing an inward smile, then I continued on my course.

15

The ranch hands were playing a stick game outside the bunkhouse and were quite boisterous. They were sitting on the ground in two rows, four men to a row, facing each other, each man in his turn trying to guess in which hand his opponent was hiding an elk's tooth. The men's eyes were fiercely rapt. They pawed at the ground and made animal sounds, invoking the spirits of the bear and wolf to aid them in discerning which hand held the tooth. Shouts of triumph and groans of ruin ejaculated rhythmically across the two lines as the tooth was revealed. No one noticed my approach. No one would have noticed a stampede of wild horses, either.

Walking past, I noticed a sizable pot of silver coins spread out on a blanket in the center. Coins and dollar bills glittered and fluttered onto the pile as the tooth was passed down the line, back and forth. Sy's team was winning, according to a quick count of the colorful tally sticks in front of him, and they all wore smiles. The men in Jimbo's team, with only three of the fourteen sticks left, each wore a hangdog look; these contributed much to the groans of ruin. I shook my head and chuckled to myself.

Earl Thomas strummed his guitar from a ladder-back chair, a cigarette dangling precariously from his lips as he kept furious time with the rhythm of the game.

Sammy was sitting next to him; it seemed the sweat lodge Sy built had done him some good by the look of him. His eyes, alert and clearer now, followed me guardedly as I ascended the steps onto the porch.

"Hello, Earl," I said. "Good game, huh?"

Earl smiled big-cheeked at me, his little black eyes disappearing into the mounds of his happy nature as he squinted through a fog of cigarette smoke. He continued his ferocious cadence.

I glanced at Sammy and nodded cordially.

He regarded me for a moment, then nodded back.

I leaned against a post and watched the game. But my mind was elsewhere.

Glancing across the steading to the ranch house, my mind drifted back to the dinner table, found Papa's glaring eyes waiting to pounce on me, then reeled away with something that moved dangerously close to hatred. I felt something smart in my soul as though from a lash. Looking quickly away from the house, I beheld the sun glaring white on the face of the barn, the barn's single unblinking eye peering into the sum of my transgression with the merciless scrutiny of an Old Testament judge, the Law accusing me, convicting me. I shuddered under its condemnation.

A victory howl jolted me from my thoughts. Jimbo's team had finally scored a point, and Sy grudgingly tossed one of his colored sticks back across the blanket. Jimbo pumped his head proudly and bayed like a wolf. The others on his team did likewise. Several tally sticks were reclaimed in quick succession, the pot grew accordingly, and the game ascended or descended (depending on one's perspective) to a new level of boisterousness.

I was swept along by the roar and found myself laughing, sometimes groaning, sometimes howling, reveling in the simple freedom of these men. They bequeathed to me a blessing of unfettered laughter, and the judgment lifted off me and roosted in the shadowing live oaks, there to wait and watch.

Sy's team rallied and made a roaring comeback, and at last all of the tally sticks were collected onto his side of the blanket. Sy divided their winnings, a sizable plunder. Jimbo chided his team to shame as they slunk into the bunkhouse to fix supper. Earl Thomas, still smiling squint-eyed and big-cheeked at everyone and at no one in particular, followed after them with his guitar.

I alone was left on the porch to bask in the warm glow of the spirited game and to consider myself a richer man for having observed it. I sat down on Earl's chair, leaned back against the wall of the bunkhouse, and glanced at the bluffs in the west.

The sun was falling quickly now, speeding to its rendezvous with the sea. Shadows collected in the shrubs and trees and fingered over the steading. A hush fell in which sound carried from great distances. I could hear cattle lowing, pigs snorting, and the looping call of a crane down by the river.

I looked across the yard at the house as Mama came out onto the porch and took up her vigil in the swing. Our faces met for an instant.

"You all right, Tyler, honey?" she called, her voice carrying clearly on the cool off-river breeze.

"I'm fine, Mama."

She looked away and stared across the yard.

Jenny came out soon after and sat next to her and laid her head on her shoulder. They swung for a while, in one of those mother and daughter embraces, neither of them speaking that I could see, and then I heard Jenny's voice lifting clearly on the wind, asking, "What's it like when you die, Mama?"

I could see Mama look at her, a little surprised. "I don't know, honey," I heard her say. "We go to heaven."

"Does everybody go to heaven?"

"Not everybody," Mama said. "You know that from your Sunday school."

"Who, then?" Jenny persisted. "Who goes to heaven and who goes to hell?"

"Jesus' lambs go to heaven, and the devil's goats go to hell."

"Are we lambs or goats?"

Mama looked at her sharply. "Now what kind of thing is that to ask?"

"I was just wondering," Jenny said, looking out over the yard wistfully, strangely, it seemed to me. "I was wondering what it would be like in heaven, goin' through them pearly gates and walking on the streets of gold. I was wondering if Saint Peter would come up to you once you got in and then, finding out you were a goat that got past him, whether he would throw you out."

"That's quite enough wondering for one night," Mama said, closing the subject. And they fell back into the mother and daughter truce, rocking quietly, and the wind died down and buried their voices.

I shook my head.

Trout was hunting something along the side of the house with a stick, Mutt and Jeff sniffing along behind him. Then Billy came out and sat down on the steps, and each of their shapes grew dark in the retiring light. Big-eared bats boiled out of their haunts and frolicked against the furious hues of the sunset.

The voice of Billy's harmonica rose over the silent exhale of the day, and something immediately changed in the atmosphere, like the switch of a light turning on. I knew in that moment that the lingering demons of Sunday morning had finally taken wing, taking their little hell with them, and a peace descended over the ranch.

I was reminded of Mama's belief that the voice of God consisted of eight notes, and how the devil could not abide the sound of it. When Billy and I were small children, she often told us the story of

David the shepherd boy at bedtime, citing how, when he played his harp for the tormented King Saul, the devil had to run away holding his ears. She added that last part, but I thought there was some truth in it. That's why she sang to us each night when she tucked us in, and why we knew we were safe from the boogeyman until the last strains of the music wore off.

Mama says her love of music was a blessing of her Dublin roots, and she made it her calling in life to infuse as much of the voice of God as possible into the rearing of her four children. We had an upright piano that was probably tuned at one time, and on birthdays and Christmas Mama would gather us around and sing: mostly hymns and spirituals but also some Irish ditties and love songs she had learned from her parents.

Papa was a fair hand with the flattop guitar, and he would sing along as he picked out the melodies with Mama. He had a fine baritone voice that came out silky smooth after a few belts of Tennessee whiskey. Those were such sweet times that even their memory was a balm.

None of us children, however, had much in the way of acumen when it came to music except Billy, who could play the harmonica to make you cry. He had an impressive repertoire that he worked through on cool summery nights or during those times when Papa, Sy, Jimbo, and I would drive the herd to the railhead in Columbus. He said it soothed the cattle, which it did, but when he played "Shenandoah" it brought tears to our eyes, it was so sad.

"Your brother plays good mouth harp," Sammy Two Feathers said, suddenly appearing at my side.

"Whoa!" I cried, jumping to my feet. "You liked to scare me to death!"

He chuckled. Then he went to the porch rail and gazed out over the calming steading. I watched him carefully.

"What's that song your brother's playing?" Sammy asked. "It is a good song."

Surreptitiously I wiped a tear from my eye. "It's called 'Shenandoah.'"

He looked at me. "'Shenan-doah'?"

"It's an Indian name for a valley back in Virginia," I said.

"What Indian?"

"Shawnee, I think."

"It's a good name," Sammy said. I could see him sounding it out in his mind. "A good Indian name. It has the voice of tears in it."

144

I glanced at him. The lowering sun glistened over his black, watery eyes and shone on his face a deep reddish brown. He was a handsome Indian; he had a high brow and cheekbones with a square jaw, giving him the hint of a Spaniard. Silver highlights danced in his hair.

A silence fell between us as we listened to the mournful cry of Billy's harp.

"It is a lonely place, this Shenan-doah?"

"I dunno—never been there."

The song trailed off. Billy allowed an appropriate interlude of quiet to let the stirred feelings settle, spread out, and dissipate into the night. Then he charged into a spirited rendition of "Little Brown Jug."

My foot tapped of its own accord to the lively rhythm.

Sammy glanced over at me. "Your father is a good man," he said, changing the subject with the mood swing.

I stared at him defensively. "Good man. That why you pulled a knife on him?"

Sammy's eyes narrowed. "If he were not a good man, I would have cut him."

I grunted. "You would have tried. I ain't never seen him bested yet—leastwise not by no cocksure-of-himself punk with a knife." It was too strong a retort, but I let it stand.

Sammy looked away, chuckling. "Then you agree with me." There was a note of irony in his tone.

"What are you talking about?"

"There is pride in your voice—the pride of a son."

I just stared at him. Then I grunted. I had nothing to say.

"Your father has two mountain lions in him," Sammy continued, "one good, the other bad. He goes to feed the one that is bad now. I know this lion. When it has fed, it will sleep; then the good lion will come out of its hiding."

Then I had something to say. "I expect Sy'll be looking over his shoulder now that there's another prophet on the ranch."

Sammy smiled. "I think maybe there are two cats in you too. Which one do you feed now?"

I looked away from him, feeling suddenly without a defense.

A laugh rose inside the bunkhouse. I glanced through the screen door at the men sitting around the table. Supper cleared away, they were smoking now. A yellow pall of smoke swirled around the kerosene lamp. John Thorpe was recounting the highs and lows of the stick game, demonstrating once again his bear growl that enabled him

145

to see the elk's tooth through Jimbo's fingers. Jimbo was waving him off with a growl of his own.

"Why aren't you inside with the others?" I asked.

"I wanted to see the sun set," Sammy replied. He filled his lungs with a draft of the fresh night air. "I wanted to see the moon rise—see the stars come out." He took another draft of air as though he had suddenly remembered how to breathe. He tasted it greedily, then reeled in the heady brain brew of river, trees, put-up hay, and animal smells. He gazed upon the hills and trees and colors of the sky as though seeing them for the first time. "It is a good night, no?"

I glanced up at the first stars, twinkling low in a band of turquoise and orange over the purple rim of the river bluffs. "Yes . . . yes, it is good."

"My mother says the stars are angels, watching over us," the Crow youth said. He turned to me. "The priest at the mission told her this—you know Father Inglesia?"

"I've met him."

"He's a good man too. He told me one time he prays for me every night—tonight, maybe, too. What do you think the stars are?"

"The stars? I don't know—big balls of gas, I suppose."

Sammy turned away with a shrug of disgust. "I think they are angels."

It seemed strange talking to Sammy like this, him being sober for the first time in months perhaps. I was suddenly intrigued by him. He had always been just a drunk to me, a wretched soul who'd end up either in jail or dead in some ditch or bar. I wasn't quite sure what to think of him now. Then I noticed a chill shudder over him, a bit of poison winnowing out through his pores.

"The snows will come soon this year," Sammy said, covering up for it. "I can smell it." He took an exaggerated sniff of air. "Indian have better nose than a white man."

"I expect Papa's part Indian then."

Sammy looked at me queerly.

I chuckled. "You best turn in. Dawn comes pretty early to the Hochreiter ranch."

Sammy stared at the jagged line of trees along the bluffs, raking through the glittering starfield. He smiled. "I would like to see the dawn." Then he looked at me, nodded his head, and turned away.

"Sammy?"

He stopped at the door. "Yes?"

I wanted to tell him I was sorry about his father's dying. Tell him I was sorry about some of the things I said.

He stood in the doorway, looking at me with his shining black eyes.

"See you in the morning," I said, clearing my throat.

"See you in the morning, rancher boy."

I watched Sammy go inside, then stood on the porch for several minutes thinking about him, thinking about what he said about Papa and me having two lions in us. It certainly felt like it at times—now, for instance.

"Amazing Grace" descended over the steading—Mama's favorite. I looked up at the stars, studied them, noticed how quickly they multiplied in the blackening night, angels filling in the ranks, and I swear I felt one of Father Inglesia's prayers wing by. Then everything was quiet.

"You comin' in, Ty?" Billy's voice echoed across the yard.

"In a bit," I called back.

"You come in now, Tyler. I want you inside before your father gets home."

"I'm coming."

I stepped off the porch, walked slowly across the yard with a prayer birthing in my heart and joined Mama's dark silhouette on the porch swing.

"It gets away from him sometimes," she said.

"I know."

"He loves you, Tyler. He just doesn't know how to say it always."

"He has a strange way of showing it."

"I'll admit he's clumsy."

"Good night, Mama."

She looked at me. "Good night, son. I'm praying for you."

"Thank you."

I went inside, paused at the foot of the stairs, thinking about my father, thinking about the times I had wanted to tell him how much I loved him, but he always seemed just beyond my reach. It seemed there was a chasm between us. The hall light cast a pallid glow along the stairwell and on the frozen dead faces of my ancestors, who followed me with their eyes.

I shook my head as I ascended the stairs, and then the Model '95 clutched tightly in Bapa Otto's hand arrested my attention. I turned and stared hard at it for several moments, given to a kind of melancholy trance as my mind resurrected a long-buried scene.

I recalled the look in my father's eyes and the intensity of his smile when he brought the rifle out for me to hold on my sixteenth birthday. It was one of those inaugural looks that could either commemorate great moments of human endeavor or send armies off to war. After Bapa Honus was killed, the rifle had fallen into Papa's estate, along with the ranch, and now it was to be passed along to me, the heir apparent to the gift.

But I didn't want to touch it. Not that rifle. Not with its history. However, as I took it I felt a link with my father that I had never known, like a little bridge going up between us. And as I smoothed my hand over the stock, as I smelled the linseed and gun oil and levered open the breech, I felt the first stirrings of manhood in me, felt the pride of my roots begin to awaken. For the rifle, it seemed, was a scepter of the clan, a talisman that possessed some mystical bequeathing power of life. It was a blessed moment.

But as I touched the cold barrel, gazed along its length and caught the first glimpse of the muzzle, a shudder went through me, and then there was nothing left of the moment but the cold of the metal.

Papa rustled my hair and said fiercely, "Someday it will be yours, Tyler. Won't that be grand?"

It was too grand a thought for me to comprehend, and so I just blinked at him and said with a tentative voice, "I think maybe Billy'd want it, Papa."

I felt the snap of his eyes, the reel of his countenance, as I handed him back the rifle, the connection broken, the little bridge twisting over a chasm of shards. And from that moment on, I sensed his prophet's glare upon me, searching for the blessing of the gift amid the leaves of my budding manhood. Otto and Gertie glared at me now from their perch, and, breaking free of the trance, I turned away with a sigh and climbed the stairs, forgetting the rifle, forgetting the little bridge, thinking of Papa.

Later, as I lay in bed listening to the sounds of Billy sleeping and the porch swing creaking softly back and forth, I heard the truck rumbling down the road, the fourth cylinder missing rhythmically, then grinding to a halt in the yard. I heard the door slam, then Papa's voice—in a fine whiskey baritone—loudly singing an Irish love song that Mama taught him. I heard them on the porch, then heard Mama helping him into the house and up the stairs—Papa still singing, and Mama shushing him—and after his voice trailed off into the night I felt a heavy peace descend over the ranch like a down comforter. I curled up in it and breathed out a prayer, hoping that the devils would give us rest for a season.

They did. For a season. A week. And then all the devils in hell broke loose.

16

By first light Monday morning, the tractor was purring over the windrows like a contented cat. Papa, with his hand thrown carelessly over the wheel, glanced across his fields, their perfect pleats ess-ing over the gentle swells of earth, exulting in the glory of them, and the gleam in his eyes marking them with a pride that was hammered and honed on the anvil of his soul for generations.

Then he glanced up at the western sky. There was a lowering band of red on the horizon, dark and mean around the edges, a clear sign that the weather was turning, and he smiled. He would beat it. He knew he would beat it, and he laughed. He actually threw his head back and laughed.

Billy and I, both working the baler, jumped with amazement, then looked at each other and shrugged our shoulders. We both sensed it at once: there was something strange in the air, a reprieve perhaps, a benediction of grace lowering over the ranch. For some inscrutable reason, whether because the tractor was running smoothly, or because of something Mama might have said to him last night, or because this was the final week of baling, Papa acted as though yesterday afternoon had never happened.

Throughout the day he smiled and joked with Sy and the other hands, winked at Sammy and those bucking bales as the tractor purred happily past them, glanced back at Billy and me and grinned. More than once the thought crossed my mind that Sunday afternoon had indeed never happened, that it had either been a figment of my imagination or some clever mind trick of the devil.

Kate came out on Tuesday and helped Mama and Jenny with preparations for the upcoming barbecue. She was wearing jeans with the cuffs rolled over her ankles, a red plaid work shirt with the sleeves rolled past her elbows, and a pair of black-and-white saddle shoes. Her hair was pulled back loosely and tied with a red bow, and she looked prettier than the first rush of autumn.

I saw her only at lunchtime, when she brought out sandwiches and lemonade, and when it was time for her to leave. When we had a moment to ourselves she asked me how things were going. She listened intently as I told her about Sunday afternoon. I saw the edges tighten around her eyes, her lower lip stiffen beneath her teeth.

Then as I explained that things had quieted down and that Papa was in good humor, I saw the tension ease, the tight lips swell into a full, warm smile. She said everything was going to be all right, I believed her, then she gave me a quick peck on the lips.

"That all I get?" I moaned.

"Till Sunday, yes."

"I'll wither away before then."

"You big whiner." She smiled, then really laid one on me. "How's that?"

"That oughta hold me till next year."

"It better not."

"Then you best take some of the shine off it."

She gave me another that left me weak in the knees. And as I watched her drive away in her father's old Packard, I was wondering if I could wait another four years to get married. *Not a chance*, I thought.

Wednesday and Thursday we worked hard from sunup to sundown, putting up the rest of the hay in the barn until the muscles in our arms and legs and backs ached with numbness. Then at last, on Thursday evening, we all collapsed on the porch—Papa too—every part of our bodies and souls feeling good and clean and spent.

Work was a sacred thing to us—like a divine rite—and by it we kept a ledger of our right standing before the Law of the land. We had all partaken of the rite, done our fair part in sweating out the Curse, and for now the ledger was balanced. And as we sat on the porch with a holy satedness, our legs outstretched, with the travail of our labor draining out through the soles of our feet and beading upon our brows, every one of us saw that it was good. Even me. Never had I felt closer to the land or to the wily magic that held my father in its spell.

Mama and Jenny brought supper out onto the porch, and we ate in silence, listening to the sibilant breezes whispering through the cottonwoods, listening to the distant rustle of the Stillwater and the cattle lowing in the fields. Thunder rumbled petulantly in the distance, and we all looked up at the black skyline and pondered the threat.

A happy indolence descended over the ranch like a billowing sheet, spreading out smooth and silky. Then the sweet strains of music soughed over the steading as Earl Thomas plucked his guitar, and we listened to that too. It was like a hymn, like a prayer of the ancients ascending, and our hearts were moved by it. He gave it up after a while, and everyone went to bed, each in his turn, Trout, Jenny, Billy and me, then Mama and Papa, secure in the swaddling shroud of night.

As I lay in my bed I listened to the slow, sure creak of the windmill, its metal vanes marking the passage of the breeze. Slowly I began to drift into a long, black tunnel of thought, passing thoughts of the ranch, thoughts of today's labor, of tomorrow's, of Kate's pretty face—that kiss, that lingering unsettling kiss, holding it, losing it, searching for it, the tunnel darkening, filling in, taking me, and at some point I must have slipped away.

Suddenly I was awake and staring at the ceiling! What was it? Something was different, but what? And then I heard the vanes of the windmill humming a warning. The breeze had stiffened—storm coming—the advance guard approaching stealthily while we slept, and I wondered if Papa was listening too.

I wondered if the land and sky and rivers whispered to him in his dreams, or was it the other way around? *Do they bend close to you at night to hear the dictates of your slumbering soul?* I was too tired to think about it, so I drifted back into the tunnel, let some inky flow smooth me along to . . . *there you are.* Ah, that kiss . . .

By Friday noon it was finished—the Soul's propitiation to the lord of the harvest was complete. The barn was crammed to the rafters with hay, until they groaned and bowed under the great weight. The stubbled acres gleamed in the sun, with stacks of round bales and square bales rising over the fields like green and gold monuments. It was good, this testament to our zeal.

Billy and I saddled our horses, then rode out with Papa to select a suitable offering for the barbecue. There were several young bulls in the east section of the herd from which to choose, big lean beeves packed solid with meat. But Papa knew the one. His sleuthing eyes had already chosen the perfect sacrifice to appease the unbending gods that drove him. The rest of the bulls would be dehorned and cut and herded off to the railhead in Columbus next week, to be sold along with the surplus cows.

We didn't talk much on our way, for there was a kind of reverence that encompassed us. The sweet incense of cut alfalfa preceded us and swirled about our heads. I glanced at the Beartooth Range in the distant west, and the sky was dark there, almost black, the broken ridge line looking ominous and mean. However, there were golden grottoes of sunlight sweeping over the ranch, driving back the cool shadows under the advancing clouds. The contrast of gleaming light and encroaching dark was dramatic and stark and thrilling. I filled my lungs with the enlivening air and blew it out hard. I felt almost giddy with excitement.

Then a flash of light caught my eyes, and I glanced up to see a bald eagle circling overhead, hunting victims. Marmots and chipmunks scampered into their holes as the shadow knife passed over them, but not before Billy shot them with his finger. I chuckled, feeling good and clean.

When we approached the east section, I dismounted and opened the gate. Papa and Billy rode through, and I closed it behind.

"You stay here, Tyler, while Billy and I go on ahead," Papa said, looking back at me. "I want you to check the fence along the west section here," he added, gesturing. "I thought I saw a wire down a few days ago."

I looked up at him, perplexed. Then I glanced along the fence. There were no wires down, I knew. I'd been along there myself during the week. Then as I looked back up at Papa, our eyes met in a swift passing, and in that briefest of exchanges I caught the uncertain light in them, that bit of crimson flare that had been smoldering behind the smiling eyes all week long. I knew then that last Sunday afternoon had been no figment of my imagination.

I felt the kick in my stomach, then Papa nodded his head at Billy, and I watched the two of them ride away.

A chilling wind knifed over the fields, and standing there watching, I suddenly felt alone. Abandoned. A terrible isolation closed over me. The glory flown in a cry of Ichabod!

I checked the fences, and they were fine. Of course they were fine. No need of fence-mending here—only the mending of the first-born. Walking back to my horse, I picked up a stone and hurled it at the sun.

An hour later they returned, driving a fine young Brahma bull.

As we rode home, Papa paused at one point, looked back over his gleaming fields, then took a deep breath as though he wanted to possess the sum of his eyes in his chest. He let it go, and immediately a cold wind blew from the north. It was as though the land, breathing in tandem with Papa, gave a final exhale until spring. The land would die now. Winter would come—was coming. Lightning flickered in the dark cloud wreaths of the mountains, followed by an angry rumble. I felt the death shudder, looked away at the Beartooths looming dark in the west, and a chill went over me. We rode home in silent expectation.

Papa slaughtered the bull without mercy or ceremony, then Billy and I hoisted it up the side of the barn with the Jackson fork to drain the blood. Afterward we dressed it out and quartered it, covered the meat with burlap, then hung the quarters from one of the rafters in the smokehouse.

Papa came in and inspected our progress. He didn't say anything; he just nodded at our work, looked away, and threw more hickory onto the fire. There was an air of mystery enveloping him, a cold and deliberate aloofness. I saw the change working over him like the movement of the seasons, the colors of his mind subtly advancing to the next phase of the Soul's orbit.

Thunder boomed again in the distance, and the air darkened with the slow advance of the storm. I felt the atmospheric shift even inside.

"Think it might rain tomorrow, Pa?" Billy asked.

"Might."

"It'd ruin the barbecue if it does."

"I won't let it rain then," Papa said, flashing a defiant grin.

Billy and I chuckled at his joke, but I wasn't quite sure it was a joke.

Papa left the smokehouse with an exultant laugh.

Saturday was a nothing day, the kind of day when nothing happens of any significance except to define and bridge two more significant days with a nothing span of time. Aside from our regular chores it fell to Billy and me to wrangle some two-year-old horses for tomorrow's festivities.

Billy had a gleam in his eyes. "I got my eye on a strawberry roan —cute little filly's gonna throw ol' Tom Baxter good." He chuckled at the thought. "Thinks he's so smart, always trying to catch Laura Miller's eye. He'll catch her eye, all right."

Later that afternoon we herded a small string of horses into the corral, then helped Mama with the final preparations for the barbecue. We made a few tables from a stack of planks we kept in the barn for the purpose, set several bales of hay around for people to sit on, and we butchered some of the meat into steaks and ribs, leaving the haunches to smoke. We actually felt guilty from our lack of enterprise and made silly efforts to look busy.

And then there was Sunday.

17

After the morning service, cars and pickups began to arrive at the house, first a trickle, then a long parade of them, then a trickle of stragglers. Immediately the men and a few interested girls collected around the corral adjacent to the stables, some sitting on the hoods of their cars and trucks, others on horseback. But most stood on one side of the corral with their feet propped on the bottom rail and their elbows draped over the top.

Jimbo and John Thorpe rigged a makeshift chute out of the cattle loader and worked the gate, and with Big Bob Baker manning the stopwatch, our little rodeo commenced at eleven o'clock sharp.

Billy won the steer roping event with a time of twelve and a half seconds. I came in third with a fourteen-two, behind Tom Baxter. Kate, watching from the running board of her father's Packard, said I looked wonderful and manly. And I told her that, in a field of seven, third isn't so wonderful.

The next event was steer wrestling, and Billy won that event hands down. I came in third behind Tom Baxter, with a bruised rib where the horn grazed me as I dug the head into the ground. Kate said I looked wonderful and manly, and I just let it lie at that.

The final event was the bareback bronc riding. This was the big one, the event that separated the men from the boys and the latter from the backs of their broncs.

Billy was scheduled first. He had drawn a spirited buckskin we'd named Cyclone to add color to the proceedings.

I grinned down at him from the rail of the chute as he wrapped the rope around his hand.

He looked up at me and grinned. "Can't live forever." Then pulling his hat down on his head, he nodded to Jimbo, and the horse bolted with the gate. He lasted seven seconds before Cyclone sunfished and tossed him into the dirt. The crowd roared with laughter.

Billy climbed to his feet, grabbed his hat and slapped the dust off himself, then limped over to the rail. Laura Miller was there to greet him, and when he saw her, I swear his limp became more pronounced.

Tom Baxter drew a surly black we'd named Thunderbolt and got summarily tossed off in five seconds; his brother Steve was clawing air after three seconds on Jackhammer; little Petey Werton lasted two on Stick-O-Dynamite, and then it was my turn.

I had drawn Billy's strawberry roan, a real widow-maker Billy had christened Hell Fire.

Enos Stubbins had some side bets going that I wouldn't last four seconds, and there were plenty of takers.

I climbed down onto Hell Fire's back and felt his hide shudder menacingly, as though there were a legion of demons crawling just under his skin. "I expect you're one of the four horses in the Apocalypse," I said to him. The strawberry roan looked back at me with a glaring red eye and snorted.

Terrific.

Billy clapped me on the shoulder and grinned. "Say, Tyler—you know that flying eagle collection of yours that I've been coveting since second grade? I just want you to know that it'll fall into good hands once this old boilermaker stomps the living stuffings out of you."

"You were always the thoughtful one in the family, little brother."

He chortled. Jimbo snickered. John Thorpe looked at me kind of funny. And Kate, climbing onto the rail with an anxious look, waved at me and blew me a kiss.

I blew a prayer heavenward, flattened my hat down on my head, and cried, "Let 'er go, Jimbo!" The gate swung open, the roan jumped out of the chute as though his feet were on fire, and during the next several seconds it felt as though I were tied to a pile driver.

Billy had picked a good horse for Tom Baxter; only the luck of the draw picked me. He was an angry one, that roan. Time and again the earth fell away from me in a dizzying retreat, the horse cresting, head down, feet extended to arch his back in a violent bow, then rolling, to rush the earth with a bone-jarring hammering. And then again he jolted away in an angry lurch, twisting, again sunfishing, and again kicking high to throw me, snorting fiercely when he failed, and I with my right hand thrust high and cutting through the sky like a rudder as I sailed over the earth with an exhilarating lightness in my stomach and my legs threshing along the flanks of the pile driver.

Then after what seemed an eternity, I heard a horn piercing the dull roar of the crowd, and immediately there was an angel of mercy alongside me on the pickup horse, wearing the broad grin of Cleat

Patterson, and then I was leaping across the chasm from Hell Fire's pitching back to safety.

The earth reeled beneath me as I strode off the field to thunderous applause. I thought my knees would give out over the unsteady plain of the arena. And then I saw Kate waving and everyone howling along the rail, and it felt good inside knowing I had won the event, and I found my legs.

Enos whistled as I walked past him. "Well, I'll be a dirty word."

"Thank you, Enos." Charley Reese grinned, snapping a sheaf of bills out of his hand.

"That's some fine riding your boy did, Hank," I overheard Big Bob Baker tell Papa as I walked past a group of men. "A regular Curt McCarty."

Papa grinned a "what did you expect" grin, then he and the men headed toward the house.

Kate ran up, threw her arms around my neck, and gave me a big kiss. "You were wonderful, Tyler! Just wonderful!" Then she gave me a squeeze that liked to break my neck.

"I got lucky." I shrugged.

"Ain't no such thing as luck, big brother!" Billy beamed as he strode cockily up to me, sporting Laura Miller on his arm. "That ride was prettier'n a bride at the altar!"

Laura Miller giggled prettier than a bride anywhere.

"Thanks," I said.

"The Hochreiter boys ride again!" Billy howled. "Let that be a lesson to the rest of you two-bit greenhorns!" he shouted at the other contestants, the latter throwing their arms at him and saying, "Aw, go on! Lucky! Lucky!"

"Let's not be bragging now," I said. "Nothing worse than a bad winner."

"Are you kidding? Why, I'll crow to make Sylvester weep." And he threw his head back and crowed like a banty rooster.

Laura Miller giggled, and I saw a thrill go over her, looking at him.

Kate gave me a nudge and escorted me away.

An hour later Papa had the fire going in the stone pit and the big pieces of meat and the ribs slowly turning on spits. On a table beside him were potatoes and corn and steaks stacked on a plate awaiting their turn. A sweet aroma of meat and marinade curled off the pit into the air like a burnt offering. But a steady wind from the north beat it down and flattened the smoke into a blue pall, and people angled their noses to it and smiled.

The women flowed back and forth from the house to the tables with bowls full of potato salad, cole slaw, beans and chili, assorted breads, and salad. An intense pride of service burned in their eyes; their teeth flashed with furious duty.

The men cooled their heels around Papa at the barbecue pit, discussing ranching and the soon opening of hunting season, and dabbed their fingers into the marinade. Once Nils Johansson arrived with the keg, they traveled to and from it under the censuring eyes of their wives. However, Enos Stubbins, having elected himself Justice of the Draft, doled out his sentences with a liberal interpretation of the law and overruled any objections from the prosecution.

Trout herded a string of boys to the river, some with fishing poles, others with buckets or other receptacles, and the teenagers gathered into gender huddles and eyed one another wonderingly.

The Indians brought out their wives and families, if they had them, but stayed to themselves. The men sat in a semicircle in front of the bunkhouse, talking and smoking, their hands rising and falling over the currents of conversation. The women chattered busily inside over the meal preparations, and flowed in and out of the currents.

Some invisible line had been drawn between the two camps, separating the Indians and the whites into two social classes. No one had drawn the line, no one had articulated it, but it was there, as plain to see as the Great Wall of China. We were free to cross over into their camp, but they were not free to cross over into ours. It was understood. They had their own celebration, their own place in the sun, and they seemed content and happy.

Except Sammy. Sammy crossed the line.

His body and brain seemed sweated clean of the alcohol poisons. His eyes had cleared of their rheumy glaze and steadied in their sockets. It appeared he had awakened to a new knowledge of the world, and he clambered up into the seat of the tractor, which was hunched stolidly off to one side of the yard near the well, to explore it. He was safe there, he knew—his mastery of the thing had granted to him an inviolate dominion—and he watched with guarded fascination the unfolding drama. His dark, soulful eyes gazed intently at the goings-on, as though peering across into another realm, a realm veiled in a shroud of mystery, a forbidden realm.

Carrying a large pitcher of lemonade, Mama caught my eye.

"Tyler, set another table up for me, won't you? The whole county's showed, it appears, and Billy's run off somewhere."

I chuckled. Billy hadn't run off anywhere; I had seen him tooling along the road with a giggling Laura Miller. "I will, Mama." *That Billy*, I thought, walking over to the barn. *All he needs to do is name the tune, and the world will play for him.*

As I approached the barn I waved at Sy, Jimbo, and the others. They all paused, looking over at me, and waved back.

I went inside the aged barn and walked into a thick-smelling wall of hay and wood and leather and dried manure. It was a comforting smell. And then suddenly, unexpectedly, I was struck by the immensity of the barn.

I looked up at the sagging roof and around at the walls—blades of light sliced through the gaps in them and dissected the floor—looked at the rusting equipment and tack wanting neat's-foot and oil, as though seeing them for the first time. The barn seemed to encompass the very sky and earth, so immense it was, and for just a moment it took away my breath.

Then my senses tingled as though the nerve endings were on fire, and it dawned on me that I had entered either a very dangerous place or a holy place. A rush of chills raced along my spine as I became suddenly wary. My pulse thickened in my throat. It was like that time, nine months ago, when I awoke out of a dead sleep and felt the penetrating gaze of some fierce Presence in my bedroom—so real, so close and all-encompassing was its gaze, almost suffocating, so wonderful and yet terrible at the same time.

Do you love Me, Tyler? A voice had spoken to me on that wonderful and terrible night, not in words audible to the ear or measured by time but in a single brand of fiery thought that pierced the depths of my soul. I felt as though I might be struck dead any second.

"Yes, Lord, I love You," I whispered, not trusting my voice. I gaped awestruck into the inscrutable darkness, my heart burning, pounding in my chest as the room fell away from my senses in jolts.

And then, *Will you serve Me, Tyler?*

"Yes, Lord, I will serve You," I whispered stupidly. "I will go to deepest, darkest Africa, if need be."

I will teach you mercy.

I was mute. *Mercy*, I thought, pondering the word. Yes. *Mercy.* And then it was as though the ceiling were suddenly removed, showing a host of blazing stars, followed at once by a furious stirring in the air like the fluttering wings of a thousand angels pouring through the

159

opening and swirling about the room, whooshing past my face. I shuddered in terror. I was undone by the unapproachable holiness, the fierce light. There was a rushing sound, a furious beating, and then there was nothing. Silence . . . silence. A pristine silence that spilled over into a deafening void.

I blinked tentatively about the room, swallowing down the fear in the lingering hauntedness of the night. Then slowly, cautiously, the night sounds returned on a sea of waveless black, at first subtly billowing the curtains. Then the sounds edged into the room full-voiced over the quiet—the cricket song, the river, the music in the trees, the soothing creak of the windmill. And then at last there was the contented moan from Billy as he rolled over in his bed. I looked up at the ceiling and saw the vague shape of it, secured by its four corners. And I knew that I was safe again.

The next morning I arose to my desk and wrote the Chicago School of Divinity, sure that God had called me into some glorious ministry. I would set the world on fire.

Now I continued into the barn with the reverence that I had felt that night, my knees trembling at the prospect of walking upon so holy a ground. "Is it You, Lord?" I whispered at the stacks of bales along the left wall. "Is it You again?"

No response.

"I have told Papa that I would go."

But there was no response, no fierce fluttering of wings. There was only the feeling of a terrible weight upon me that I once felt in this place as a little boy, that humbling dread of a world much larger than myself, a world whose piercing gaze saw through to the least of my sins and condemned me.

I went over to collect the planks that lay against the right wall but paused in my business when I heard giggling. It was coming from the other side of the barn. Curious, I edged surreptitiously around the hay mountain, not sure what villainy I would find. My mind supplied at least one suggestion.

I peeked around a stack of bales, readying myself for it, but there instead, sitting in a square of incriminating light, was Took Johansson, intent on some mischief. Relief spread over me.

I sneaked up behind him and looked over his shoulder to see what it was. I smiled. He had placed a piece of wet taffy next to an ant hole, and as the ants streamed onto it, he was angling a small magnifying glass over them and drilling them with his fiery caprice. His shoulders bounced with delight.

"That how you smoke bees?" I said, after observing an ant disintegrate in a tiny wisp of smoke.

Took reeled and looked up at me astonished, caught in his crime. He thrust the glass behind his back. "Er . . . no. No! What'ya mean?"

"It's all right, Took." I chuckled. "I used to fry ants when I was your age too, I confess. Stinkbugs too. You don't want to hear what I did to salamanders." I sighed for effect. "It's a sad commentary on the human condition, I'm afraid."

Took blinked up at me. His pale blue eyes spread behind the thick glasses, struggling to let in some cogent light. I could see I wasn't getting through.

I looked down at the swarm of ants. "That piece of wet taffy you got there is a slick trick. I never thought of that. Got them ants riled good."

Took stared off to one side of the ant pile and said, "I asked Pa if they had feelings. He said they don't—none to speak of—so I figured it was OK. But they's your ants."

"It's OK, Took, you can fry 'em if you want. We got plenty."

A thought cleared on Took's brow, and as soon as I started to turn away, he was at it again. I left the barn feeling relieved with the weight lifting off my back.

The supper was a grand success, and the women cackled happily as they cleared away the plates and tableware. Each woman wore a look of satisfaction; none had stood above the others; every dish had been tried and fancied, and now there were only dishes.

The men pulled out their pouches, and, as a great cloud of smoke ascended over the steading, a wheel of philosophy began to turn. It began with a discussion concerning the price of beef. Then it turned to the local politics of Stillwater County, after which it turned to politics on the state level, and then to the national level, to FDR, to the war in Europe, to Hitler, Mussolini, and then the wheel turned back to the price of beef in Stillwater County and war.

War, be it ours or theirs, would need to be fed; war was market-driven, an economy of have and have not, of supply and demand. War craved fields of waving grain and high yielding meat per pound steers. There was considerable nodding of heads and looking thoughtfully at the ground and pulling on lips and grunting and spitting and tipping of small tin flasks as the great wheel of thought made its rounds, and men calculated the wealth of their herds.

Papa was the hub and held the spokes together, the flow radiating out from him and back to him. His word was law and unassailable—he had the gift, the gift of profit—and the men's eyes were never long from his.

Billy, wearing a big smile, sidled up beside me on a bale and asked if I wanted a pinch, and I told him what to do with his pinch. He lipped one into place, grinning cockily, as Papa might have grinned when he was seventeen years old and on the brink of manhood. And then he glanced over at Laura Miller—pretty Laura Miller, prettiest girl in Stillwater County Laura Miller—who at the moment was looking like a flower in bloom and out of place among the chattering stream of women and dirty dishes.

Billy chuckled and shot her a wink as he squirreled his round tin back into his shirt pocket.

Then Trout, covered with mud from head to toe and grinning as though he'd discovered a lost gold mine, returned from the river with the string of boys and wondered what was for supper. With a collective shriek, a flock of mothers descended on them and, taking hold of earlobes and elbows, whisked them off to the well.

Nearby, Sammy sat perched upon the tractor, watching everything with interest. I noticed his eyes wander to Jenny from time to time, make a secret appraisal of her, then look away as if he didn't notice. But I knew that look. He noticed all right.

Jenny, on the other hand, ignorant of or indifferent to his glances, floated through the crowd like a ghost. I caught a certain look in her eyes too, a look similar to the one she wore at the supper table last Sunday, like a scared mouse trapped in some corner, ready to roll over or lash out.

Jenny was strange to me, like a creature in one of those Flash Gordon comics Billy read all the time. I couldn't figure her, and I didn't try. She was pretty though, I had to admit, truly pretty, and I chided myself for not having told her. It wouldn't have cost me anything.

At some point Nils made another keg run. Enos presided over the second court more liberally than the first, making thunderous rulings, overturning all convictions, and the afternoon was off to a fine start.

Holly Dunbar, the dentist, pulled out his fiddle and began to rosin his bow. Cleat Patterson and Papa took his cue and tuned their guitars to one another; Big Bob Baker got out his banjo and plucked "My . . . dog . . . has . . . fleas."

162

The air was suddenly charged with excitement. Children appeared from their furious play as the first discordant notes popped into the air. The women gravitated to their men and fixed their hair. The girls giggled as they looked at the boys. The latter looped their thumbs in their trousers and shrugged their shoulders at one another, daring not to appear interested. They knew what was coming, though, and wore secret smiles.

The caller, a wizened old seed from Absarokee, stood up on one of the bales and, smiling amiably at the crowd, told everyone to make up squares.

I looked at Kate and said, "Do you want to?"

"Do I *want* to? Now what kind of question is that, Tyler Hochreiter?" she scolded. Then she took my hand and pulled me out into the clearing.

We were quickly joined by Billy and Laura and two other younger couples to fill up our square. There were six squares in all, and we had to move some bales out of the way to give us kicking space.

The old seed smiled upon us as a grandfather might. "Gentlemen, bow to your ladies," he began in a singsongy voice.

And I bowed to Kate.

"Now bow to the gal on your left!"

Then I turned and bowed to Laura Miller. She smiled embarrassedly at me and, feeling the cool smooth texture of her hand in mine as our square made a circle, a rush of embarrassment went through me too.

The music started with a burst. First the fiddle, calling the music to order; then the guitars, defining the rhythm; then Big Bob on the banjo, kicking it in the seat. Feet began to pound and tap, and hands clapped to the driving cadence.

"Circle to the right," the caller called, and we all, hand in hand, turned a wheel to the right, six wheels turning round and round like the gears of a clock, with everyone smiling and intent on their feet.

"Circle to the left." And we all whirled, chuckling, to the left, getting into it now, and kicking out the embarrassment and concentrating on the voice of the caller as it ducked in and out of the ebb and flow of the lively reel.

"Left allemande!" And we all turned with a stomp and a clap, the men then going one way and the women going the other, hooking our arms through the laughing flow.

And then, I confess, the rest of the dance was a whirl of pretty smiles and flushed faces, with the squares moving in and out, then

163

back and forth, then changing partners, losing Kate, then rotating through the stations and back to Kate, with the colorful cottony dresses twirling like bouquets of flowers and the boots stomping, the heads dipping, and, "Here we go," then promenading the gal around, and everything moving and turning and dipping and smiling against a swirling wall of onlookers, and the intent eyes of Sammy Two Feathers.

After a few dances, as we do-si-doed, shoulder to shoulder and passing, Kate whispered through a smile, "Want to go for a ride?"

I looked at her surprised, the way she said it. I waited until she rotated back to me, and, promenading her, my right hand lightly guiding at the small of her back and her left hand lightly resting in my left, I whispered, "Yes."

At the first punch break we slipped away discreetly, quickly saddled two horses, then rode away across the west fields, escaping the music and laughter that called after us.

She was a fine rider, my Kate. She sat a horse as pretty and natural as any woman I've ever seen. I watched her hair lift and fall with the gait of the horse, her dress catching the wind and billowing behind her like the meter of a poem, as we cantered across the fields toward the river and Big Medicine.

Then we slowed to a walk and rode silently for a while, Indian-like, as Sy and I had done so many times, taking in the wonders of Montana: a half dozen mulies moving silently along the bluffs, a bald eagle keening overhead, the Beartooth and Absaroka ranges cutting a great masculine scar across the endless western sky. The sky was black there and threatening, moving in, but kept at bay by the force of Papa's will. The views were striking, the contrasts exhilarating, more than one could take in at a glance.

It was cool in the shade of aspen stands and cottonwoods along the river. The smooth round stones popped and grated beneath the horses' feet as we guided them along the banks. The sun, slanting overhead, flashed through the nervous leaves and traced filigree patterns over the earth. And the leaves were beginning to change, some yellow now, some red, some browning around the edges like a fire going through them, all shimmering in the bellowing breezes. The cold white winter was coming behind a prelude of color.

Once we came to Big Medicine, we let the horses graze, and we walked, hand in hand, to the great willow. I parted the spray of leaves, holding it open for Kate as she went inside, and I followed her. We both paused and looked about.

There was a sudden feeling of safety in the little dome—a feeling that nothing could touch us, could harm us—as a soft green glow, like diffused light shining through the stained-glass windows of a church sanctuary, filtered through the veil of leaves. It played softly on Kate's wondering face.

"Sy showed me this place when I was a boy," I said, reading her thoughts.

She looked at me.

I smiled. "I come here a lot to think. I wanted to show it to you before I left for school." I glanced about the inner walls of the dome like a man showing his bride their new house, one bare of furniture, carpeting, and trappings but one that seemed tailor-made for the couple—one already possessing a soul. "Pretty swell, huh?"

"It's wonderful!"

I chuckled. "Sy told me once that it's a good place to die. That the evil spirits can't touch your soul in here when it flies."

She looked at me strangely.

We sat down with our backs against the trunk of the great willow and for a time gazed out through the translucent veil of leaves, feeling secure from the evils of the world and a freedom in the other's presence. The river eddied beneath the stroking fingers of the willow. Ripples drifted softly against the muddy bank.

I pulled off my boots and socks in that freedom and rolled up my jeans to my calves. Kate slipped off her shoes, and we let our feet swirl in the current, feeling the gentle pull of the water, cold and sharp and startling at first, then numbing and cooling, then tingling to a pleasantness.

Neither of us talked much. Talking would spoil it. I watched Kate strip a blade of grass, then toss it into the river, and the current, uncertain at first what to do, played with it, twirling it slowly round and round, then sweeping it out and taking it swiftly north.

A chilling wind fingered through the leaves and troubled the calm eddy at our feet.

Kate looked at me suddenly, her eyes starting with a thought, then she smiled embarrassedly and looked away. Then I felt her cool fingers smoothing over my hand and, looking up, saw that she was peering into my eyes. I kissed her. And again.

Then I stood up. "We'd best be going," I said. "They'll be wondering."

"Tyler."

I looked down at her and saw a shiver go over her.

165

"Won't you hold me?" There was a worried look in her eyes, a shade of some dark thing crossing her brow. "I need you."

I helped her to her feet and took her in my arms. The papery limbs of the willow enfolded us in its holy light. We were safe. The wind was withheld, the dark thing kept at bay. I held her face in my hands and gazed into her eyes. Then I bent toward her and kissed her lightly on the forehead. "We'd best go," I whispered.

"Yes, we'd best."

We rode back toward the ranch house in a desultory manner, pausing here and there for no particular reason other than to take in a sight or a thought. The sky was an angry soot black in the distance, crouching over the bluffs pantherlike, the storm ready to leap. The temperature had dropped quickly, and I felt winter coming.

Might snow, I thought. *That Papa, he had the gift all right.*

It was as we came over the last low hill before the fields dipped into the steading proper that I saw a plume of black smoke. It rose from behind the colonnade of trees, curling into the soot of the sky like a slow-dancing snake. It did not register in my mind at first what it was.

Kate said it. "Tyler, isn't that your barn on fire?"

18

When at last we rode into the yard, it took a moment for me to comprehend the import of what I saw. At first glance it seemed we had ridden into a dream: people were streaming every which way like frenzied insects, and the barn was engulfed in a whorl of orange and red and yellow tongues. Its single, unblinking eye narrowed upon the steading with fiery indignation. Thick black smoke twisted from its various ports and screwed heavenward, the heavens sucking it up in a draft of wind, with the sound of a continual roaring.

Some of the people, women mostly, stood in astonished clusters and gaped at the fire. Gasps attended each leap of flame, each bringing a host of hands mouthward. Heads shook incredulously and tongues clucked. "My . . . my, isn't that something?" Children clutched their mothers' knees, trembling with excitement, their eyes wide with amazement. Animals stood in huddled silence. A calm, almost serene, wonder enveloped the scene.

The Hochreiter barn was going up.

My mind reeled behind a protective wall of shock. Time slurred to a surreal, underwaterlike crawl. And then it felt as though I was in one of those dreams where some ghoul is chasing you, threatening to overtake and commit some heinous atrocity to your person, and your feet get caught up in a taffy pull. You know in your dream that you must wake up lest it kill you, and so you force yourself awake just before it strikes.

But there was no waking from this—there was only standing there, leg-numbed and hollow-bellied, and watching helplessly as the spectacle of horror shaded over me and, lurching, dragged me under.

At some point I must have dismounted. I don't know what became of my horse or of Kate, but I felt myself running—taffy-legged running as in the dream, only now I was running toward the monster.

Sounds leaped suddenly from the wall of shock. I heard men calling out to one another—their voices jumping in and out, here and there, in a series of non sequiturs—and then I saw that they were passing buckets and pans, even Stetsons, along a long line that ter-

167

minated at the well. Those at the head of the line were rushing forward with their buckets and tossing water upon the blazing edifice, while the others rushed to bring up reinforcements.

It seemed a futile effort. For the flames lashed out at the men like one of those Greek chimeras I once read about, the multiheaded thing stabbing angrily against their faces with tongues of fire, and the men were forced back from the roaring heat.

The Hochreiter barn was going up.

Something cold and deliberate awakened in my brain as I ran, an inert and primal sense of something fanned to life. Emotions fled. Fear fled. The one thing remained, the primal thing that connected me with the other men and impelled me forward. I moved with the cold, well-oiled efficiency of a machine or of a soldier.

And charging over to the front of the line where Papa and Billy were fighting desperately, I grabbed a bucket from someone, rushed forward, and tossed its contents into the roar of blazing light. But I might have tossed a thimbleful for all the good it did, for the fire hissed at me, spewed a black blast of smoke from its nostrils, then licked up the face of the barn as though invigorated by the water.

I glanced at Papa, passing the bucket behind me and taking hold of another one. His face was intent, his jaw set and grim as he fought to save his barn. He seemed suddenly a heroic figure to me, orchestrating the players in a dramatic tragedy.

I felt caught up in a swell of pride as I rushed forward again and again, back and forth, in a kind of rhythmic bucket dance. "Promenade left, promenade right, swing that bucket and bring her on down." The Hochreiter magic worked strong in me, loosed from my brain some fettered creature, and I heard myself laugh, like a fool or a madman or a keeper of the Soul:

> " 'Half a league, half a league,
> Half a league onward,
> All in the Valley of Death
> Rode the six hundred.' "

Again and again we rushed with our buckets, and again and again the fire repelled us. The ancient planks screamed and moaned as they released the ghosts of dead seasons.

Then, at some point, a disturbing noise began to click in the back of my head, finding my inner ear amid the tumult of the crowd. I paid it no mind at first, but like a troublesome bluebottle that buzzes around your ears and neck and alights when you ignore it, it would not give me peace. It kept droning through my head, occasionally alighting on some untended patch of my subconscious, then stroking its iridescent belly and tickling me. I swatted distractedly at it.

"Here! Give me another bucket!" I shouted amid the ebb and flow of the pails, taking one, rushing forward, and sprinkling its contents against the blaze.

However, the mind fly continued to drone annoyingly louder and louder in my inner ear, gnawing, needling, worming its way to the surface, really tickling now, then crossing some threshold so that at last I heard a voice in my outer ear. I started at the sudden sound of it, and, turning to my father, cried, "What is it, Papa?"

But Papa wasn't there. He and Billy had rushed into another sortie with their buckets. I glanced back upon the long line of men. Here and there a face leaped out of the crowd as the light of the fire flashed upon it. Their faces were grim, set, fiercely intent, moving in concert. And then I saw Nils Johansson, and my chest went suddenly cold.

The big Swede was moving down the long line of men, crying, "Haff you seen Took? Haff you seen Took? Has anyone seen my Took?"

His wife, Ilse, was behind him, small and sickly looking as she peered into the men's faces, her rabbit eyes looking away to the next face as each head shook.

"No, ain't seen him, Nils . . . You, Tom? . . . No, not me . . . Ain't seen him since you come in . . . Me neither . . . Sorry, Nils. He'll turn up, you'll see." And so on down the line they came.

"Yes, I saw him," I shouted.

Nils fixed on me and came running, Ilse behind him.

Nils took hold of my arm. "You saw my Took?"

"Yes—earlier," I said. "He was in the barn, playing with—" And then I saw the beam of light narrowed on the piece of wet taffy, and the cold in my chest turned suddenly hot with terror. The mind fly was caught in a sudden updraft and twirled away, laughing, in a fiery blue brilliance.

"The barn!" Nils's face went white as the words spread over him. Ilse threw her hands to her mouth. Then I saw a madness sheet over Nils. He reeled about and faced the barn, his mouth agape with a question. Then, stepping heavy-footed toward it, he lifted his hand before him in a reach and cried, "Took . . ."

"Here I am! Paw, here . . . in here, Paw!" a voice cried in retort.

We all looked at once, and behind the open bay we could just see his wavering form through the flames. His eyes were wide with animal terror as he waved his arms.

Seeing him, Ilse slumped to the ground in a faint. Two men rushed to her and pulled her to one side.

"Paw, help me . . . help me, Paw . . ." And then a rafter fell, sending a crash of sparks into the air, followed by a riot of fire shards. We saw Took jump away from the opening, and the rise of flames and smoke obscured all but a frantic shape running back and forth.

Nils picked up his pace as the madness consumed his reason. "O my God," he cried. "O my God, haff mercy!" He broke into a run.

I ran and tackled him around his legs, and, hitting the ground, he began to fight me. His big fists beat wildly against my chest, some blows glancing off my head. I ducked most of them, though, then struck his face with my open palm. He looked at me suddenly, a fierce light glazing over his eyes. "No! No! My son is in there!" he bawled. "Leave me be!"

"Somebody help me!" I cried.

Big Bob Baker was suddenly beside me and pinned his arms.

Nils threw his head back and wailed.

I glanced around at the spectacle. People moved swiftly in the light of this new horror, men shouting, women weeping, children wondering what cue to follow. My mind dissected the tumult into its separate sounds, each sound clear and distinct from the others, every sound and syllable cut away from the whole—my boy . . . my boy . . . give me another bucket . . . a rumble of feet . . . over here . . . watch it now . . . stand back, Charley, that wall's giving way . . . the sky darkening and a brilliant flash of lightning followed by a thunder crack . . . another trampling of feet . . . let go of me—can't you see my boy's in there—my boy . . . Took! Took! . . . the starter of a truck *cah-cah-cah*-coaxing a listless engine to life . . . the engine coughing . . . roaring . . . and then a squeal of tires.

I looked up as a pickup sped past and recognized it as the Johansson's. I jerked my eyes down at Nils pinned beneath the powerful arms of Big Bob, wondering how it could be. The big Swede lay on the ground, subdued now, the madness going out of him in a quiet whimpering.

Then I glanced up in time to see the pickup disappear into the flaming bay, the firelight flashing for an instant on the side of a face, as though the mouth of hell had swallowed the truck whole. I lurched forward, feeling I'd been kicked in the stomach by a mule.

"Billy!"

It was Papa's voice I heard.

Jumping to my feet, I saw him running toward the bay, but a belch of flames threw him back to the ground. A section of the roof gave way, and we all had to jump back out of the way of the intense heat and flaming debris. I tripped and fell. I lay in the dirt a moment, stunned, the separated noises rushing together in my brain to reconstruct the tumult. Then I staggered to my feet and stared dumbfounded at the barn, black amid the brilliant orange and yellow.

The men along the line stopped and stared stupidly, each man holding his bucket. A collective wonder fell over the people. A terrible silence thickened in our throats. The fire roared and hissed and crackled with delight.

Then I saw Mama running across the flickering aureole, screaming, "William! O God, not my William!" But one of the men took hold of her and pulled her back. She fought him for a moment, then went slack in his arms, crumpling, one arm crooked around his neck, the other clutching her face in anguish.

A bolt of lightning jagged wickedly across the black sky, followed by an immediate deafening report, and I took an involuntary step backward from the force of it. The tail of thunder whipped along the bluffs into a distant quiet, and then the sky flashed again with a terrific thunderclap. The storm had stalked us in our distraction, the chimera had leaped upon us with a terrific roar. It seemed the world was coming to an end.

Suddenly the west wall of the barn seemed to explode before a speeding black shape. Everyone turned with a gasp. Thick black smoke and fiery cinders scrolled off the shape, revealing that it was Nils Johansson's truck speeding away from a jagged yellow hole in the wall, gluttonous tongues of fire licking out after it. The truck swung around the barn with a grating of gravel, trailing thick tendrils of smoke from its wheel wells and windows, and screeched to a halt near the water pump.

Immediately the cab door swung open, and from it the form of Billy belched out in a wreath of smoke, coughing and sputtering and carrying the still form of Took. Their faces were both black. Their hair was singed, and smoke rose off their forms as if they were two smoldering wicks, and a little spear of flame kindled on Billy's shirt. A man appeared with a bucket of water and doused him.

"Give way," a voice cried out, "let them through!"

The men made a small clearing as Billy laid Took on the ground.

171

"Give him air . . . give him air . . . water! More water!"

Sammy pushed through the onlookers and quickly loosened Took's trousers. Then he pressed lightly against his stomach, forcing bad air from the boy's lungs. Then he pulled up on his arms, working the diaphragm, out and in like a bellows . . . out and in . . . out and in.

"That's good. Keep it up," a woman's voice said. It was Kate, settling next to the boy. "Hold it."

Sammy paused as Kate pressed her ear against Took's chest. She looked at Took's face. There was soot around his mouth and nostrils, bits of char clinging to the roof of his mouth.

"Again," she said.

Sammy lightly pressed the boy's stomach, then pulled up on his arms. He did this several times and, when he paused, Kate listened again.

Nils appeared and gazed gravely down at the quiet form of his son. His lips trembled. "Is he . . ."

"Someone get Doc Turner," Kate shouted.

"I'll fetch him," a voice cried. And a moment later a truck was roaring down the road. Heads turned and followed it momentarily, then quickly returned to the tragic little scene, eyes taut and anxious.

Kate had a towel in her hand and dipped it in a bucket of water next to her. Took's thick glasses were hanging off one ear. She removed them, handed them to someone, then gingerly dabbed the boy's face. Black-and-pink streaks appeared beneath the outer layer of soot, revealing wicked-looking blisters.

Nils searched Kate's eyes and then the blistered face of his son. "My boy . . . is he . . . is he dead?" he asked, his voice breaking.

The boy stirred at the sound of his voice, then coughed.

"That's enough, Sammy." Kate smiled. She dabbed the wet towel over Took's face, mindful of the blisters, and looked up at Nils. "No, Mr. Johansson," she assured him. "He is not dead."

Took moaned and rolled his head from side to side. "No! No!" He was still fighting the fire. Then his eyes blinked open, started wide, and finding the worried face of his father looming over him, he coughed. "I didn't mean to, Pa."

Some pent terror was loosed from the crowd, and a cheer went up. People clapped each other on the back the way they do on New Year's, clambered around Billy and clapped him on his back too. Women giggled out a knot of nerves. Men laughed and shook their heads, pulled out neckerchiefs, and wiped their necks. Brown streams of tobacco juice spattered the ground, as the air cleared of the specter

172

of death. It was like a New Year's all right, like a new something anyway.

Billy sat back against the wheel of Nils's truck and poured water over his head. Blinking, his eyes showed white through the soot like Al Jolson's.

Mama grabbed his neck and wept. "Thank You, Jesus! Thank You, Jesus!" She kept smoothing her hand over his face with a wet cloth, weeping and kissing his cheeks.

Billy caught my eyes and grinned. *Just like Al Jolson*, I thought. *That Billy—the heir apparent*, and I was proud of him.

My cheeks were wet with tears, and as I looked around at the happy faces, I didn't see a dry eye but one. Papa's jaw was set tight, and his lips were compressed into a grim smile. He just kept nodding his head, then shaking it, taking hold of the back of his neck as if he didn't know whether to laugh or cry.

There was a sudden loud noise, like the crack of doom, and as everyone turned to the barn, what was left of the roof fell in on itself, and the whole of the thing went up in a glorious pyre. Showers of cinders shot heavenward, careering every which way like the Fourth of July, and intense heat pushed outward against the crowd. Sy and the other hands hurried about the steading, looking for touch-offs.

A blaze of light shot across the sky, and the thunder boomed. And then flakes of ash, some quarter-sized, some half-dollar, began floating down upon us. I looked up, and the flakes were gray against the sky, a few falling at first, twirling, then more, lighting in the live oaks, in the shrubs, in our clothes and hair. One flake landed on my nose. It was cold at first, then it melted, and looking up at the falling flakes, now white and smaller and driving from the north, I realized that it had begun to snow.

The following morning the world was covered by a thin white sheet. It appeared the world had not come to an end after all. It was only newly clean. The trees stood out a dark gray beneath the light dusting, and birds chirped their winter warnings in the branches.

The sky was dark and roiling—a blood red smear over the rim of the earth—though clearing in the east with the sun now climbing over the hills and herding the storm toward the mountains. The clouds were black and gray strokes overhead, showing brilliant white on top, as though the sky painter had used a palette knife over the canvas in order to achieve a bold and dramatic effect. It was dramatic all right.

There was a muttering of thunder in the distance, accenting it, but I knew it to be only thunder.

For a long while we stared at the immense black square of soot that was once our barn, none of us saying much, each of us kicking numbly at things amid the ashes.

Thin smoke ghosts rose silently from shards of burned wood and timbers that jutted from the ashes, from the few blackened bales of hay that survived, and from some old machinery—all that remained of the barn that Bapa Otto built, that chronicling keeper of three generations of hard work. Clawing out of the ruins was the harrow bed, a twisted black skeleton, its curving ribs charred as though from cremation.

Papa pushed back his brown fedora, spat an arc of juice into the ashes, then gave the harrow a kick. It shuddered and collapsed on one side. He stared at the thing a long while.

I glanced at him out of the corner of my eye, trying to translate the language of his body. But I couldn't see through the veil, that air of mystery that earlier enshrouded him and deflected all inquiry.

Mama went over to him and put her arm around his waist, and I thought I heard him chuckle.

Then I noticed Sammy fiddling with the entrails of the tractor. Every so often he'd glance up furtively, gaze at something across the yard, then go back to his jiggling. I followed his eyes to the house.

Jenny was on the porch swing, rocking slowly, pensively, her knees drawn up to her chest in a kind of bulwark against the world. Her eyes were taut, almost wild like an animal's—that cornered mouse look again—staring out at us from the shadows of the overhang, as from some secret place or knowledge.

The thought struck me that perhaps from her perspective the smoldering ruin was something more than an accident of nature or mishap of a retarded boy's play; that it was, instead, a kind of judgment that had been unleashed against some transgression of the ranch and that the porch was a sanctuary that she dare not leave lest it strike again. When our eyes met she quickly looked away. The Indians stood about in quiet huddles, muttering to one another in their Crow tongue. This was a powerful sign from the Akbadádéa—the All Father—a good sign or a bad sign they hadn't yet determined, and they debated among themselves for the meaning.

Jimbo scratched his head. Sy was silent and stared away at the lowering clouds in the west, as though listening to a distant voice or reading an epitaph carved into the granite teeth of the mountains.

"Lookit I found," Trout said, holding up a small metal object. He brought it over to Papa. It was the magnifying glass, the glass shattered out of it.

Papa looked at it, grunted, then tossed it back into the ashes.

We looked up when Nils Johansson's truck rattled into the yard. He climbed out of the cab, and we gathered around him.

"Morning, Nils," Papa said.

"Good morning, Henry." He glanced over at the burned-out scab of earth. It seemed a shade passed over his face, and I saw a little shudder go through him.

"How is your boy?" Mama asked.

Nils nodded at her. His eyes moved reflectively to Billy's face, to the bandages on his hands, then back to Mama. "Doc Turner said he's goin' to be just fine," he said quietly. "He's resting nicely. Doc Turner said if Billy hadn't got to him when he did . . ." Then his voice thickened, and he choked. He looked quickly at his feet, rubbing his brow with his big fingers, and when he looked up at Billy his eyes were streaming. He started to say something but couldn't.

Mama put her arm around Billy's waist and drew him close, smiling.

"Yes, well . . ." Nils said, clearing his throat. Then he reached into his cab and pulled out a long package. Smiling at Billy, he handed it to him and said, "This doesn't begin to pay for what I owe you, son. But it's something."

Billy looked down at the package. "No, Mr. Johansson, I can't accept this." He started to hand it back, but Nils pushed it away.

"No, son, this is for you. From Ilse and me and . . . Took." His voice cracked. "Please, take it."

Billy looked embarrassedly at the package in his hands, then back at Nils. "Thank you." He chuckled. "Thank you very much."

Nils's brow cleared as he turned to Papa. "Henry, we are goin' to build you a new barn," he said. "You never saw such a barn as we goin' to build. No, sir . . ." He struggled to finish his thought.

Mama went over to him and took his arm. "Now don't you worry about a thing, Nils. We've been meaning to tear down that old barn for some time, isn't that right, Henry?"

Papa glanced over at the burned square and scratched the back of his neck.

"No, we goin' to build the biggest barn you ever did see," Nils said quickly. "And don't you worry about your hay, Henry. We got plenty hay."

"Nonsense," Mama said, "we have plenty of hay. You just quit your fretting and get home to your family."

Nils smiled awkwardly at her. Then he looked again at Billy, his head did a little bobble, and he climbed back into his truck. We watched his pickup grow small down the colonnade of trees.

"Hey, Billy, what'd he give you?" Trout asked, allowing an appropriate interlude of silence to pass. "Ain't you gonna look inside?"

Billy just stared at the long package, feeling the certain weight of it. He didn't open it. He didn't have to. I could almost feel the joy of it coursing up into his arms.

19

That night as I lay in bed, my mind was a black square in a field of white. I couldn't shake the image. Every time I closed my eyes there it was, rising out of the depths of my mind and settling over me like a pall, leaving me with a deadness sucking away in my chest.

I lay there thinking about how not to think about it. I tried thinking of Kate, of those strawberry lips, of going off to college in two weeks; even Booster made his rounds through my thought repertoire. But none of it worked. Sooner or later the black square would descend, envelop me, and there I was, telling Took it was all right for him to fry ants. We had plenty of them. *Go ahead, Took, fry the ants and burn down the barn.* I rolled over for the tenth time and rehearsed my repertoire from the beginning.

And then at some point, in that silky place before you slip over the brink into sleep, I heard the most eerie sound. I thought I was dreaming at first. It was a lonesome, chilling sound, a chilling to the bone sound, sounding like an abandoned baby crying for its mama, and it kept up for the longest time. Everything would go quiet, and I would wait, knowing, and then sure enough it would start up again, that awful sound, that baby abandoned somewhere up in the mountains and wondering why its mama had up and left him sound. It sent shivers up my spine, for I knew what it meant.

"Hear 'im, Tyler?" Billy asked.

I could see his silhouette rising into the square of the window, the moonlight bright on the sill. "Yeah, I hear him."

"We're gonna have to get after 'im, you know."

"I expect so."

"Mutt and Jeff won't be worth a lick," he said, thinking out loud. "Maybe Izzy'll loan us his hounds."

"He'll want to come."

"Fine with me." Billy chuckled. "Izzy's all right. Couldn't hit the broad side of a barn if he fell on it, though."

"You might've used another figure of speech."

"Sorry if my command of the language ain't as pretty as yours, Ty. Still, it don't make Izzy any better a shot."

"All we need are his hounds, so long as you and your shiny new rifle tag along."

"Now there's a truth." Billy chuckled again, then lay back with his hands behind his head on the pillow.

We listened for a while until the baby crying finally trailed off into a long silence. We waited for it. Nothing. Then the white sheet with the black square began to settle over my mind.

"What made you do it, Billy?" I said, resisting it.

"Do what?"

"You know what—drive into the fire like that yesterday."

"I don't know. Something just come over me. Had to, I guess."

"*Had* to?"

I could hear Billy thinking about it. "Think I'm crazy?"

"You know better'n to ask me that." I chuckled.

"Pretty scary, huh?"

"Yeah, pretty scary."

I saw the moon flash on his eyes as he glanced over at me. "You're a hero, boy," I said. "A real bona fide hero. I expect they'll be writing songs about you. Naming streets and babies after you too. Billy Avenue . . . William Square . . . Brave Billy's Five and Dime . . ."

"Knock it off."

"Good night, sweet knight."

"Shut up."

Billy lay down and quickly augured into a deep well of sleep. I spirited away at some point, dreaming of babies with fiery eyes and long fangs and sharp claws romping after me. I woke up with a start, feeling the hot breath on my neck. Then, realizing that it was only a dream, I breathed easier.

I lay there for a long while, blinking at the ceiling, staring into each of the four corners, listening to the sounds of the night closing in and Billy's snoring. *Is man a trichotomy or a dichotomy?* Only two more weeks and I'll know. Fourteen revolutions of the earth. I liked the sound of two weeks better.

Kate, where are you, Kate? Where have you flown? Come and kiss me, Kate. "*Hearing thy mildness praised in every town, / Thy virtues spoke of, and thy beauty sounded, / Yet not so deeply as to thee belongs, / Myself am mov'd to woo thee for my wife.*"

178

And then the black square folded me in nothingness, and I slept fitfully.

In the morning Papa found the tracks right off in the soft bank of the river, about a half mile from the house. "It's a big'un," was all he said.

Billy looked at me and smiled. "Lucifer."

The Labs sniffed around and growled, but I knew their hearts weren't in it. They did all right with deer and upland birds, but you needed a good blue tick or bloodhound to get after mountain lion.

Papa mounted his horse, and we followed the Labs downriver, eyeing the trees and the pine-covered bluffs. The sun was just working down to the glittery tops of the aspens along the opposite bank.

The calf was lying beneath a rotted-out cottonwood, debris tossed over the carcass, with the flies already at work around its eyes and mouth. A big section of its right hindquarters was missing—the flies were busy there too—and the grass was all flattened where the big cat lounged about after eating. The smell of lion clung to the air like a morning mist; even I could smell it. Mutt and Jeff sniffed at the spoor, making short forays into the trees and high grass with their hackles up and quivering, but I could see their hearts still weren't in it.

Billy eyed the carcass from his horse. "Don't look like he'll be straying anymore."

Papa cursed.

I held my tongue.

"Want Tyler and me to get after him, Pa?"

Papa looked back in the direction of the ranch, then he glanced up at the bluffs and beyond, and I knew what he was thinking. He was thinking we had plenty of dehorning and castrating to do before the drive next week, and we didn't have time to go flying off on a lion hunt.

He was also thinking that a mountain lion prowling about was nothing to fool with, especially a stock killer like Lucifer. Ranchers had been after that old boy for years. He was a notorious rogue. He didn't stick to his own territory like most big cats but ranged about, killing cattle and sheep, hogs, chickens, you name it; been known to kill other mountain lions. A man-killer too. A woman was found mauled to death and half-eaten up Big Timber way about a year ago, and Lucifer got the blame for that. It was that thing of reputation again; once it gets hung on you, there's no retreating from it.

Papa cursed a second time; he hated decisions being made for him. "You'll need Izzy's hounds."

Billy grinned that big grin of his. "I'll give him a call."

"Like to go with you boys," Papa said, swinging up into his saddle, "but somebody's got to stick around here and do some ranching, 'fore everything goes to fertilizer." He reined his horse toward the house, gave a short jab to its flanks, and the Labs were only too happy to lead the way.

When we got back to the house, Mama had a big breakfast set up, and the smells breezed out through the screen door to welcome us on the back porch. Billy's eyes lit up as we banged into the kitchen.

Mama looked at us from the stove.

"Lucifer," Billy said, reading the question on her face. "Took down that renegade calf."

Mama shoveled grease over the egg yolks and clucked her tongue. "That's a shame."

Trout gaped at us intently. "Lucifer! It's really Lucifer? You gonna get after him, Tyler?"

"We're going to try." I passed by the table and gave the biscuits a big sniff, then glanced back at Billy. "You call Izzy while I go upstairs and get my rifle."

"Yes, Papa."

Mama shook the spatula at us like a switch. "You boys are going to eat some breakfast before you go off into the hills, hear? I didn't go to this trouble for the Labs."

Billy winked at her. "Don't you worry, Mama. Breakfast will get et if I have to eat it all myself."

Mama grunted, then, working the edge of the spatula under the eggs, asked, "Where's your father?"

"With Sy. He'll be along directly."

"Can I go too?" Trout begged. "I never been on no lion hunt before."

"Sure," Billy said, then leaned close to Trout's ear and grinned. "We could use you for bait—stake you to a tree maybe. Wait till Lucifer got to sniffin' your belly button . . . then—" With a ferocious roar, Billy snagged a strip of bacon off Trout's plate.

Trout screamed and jumped about a foot off his chair.

Mama dropped the spatula on the floor, spattering hot grease everywhere. "Mercy, William!"

"Hey! That's mine!" Trout squealed, watching Billy devour his bacon. "Mama, Billy swiped one of my bacons!"

"You hush now, Joseph," Mama scolded. She wiped up the floor, then slid another strip of bacon onto his plate. "Billy needs his strength to get after that mountain lion."

"Why can't I go?"

"'Cause if that lion ate you, he'd get such stomach cramps we'd never get any sleep at night."

Trout blinked at her, sorting it out in his eight-year-old mind.

Mama's voice chased me up the stairs. "Tyler, fetch Jenny for breakfast, won't you?"

"Sure 'nuff," I said, rounding the corner into the hall. Jogging past Jenny's room, I sang, "Breakfast! Last one there's a two-dollar mule!"

But there was no response. I pulled up abruptly, seeing something through a crack in her door. Peeking into the room, I saw Jenny curled up on her bed like a baby. She was crying. A shaft of yellow light pushed in through the window dividing the shadows, and there were dolls and stuffed animals walled around her, staring down at her with benign ferocity. Her shoulders rolled slightly as she whimpered.

I poked my head in farther. "You OK?"

She looked up at me startled. Her eyes were red, and tears shone on her face. "Don't you know how to knock?"

"I heard you crying."

"I'm not crying."

"Red eyes, wet face . . . I get it—you were laughing hysterically."

"Leave me alone."

I grunted. "Mama wants you for breakfast."

"I'm not hungry."

"Suit yourself."

"Tyler, don't go," she said quickly.

I turned and looked at her, and there was that cornered mouse in her eyes, ready to fight. "All right, Jenny. What gives?"

She stared at me for a moment, and I could see a thought working behind her eyes, the mouse looking for a hole or a bit of offered cheese. And then she said quietly, "Nothing. Nothing's the matter. Just leave me alone."

"Fine. Why don't I just leave you alone?" I shook my head as I closed the door, convinced that Jenny would be better off in an institution. I went and grabbed my Marlin, and when I passed by her room again, the door was closed.

Breakfast was a blur. We chased it with coffee, and afterward we heard an unholy row roaring toward the house. It sounded like something was being torn to shreds, but we knew it was only Izzy and his hounds.

Billy and I stepped onto the front porch as his truck slid to a halt behind a squall of chickens. A cloud of dust and smoke caught up to and billowed over the truck. Trout banged out after us. The dust clearing, it seemed Izzy's truck was alive with a boil of barking dogs— three or four in the bed, panting and slobbering, with their paws reaching through the slat rails, and at least one in the cab with Izzy.

"Lookit them hounds!" Trout squealed.

"How do, fellers." Izzy grinned, stepping out. The dog in the cab, a bloodhound, immediately stuck its copper head through the window and barked deep-throatedly through a corrugation of loose skin.

The hair went up on Mutt and Jeff's backs. A low growl rattled threateningly in their throats as they crept off the porch. They circled warily toward the truck and showed their fangs.

"How do," we returned.

Izzy ranged toward us and put his long hands out to the Labs, showing his palms. The Labs eyed the palms and approached him guardedly, the threat tempering from their growls.

"Hey, fellas." Izzy smiled. "No need for that. You remember ol' Izzy, don't you?" Mutt seemed to and stepped forward, and Izzy put his hands all over him, chucking his neck and ears. "There you go— see? I ain't gonna hurt ya." He looked at Jeff and offered a hand. "Come on, big fella—there's a boy!" Not to be left out of a good ear scratch, Jeff warmed up to him and licked his hands.

Izzy shot us a wink, then he stood up and tromped over to the porch, and the Labs followed him, smelling his ankles. He was a tall, loose-limbed, rangy-looking man in his mid-thirties, with a mess of black hair sticking out every which way from his cap. He was wearing a pair of worn-out overalls, patched from sunup to sundown, a red plaid work shirt with the elbows torn out, and beat-up work boots. From their deep sockets his little blue eyes twinkled with the lust for killing.

"Lucifer, huh?"

"The devil hisself," Billy said.

Izzy pulled his long fingers over a three-day crop of whiskers. "I get the pelt, right?"

"You betcha. Sounds like your dogs are rarin' to go."

Izzy spat into the dirt, then wiped the dribble off his chin. "Billy, you ain't seen dogs." He glanced at his truck. "Ain't that so, Dollar?

Buttercup? You and your compadres ready to catch us a mean old cat?"

The hounds threw their heads back and howled, their heads pitching and yawing something fierce. Izzy threw his head back and howled too, then danced a little high-elbowed stomp in a circle, hooting like a scarecrow on the warpath.

Billy and I laughed.

Mama looked at him through the screen door and shook her head. "Well, look what the cat drug in." She smiled. "Want some coffee, Izzy?"

Izzy tipped his cap. "Thank you, no, Mrs. Hochreiter. It don't set well with my stomach."

"Don't look like anything's been setting on your stomach by the look of you. You look about a skin shy of a corpse."

Izzy grinned. "Don't you fret about ol' Izzy, ma'am. The Lord takes care of fools and mountain men."

"And which one are you, Izzy?" Mama grinned impishly. Mama liked Izzy.

Then he smiled broadly at her, showing the brown tobacco stains on his teeth. "I'll take some buttermilk, if it ain't too much trouble, though."

"No trouble at all."

"Hey, I'll take some buttermilk!" Trout said, rushing back inside.

"You'll finish what's on your plate first."

Bang! went the door.

"Aw, Mama, I ain't hungry no more."

"You're *not* hungry *any*more."

Trout stared at her as if she had lost her plumb.

When we were set to leave, Mama handed me a tote of food— some sandwiches wrapped in waxed paper, some strips of jerky, a few apples—and said, "Supper's up to you and what the good Lord provides. I don't expect you'll starve."

"Not likely." Billy grinned.

We grabbed up our rifles, and, seeing Billy's new Winchester, Izzy blew out a long whistle. "Whoo-ee! Will you looky there!"

Billy held up the rifle for Izzy to inspect, his right eyebrow cocking into his hairline like a brand new father's.

Izzy ran his fingers along the barrel. "I swear. It shines like Miss Abbie's eyes in the spring." He looked up quickly to see if Mama had heard him, but she had gone back inside. He chuckled, then hefted his Springfield '03. "My old Hun-buster ain't seen the color blue since Elijah got spirited away. But I don't expect it matters spit to a bullet what color a barrel throws it."

Billy extended his rifle to Izzy. "Want a look?"

"I'm afraid it might break, it's so glassy-looking." Izzy, taking it, eyed the Model 70 admiringly, the straight walnut grain and all the other fine points of a well-made rifle. "My, my . . . fancy scope and everything."

"Weaver, four power," Billy said proudly. "Even you oughta be able to hit something with it."

Izzy frowned at him, then he pulled the stock to his shoulder and peered through the scope at one of the pigs across the yard. He lowered the rifle and squinted. "So that's what that thing is—a pig. And here I thought it was one of them Hochreiter boys about to get a whoopin' if he didn't mind his tongue." Billy chuckled.

I cleared my throat. "We gonna stay here all day ogling your rifle, Billy, or are we going after that cat?"

Izzy threw his head back like a hound and howled, "Yooo-iieeee!"

The hounds joined him and raised another racket. Even Mutt and Jeff got into the mix, and the chickens high-winged it across the yard, cackling furiously. It seemed a little wildness had gotten loose in the yard.

Izzy looked at us suddenly, his eyes brightly twinkling again. "What're you waiting for? Lucifer to come up and introduce his sorry self?"

He trotted over to his truck and lowered the tailgate for the Labs. They hopped up into the bed and introduced themselves to the hounds. There was a lot of initial sniffing and snorting on the hounds' part, but it was friendly sniffing and snorting, for a stronger thing was pulling at them now.

We piled into Izzy's truck. There was no room for Dollar with the three of us in the cab, so the bloodhound straddled himself across Billy and me, his hind legs lost somewhere on the floorboards under Izzy's feet and his front legs jockeying for position on the seat between my legs.

It was close quarters, and a thick smell of dog pervaded the cab. I leaned out the window to catch a bit of air, but there was no escaping it. Then Dollar, his dark watery eyes admiring me over the drooping, blood crescents of his lids, began to pant happily, adding hot dog breath to the fragrance.

184

Izzy popped the clutch, Dollar's slobbery, corrugated face pressed against my face, and we roared out of the yard with Izzy howling out the window like a lunatic.

At the kill site, the hounds made quick forays into the brush around the dead calf, crisscrossing one another's path with their noses working excitedly through the grass. Dollar picked up the scent almost immediately, flapped his head back and bayed, and a contagion of blood lust raced through the air. The ancient clarion of hounds trumpeted to a fever pitch.

Izzy released them with a command, and the dogs bolted along the river toward a land bridge a quarter mile downstream, yelping and barking as though they were being shot. Once over the bridge the hounds cut back and traversed up through the steepest section of the pine bluffs, showing us the very route the cougar took, as clear as if there were red flags marking the various turns in the trail. And I swear it sparked something in me; something old and primal reached up from my belly and bubbled in my throat, tingled up along my spine until I felt the fever burning behind my eyes.

"Let's get after 'em!" Izzy cried. He let out another howl, hefted his Hun-buster, and bounded away.

Billy and I looked at each other, both of us let out a hoot, then we ran after him howling like banshees.

By the time we reached the summit, I thought I was going to die. I bent over, right hand holding my rifle as a cane, left hand on my knee, and tried to catch my wind. The sun beat down on my back and reflected off the ground into my face. I glanced over at Billy, and he was doubled over as well, only his rifle was slung across his back.

"Some climb, huh?" I said.

Izzy was ahead of us by fifty yards. He turned, waved us forward, grinning, looking barely winded, then galloped away.

We looked at each other.

"Why don't I wait here?" Billy wheezed, chuckling. "Let you and Iz herd him back into range."

"Nothing doing." I kneaded the stitch in my right side, then hefted my rifle. It was heavier now, I swear it was heavier. "We'd best be going, or we'll never live it down."

"It was just a thought."

Then Billy took off, and I loped after him.

Spread out before us was a thin veil of lacy snow covering the ground, with rocks and wheatgrass showing through the holes in the lace. The dogs were nowhere in sight, but we heard them off in the distance, their fitful baying dipping in and out of the rugged terrain.

We soon got into a rhythm, up and down steep hills, mostly up and moving higher up into the trees, pine and spruce and fir, back and forth, climbing higher and more steeply, up around boulders and wending up through the trees.

My feet were wet from the boggy ground and the creeks that we splashed through, but I was feeling better about it now, feeling the sure pound of the earth drumming the steady cadence and a flutter of excitement in my belly. And all the while the dogs were baying somewhere ahead, out of sight, their voices bouncing off the hills to fall echoing upon us as though from another world.

Occasionally we'd lose the dogs, and Izzy would pause in the houndless quiet and listen, with his long fingers cupped behind his ear. Then, scanning the dazzling white vistas and the glowing embers of the leaves set against the backdrop of the Beartooths, rising sharp and jagged and majestic, he would sniff the air as a hound would sniff and take off in a likely direction. Sure enough, it wouldn't be long before we'd hear the hounds howling like there was no tomorrow, and the fever of the chase would resume in full fury.

An hour passed. Then another. And then we came upon the Labs. They were lying in the shade of a spruce, looking at us as we came into view, panting as if they were about to die. They were quit of it.

Izzy made some deprecating remark as he jogged past them, chuckled, and asked if we wanted to stay with our dogs and take a little nap.

Billy and I glowered at the Labs. They groaned to their feet and followed us, dragging their tails in shame, with their tongues lolling.

Another hour passed, and we were in high country now, the terrain grown rocky and desolate with conifers, lichen, and sage, and only the sound of the wind soughing through the trees. The baying had dipped again, and Izzy glanced about him for sign.

I heard a shrill whistle and looked off to my left to see several marmots standing at attention over their earthen forts like hairy sentinels, eyeing us curiously. Just off to the right a couple of chipmunks scurried about on a fallen log in an unending game of tag. Fifty yards beyond them, a red fox trotted along the shrub line and paused, studying us with its quick black eyes before bounding away through the snow. Filtering through the distance came the sound of a woodpecker knocking against the thick mountain quietness.

We paused while Izzy shinnied up a tree. There hadn't been a sound of the dogs for a while now, and we feared we'd lost them for good. He cupped his ears to the wind.

"Over there, Billy," I whispered, pointing across a broad, rolling meadow that splashed against a bank of dark trees.

Billy looked, and I saw his face change. He quickly unshouldered his rifle and peered through the eyepiece. "Will you look at that!" he breathed wonderingly. "It's him!"

"Let me see."

He handed me his rifle, and I looked into the scope. Moving into the bright circle of light was an elk, an imperial by the count of his massive seven-tined rack of antlers spread over his back. There were fifteen cows grazing ahead of him. The bull raised his head and looked at us inquiringly, challenging, as though he owned everything in his sight. I do believe he did. I lowered the cross hairs a touch over his shoulder . . . *Pow!*

"I've never seen such a rack!" I marveled, handing Billy the rifle. "That's one for the *Boone and Crockett.*"

"Yeah." He peered through the scope. "And once the season opens he'll be gone to kingdom come."

The elk grazed away into the cover of the trees, and then a whistle of wind brought a spray of snow sprinkling onto our heads. It felt good, shivering down our necks.

Suddenly Izzy let out a holler and came shinnying down the tree as if hornets were driving him. "They're onto him!" he shouted, hitting the ground and pointing toward some high country. "They got him treed, sure!"

I strained my ears but heard only the panting of Mutt and Jeff.

But we caught the fever again, that rush of blood as when you first bust a covey of grouse or pheasants and their short wings chop furiously through the air over the sweep of your barrel. You pull the trigger, and, not hearing the muzzle report, you see the smack of feathers and the drop of the bird. But you miss the second shot in the excitement, and the birds career away, laughing, in fast arcs behind trees and shrubs and knolls, and you get after them, pumping shells into your gun and knowing you've got a hunt after all. You feel your adrenaline surge and that primal thing tingling over you, burning like coals behind your eyes, and you forget about the pain and boredom of before, and all you think about is getting after those birds.

Cresting a rocky incline, we heard the sudden baying of the hounds through a tract of woods ahead. I heard Izzy howl and Billy shout, and something was coming out of me too as I levered a .30- 30 shell into the chamber. It was full tilt now, all the stoppers in me blown out as I ran pell-mell toward the confusion.

Billy was off to my left, and I could hear jerking in his throat the *huh-huh-huh* sound of wind blown over the fever, and I knew we were in a footrace. I didn't know where Izzy was—forward or hinderward, to right or left—and I didn't care. My mind was trained on the hounds, on the beckoning call of Dollar's voice, and knowing that I was going to get to them first.

The wood opened into a narrow strip of meadow, rising steeply toward a long palisade of rocks and boulders beyond, broken and piled high, and immediately I saw the hounds. They were in a furious scramble at the base of several huge boulders. I saw them leaping up the broad face, climbing to a cleft in the rock, and clinging tight-shouldered to it with their claws, then falling back to the ground. Up again and down again they leaped, their barking high-pitched and frenzied.

I looked above them in time to see a tawny flash through the rocks. The air suddenly shook with the concussion of Billy's rifle. The shock of it pushed a long and narrow corridor into the air, and the echoes rippled back with a stuttering report, and then there was nothing but a curl of wind.

I heard Billy swear beside me, and then Izzy swore.

"If that cat ain't the devil, I'm a two-tailed skunk!" he snarled.

"Do we get after him?" Billy cried, chambering another round.

Izzy looked at the white glare off the rocks, at his dogs leaping up at a profitless vanity, and his shoulders went limp. "It's over, boys," he said, lifting his cap and scratching his head. I could see the killing lust sheet off his face and limbs, the twinkle in his eyes dull to a gray blue. He leaned against the barrel of his rifle and tamped a lip of snuff into place, then placed the tin back in his shirt pocket.

He glanced away into the hills and chuckled. "No, I expect old Lucifer's two day's gone by now—sittin' fat and sassy on some perch, laughin' at us."

Billy and I looked at each other, then I glanced back at our trail and contemplated the arduous trek home. All that primal adrenaline pumping through my veins backed up in me all of a sudden like a muddy confluence of rivers, churning something fierce. I felt a sickness spreading out from the pit of my stomach.

I walked over to a tree and sat down against it in the shade and dug an apple out of the tote. Mutt and Jeff plodded over to me and curled into black circles of contentment. I sat there, feeling the aches of the climb easing out through my legs. I knew it would be hard getting to my feet again, but I wasn't concerned about that now; I was concerned with letting go the aches of the climb as I enjoyed an apple.

I watched Izzy find a spot against a stone in the shade and stretch his long self over the ground. He pulled his bill over his eyes and was soon snoring. The hounds were still going at it, beating their brains against the unyielding face of granite, still howling as though they were being shot.

Billy walked over to me, glancing off into the distance. "Well, it's a cryin' shame." He grinned. "Toss me one of those, won't you?"

I looked up and tossed him an apple.

He polished it against his shirt, looked at it, scraped something off the skin with his nail, then took a big bite. "Yessir," he continued, setting his rifle carefully against the trunk. He found a spot next to me and sat down. "It's a downright shame. Think of all the fun we're missing. Here we are out in God's great wilderness, two miserable wretches suffering such views of splendor, and we might be back with Sy and Jimbo bustin' horns and cuttin' steers." He took another bite of apple and chuckled. "If we time this right, we'll be home just in time for supper."

I raised an eyebrow at him. "Yeah, just in time so Pa can chew us up for missing that cat."

"Tyler, your problem is you worry too much, you know that? Life is too short to go worryin' yourself into an early grave." He took another bite of apple. "You gotta let go, smell a few flowers along the way—seize the day! You know, carpet dime."

"That's *carpe diem*, Horace."

"You said it, brother."

I settled my head on the tote, closed my eyes, and listened to the baying of the hounds. Billy was right, I worried too much. I allowed little things to pile up into big things until the weight was crushing. I needed more *carpe diem* in my life, like Billy. I don't think Billy had a worrisome moment in his life; he took each tick of the clock as it came, took what he wanted from the intervals between and discarded what he didn't.

I began to sift through the past two days, picking up scattered pieces of drift thought and looking at them like shells on a beach, turning them over, examining each one for its worth, keeping those I thought might have value for the future, discarding the others—winging them as far as I could. I felt lighter already. Is this what Peter meant when he wrote, "Casting all your care upon him; for he careth for you"? *God, here is my debris, the flotsam and jetsam thrown up from the wreckage of my soul. Take it, won't You? It is all I have to offer.*

The hounds thinned away after a time, like the tide ebbing, going slowly out from the banks of my mind and taking the discarded pieces out to sea. Then the white sheet with the black square drifted back, billowing over me as though from another world, and I didn't care. Not a bit. Sometime during my snooze, I heard myself chuckling.

20

The snow lasted only a few days and was gone, unable to abide a sudden reproach of the sun. Over the several days following we worked hard, and it felt good, for there is nothing like good hard work to shore up against the tide of melancholy.

Kate came out on Tuesday and spent the evening with us—our last for several months, we knew, until I should return from school at Christmas. She wore a new dress for the occasion, a pretty, ruffly thing that complemented her figure and lighted the house like a sunburst. She had done her hair in a new way as well, pulled it up and added ribbons to it or something—I wasn't sure—had done her eyes and put lipstick on, and she looked like a million bucks.

Seated at the supper table, Kate was the sun, fixed and glorious, and we Hochreiter males an orbit of lesser lights around her. A sudden politeness descended upon our shining faces.

"Would you like some bread, Kate?"

"Have some more peas, won't you?"

"How are your parents, Katherine? I saw your father at the station last week—said he runs the trains with military precision. I like that in a man."

Even Trout was uncustomarily genteel, not belching once and saying "please" at least once.

Mama angled her head and smiled beneficently upon Kate and me—mostly Kate—a maternal glow radiating out from her as babies skipped through her eyes.

Afterward, Billy tuned the radio to WGN, and the family sat around it and waited for the long-awaited College All-Star Game, broadcast from Soldier Field in Chicago.

Papa tamped his pipe and then lit it. He leaned back in his worn leather chair and breathed a wreath of goodwill and cheer over our heads. The wreath broke apart and thickly swirled across the ceiling. Mutt and Jeff traded contented groans at his feet.

Mama, seated on the sofa, hummed a tune down at her knitting, smiling secretly, and Jenny lay her head against her shoulder, the wildness gone from her eyes.

Billy, a die-hard NFL fan, was seated before the glowing dial, waiting worshipfully for the kick-off. "Them college pups don't stand a chance." He laughed derisively. "The Packers'll cream 'em."

"We'll just see about that," Kate said, picking up the gauntlet. She was always one for the underdog.

She was seated in a ladder-back next to the radio, peering intently at the white glow of the dial as Graham MacNamee gave the play-by-play. As she angled forward, her fists clenched menacingly. She would thrust a ruffled shoulder to block the invisible Packers, stiff-arm, and shout, "Watch it! Watch it!" as a two-hundred-fifty-pound halfback came in low. Then she'd wince painfully as they tackled the college boys and boo them with practiced contempt. When the tables turned, she hooted and jeered or jumped up and shouted with delight when they scored a touchdown.

Billy would say it was a lucky break or that the Packers were playing soft to make the game interesting, but Kate would stick out her tongue at him and, with a sneering curl of the lip, say, "Sour grapes!"

There is nothing more appealing than a pretty girl in a ruffly dress and ribboned hair acting tough. My heart raced. I couldn't take my eyes off her. Laura Miller had nothing on my Kate, not tonight.

After the game, Mama floated across the room, smiled at Papa in passing, then sat down at the piano and led out with a spirited rendition of "Skip to My Lou."

Kate pulled me to my feet and whirled me about, ruffles wheeling, with me watching her feet and trying to keep from tripping over my own. Billy cut in and took over the lead and charged around the living room, narrowly missing lamps and furniture, with my Kate gasping for breath.

Mutt and Jeff ducked for cover.

Papa got out his flattop guitar and, sitting face out on the piano bench, accompanied Mama on "Buffalo Gal."

Billy twirled Kate, laughing, into my arms and, not missing a step, scooped Jenny off the sofa. She resisted at first, but whatever dark gloom had been overshadowing her was no match for the fiery wind of Billy, and soon she was skipping airily about, laughing and singing along with everyone else.

Trout, wanting to cut in now, poked me on the arm, and Kate gave him a few turns around the room. He kept looking over at Mama to see if she was watching; then, glancing up at Kate to see her smiling at him, he'd let out an embarrassed giggle. I caught her eyes as they rounded their circuit, and there was a look in them of holy fire blazing that caused a thunder to resonate in my breast. She twirled past me, her ruffly dress brushing my leg, and I felt a rush of breath escape and tremble away.

Mama softened the tempo with "Barbara Allen," followed it with "Greensleeves," and then as we gathered around the piano she led us in a few quiet hymns, those tried and true hymns of Charles Wesley and Fanny Crosby. Billy fetched his harmonica and added a soulful counterpoint. A reverent glow descended upon us like a dove, a peace secured by a feminine tyranny. All was well in the Hochreiter home, and the glaring, sepia eyes along the stairwell were forced to concede the evening.

Kate and I stole out onto the porch and sat down on the swing, hand in hand, looking out over the steading as we rocked. The sun dropped behind the bluffs in the west. The bats roused from their daytime haunts and curlicued across the band of light that remained of the day. It seemed they were celebrating its death.

A movement caught my eyes, and turning to it I saw the dark form of Sammy angling through the live oaks from the direction of the bunkhouse. He walked over to the burned-out square of the barn, idled there for a while, hands in his pockets, glancing up at the house from time to time as though listening to the music. I don't think he saw Kate and me, for we were in the shadows, and when I called out to him, he turned quickly away as if he'd been caught at something.

"He's a lonely soul," Kate said, her eyes following him across the yard. "What will become of him now that summer's over?"

"I think Papa's going to keep him on after the drive."

"Really? I think that's decent of him."

I chuckled. "Papa'd keep Jack the Ripper on if he could keep that tractor running."

She frowned at me. "You don't give your father credit. A minister must be generous in mercy. If he isn't, who will care for the sheep?"

I said nothing. She'd said it all. I drew her close to me. We watched as Sammy disappeared into the dark folds of the trees, then reappeared as a silhouette in the yellow glow of the bunkhouse door.

"He's in love with Jenny, you know," Kate said.

I looked at her quickly.

She smiled as though she were privy to some well-guarded secret. "You should've seen the way he looked at her at the barbecue."

I grunted. "I did." The poor fool. Jenny's world of late was big enough for only one star to light it, and it wasn't Sammy Two Feathers. "Do you want me to write you a tragedy?"

"Must you?"

I bowed to the ovation of my audience, then gestured theatrically. "'Is this a dagger which I see before me, the handle toward my hand? Come, let me clutch thee. I have thee not, and yet I see thee still.'"

Kate slapped my knee. "You thief."

"Better to steal a pearl, my love, than to offer you a pebble."

"Better to have a pebble hanging around my neck than a millstone."

There was no arguing with her.

Billy's "Shenandoah" filtered through the screen door, changing the tenor of the mood, and we rocked gently back and forth, neither speaking as we listened to the sweet, sad melody pull the stars from their hiding. An amber glow crept out of the house and spread against the encroaching night.

Kate let out a long and wistful sigh.

I looked over at her and could see a tear, glistening like a fiery jewel in the light, trickling down her cheek.

She wiped it away, angry at herself. "I said I wasn't going to do this. Now look at me."

"I am."

She looked quickly at me with those big hazel eyes. "You silly." Then she looked thoughtfully down at her hands, one cradling the other as though it were a fallen bird. "I'll write you every day."

"You'll run out of things to say. Day—say. That rhymed, didn't it? I wrote half a poem." I chuckled stupidly.

The bird fluttered to life and winged to my cheek, smoothing over it with a downy touch. Then she buried her face in my shoulder and cried, "Oh, Tyler."

I kissed the top of her head, and we continued to rock back and forth, listening to the music of the night. And then there was only the creak of the swing.

The next day we drove two hundred head to the railhead to thin out the herd over winter. Billy and I went along with Papa to see Kate's father at the station and arrange for the freight, while Jimbo and the other hands stayed with the cattle at the stockyard, looking proud as Crow warriors on their horses.

The train station was old, old as the rails, as they say, with the color leached out of the wood siding and long gone downriver. The grain elevators looming over the tracks just beyond looked old and rusted and sad against a brooding morning sky, and you got the feeling that they might go sliding down into the Yellowstone at any moment.

As we walked along the platform toward the office, there was an oily smell of train lingering over the rail bed, rising up and smacking me in the face; a pungent smell of creosote and steel and gravel mingled with the stockyard smells breezing along the banks, and it evoked in me a pleasant feeling, one reaching back into my childhood and stirring in me a kind of wanderlust.

I remembered how I'd lie awake at night listening to the far-off sound of a train, moaning through the hills, its siren pipes calling me to wonder where it was bound, to imagine what grand adventure I would have once I stole aboard it. I loved trains, and I loved that feeling.

Looking across the street, I saw two men in the window seat of the corner diner. One was gesticulating wildly as he addressed the other man; and the other man was watching him quietly and smoking a cigarette.

The quiet man looked out and, seeing us, stood up quickly, stabbed out his cigarette, and headed for the door. The wildly gesticulating man seemed surprised; his hands froze in midair as he saw us, and he hurriedly followed the other out of the diner. They waited impatiently in the street for three westbound trucks to pass, then loped across and over the tracks.

"Hank?" the quiet man called out.

Papa turned and watched the two men climb the steps of the platform. Both were of medium height (the quiet one being of medium build, while the other was slighter and wiry); both were in their mid-fifties. Both, I knew, had fair-sized ranches along the Yellowstone. Their boots thundered hollowly over the thick gray planks, and their eyes were blazing.

Papa smiled affably on them. "Hello, Wade—Ned!"

"Did you hear the news yet, Hank?" Wade Wanamacher asked.

Papa held out his hand, and Wade took it. "Good to see you fellas."

"Did you hear the news, Hank?" Wade repeated.

195

Papa reached for Ned Dilbert's hand, but the latter seemed too agitated for such amenities and shook his hand with a quick snap. His feet shuffled anxiously from side to side.

Papa laughed. "What on earth are you boys all fired up about?"

Ned turned quickly to Wade. "He ain't heard." Then he spat over the edge of the platform.

Papa narrowed his eyes on the two men. "Haven't heard what? I swear, you two are acting like a couple of schoolgirls."

The two men rushed to speak at the same moment. Wade shot an irritated look at Ned, and the latter conceded, "You tell him."

Wade looked Papa square in the face and said, "Josiah won the beef contract with the government. Just got word of it this morning."

Papa's face flattened. "What do you mean?"

Ned stepped forward. "Just like he said, Hank, that two-bit snake—"

"Won it for the grange, you mean?"

"You don't understand, Hank!" Wade said. "He won it for himself! He stole it out from under our feet!"

"He can't do that—the grange—"

"The grange!" Ned barked a laugh of contempt. "Them old ladies!" He nodded at Billy and me as though we were in agreement with him, trailing his laugh with an anxious chuckle.

Papa looked hard into Wade's eyes, bore a steel blue hole clear through his skull. "He can't do it," he said coldly. "I won't allow it."

"Well, he's done it!" Ned said, almost in a shriek. "Got a congressman up in Helena in his back pocket."

Papa eyed the two of them while the news worked its way into his brain. I felt cold all of a sudden, as when the finger of icy wind found an opening through the willow leaves—however, now finding my soul and touching me lightly, but touching hard enough for the cold to infiltrate. Billy and I looked at each other, and I could see the cold in him too. The air was suddenly charged with danger.

Ned seemed pleased with the reaction in Billy and me, for he kept saying, "Yep, yep, y'see?"

Papa leveled his eyes on them. "When did this happen? Why didn't somebody call me?" His voice was angry but edged with a chilling calm.

"Jim Skeller called you first," Wade said, "but you was gone with the herd. He told us to look for you when you got in."

Ned nodded fiercely.

Wade said calmly, "He's getting a meeting together at the grange, Hank—calling everybody—don't matter they got two head or two thousand. I expect the hall's buzzing by now. It's people's lives we're talking."

"Yep, yep . . . that's right," Ned agreed, then elbowed him. "That ain't the worst of it. Go on, tell him, Wade. Just wait till you hear this, Hank."

Wade looked at Papa. His expression constricted, almost painfully. "He's undercut us, Hank. Got it fixed clear across the state. You'll be lucky to get feed out of your herd now."

I felt the shock of that one. I looked quickly at Papa and saw a fierce light jump his eyes, and he looked suddenly deadly.

"We'll take him to court," he said, holding it back.

Wade grunted. "That's just what he wants us to do. Him and his fancy Billings lawyers. Fisk can hold out—he's so big. But us, we can't hold off sellin' our beeves. Can you? We'll go under. He wants it all, Hank. That skunk won't be satisfied till his brand is on every last steer in the state."

No one spoke for a moment as a collective thought reflected over a placid pool of quiet. Suddenly I could hear our cattle bawling in the stockyard, troubling the quiet like a cast stone.

Papa glanced off in their direction, and I knew what he was thinking.

"Hank, we were all supposed to get a share of that contract," Ned cried. "It was going to finally pull us through—get us out of playing this catch-up. I can't make it through another lean winter. That last one about finished us." He was on the verge of tears now. His lower lip trembled. His hands began to work out his thoughts, pleading, as though Papa could just wave a magic wand over the problem and make it disappear. "Hank, we just got to get this contract. I lose my ranch, Hank, I swear . . . I swear . . ." Then his expression went dark. "I swear I'll kill him, Hank! I swear it! I'll make him pay! I ain't gonna end up suckin' wind like Rube—not with no six mouths to feed. No, sir!"

Papa ignored him and pulled out his wallet. He drew out a sheaf of bills, counted off a number of them, then turned to me. "You square accounts with Tulane," he said, handing me the money, "then get over to Jimbo and tell him to load up the beeves without me."

I looked at him, confused. "We're sending 'em, not knowing the market?"

Papa glared at me. "Did I stutter or something?"

"No, sir."

"Then do as I say."

There was no arguing with those eyes. "Yes, sir."

"Want me to go with him, Pa?" Billy asked.

"No, you come with me. You need to be a part of this." Papa wheeled around and jumped off the platform, then took off in the direction of the grange hall. Billy and Wade followed him without a word, and Ned, trailing behind, was talking to himself, his hands gesturing to no one in particular.

I was alone on the platform, watching the four of them disappear around the corner, feeling as though I were somehow to blame for negotiating the contract for Josiah. I felt something rising in me, a dark thing, and I fought it with anger. Then I strode toward the office, the hollowness of the planks reverberating up into my chest, sounding a dread, and the smell of creosote turning in my stomach.

21

Tulane Morgan was attending to a woman as I entered the office—someone from out of town, I suspected by her city apparel and just by the look of her.

She was asking if the eastbound was the Northern Pacific or some other line. "They have such lovely Pullmans, don't you think?" she said. "And the club cars are just wonderful."

She was from out of town, all right; leastwise I'd never seen her before.

Mr. Morgan nodded, glancing at her curiously when she wasn't looking at him, then, smiling appropriately, he told her that "yes, the Northern Pacific would arrive at 11:45." But he made no comment on the club cars.

"Is it on time?" the woman asked.

"My trains are always on time," Mr. Morgan said proudly, the smile wearing a little thin. He eyed her again when she looked into her purse, and shook his head; it seemed with an air of contempt.

I waited, my lips drawn taut over a thought, looking aimlessly around the station so as not to seem impatient. I was anxious, though, anxious like that night at the supper table when it felt as if my stomach was twisting into knots. I looked back at Mr. Morgan, and he saw me behind the woman.

"Be with you in a minute, Tyler," he said over his eyeglasses.

The woman, in her late thirties, early forties, and pleasant-looking I saw now, glanced at me quickly and smiled. There was a hardness around her eyes though, something hidden just beyond the corners.

I looked away, a smile dying on my lips, for I was a little embarrassed for my intrusion.

There was an old smell of dust and wood in the place, a good warming smell of going places, of adventure, and the two rows of wooden benches, facing the door and the platform, looked worn and comfortable. Sun streamed through the east windows and stood sharply on the floor, and dust floated through on a windless current and twinkled in the light. The regulator on the wall opposite the benches tick-tocked a comforting rhythm, its tiny death knells ticking off the eternal leaps of time, sounding once and solidly as the long, black minute hand reached the half hour.

A Sioux Indian man (thin and wrinkly) and woman (smooth and round) sat against the far wall on a flat bench perpendicular to the two rows of benches. The man looked at the regulator as it struck, then he looked at me and stared impassively.

I nodded at him, and he looked away slowly—proudly, I should say, or unimpressed—and he stared out the window. The Indian woman was looking down at her delicate brown hands. I wondered what adventure they were having.

"Here you are, Miss . . . er . . ."

"Miss." The woman smiled without embarrassment.

Mr. Morgan handed her a ticket, along with her change, which she scooped into her handbag without counting.

Stepping away from the window, she looked over at the regulator, checked her watch against it, then slipped the watch into her coat pocket.

I had to step out of her way to keep from being stepped into. "Excuse me," I said, nodding apologetically.

"Oh, pardon me," the woman said. Then glancing at me more thoroughly, she smiled. "Going east?"

"Uh . . . yes, ma'am."

The woman seemed slightly taken aback. "Ma'am? Isn't that nice?" She smiled, regarding my face. "I'm heading east as well. Perhaps we can chat along the way? It's always better to travel with someone, don't you think? Helps pass the time."

"Oh, but I'm not leaving for a couple of days."

She shrugged her shoulders and said, "Pity. You seem like a nice boy. I'll bet your mama's proud."

I got a little embarrassed. "Thank you, ma'am."

She shook her head amusedly and walked away. She sat down pertly on the smooth wooden bench nearest the door, settling comfortably into position like a hen settling, or a cat, then pulled out a pack of Chesterfields, tamped the end of a cigarette against her thumbnail and put it into her mouth. She lit the end, shook out the match, then, smoking, stared at the slow ascent of the minute hand.

"Tyler?"

"Huh?"

"Was there something I could help you with?"

"Oh, hello, Mr. Morgan."

200

I stepped forward to the window, and for just a moment there was an unspoken understanding between Mr. Morgan and myself about the woman.

He grunted, again with an air of contempt. "I heard about Fisk," he said.

"I expect everyone has by now."

"Yes, I expect so." He studied my eyes. "How is your father taking the news?"

I averted my eyes as I pushed the bills across the counter. "Here you are. Two hundred head for Billings."

He looked at the money and then at me, drawing my attention. "Your father sure he wants to load 'em?"

"He's sure."

I saw a flicker of Kate around his eyes, playing at the corners of his mouth; the way his brows raised on one side when he was thinking lived on in her. She was everywhere in him, the feminine showing through the masculine, peeking out at me in subtle turns of expression.

He smiled, took the money, counted it, then stacked the bills into a wooden tray, the twenties here, the tens there, and so on. He wrote the amount in a ledger with a small, finely sharpened pencil, how many head, the time of departure, the destination, the name of our ranch. Everything was written neatly and carefully. Mr. Morgan ran a tight ship.

"Is it all there?"

"To the penny," he said. Then he eyed me curiously.

"I have to go now," I said, turning to leave. "Pa's expecting me."

"Tyler, are you all right?"

"Huh? Sure. Everything's fine, Mr. Morgan," I said unconvincingly. "Everything's just fine."

He smiled at me, his blue eyes twinkling bright and knowing, and I knew he could see through me, just as Kate could see through me. "Stop by the house before you leave for Chicago, if you can, won't you? We'll have a big send-off."

"That would be swell."

"Friday night?"

"Sure, Friday night."

I turned and left, knowing that I wouldn't be there, and I felt three pairs of eyes on the back of my head. I don't know about the Indian woman, though.

22

The dirt lot outside the grange hall was jammed with pickups and cars and two or three wagon teams, and several horses were tied at the hitch rail. I think every rancher in Stillwater County had come to the meeting. "It's people's lives we're talking," Wade Wanamacher had said.

Inside there was standing room only. As I squeezed through the back door I smelled it at once, smelled the fear clinging to the air as a horse can smell fear on a man. It crackled over everyone's head like an electric current, like a corporate pulse going through everyone's chest.

Big Bob Baker was manning the door, and I nodded to him as I closed it behind me. He nodded back but didn't see me, I knew, for I could tell that he was intent on the business at the front of the hall. I saw it on his face too—the quick taut eyes and mouth, the narrowed, wary glare, that hunted look of fear that, once the animal was cornered, was so capable of violence.

And seeing it on his face I caught it too, felt the spark of it buzzing in the pit of my stomach, pulsing through me and out to connect with the corporate pulse. I turned away from him with a little shudder.

I stood on my toes and looked for Papa and saw him in front standing next to Billy, where I knew they would be. I threaded my way through the crowd, mindful not to look at anyone's face, and finally pushed next to Billy.

Jim Skeller had the floor.

"Carl, I'll say it again, Fisk would take ten percent of every head sold," Jim Skeller repeated, it seemed from his expression, for the tenth time. "According to him it works out cheaper than paying the freight to Chicago."

"That's a load of fertilizer," someone called out.

Someone else called out, "What if we just do an end run on him?"

"I expect he'd lock us out," Jim Skeller said. "He's got the government contract—according to him, anyway—and if we want to sell cattle in this county, then we got to comply."

"That sounds like extortion."

"Who says we got to comply?" another man said angrily.

"Yeah! What do we care what he does?"

Jim Skeller looked at him. "It's what Fisk says we got to do. Now that ain't what I'm saying we got to do, let me make that clear."

"Then what are you sayin', Jim?"

"Yeah, you're the president here, Jim. What are we supposed to do? Just cave in?"

"Nobody's caving in to nothing," Jim said. "I'm just saying that we need to think this thing through, is all." He looked over at Papa, exasperated.

"Well, it ain't legal. He can't do it, can he?"

"That's what we're trying to find out, Pete," Jim Skeller said to him. "We got a call in to Lance Hoolihan."

"What can he do? He's just another fancy-pants lawyer out of Billings."

"He can do plenty," someone snapped. "So shut up."

"Who are you telling to shut up?"

"I'm telling you to shut up."

Jim Skeller waved his hands. "Settle down, men. Let's not be fighting amongst ourselves."

"I can't afford ten percent," a portly man near the front said. "I'll have to sell out. Maybe Josiah'll take less than ten?"

"Will you pay him less?" the man next to him snarled.

The portly man shrank back from the other's glare. "Uh . . . no, that's not what I meant. I just thought we might ask."

"Leave him be, Enos."

"I thought I told you to shut up!"

I looked around and saw the fear becoming an ugly surliness in their faces. Men began poking one another, their voices rising, their fists wagging. I thought it might go to blows.

Jim Skeller waved his hands again. "Hold it! Hold it!"

But the men paid him no mind, and the mood continued to degenerate.

So he picked up his gavel and banged it against the tabletop. "This is no time to go to pieces! Enos—Pete, knock it off! We've got to stick together in this thing."

"I know a way to handle this," a voice cried out.

"We'll have none of that in here, Ned," Jim Skeller said. "This ain't no lynching party."

Ned Dilbert shook his fist at him. "Josiah's got his noose around our necks, don't he? It'd be self-defense, and you know it. Besides, if we stuck together in this, like you say, then who can do anything about it? They can't arrest the whole county."

Several of the men around him agreed—good, respectable men that you'd never think capable of such a thing—and an angry murmur buzzed through the crowd.

Billy shook his head in disbelief.

"What's Hank Hochreiter got to say about this, anyway?" Big Bob called out from the rear of the hall.

"Yeah, Hank. What you make of this thing?" another added.

The tumult simmered down to an anxious quiet.

Jim Skeller looked over at Papa and waved him up to the table to speak, obviously happy to yield the floor.

As Papa stepped forward I could feel the immediate release of tension in the room, as though a taut wire had suddenly gone slack.

"What do you say, Hank?" Carl Peterson called out.

"Let's hear him," someone else barked.

Papa pushed back his fedora, allowing the light to strike the hard, warrior lines of his face, then he threw his hands on his hips. He glanced over the expectant faces, the fiery blue bolts of his eyes penetrating the crowd, ferreting out the weakness like a general. "Listen, men, I don't know any more about this than you do. One thing I know, though, I ain't gonna lose my fool head over it like a bunch of crybaby women."

Several men briefly lowered their heads beneath the steel blade of his eyes.

Papa turned to Jim Skeller. "Now didn't you say that you called Lance Hoolihan?"

Jim nodded. "That's right."

"Well, Lance is a good man. You all know that," Papa said, turning to the intent faces in the crowd. "He's a ranching man—knows the law better'n anybody I know. I've known him to find loopholes in so-called airtight contracts that you could throw a cat through. Ain't that so, Dewey?" he said, singling out a tall, thin man in the middle of the crowd. "Didn't he beat off them banker wolves that was coming to foreclose on your place, two years back?"

Dewey nodded sheepishly. "That's right, Hank."

"Shoot if he didn't. And didn't he settle that business with the IRS, John?" he said, pointing to the portly man in front.

"Yes. Yes, he did, Hank. Gave me a new start."

"See there?" Papa growled. "Lance Hoolihan is a good man—he knows the law, like I said. If anybody can get to the bottom of this, Hoolihan can. Ain't that what he always says? He'll find the flaws. He'll find the loopholes. If there's been a breach of covenant, he'll unbreach it. The law's on our side here, boys—you can bet on it. Let's just hold off on the lynching till we see what Hoolihan says, what do you say? If Lance says it's a bust—well, then, I'll throw in with you, Ned, and provide the rope!" He said this last thing with a big grin.

I could see the fear slinking off the men's faces as they listened to Papa's commanding voice, his compelling reason. I could feel the cold tentacles of fear unwinding in me as well. Papa even cracked a joke about Adolf Hitler, comparing him to Josiah Fisk, and everybody laughed. Papa had what it took all right, and a warm glow of hope descended upon the grange hall.

"Hank? Hank Hochreiter?"

Papa turned abruptly, as a thin, rapier voice pierced the clamor of the crowd. I immediately recognized the voice, and as I turned I saw Tulane Morgan pushing his way toward us.

"What is it, Tulane?" Papa asked, grinning, once Mr. Morgan came up to him. "Something wrong with the herd?" He was still grinning.

"It's Jenny, Hank," Mr. Morgan said quickly, then handed him a little slip of paper.

"Jenny?" Papa read the note, and I saw his face go white. I'd never seen that look before. "O God, no," he said, staring at the words. A visible shock went over him, and he took a step backward.

"You need to hurry," Mr. Morgan said anxiously. "Doc Turner's on his way."

Papa brushed past him, and the crowd opened before him, the expression on everyone's face changing to bewilderment.

"What is it, Pa?" I called after him. I took hold of Tulane's arm. "What is it, Mr. Morgan?"

He looked gravely at Billy and me. "Jenny's slit her wrists."

"What?"

It took a moment for the words to pass through the infinite length of my body and then fight their way up into my brain. "Is she—"

"I don't know, son."

Billy and I rushed after Papa. Then just as we got to the rear of the hall, the back door swung open, and Josiah Fisk, along with his three sons—Booster, Arly, and Nate—entered the building.

Sheriff Bonner and his deputy were with him too, as well as the federal marshal from Helena. The marshal, a heavyset, mean-looking fellow, wearing a big Colt with staghorn grips on his hip, was holding a pump gun and looked like he was prepared to use it.

Papa halted briefly and glared at Josiah. I saw the deadliness jump into his eyes again as he looked deep into the man's eyes. "You've got a nerve, Fisk."

Josiah looked at him, astonished. "Why, Henry, last I remember I was still an upstanding member of the grange. Ain't that so, Sheriff Bonner?"

Sheriff Bonner looked as if he did not want to be there. He fidgeted uneasily, averting his eyes from Papa to look down at his feet.

"I've just come to see if the grange has considered my offer," Josiah said, showing his teeth. "I think it's a fair offer, don't you, Henry?"

Papa's hands doubled into fists.

The big marshal took a step forward and looked at Papa aggressively, flexing his hands on the pump gun to remind everyone that he was still holding it and that he was prepared and happy to use it.

Papa did not take his eyes off Josiah, and I don't think he ever gave the marshal a thought.

"Good afternoon," Josiah said, tipping his white beaver Stetson with a grin.

Papa brushed past him, Billy and I following, and as I passed by Booster I heard that wicked chortle of his.

23

As we galloped through the colonnade of trees, the leaves all turning red and yellow with winter's breath upon them, there was the house at the end of the way, the old clapboard ranch house that had stood through the advent of automobiles and flying machines, the war to end all wars, Prohibition, and the Great Depression. I wondered if it could stand this day.

And then, seeing the solid rise of it over the yard, I knew that it would stand this day and tomorrow and the day after tomorrow, that it would stand until the last of us Hochreiters was tendered cold beneath the gentle swell of live oaks.

Doc Turner's Model A Ford was parked in front of the porch, next to our truck, and Sy and Sammy were waiting on the porch, both of them turning at our approach. Seeing us, they came down the stairs to tend to our horses. Their faces were sober and pensive, Sammy's particularly, and there was something else in his eyes, but I didn't think about it.

"It's Miss Jenny," Sy said, taking Papa's reins.

Papa nodded, glancing briefly into his eyes for any telling signs.

Sy shook his head and added, "The doctor's inside with her now, Mr. Henry."

Sammy led the horses away, looking back at us with that something else in his eyes.

As we entered the house, Mama was coming down the stairs, holding a basin of bloody towels. Her eyes were wide with a mixture of bewilderment, fear, and anguish, and seeing us she set the basin on a side table, rushed over to Papa, and threw her arms around his waist. "Henry! Thank God, you've come! Oh, Henry!"

Papa held her, patting her lightly on her shoulders. He was looking up the stairs. "Any news?"

She shook her head. "Walt's with her now." Her shoulders trembled.

"Why aren't you helping him?"

"I did," she said. "I helped carry her into bed. Helped him with her clothes, but—" She broke off suddenly. "Henry, her wrists. I couldn't look at her wrists." She clasped her face and began to cry. "O Jesus, my little girl!"

Papa moved toward the stairs, but the sound of the bedroom door closing upstairs withheld him. He drew up sharply and waited for the heavy, hollow report of footsteps to produce the form of Doc Turner.

We looked expectantly up the stairwell as the gray-haired doctor descended, his left hand holding his worn leather doctor's bag, his right hand resting lightly on the smooth wooden rail, the dead Hochreiters glaring at him from their oval perches on the left wall, and the McInnises smiling at him from the right. And then his own gray, bespectacled eyes met those of Papa.

"Henry."

Papa nodded cordially. "Walt."

Mama studied the doctor's eyes.

"Hello, boys," he said, glancing at Billy and me. Then he looked from Mama to Papa. "She's lost a lot of blood, Henry. But we got to her in time, thank God. She's young and strong. And with plenty of rest and fluids I think she'll pull through."

Mama cried, "Thank You, Jesus! Thank You!"

A change went over Papa's face, from concern, quickly through relief, and now into something that I didn't recognize. "What happened, Walt?" he asked. "She cut her wrists?" It was more a statement than a question.

"Yes. Thank God not deep enough to sever the arteries."

"Why on earth?" Papa said, more to himself. "Why?" And then a thought occurred to him, or so it seemed by the shift in his expression. "Who found her?"

"Joseph did. Had to go to the bathroom," Doc Turner said, smiling over at Trout, his warm eyes twinkling paternally. "Isn't that right, Joseph?"

Trout was standing next to the sofa, his small dirty hand fiddling absently with the linen head cover as he stared across the room at the basin on the side table with dark, inquisitive eyes. He made no response.

The doctor looked at Papa and lowered his voice. "Found her in the tub. If he hadn't—" He shook his head. "What gets into their heads? Is the world so brutal—so hostile—that she would destroy God's most precious gift? I told her you would understand."

Something dark went over Papa's face. "Understand? What do you mean, Walt?" he demanded. "She tried to kill herself. We're supposed to understand that?"

"I think if you knew why, Henry, it might help you to."

"She told you why?"

"She didn't have to." Doc Turner glanced from Papa to Mama. He smiled at Mama and patted her hand, then he looked Papa square in the eyes. "You didn't know that Jenny was going to have a baby?"

For a moment there wasn't a sound. The silence thickened like that of a heart skipping a beat, swelling with pressure during the interval.

Papa's head reeled with a cough. "You mean—you mean she's *pregnant?*" He about choked on the word.

"Yes. She's three—maybe four—months along now," Doc Turner said. "She hid it well, I see."

Papa stared at him murderously, and then his eyes wandered up the stairs. A thick pulse beat in the room.

Mama sat down slowly on the ladder-back chair, not taking her eyes off the doctor. He let go of her hand, and it settled softly on her breast. A word formed on her lips, then blew away. Then she stared at her hands, and I could see her mind working over them.

Everything came into focus for me too—Jenny's mood swings, the wary look in her eyes of late, the secret trysts with Nate Fisk. I saw the fear crawling into Mama's eyes as she looked up at Papa's darkening face. I heard Billy, next to me, blowing out a silent whistle.

Doc Turner looked at each of us. "Jenny's lying in her bed right now, thinking her world has come to an end." His tone and demeanor had become that of a professional. "She needs all of your support— yes, and your understanding."

He turned to Mama. "Can you fix a strong beef broth, Beulah? It will help her body replenish the lost blood. It's too early yet to tell about the baby. We'll know for sure in a day or so."

"Yes, yes, of course." Then everything hit her at once, and she stood quickly to her feet. "My little girl—my baby!" she cried. "I'd best go to her."

Doc Turner touched her arm as she passed. "She needs a moment, Beulah, just a few minutes. She's asked to see Tyler. I think it's a good idea."

"Tyler?" Mama looked at him desperately, then threw her hand to her mouth.

I turned to go upstairs, but Papa snatched my arm like a trap, his face a black scowl. "Wait a minute, Walt! What do you mean she doesn't want to see anyone but Tyler?"

Mama shook her head and cried, "Henry, not now."

"I'm asking a question," Papa snapped. He glared at the doctor, his eyes a pale blue deadliness. "What do you mean she won't see her mother? What kind of thing is that to say? Can't you see how upset she is?"

"That's not what I said, Henry," Doc Turner said calmly. "Jenny's frightened. Embarrassed too, I'd expect. She just needs—"

"She too embarrassed to see her mother?" Papa said, his voice climbing. "She'll see her mother. Embarrassed," he grunted. "Imagine that! She'll see me too, you can bet, or I'll kick her sassy little tail from here to kingdom come!"

Doc Turner held his hand up and gently smoothed back Papa's words. "She just needs a little time, Henry. We have a distraught little girl upstairs. It's a delicate matter, a matter best handled by a minister. I don't have the tools to go fiddling around in her head, and I daresay neither do you. You go storming up there now, and who knows what she's liable to do."

"And just what's that supposed to mean, Walt?" Papa growled. "You think maybe this is my fault? Is that what you're saying? Jenny's upstairs all cut to pieces because of me?"

"No, Henry," Doc Turner said. He breathed out a frustrated sigh. "I'm not saying it's anyone's fault. And there's no need to raise your voice."

"Papa?"

"Shut up, Tyler!"

"Think of Jenny, Papa!"

"I said shut up, sissy boy!"

I felt a jolt of rage shoot through me, and then something clicked. "No, I won't shut up," I heard myself say, as though from a great distance.

I stared at Papa through a burning haze of fear and anger, the sum of nineteen years of fear and anger mounting in my chest, racing the other, neck and neck, and then the anger finally catching up to the fear and passing it.

Papa turned on me with those deadly metallic eyes of his, and I knew there was no going back.

"Tyler, don't!"

210

"I'm tired of shutting up, Mama," I said, swept along by it. "All I ever do is shut up. Well, I won't shut up. Not when Doc Turner's right and Papa's wrong. Jenny's hurt bad and needs help."

There was a flash of stars, what felt like a mule kick to my head, what seemed an interminable reach of space, and then the hard, jarring fetch of the floor.

Somewhere in the sudden blackness I heard Mama scream, "Henry!" followed by, "Don't you ever talk like that to me again, do you hear me?" Then the room reeled out of black to a fiery swirl of colors and into a watery focus, and Papa was standing over me with his big index finger wagging in my face. "I said, do you hear me?"

Billy rushed over and helped me to my feet. He stood up deliberately, his fists clenched. He glared at Papa. "You shouldn't have done that, Pa. Ty's right."

Papa stiffened like he'd been slapped.

"It's all right, Billy," I said as calmly as I could. "I'm all right. It doesn't hurt."

Then something suddenly went out of Papa. He glanced past Billy as though he didn't see him, rubbing his hand and looking dazedly at it, then looking at me. Mama rushed over to Billy and put her arm through his and stared at Papa, frightened.

Doc Turner came over to me and looked at my mouth. I could feel a trickle of blood going over my lip and the slow-swelling numbness spreading through it. I dabbed the corner of the lip with my tongue, and it tasted of iron and salt. "It's all right, Doc. I'm fine. Honest."

He ignored me and began to clean up the wound with a cloth. "Henry," he said, now applying iodine to the corner of my mouth with a cotton swab. "I've never said this to anyone in my life before, but you're a pigheaded fool. There, that should do it, Tyler. No broken teeth that I can see. Jaw working fine?"

"Fine. Really, I'm fine," I lied.

The doctor grunted. "Now if I can just get out of here without having to mend anymore broken Hochreiter children, I'll consider the day a success."

Papa just stood glowering at him while Doc Turner packed his bag.

"Jenny needs rest, Beulah," he said, snapping it shut, then reaching for his frayed black coat. "She needs a whole lot of love and understanding and whatever else it is the good Lord equipped mothers to give. In His infinite wisdom and mercy He saw fit to spare her life—and the life of her baby, I might add—so bear that in mind, won't you?" The question was directed at Papa. "I'll send Emily by tomorrow morning to check on her. Call if you need me."

Mama forced a smile. "Yes, Doctor. And thank you."

The doctor slipped his right hand into the old coat sleeve that held the form of his arm from years of use, then he shrugged it over his back, and the other hand adroitly found its sleeve hole. "Don't forget that beef broth; her body needs it." He smiled at her, then, glancing over at Papa, nodded and said, "Henry." Then he left.

Mama looked at me.

"I'd best go see her," I said, not looking at Papa. I could feel his eyes on me as I walked up the stairs.

24

As I passed the open door of the bathroom I glanced inside, saw the dull glint of the razor on the edge of the sink, felt the kick of the image in my mind, then moved quickly along the hallway. I stopped outside Jenny's bedroom. I listened for a moment, and, hearing nothing, I took a breath of cleansing air and prayed, *Give me a tool, Father, a word in season to help my sister.*

Then I knocked. There was no reply. I thought she might be asleep, so I quietly opened the door and poked my head in, my mind turning, then fast becoming a whirl of thoughts and images. Out of the whirl a thought occurred to me, a terrible thought that kicked up from the pit of my stomach and clutched my throat, but when I saw her staring out the window, saw the gentle heave of her breathing, the thought withered away.

"Jenny?"

Her eyes moved heavily, wanly, in a slow-footed sweep to mine. It seemed to take an eternity. Then, when at last our eyes met, I felt a hot snap, like a lash laid smartly across the breadth of my mind.

For the person I beheld was pale and drawn, a frail and helpless-looking creature that I did not recognize at first, and for just a moment the thought occurred to me that it was someone else lying in Jenny's bed.

"May I come in?" I asked.

"Hi, Tyler," she said weakly, then looked out the window. "I saw you ride up."

I stepped into the room and drew up a chair next to her bed. "How're you doin'?"

"Swell."

"You look awful."

She glanced at me, saw my grin, then looked back out the window. "Thanks, Tyler," she said sluggishly. "I knew I could count on you for moral support."

"Don't mention it."

She stared out the window, her arms folded loosely over her stomach, watching as Doc Turner drove away through the avenue of trees, listening to the Ford sputter and cough, a northerly wind smoothing over it and then quieting until there was only the sound of the chickens chuckling in the yard below.

I studied the pale lines of her face, and when I caught flashes of her eyes, as the light struck through the window, I could see that the wariness was gone from them. She only looked scared now. Then I noticed her wrists, and how the fingers of one hand moved in a brittle and tentative dance over the gauze bandages of the other, the fingertips tap-tap-tapping the beat of an internal struggle.

"Everybody knows, I suppose?" she rasped painfully, glancing at my eyes to catch the truth in them.

"About you having a baby? Yes."

Jenny groaned, waited, thinking, I saw. "What was all the noise?" she asked, glancing at me again. "I heard Papa." Then, looking steadily at my mouth, she added, "Superman beat up all the bad guys?"

I chuckled. "I guess so."

Then she gazed out the window for a long while, her eyes drifting to the clouds banked over the bluffs. I could see the struggle in her eyes, the labor of a tear swelling at one corner, then trickling down her cheek. It flashed like a flash on the river as the sun struck it.

"I'm scared, Tyler," she said, still gazing out the window, then closing her eyes.

"I know you are, Jen."

"You don't know how scared, Ty."

"No, I don't. But I tell you I was plenty scared when I heard about it. I'm still scared." I waited several moments. "Why'd you do it, Jen?"

She looked at me, her eyes narrowing. "Do what? You'll have to be more specific. Which crime are you talking about? God knows I'm guilty of a mess of 'em."

My eyes lowered to her wrists.

She chuckled weakly. "Oh, you mean *this* crime."

"Quit acting tough, Jenny. It's me, Tyler, remember?"

"That's right. I could never act tough around you, could I? I could only act tough around Billy. Only with Billy it wasn't an act."

She looked out the window again at the clouds over the bluffs. Her eyes glistened in the light coming through on her face and showing the downy fuzz on her cheeks, streaked with the recent tears.

214

"You ever dream you were a bird and could just fly away?" she asked wistfully. "Just grow feathers, or just have them, and go soaring off like an eagle?"

"My dreams never had wings," I said. "Only swift moving currents and pretty hazel eyes." She didn't hear me, I could see.

"I used to lie awake at night," she continued, "imagining I was circling over the ranch—way up high—and looking down at everybody. No one could ever touch me, I was so high. I'd laugh, seeing everybody's faces as they tried to catch me, then off I'd go, soaring over the bluffs, and keep on going till I got into the Crazies. Everything was so quiet and peaceful there—just me and the other eagles."

A groan fluttered out from some deep place in her. "Oh, Ty. When Nate came along, I thought he was going to give me those wings. He treated me kind. Everything about him—the way he talked to me, the way he looked at me with those beautiful eyes of his—how he told me I was so pretty and special."

"Does he know about the baby?"

"Did you ever look at his eyes, Tyler?" Jenny sighed. "They're so blue—like a field of lobelias."

"What about the baby, Jenny?" I repeated.

She smiled weakly, painfully. Then she rolled her eyes and stared at the ceiling a long while, a few tears leaking over her cheeks. "Am I going to go to hell, Tyler? Am I one of the devil's goats?"

"You didn't answer my question."

"Am I?"

I shook my head. "I'm not your judge, sis."

"Reverend Jacks says if you take your life it's like murder."

I stared at her, racked the theological portion of my brain for an appropriate answer but found none that I cared to relate. "Jesus died for murderers too," I said, then wincing at how trite the words sounded.

But why did they sound trite? I believed them, didn't I? Yes, I believed them. Of course I believed them, and I clung desperately to the triteness of them with all my heart and soul and mind. *God have mercy,* my soul cried. Or was it my heart? Perhaps my mind? *Have mercy, God, whichever. Have mercy.*

I looked up at Jenny's side-turned face. The tears breached over her pallid skin, then abated, then breached again to a tenuous pulse.

"What are we talking about murder for? You're still alive, aren't you?" I smiled. "You got to have a habeas corpus to have a murder. I read that in a murder mystery once."

She turned her head, closing her eyes as she did, then opening them to gaze at the palisade of stuffed animals along the wall. She chuckled throatily. "Yeah, I botched that one up good, didn't I?"

"Yes, thank God." *Yes, thank You, God.* I grinned at her like an older brother, suddenly reminded of the fact that I was one. "You're the only sister I've got—for better or for worse."

"Don't forget till death do us part."

"Knock it off."

"OK. I guess you're just stuck with me, aren't you? Warts and all."

"Stuck to you like glue. Hey—'you, glue.' I made a rhyme! Watch out, Willie boy!"

She giggled. "You're crazy, Tyler."

"Certified."

She rolled her eyes, then looked out the window again and breathed deeply, letting our words trail off somewhere.

Neither of us said anything for several moments, and the room breathed a quiet exhale, in and out, our thoughts drifting to and fro on invisible currents, like little boats crossing, coming alongside each other, touching, knowing that we touched, then moving on in that quiet breathing silence.

The tractor fired up outside. I looked out and saw Papa talking to Sy and Sammy, giving them instructions, then pointing over to the burned barn.

Jenny sighed. "How's everybody taking it?"

I made a so-so gesture. "Mama wants to come up and see you. She's very concerned, as you might expect."

"I want her to." Then she knit her brows together. "What about Ghengis Khan? Is he concerned too?"

I remembered the look on his face when he read the note Kate's father gave him at the grange. "I think so, Jen. I just don't think he knows what to do with it just yet."

"So he hits you on the mouth."

"So he hits me on the mouth. Then he punishes himself until he's made some adequate propitiation to himself."

"You mean he'll get drunk and beat somebody up," Jenny said, a weak red color rising into her face.

"Yes, the absolution of the sinner."

Jenny's expression grew desperate. Tears came in a faster pulse. "What am I going to do, Tyler? School starts in a week. Everybody in town will know." Then she wept bitterly. "My life is ruined."

"No, it's not. You're going to live and have a baby and be happy for the rest of your life. We'll get through this, Jenny, I promise."

"How? How're you gonna make good on your promise? You're goin' off to college. It'll get better for you, you mean."

I felt that one.

Then a darkness went over Jenny's face as it had over Papa's, her eyes red and burning through the darkness. "No, Tyler, it ain't gonna get better. Papa's gonna kill him."

"Who?"

"You know who."

Her words struck me solidly. I just stared at her, blinking, looking through and beyond her, as the weight of the day crept onto my back like some scaly reptile. First the business with Josiah, and now this of his son, and Jenny's attempted suicide. Yes, he would probably kill him. He would kill him, and then he would kill Fisk and Fisk and Fisk, until there was no more threat to the Soul, and then he would turn the rage on himself.

Isn't that what Bapa Honus did—looking over the black muzzle of that .45- 70 and down the long blue run of steel, and then the firm, cold touch of metal tang that—pushing—tore mind from soul from body in a hot blinding flash? Yes, and there's no going back from that one either.

"Does he know about the baby, Jen? Tell me."

Jenny let out a low painful groan. "Yes," she said, struggling with it. "I told him last Sunday how I'd missed my time three months now." She cleared her throat, choking, a fresh stream of tears sparkling on her cheeks. She looked suddenly confused and panicked and like a little lost sheep. "Know what he said, Tyler? He said how did I know it was his."

I felt a rush of anger in me, my fists involuntarily doubling over the anger.

She grunted. "I told him I was sorry, but he wouldn't listen. He just laughed at me and told me I was a stupid little girl. Then he walked away, telling me I should get hold of a little bit of baling wire. Papa's gonna kill him. I just know it."

I might kill him myself, I thought. I sat there looking at little Jenny, heiress of the curse, of the infinite crime, and the dark clouding thought of it about overwhelmed me.

Suddenly Jenny's eyes got wide, then she clasped her face with her hand, and her shoulders began to heave. "O God, forgive me.

Forgive me. Won't You forgive me?" she wept. "It's no use, Tyler. I'm lost. Lost. It would've been better if Trout never found me."

"You're talking nonsense, Jen. There's nothing we can do that God won't forgive," I said, meaning it now. I meant all of it now.

"I've been praying real hard, Tyler, for weeks now. But God keeps slapping my prayers back in my face." She sighed, her chest heaving with sorrow. "Everything I do, it seems, keeps getting slapped back in my face."

"It isn't God slapping you, Jenny."

She looked at me suddenly.

"That's right. It's you. You've got to forgive yourself too. Ain't none of us good enough to walk the streets of gold. Don't you see? He's merciful, Jenny. He took all the weight of your crimes on His bleeding shoulders, so you could mount up with eagle wings and soar—soar beyond the Crazies to the highest peaks in heaven and never look back on this place."

I saw the tears brimming, then it all came at once, and she clasped her face with both hands. The fountains of the deep broke loose, and I knew that it was a good one, that there was no bitterness in her tears.

I stared at the gauze on her wrist for a moment, then looked outside again, allowing her a privacy. Sy and Sammy were attaching the discs to the Fordson, while Papa, sitting on the tractor, was looking away at the hills. I wondered what he was thinking. But I knew, didn't I? Yes, I knew.

After a good cleansing time of it, Jenny looked at me and wiped her cheeks with the back of her hands. I handed her a handkerchief, and she blew her nose. I chuckled. "That's some tooter you got," I said. "You sound like a bull moose in spring."

She laughed as she wiped her eyes, gently dabbing under each one and at the corners. "You should talk," she said, folding it, then handing me the handkerchief.

I made a face. "You keep it," I said. Then I patted her feet under the covers and stood up. "You OK now?"

She smiled. "I'm OK."

"God is merciful, little sister," I said, as Mama had said, and said, and said, as she beat back the curse time and again. "You will see." And then I walked to the door.

Looking back at Jenny, I saw the sun shine kindly over her face, giving it a warmth and glow that was absent from her veins, and in that moment of time she was forever changed in my mind. She looked small and weak lying in her bed, and suddenly she was ten years older. My little sister was gone with a single self-destructive impulse, and she was something else now. Weren't we all? Changed, I mean.

"Anyone ever tell you you were pretty?"

Jenny grunted. "Not in this house."

"Well, I'm telling you."

She blushed. "When are you leaving for school?"

I hesitated. "Day after tomorrow."

"Day after tomorrow," she repeated, then thought about it a couple of seconds. "I'll miss you."

"I'll miss you too. But I'll write, if you do." Then I corrected myself. "I'll write even if you don't." I smiled at her, then turned to leave.

"Tyler?"

"Yeah?"

"Thanks."

"For what?"

"For everything."

"Don't mention it. If you do, I'll deny everything." I walked down the hall and waited for it.

"Pig face!"

There it was. *Thank You, Father.*

"Pig face!" I called back.

I passed Mama coming up the stairs, holding a steaming bowl of beef broth.

She looked at me horrified. "Who were you calling that name?"

"What name? Oh, you mean *pig face?*" I grinned for effect. "Why, Jenny, of course!"

I left Mama staring at me, then descending the stairs between smiling Mount Gerizim on my left and scowling Mount Ebal on my right, the blessings and the curses, I wondered what lay before me in the valley of decision. I felt a darkness rising in me, and my mind turned on a single wheeling thought.

Was I changed? Changed as Jenny was changed? I didn't know. But I knew I wasn't the same person I was ten minutes ago. And I knew I could never go back. Not very likely.

No, not ever.

25

I went outside and sat down on the porch swing to clear my thoughts. Billy was on the steps, bent over his rifle with an oil cloth and giving it a tender wipe. There were four cartridges standing in a shining line next to his leg.

He looked up at my approach, allowing the oil cloth to dangle over his knee. "Jenny OK?" he asked, looking at me with those young Hochreiter blues.

I nodded. "Mama's with her. She'll be OK. She's a tough girl."

"Yeah, she's a tough girl," Billy said. Then a dark look came over him as he ran the cloth inside the blued action. "It's Nate, isn't it?"

I looked at him.

"Thought so," he said, pushing the bolt home, then raising the rifle to his shoulder and sighting on an imaginary something. "Tell you what I'd like to do. I'd like to put a neat little hole right between his eyes." He squeezed the trigger. *Click.*

I shook my head. "That would solve all the problems, all right. They'd haul your tail off to prison and probably hang you."

Billy grunted contemptuously. "I'd like to see 'em try it."

I glanced over at Papa. He was angling the discs back and forth over the large black rectangle that was once our barn. Sy was pulling charred bits of debris from his path, using a rake with the smaller stuff, and every so often Papa would get down and help him with a larger piece.

Sy was showing his age, it seemed. Whatever age that was. Old as dirt, that's sure. He moved as though he might break—maybe "brokenly" would be a better way to describe his movement. Whatever, he was showing his age. And Papa was showing something else.

"We should help," I said, rising to my feet.

"I already offered," Billy said. "Pa said he didn't want any help but Sy's, and I wasn't about to argue with him."

I sat down.

"What are we gonna do about it, Ty?" Billy asked. "We're her brothers, ain't we? We've got to stand up for her honor."

"Not with no .30-06 we don't."

Billy swore. "I'd like to kill 'em all—every last one of 'em."

I could see he meant it.

The sound of the tractor pulled my eyes back to Papa, and I saw the plume of blue smoke trailing off, slanting, then splaying out into nothing over the wind, and Sy standing there, his hands lowered to his sides, hanging heavily, looking away at the bluffs in the west.

I could only see Papa's bent back through the disced-up cloud of ash and dust, but I could tell by the set of his head and the thrust of his arm over the wheel what he was thinking. Every so often he would spit off to one side, then he would sit back into a grim hardness, the arm thrust rigidly as he took the blows of some hammering gavel.

"You sure he doesn't need help?"

"You go ask him. What're you so all fired up to help him for anyway? You should see your lip."

I touched it lightly, and it smarted.

The porch swing creaked pensively, the sound of it sounding hollow and remote. A fine haze spread over the yard and against the hills, softening and pushing everything away as in the first fluid moments of a dream. I let it take me for a while, and thoughts floated lazily. Chickens wandered into the dream and struck hammerlike at the banks.

Then Trout crept into my field of view from the right side of the porch, holding a pail in his right hand; he stood and stared at us. He had a funny look in his eyes, as he had before in the house.

I roused out of my dream. "Hey, Trout!" I said. "What you up to?"

He stared silently at us for several moments, his eyes dark and fixed and inquiring. I could see his mind working behind them, how it was turned inward on his eight-year-old world.

"I see you got your pail," I said, trying to coax it out of him. "Goin' down to the river?"

He glanced down at his bucket, then stared at me with those inquisitive eyes.

Billy said, "Cat got your tongue, Trout? Or have you gone spooky on us?"

"Easy, Billy," I said.

Billy chuckled.

Trout fidgeted with the pail. Then he kicked a stone under the porch, and one of the Labs groaned. "Why'd she do it?" he asked, staring darkly. "Cut herself like that."

"I don't know, Trout," I answered.

His eyebrows pinched together. "It don't make sense."

No, it doesn't make sense, I thought. *But I'm not Jenny.* "People do things all the time that don't make sense."

He didn't buy it. His eyes shifted briefly to Billy, then back to me, and continued to stare. "Is Jenny crazy?"

"No. Just scared."

He screwed his face into a scowl. "Scared?"

I could see that was too lofty for him. "Trapped," I corrected. But that didn't work either.

"Did you see the tub?" he asked, screwing his upper lip.

"No, I didn't."

"I did. There sure was a lot of blood in it. How come there's so much blood?"

I tried to explain to him that the tub was filled with water, but that only seemed to complicate matters.

He disregarded me and turned his attention to Billy. Billy pushed each of the cartridges into the magazine, then he ran the bolt over the last one, pressing it down with his thumb as the bolt slid over it to keep the chamber free. He pulled the trigger. *Click.*

"Pa says you shouldn't dry fire," Trout said. "It'll wreck your gun."

Billy ignored him.

"You gonna shoot Nate, Billy?"

Billy grunted.

Trout grinned at him. "I'd shoot 'im if I had a gun." The darkness went out of his eyes, and then he picked up a clod and winged it at a chicken. The chicken squawked across the yard, wings back and high, causing a row as it settled in with the others.

Trout laughed. "Stupid chickens!" Then he sauntered away toward the river, swinging his pail and every so often throwing it ahead of him, the pail hitting with the sharp sound of tin. Mutt and Jeff crawled out from under the porch and wagged after him.

I shook my head.

I looked up as Jimbo and the others were just returning from Columbus, trotting through the trees and hazily into view. They headed over to the stables beyond the barn. We exchanged waves. Those Indians sure looked fine riding into the yard, like a war party come

222

home. Never an Indian sat a finer horse; even Earl Thomas rode with an air of pride. Jimbo's tooth flashed dully in the sun as he talked to Papa and Sy.

Papa turned off the tractor, and they talked a long while, Jimbo's hands describing the various points of interest.

Then Sammy came out from behind the house and made his way toward the stables.

"Where'd he come from?" Billy said. He stood to his feet, holding the rifle cupped under the magazine.

"Beats me," I said. "Hey! Sammy! Where you been hidin'?"

Sammy just walked away without answering.

"How do you figure him?" Billy asked.

"I don't."

The phone rang.

"I'll get it," I said, rising from the swing.

I lifted the receiver and spoke into the mouthpiece. "Hello?"

"That you, Hank? Jim Skeller." His voice was quick and agitated. "You best get on down here. Lance Hoolihan just come in and took a look at the contract. He says it don't look good, Hank. Can you come? Things are gettin' ugly here—say, how's Jenny? Morg told me about it. I'm sorry to hear about that, Hank."

"She's going to be fine."

"Hank?"

"This is Tyler, Jim. Pa's outside."

"That you, Tyler? I swear, you sound just like your Pa. Is he there? Get him quick, won't you? Hurry, son."

"I'll get him."

I went outside and called Papa. He looked up at me from the tractor, and I waved him in. "Jim Skeller's on the phone!"

Papa leaped off the Fordson, then strode to the porch, his arms swinging, stiff with the fists clenched. He took the porch in two steps.

"Jim Skeller's on the phone," I repeated as he passed by, pulling a draft of warm air behind him. But he didn't answer me. He just looked ahead, his eyes, hard as cement, were glaring in thought as he pushed through the screen door. I looked over at Billy and raised my eyebrows.

We both listened from the porch.

"What is it, Jim?" Papa said. "What do you mean? That don't make sense." There was a silence. "Sure I will. Where's he now?" Another silence. "He's sure of it? Ain't no way, Jim . . . no . . . Jim, listen to me, Jim . . ." Long silence. "Jim, listen . . . yes, she's fine . . ." Short silence. "I'll be right down there." Papa cursed as he slammed the receiver home. We listened as his heavy footsteps quickly ascended the stairs.

Two minutes later the footsteps descended, then the screen door banged open, and Papa strode across the porch carrying the .45- 70.

Mama followed after him. "Where are you going, Henry?" she asked. "Who was that on the phone? What's the rifle for? Henry?"

"Just going into town," Papa said, taking the steps one at a time, quick and heavily. He had a killer look in his eyes.

"Henry!"

"What's goin' on, Pa?" Billy asked him.

"Nothin'." He headed toward the truck, setting his hat forward on his head, then looking away into the distance.

"I'm comin', Pa!" Billy cried, then he ran after Papa, hefting his Model 70.

"Billy, you come back here!" Mama called after him.

But Billy had caught up to Papa, and the two of them got into the truck with their rifles.

Mama's right hand went to her face. "O Jesus . . ."

I sat back down in the swing and watched the truck curve out of sight into the trees before a big cloud of dust. I looked past Mama at Sy and Jimbo. They were walking slowly toward the stables, Jimbo leading his horse and neither of them talking.

Mama, still looking down the road, took a deep breath and shook her head wearily. I could see the strength go out of her small frame. Her shoulders sank, and she sagged into herself like the air seeping out of a tire. Her left hand came up to support her right elbow, for it seemed a great heaviness to her.

She looked over her shoulder at me, her hand still touching her cheek. And then I saw something flit across her face that I had not seen before. I saw it again in the angle of her head, along the line of her jaw, I saw it glaring out from her eyes in a silent cry for help, and for just a moment I could see Jenny.

26

Mama sat down beside me on the swing, and we both stared out from the porch at the chickens nestling in the remaining warmth of the dirt. A coolness settled under the eaves of the porch, curled around our heads, and whispered the change of weather. *Snow's in the air*, I thought, seeing the thin, dark line of clouds over the northern buttes in the distance, giving them a purple tint. *Gonna be a hard winter.*

"It'll be all right, Mama," I said, breaking a long silence.

Mama began to cry, softly at first, and I put my arm around her and drew her close. She caught herself, then pulled out a handkerchief and blew her nose. "Look at me. Blubbering like a schoolgirl."

"You're entitled."

She looked at me. Her eyes were red and wet, and I could see she was fighting it. "It was a fine thing you did for Jenny, Tyler," she said, forcing a smile.

"Is she all right?"

"I got some food down her. She's sleeping now." She patted my knee. "I don't know what I would do without you, Tyler. You're a comfort to me."

I looked down the road, at the trees arching colorfully over a long tunnel of brightness, and then it came to me.

There are a thousand and one things that happen in a day that change a man from one thing to another—a telephone call, a newspaper headline, a conversation with someone, a rap on the mouth, a pat on the knee, but rarely do we stop and reflect upon the changes. We go on blithely from one change to the next without considering the growth or regress in the world of our character until, at last, one thing leaps out at us that we cannot ignore. It is then that we look back, if we are able, and wonder what has become of us. I felt as though I had gone through a revolution.

"I'm staying, Mama."

"What do you mean staying? Staying where?"

"I'm not going to Chicago. Not now." But before she could object, I said, "I can't leave here now—not with Jenny hurt. Not with everything else so turned up."

She glared at me. "Tyler, I didn't mean to suggest anything. We'll be just fine. God is—"

"I know, Mama." I looked at her intently. "But you know what this business with the Fisks is gonna do. It's going to tear this family in two. I gotta stay."

Mama's expression changed. Her eyes grew moist, a darkness clouding them. Then they flashed at me. "You must go, Tyler. It's God's will you go."

"How do you know what God's will is, Mama? Did He tell you?"

"Don't you get smart with me," she snapped. Then her eyes quickly softened, and she rubbed my knee. She gave it a pat and said, "I'm sorry."

A chicken got up from one spot and moved to another.

Mama sighed. "It's just that I so want you to be the first Hochreiter to be a minister—" she gazed out over the steading "—to break free of this spinning wheel. To get off this ranch and make something of yourself. I want you to use the gifts God gave you. You've got such a mind." She looked at me earnestly. "Don't you see, Tyler? You must go."

"No, Mama, I mustn't. I've been doing a lot of thinking—praying too. It'd be wrong for me to leave right now. I just can't. Not now. Maybe next semester, after things settle down."

Her eyes brimmed with tears. "Oh, Tyler."

"It's the right thing, Mama, you'll see." I patted her shoulder, then stood up.

She looked up at me, panicked. "Where are you going?"

"Into town."

"No, you aren't."

"I got to know what's going on," I said, walking to the edge of the porch. "Jenny's all right—you said so."

"Tyler, no!" She stood up fiercely. "I don't want you going into town."

I frowned at her. "Mama, I'm nineteen years old. I'm not a kid anymore. Don't make me buck."

She rushed to me and held me. "Oh, Tyler, my sweet boy. Hold me. Just hold me, won't you?" She cried desperately. "I couldn't bear it should anything happen to you."

"Nothing's going to happen to me, Mama. Everything's going to be all right," I said, feeling the rage of frustration rising in my chest. I patted her on the back. "I won't go to the grange. I'll just hang around Johansson's a while. Nils will know what's going on. That place is like a switchboard."

She looked up at me, her eyes streaming with tears. "You promise? Promise me, Tyler."

"No grange, I promise."

She smoothed her cool palms over my cheeks. "Oh, Tyler, I'm so frightened. What's happening to us?"

"I don't know, Mama." I held her out from me and looked into her wet, worried blue eyes, and she reminded me of a teenager. She sniffled. "You all right now?"

She forced a smile.

"That's my girl," I said, patting her shoulders. "Anything I can bring you from Johansson's?"

She wiped her eyes with the handkerchief. "Let me just get you a list," she said, then went inside the house.

The temperature had dropped, so I went inside to fetch my jacket.

"You promise?" Mama said again, handing me the list.

"I never break a promise."

She kissed me on the cheek, then I went outside and walked over to the stables. I glanced back once, and Mama was framed by the screen door, her right hand touching her cheek.

Sy was standing beneath the live oaks overspreading one side of the paddocks that came out from the long row of stalls. The sun made patterns across the grooves of his caramel features and his dark, moist eyes. He was looking away at the bluffs, still holding the rake, holding it like a shepherd's crook, and his body was swaying slightly and he was chanting quietly. A light cold wind was blowing through the leaves, and his body waved with it like a stalk of grain.

"Hello, Sy," I said, walking up to him.

He continued to sway and chant softly as though he hadn't heard me.

"Sy?" I looked into his eyes, and I could see they were reaching far beyond the ranch into the west. Beyond the Beartooths even. He had that sad look in his eyes as when he told a story from his past or when someone was telling him a sad story. I couldn't tell which it was. "You all right, Sy?"

His eyes twinkled to life. Then he looked at me, and they were wistful and dreamy and melancholy. "My soul flutters like eagle down on the wind," he said. "I have lived too long. I have seen too many things."

"What're you talking about, Sy?"

"Soon the great blue heron will come for me—take me to the tepee of the Akbadádéa."

"No, Sy."

Something changed in his features. His brow cleared, and it was the old Sy again, the story told and flown over the bluffs. He smiled at me, then turned away and walked into the bay of the stables, his gait slow and brittle. I followed him inside along a sharp wedge of light, keeping my eyes on him.

There was a heavy smell of sweating horses in the place, a sweet and sour pungency of manure and leather and neat's foot oil and a muskiness born of time. The horses poked their heads over their doors and followed us, chewing their hay and whickering. Several fat cats lazed about on bales and grain sacks, with their tales flicking satedly in the afternoon sun striping the shade. Flies droned lazily in the still air and clung to the walls. A mouse scurried across the hard pack of ground, and one of the cats looked over at it but did not bother.

"You need your horse, Tyler?"

"Yes. But that's all right, Sy—I'll take care of it," I said, still watching him.

The horse at the end of the row thrust its head out and whickered at the sound of my voice, then thumped its hoof against the stall.

"I'm coming, Ginger," I said.

Sy went over to one side and laid the rake against the wall.

I raised the wooden lid off the grain bin, grabbed a handful of oats, and ate some. They tasted good and dry and powdery. I gave the rest to my horse, who lipped them greedily from my palm. I patted her thick neck, and she threw her head up and down.

"That's a girl," I said. "That's right, we're going for another ride." I chuckled. "There's no rest for the wicked."

I went over to the tack wall, and Sy handed me the bosal.

"Thanks," I said. "The men getting packed?"

"Yes," he said, then carried the blanket over and put it on Ginger's back. I smiled at him. *That Sy,* I thought. "I wish there was more work for them," I said. "They're good men."

Sy said nothing. He sighed heavily.

"I'll get the saddle, Sy."

The old Indian picked up a muck rake and went into one of the stalls.

"That's Sammy's job," I objected. "I'll go call him."

"He's gone," Jimbo said, coming into the stables, smiling.

"What do you mean gone?"

"We passed him on our way in. He said Mr. Henry had a chore for him in town."

"A chore?" I noticed the empty stall next to mine. "He riding Buttons?"

Jimbo nodded.

"Well, it's the first I heard of it," I said. "He said Papa sent him to town?"

Jimbo nodded.

I thought about it and shook my head. "I'd like to know when it was he talked to him."

Jimbo shrugged. Then he took the rake from Sy and started to rake out the manure. Sy went over to the saddles and bridles and began to soap them.

I saddled my horse, smelling the wet soapy leather, savoring the smell of it, then, looking once more at Sy, rode out of the stables and across the yard, waved at the few hands who had collected on the bunkhouse porch—waved at Mama, who was still framed inside the screen door, watching me leave—and trotted up the road through the trees.

The iron shoes grated a jaunty tempo against the gravel road. It felt good to be doing something, going somewhere, even if it was only to Columbus. A wind soughed through the bowery, sounding like a moan. And exiting the trees into the sudden brightness of the fields on either side of the road, I looked over at the low swell of live oaks off to my left, where the headstones were sunk and tilting and marking the quiet deterioration of my ancestors. I felt a pang of anger knife into my chest.

"What do you think about this, Bapa Otto?" I said aloud. "This what you had in mind?"

No response.

"How about you then, Bapa Honus? No, I don't expect you gave it a thought, either. You had other things on your mind. How about you, Uncle Fredrick?"

No response.

"What am I asking *you* for? You're only a headstone. The rest of you is buried who knows where. What about the rest of you Hochreiters then? Nana Gertie? Grandma Wilhelmina? Does anybody got anything to say? Any pearls of wisdom for your great-grandson? The fruit of your loins? No? Then tell me how to stop this wheel you got to turning."

A hot wash of tears suddenly made everything blurry.

Ginger looked back at me.

"I'm all right, girl," I said, chuckling it away bitterly, then patting her thick neck. "We humans get a little crazy sometimes, didn't you know?"

No response.

"It's in the genes. You didn't know that either? Sure. Mendel's got it all worked out. I studied it in biology. Got an A on the test. Got an A on all the tests."

The horse snorted.

"It's true. Like father like son . . . or, 'The apple don't fall far from the tree,' or, 'Say, ain't he the spittin' image of his old man?' What's spit got to do with it anyway? I got them there, don't I? I don't chew. Now if they were to say 'the spirit and image,' why, then I might have to concede that." I grunted.

Then I left my ancestors to their quiet industry and looked beyond the rise at the trees along the river, smoothing along low through the rocky trough of land and sounding like a continual ovation to God's good work. The aspens crowding the banks were bright and sprinkling the air with coins of yellow gold; the cottonwoods and maples blazed rust and red and bright orange; and the sycamores and elms were gone to the browns and something indescribable.

A great blue heron lifted off from the rushes, pumping heavy-winged upstream, then spreading its broad wings flat and smooth as silk over the current. I thought of Sy's light soul and smiled.

Thank You, God, for Montana, I thought. *No other place like it on earth, though I'm sure I wouldn't know.*

A cloud of gnats found my head. Getting their last licks in, I suppose, before the cold took them. Gnats were a result of the Fall, I was sure, spawned in the sweat of Adam's brow and thenceforth swarming back to the brow of man. I clapped a few of them, but it was no good. They were persistent devils, so I put Ginger into a lope.

In the distance the thin, dark line of clouds had thickened over the buttes, and I knew we were in for snow. A good one this time, by the look and smell of it. The wind shrilled down the hills off to my right to confirm it, whistled over the cut grass, all reedy and graying in the thinning air, then found my ears and nose, and I was glad I had thought to wear a jacket. I buttoned it to my neck, turned up the collar, pulled the leather gloves from my saddlebags, and rode ahead into the wind. It was a fine day for a ride, I thought, looking up at the sky.

No response.

230

27

As soon as I crossed the bridge into Columbus, it was like riding into a wall of fear. I could smell it on the town as I had before in the grange hall. It was everywhere, pervading the air. There were a few random people moving quickly along the street, not with the broad ranging eyes of commerce but with eyes reined in close to their quick and scissoring steps, no one looking into store windows, only moving from one point to another and quickly disappearing around corners. I saw it as they drove past me in their cars, their dark, in-turned eyes glancing quickly out their windows at me then looking ahead and speeding away.

There was a gray cast to everything. The river was gray. The brick walls and storefronts were gray. The streets were gray. Even the wind that swept along the street in blustering swirls, leaving little piles of debris along curbs and door niches, seemed to strip the bright colors from the flying leaves. The air felt tight, constricted, as though the oxygen had been sucked out of it. Some dreadful thing was quivering in the air.

Josiah Fisk had a contract on the soul of the town.

I tied Ginger in front of Johansson's and went inside, and the little bell over the door sounded my arrival. It was a familiar scene. It was warm, and there were the immediate warming smells and glow rising off the floor and the counters, along the shelves and spreading through the air and drawing me in with a friendly welcome. The refrigerators in the rear hummed a single monotonous note that was somehow comforting. The elk was in his place over the storeroom door like some gargoyle perched over a cathedral, staring dully at everyone who came into the place, warding off evil spirits.

Took and the black-and-white cat sat in a square of sun below the display window, Took playing with dust devils, the cat curled in a contented circle of itself. The boy was chuckling happily.

Nils was behind the counter, tending to a woman customer, discussing a price. Stu Dunnegan, ensconced comfortably in his easy chair, was reading the paper. Charley was seated at a makeshift table

231

—a board set over the cracker barrel—tying flies. The dead, gray fingers of the town had not yet reached this cozy place.

There was no sign of Enos.

Nils looked at me over the rim of his spectacles. He smiled. "Why, hello, Tyler!" Then his expression was eclipsed by a thought. "How's Jenny?"

That sure got around fast, I thought. "Doc Turner says she's going to be fine."

The woman looked at me. It was Mrs. Barnhouse, a big-boned elderly woman with blue hair, who was a charter member of Mrs. Stivers's quilting circle. She got a certain satisfied look in her eyes and smiled cordially at me, showing just a glimmer of teeth, and behind the smile I could see her mind filing the information.

"Be with you in a moment," Nils said, putting her grocery items into a cardboard box.

"No hurry."

"Have some coffee," he offered. "It's fresh brewed."

"Thanks, I will." I went over to the stove and poured a cup. It smelled good and strong, the vapors curling into my face and soothing my eyes, and, holding the cup with both hands, I took a sip and felt it spread warmly and deliciously through my body. "Ahh!"

I looked down at Charley. His big, calloused fingers were pinched delicately over an elk hair caddis, wrapping the shank with a threading tool. "Spring's a long ways off, Charley," I said, making conversation.

"Don't hurt to be prepared," he said, staring intently at the colored thread going around evenly, neatly, and bunching the hairs. "Besides, I never get a moment's peace with Enos always carping."

He tied the thread off, clipped it, touched it with a dot of glue, then removed the fly from the pliers and laid it next to others of the treacherous hatch, some elk hair caddis flies and some olive woolly worms. He selected a number twelve and looked up at me. "I'm sorry to hear about little Jenny. She's all right, you say?"

I took a sip of coffee. "Yes."

"That's good to hear. Real good." Charley clamped the hook in place and shook his head. "It don't make sense, these young'uns carrying on so. What gets into their heads?"

"I don't know." I looked over at Mrs. Barnhouse, who was pretending not to listen. "Where's Enos?" I asked, changing the subject.

"At the grange, I expect." He selected some pheasant hackles and held them up to the light. "Things are getting ugly there, I hear." He chuckled. "Enos is probably having a fine time."

232

"What have you heard?"

"Just bits and pieces. It doesn't look good. Seems Lance Hoolihan can't this time." He chuckled at his joke, then chose a hackle and trimmed it.

"Nothing else?"

"Nope. Heard some shots earlier—thought that was something, but it was only crazy Ned Dilbert shooting off some rounds into the air. Sheriff Bonner told him to knock it off or he'd confiscate his gun. *Confiscate*. I like that word. It has a very German sound to it," Charley said, shaking his head. "No offense, Tyler."

"None taken. I'm only half German. The other half agrees with you."

"I don't know what's come over that man," Charley grunted. "We'll just see about what gets confiscated come elections."

I looked over at Stu Dunnegan. The headlines of his paper read: "British Flyers Hold Off German Luftwaffe!" The picture showed a downed Messerschmitt 109 pilot at the mercy of some British farmers, who were holding him at bay with pitchforks and shotguns.

He looked up from the newspaper, and his eyes went automatically to the hair around my ears.

"Hello, Tyler."

"Stu."

"Need a haircut?"

"Not today."

He smiled, saw that my mind was elsewhere, then returned wistfully to the Battle of Britain.

Nils Johansson leaned over the counter and called, "Took? Where are you, Took? Come, boy!"

Took looked up from his play, then loped to the counter and carried the box out behind a sweetly smiling Mrs. Barnhouse, her large frame almost quivering with excitement at her good fortune.

"Now, Tyler, what can I do for you?" Nils asked me, coming around the counter and smiling.

"Nothing much, Nils. Just a few things." I pulled the list from my shirt pocket and began to read. "Some gauze; iodine; some Fels Naptha—here, you can sort it out," I said, suddenly feeling self-conscious about the list.

Nils took the piece of paper and looked it over, angling his head back to see through his glasses. "This won't take but a few minutes, son." He started away and then stopped. "Oh, by the way! You just tell your pa I've got the lumber ordered for his barn. As soon as it

233

comes in, why, we're going to build him the biggest and best barn you ever did see!"

"I'll tell him, Nils."

"And Billy—he likes his rifle?"

I grunted. "He sleeps with it."

The big Swede smiled happily. "Good, good," he said, not understanding the humor, then disappeared into one of the aisles.

I sipped at my coffee and watched Charley tie flies for a while. He was humming an old tune under his breath. It was getting dark outside, I could tell. The sun squares were deepening in color, and I could just feel it, feel it like a cloud passing overhead, everything dimming and cooling at the same time, only you know that dimming is temporary. You know that when the cloud passes everything will get bright and warm again. I knew that now it would only get colder and darker.

I looked around for a clock, but there weren't any. *Funny,* I thought for the first time, *that Nils doesn't keep track of the time.*

The little bell sounded over the door. Nils only keeps track of the traffic. I looked over, and it was Took coming through the door. He was headed back to the dust devils, I could see, but pulled up short when he saw me.

"Hey, Took," I said, lifting my cup.

He stared as if he had only just now seen me. His pale blue eyes, blinking, spread over his face behind the thick lenses with a perpetual gaze of wonder. The burns on his face and hands seemed to have healed well.

"Smoke any bees lately?" I asked.

He frowned. "Pa don't let me smoke bees no more."

"That's a shame."

"He says I got to stay away from ants too."

"Your pa knows best."

He stared at me. And then he broke off, and I watched him climb into the deepening light and resume his game with the twinkling particles of dust. The cat stretched its legs and flopped over on its other side.

I drank the rest of my coffee and set the cup down next to the stove.

Charley was struggling getting a fly started. The old tune he was humming got clipped by a string of expletives as he tried to get his big fingers out of the way. It was no use. He'd made a fine mess.

"Having trouble?"

"Not that I can't handle," Charley said, cursing. "It's a good thing Enos isn't here to wear me out."

Just then the little bell sounded, and Enos, on cue, galloped into the store as though he had ants crawling up his legs. He had an impish look on his face, like the look of a kid watching a flaming building get past the firemen.

"Hoo! Hoo!" the wiry little man squealed, letting the door bang dinging behind him.

Charley glanced up and grunted. "Speak the devil's name."

Enos glanced wildly over the store. "Well, there you are, Tyler!" he said, fixing his eyes on me. "Why ain't you over to the grange with your pa and Billy?"

"I have other business."

His eyes blazed wickedly. "Well, let me tell you, boy, there's going to be some fireworks, you can bet. Your pa's fit to be tied. Hoo! Hoo!" He slapped his knee. Then he looked down at what Charley was doing. "What'ya doin' there, Charley? Makin' bugs?"

Charley, to preserve dignity, refused comment. He placed his hand over the tangle of thread and looked up at Enos with a dead stare.

Enos chuckled. "I see you got glue on your fingers again. You really should steer clear of matters beyond your reach, Charley."

Charley cleared his lungs with a grunt. "You come back just to torment me?"

"Shoot, no. I came to get you. Didn't want you to miss the doings over to the grange."

"Well, you can just about face and haul your tail out of here, 'cause I ain't going."

"Ain't going?"

"You heard me."

"You're gonna miss it, Charley. There's gonna be some shootin' or a lynchin', as sure as I'm standing here."

Charley scratched his thick bull neck with his free hand. "I swear, Enos—" he scowled "—if the sun don't rise and fall on some little wickedness, you'd consider the day a loss."

"There's gratitude for you," Enos said with a snort. He looked for the coffee can on the floor, picked it up, and spit into it.

He looked at me. "Did you hear what he said? Did you? Here's my good friend, my pal of forty-odd years, a fellow veteran of the Great War who lets me beat him all the time in checkers, talking to me like that. It don't figure. Here I try to include him in matters of some

235

importance, to repay him a little kindness, and this is the thanks I get."

He twisted an eye on the snarl of thread spilling out from Charley's thick hand and grinned, adding, "But I can see old pal Charley, here, has more exciting things to tend to."

Charley looked up at him coldly. "Yes, so I suggest you leave me tend to them."

Enos shot me a conspiratorial wink, as if I were in on his little game.

"I suppose you're right," he said. "Might be too much excitement for you, with your game leg and all." Then he brightened with a thought. "Say! Maybe that old goat Stivers and them other hens'll ask you over to speak at one of their tea parties. You're good at tea parties, ain't you, Charley? Sure you are! And you being an eligible bachelor like you are—a war hero too! You could regale all them sharp-eyed widder-women with your war stories—get their hearts to flutterin'."

"Get out before I stuff you in that coffee can," Charley growled.

Enos, still grinning, shook his head and clucked his tongue. "Well, I tried. But it's pitiful, truly pitiful."

He looked at me, the wildness jumping back into his eyes. "Hoo, hoo! Your pa! I swear, he's something! Only man in this county with any backbone to speak of." Then he turned and galloped out of the store, head thrust forward, giggling like some unfettered imp.

Charley looked down at the mess on the table, shook his head with a groan, and gave it up.

The gas bell rang outside, and Took looked out the window. He jumped to his feet and hurried to the door. However, on the way out, he was backed into the door frame by the menacing bulk of Booster Fisk. The boy tried to get out of Booster's path, stepping sideways, back and forth, awkwardly, but he only managed to block the doorway.

"Get out of my way, moron," Booster snarled, pushing him to one side.

Took stepped quickly behind the counter and stared wide-eyed at Booster.

Nils appeared from the aisles. The rest of us in the place glared at Booster. I knew I was flushed with anger.

Booster chortled, showing the gap in his teeth. He went over to the counter, pushed the bent bill of his Stetson off his face, and leaned against the glass with his elbow. "As I live and breathe," he chuckled, laying the heel of one boot on the pointy toe of the other. "If it ain't

Tyler Hochreiter. Well, what'ya know? Didn't expect to find you in here, not with your pa and brother over to the grange."

I glanced out through the door, and I could see Arly and Nate in the truck, both of them looking at the store, and I felt everything go tight inside of me.

"Hey, Hochreiter, I'm talking to you," Booster said. "Or maybe you only answer to 'preacher boy' these days."

I glared at him.

"Cat got your tongue?" He chuckled throatily. "Or maybe something else does." Then he stood up, screwing his back to us, moving slowly, lifting his feet and flapping both his arms like a chicken. *"Bwuk, bwuk, bwuk."*

I wanted to tear his head off.

Nils stepped forward. "We don't want any trouble in here, Booster."

"Trouble?" Booster made a full rotation, clucking and flapping. Then, leaning back against the counter on his elbows, boot heel on pointy toe, he scowled at me. "Who's causing any trouble? I just asked the preacher boy here a friendly question, is all. I might want him to come teach me a Sunday school lesson or something."

"Or something," Stu mumbled to himself with uncharacteristic umbrage.

"We don't want any trouble," Nils said.

Booster glanced at him. "I just come in for a tin of Red Man. Ain't this a store?"

"We don't haff any."

"What's that?" Booster laughed. "Why, Nils, I can see some right there, big as life," he said, pointing to the tins on the shelf behind the counter.

"We don't haff any for the likes of you."

"For the likes of me?" He feigned being hurt. "Now is that a Christian thing for you to say, Nils?" He looked over at me. "Tell me, preacher boy. What's your Bible got to say about a thing like that?"

I still wanted to tear his head off.

Nils stepped up beside me and frowned at the Fisk boy. "You want trouble, then I call the sheriff."

Booster chuckled, showing his gap. "The sheriff? Ain't no need to trouble the sheriff," he said. "He's got his hands full down at the grange, cooling down all them hotheads." He shook his head. "I can't imagine how it is people can't abide by the law."

Charley stood up, his big fists doubled. Even Stu folded his paper, neatly, and got to his feet.

"Maybe you're a little hard of hearing," Charley said in a low voice.

Booster looked at Charley, and I saw the grin tighten on his face for just a moment, then widen as he caught himself.

Just then Arly came in and paused just inside the store, holding the door open. He and I exchanged looks.

"Everything all right, Boos?"

Booster grunted. "Shoot. Ain't nothin' in here I can't handle, little brother."

Charley stepped forward, limping, and stood beside me. I'd never realized how big he was until that moment. Big old Charley, the ex-Marine captain, hero of Belleau Wood and Stillwater County, the faded tattoos just showing on his big forearms beneath the rolled-up sleeves.

Booster frowned at him. "This ain't none of your concern, old man," he said, hiding it well this time. "Why, you're liable to get yourself hurt, all gimped up like you are."

"That's right, Boos." Arly laughed. "Somebody may think he ain't nothin' but a lame dog and put a bullet through his tired head."

Charley picked up an ax handle from the barrel next to the counter and laid it in his hand. "You boys best be moving along," he said with a deadly tone now. "This old dog can still whoop your sorry hides from sunup to sundown."

Booster looked at the ax handle, then he grinned at me, showing off his sparse dental work. "Always got your friends around you, don't you, preacher boy?" He chuckled. "The Lord looks after His own, they say. Well, not for long He don't. We got you this time. Ain't nothin' in your Bible gonna keep your pa from gettin' knocked off his high horse. We'll see how many friends you got then. He'll come beggin', you can bet."

Arly laughed from the door. "That's right, Boos," he chortled. "I bet he don't get fifty cents on the dollar for them beeves of his. What you bet he don't?"

I compressed my lips. "You've had your little party," I said, "now clear out."

Booster chuckled. Then his expression went mean. He thrust a finger at me. "You think I'm having a party now, preacher boy, you ain't seen a party!"

Arly grinned at me.

Then Booster turned and strode toward the door. He stopped in front of Took and growled at him through his teeth.

The boy jumped back, then looked at his father and ran over to him.

Booster glared at me from the door, with that wicked grin of his spread over his face. "Guess we'll just have to go over to the drugstore, little brother, to get what we need, what'ya say?"

Arly's face went blank. "Huh? Yeah, that's right," he said, going along with it.

"Say, that reminds me!" Booster said. "I know a pretty little number over there who's just achin' to give me a big kiss. You know the one—big blue eyes, long pretty hair . . ."

Arly chortled again, getting it now. "Yeah, that's right."

I lunged at them, but Charley caught my arms.

"It's a sucker play, Tyler," he said.

The door slammed, ringing the little bell, and I could hear Booster and Arly laughing all the way out to their truck. They climbed into the cab, looking back at me through the door and grinning, and then the pickup sped away with a squeal of tires and smoke.

I looked down at the floor, allowing my thoughts to clear. But they wouldn't clear. I looked out the door again.

I felt Charley's big hand on my shoulder. "You go over there and you're playin' into their hand," he said, reading my thoughts.

I looked at him. "I got no other hand to play, Charley."

He shook his head. "No, I don't suppose you do, son."

Nils was holding Mama's items in one hand and the little piece of paper in the other. He looked confused.

"I'll be by for those in a little while, Nils," I said.

I grabbed the ax handle out of Charley's hand, then I walked out of the store.

Took followed me outside, with his eyes big and pale blue and spread out, blinking behind the thick lenses. He followed me to the street and stood staring as I mounted my horse.

28

The faces of the old brick buildings were red and glowing fiercely where the sun struck across them with sharp wedges of light. It was colder now, considerably colder, with the shadows purpling in the niches and alleyways, and I knew that the glow was only temporary, that it was a kind of last hurrah for the day and then the night would come, gathering into the shadows.

Ginger walked obediently along, her shapely head nodding happily as her iron shoes clip-clopped echoingly over the pitted and cracked asphalt street, clear of people now. Beside the hollow clap of her feet, there wasn't a sound but the occasional shrill cry of wind advancing from the northern front over the buttes. And there was accompanying it the pervading fear in the air and something that clung to my throat and made me feel sick to my stomach.

I wondered for a moment where all the people had gone—the town seemed deserted—and I wondered for a moment what Papa and Billy were doing down at the grange hall. But I couldn't think about them just now, couldn't think of anything right now, and so I put away thoughts of them and everything else.

The drugstore was just around the corner. It was situated in the crown of a long bend in the road, a sidewalk going along in front of it, with a clothing store on the far side—that is, to the east—and a hardware store on the western side, the latter being separated from the drugstore by a large vacant lot lined with big trees. Beyond, to the north, was a deep ravine that flattened away to the enormous rim of tabling buttes, stretching dark and purple, forever it seemed, against the lowering sky.

As I turned onto the street, I felt a lump swelling in my throat, preparing for it, and then I saw the drugstore ahead, and everything went flat inside my gut, smoothing the lump out into a dead cold numbness. I had hoped it would not be there, that it had only been an idle boast of churlish bravado, but it was there all right. In the long shadows spread over the ground was the Fisk truck, parked at a careless angle in the hard pack and weeds beside the store.

Nate was standing outside, next to the truck, with his arms folded —watching the place, I presumed—his head lowered in some sullen contemplation. His head shot up at the sound of my horse, and he reeled away from the truck, his eyes suddenly quick and wary, watching as I rode up to him. His head jerked several times toward the store, and then he fixed on me.

I charged Ginger between Nate and the store, to cut him off, then I swung out of the saddle and came at him, a piggin' string in my hand and pointing the ax handle at him as if I meant to use it.

He backed toward the truck, his eyes darting from the ax to inside the store where it was well lit and where his brothers were no doubt conducting some foul business.

"I got no quarrel with you, Ty," he said.

"Well, I've got one with you." I pushed his shoulder, raising the handle over my head. "Turn around."

"Hey! What're—"

"I said turn around." I took hold of his left arm and shoved him against the truck, pressing his face against the window panel. He tried to resist, but I jabbed the butt of the ax handle into his ribs, and he submitted. Then I pulled his left arm up into a half nelson and set the ax handle against the truck.

"Ow! You're breaking my arm."

"Quit squirming then."

Nate jerked his head over his shoulder at me and swore. "I said I ain't got no quarrel with you, Ty. You ain't got no call for this. I ain't done nothing."

"Is that right?" I said, grabbing his right hand and tying both of them behind his back with the length of rope. "You tell that to my sister."

"Your sister? What's she got to do with this?" Suddenly his face lost its color. "What do you mean? I ain't done nothing to her."

I jabbed him in the ribs with my fist. "Didn't do nothing, huh?"

I spun him around and glared into his face. I felt the Hochreiter deadliness rise in me, darkly, a crouching tawniness that wanted to kill him. "My little sister's at home in bed with cut wrists because you didn't do nothing. Is that what you're telling me?" I spoke lowly, evenly, in perfect deliberate control, and that's when I knew that the blood of Cain was in me. "What's the matter, Nate? You look a little peaked."

I could see the fear crawl up into his eyes. "What're you talking about?"

"Didn't hear, huh?" I said coldly.

"I told you I didn't do nothing. I don't know anything about cut wrists."

"Shut up." I shoved him against the door and tied his hands to the handle. "This ought to keep you out of the way for a while."

He pulled at the ropes, but he was held fast.

"You ain't going nowhere," I said, testing the knots. I locked the door behind him so it wouldn't swing open.

"What're you gonna do?"

"When I get through with this, you and me are going to have a little talk."

"I ain't got nothing to say to you," he sneered. "Besides, my brothers are going to kill you."

"You think so?"

"I know so."

"We'll just see about that, won't we?"

"You ain't gonna get away with this, Hochreiter!" Nate growled. "You hear me? They're gonna take you apart!"

"You just don't know when to shut up, do you?" I tore off the front of his shirt.

"What are you doin'?"

"This," I said, gagging him. "I'm sick of hearing the sound of your voice. There!"

He glowered at me, and he mumbled something through the gag.

I chuckled hollowly, picked up the ax handle, then walked away from him, walked past the streetlight on the curb, feeling the gathering darkness of the beast in me.

The two beautiful cutout figures in the display window of the drugstore, who were extolling the virtues of wearing Dr. Scholl's footwear on the beach, followed me with their gleaming white teeth and their perpetually happy eyes. I pushed the door open and went inside.

The store was bright and cheery in the incandescent lighting, and the song "Ain't Misbehavin'" was playing on the Wurlitzer. I glanced over the place with a quick sweep and saw that the store was empty but for the movement off to my right. I looked over at the fountain area, and I saw that Booster had Kate pinned behind the counter and was advancing toward her.

"Come on, Kate, gimme a kiss," he was saying, as he backed her toward the wall. "Just a little kiss." He had that wicked-looking grin on his face, his head thrust forward, chin forward, and his hat pushed back off his face, showing that he was enjoying himself. His right hand was moving along the Formica counter and the other one sliding over the chromium cook station, both of them inching menacingly toward Kate.

Kate was scowling at him, but she looked frightened. She had a kitchen knife in her hand, holding it out before her. "You come any closer, and I'm going to hurt you. I swear, I'll hurt you, Booster."

Booster chuckled, stepping closer, eyeing the tip of the knife and eyeing Kate. "Come on now, darlin', ain't no need for that. All I want is a little kiss. Ain't no harm in a little kiss, is there?"

Arly was standing between the counter and me, his back to the door. He was watching Booster and laughing, his hat tilted back on his head, getting a big charge out of it, I could tell. And as he turned to see who had come into the store, still laughing and grinning, I laid the flat of the ax handle across his brow, and he went down like a head-shot steer.

Booster looked over at the noise, and so did Kate.

She brightened when she saw that it was me and shrieked, "Tyler! Thank God!"

Booster looked at Arly, prostrate on the floor, then he saw the ax handle in my hand, and I could see the color jump into his neck and face. He came around the counter, pulling his Stetson down, never taking his eyes off mine, except to glance at Arly and then to look out the door for Nate. I could see bewilderment glint in his eyes, mixing in with the meanness. And then as he got around in front of the chrome stools, he advanced and faced me, his fists flexing and unflexing and his eyes burning with meanness and hate.

I saw Kate move behind the counter, saw a quick reflection of her in the mirror, and then I didn't see her. For all I could see now, or care about seeing at the moment, was Booster Fisk, and knowing that it was going to go to blows and wanting it to. Yes, wanting it to.

A thought crossed my mind about Nate, that he might have gotten loose somehow, and I almost turned to see if he had come into the store behind me. But I didn't. That would have been worse than leading with my right. I wouldn't make that mistake again.

"You'll pay for what you done to my brother, Hochreiter," Booster snarled. He looked at the ax handle, then glowered back at me. "I swear you're gonna pay for it."

"Anytime you want to collect," I said, with that cool deliberate deadliness.

Booster grunted. "Mighty big talk for a coward holding a club in his hand."

I tossed the ax handle, and it knocked, skittering, against the linoleum tiles. "Come on, then," I said, gesturing to him.

He glanced furtively over my shoulder at the door again, as though I didn't know what he was doing or who was outside.

"Don't worry about Nate," I said. "He's all tied up with something at the moment. It's just you and me now."

Booster grinned. But I could see his mind assimilating the information, the meanness rising, and he got a singular look on his face. And then as he edged forward, his fists doubled and rising to his chest, there was a sudden, hollow, metal sound, and his eyes shot open. He looked at me for a second, stunned, with one of his eyes losing its orbit and blinking to the center of his nose bridge and the other fixed and vacant. Then he fell headlong to the floor.

Kate was standing behind him with both hands holding fast to an iron skillet. She looked down at him, astonished. "Is he dead? I didn't mean to hit him so hard."

I was incredulous. I looked at the skillet again and then down at Booster, trying to tie the two together. It took a moment for my mind and eyes to connect, as I stooped down to check his pulse. "Well, you didn't kill him," I said, shaking my head. "But you knocked him colder than a trout in December." I looked up at her. "You all right?"

"I'm fine." Kate lowered the skillet and scowled at Booster. "That bully."

"Did he touch you?"

"No."

"If he touched you . . ."

"He didn't touch me," Kate insisted.

I stood up and glanced over at Arly, sprawled on the floor, his face flattened against the red-and-white tiles and his mouth agape. There was a mat of blood in his hair.

Arly groaned, stirring to life, but he wasn't going anywhere.

My mind cleared as I looked at the two of them lying at my feet, still breathing. *Thank God, still breathing.* A shudder went through me, jolting my thoughts into place, feeling the rush of the thing, the sudden terror of realization, and then the crouching tawniness spooking and flashing into the hills. *Thank You, God.* I shrugged off the adrenaline, feeling a little nauseous, then letting it go in a single cleansing breath.

"Are you all right, Tyler?"

"What? Er . . . yes."

"You don't look well," Kate said. "Oh, Tyler, what a stupid thing for me to say. I'm so sorry. Is it true what I heard about Jenny? That she cut her wrists?"

I looked at her abruptly. "Who told you? It doesn't matter," I quickly answered myself.

"Then it's true," Kate said, searching my eyes. "She cut her wrists. Is she all right?"

"She's fine."

"Thank God."

"Yes."

"Why, Tyler? Why would she do a crazy thing like that? She's just a kid."

"That's right, she's just a kid. A crazy kid," I said. "Here, let me take that. You might hurt yourself with it." I took the skillet and laid it on the nearest shelf.

"You're sure she's all right?"

"She's fine."

"I'll go out to the ranch this afternoon."

"No, Kate, she doesn't need to see people right now. Doc Turner says she just needs a lot of rest and fluids." I smiled at her. "Really, she's going to be OK."

Kate searched my eyes, then backed away. "Thank heavens," she said, reflecting on it. And reflecting on it, she noticed my mouth. "What happened to your lip?"

"What?" I touched my mouth. "Oh, that. It's nothing."

"Don't tell me nothing," Kate said, angling my face toward the overhead light. "It's something. Your lip is swollen. Cut too, I can see."

"It's nothing," I insisted.

"Nothing, huh?"

"Hey! Ouch! Don't touch it!"

She looked me in the eye.

I looked away.

"Tyler Hochreiter, who did this?" she demanded. "Tell me." She waited a moment. "It was your father, wasn't it? What happened?"

I grunted. "When an irresistible force meets an immovable object, something always bleeds."

"And your face is always that something."

"Not always," I said, glancing down at Booster, who lay still, the crown of his Stetson all smashed in the back. Kate had really whacked him good.

"Can I kiss it and make it better?" she asked, moving closer and putting her hand on my face.

"Do, please."

She kissed me lightly on the corner of my mouth. "How's that?"

"Not bad," I smiled. *Ahh! Those wild strawberries. Fields of them, and everything blue and bright overhead.* "Better try again, though—I was struck by an irresistible force, remember?"

"I thought you were the irresistible force."

"Maybe where girls are concerned."

She raised an eyebrow at me. "Girls?"

"Girl," I corrected.

"Well, you can be irresistible here in Columbus—" she smiled "—but I don't want any irresistible forces up in Chicago."

Uh-oh, I thought. I had forgotten about Chicago.

Booster groaned, distracting my attention. And then Arly groaned. They looked awful.

"What do we do with them?" Kate asked, frowning down at them. "We can't just leave them here. What would Mrs. Stivers say?" She clucked her tongue. "No. Wouldn't do at all."

"Hmm. I don't know," I said, feeling suddenly giddy. "We could whack 'em again, I suppose."

"We can't keep whacking them. We've only got the one skillet." She giggled.

"Swell. Never enough skillets around when you need 'em. Don't suppose we could stuff 'em in the bins out back?"

Kate shook her head. "Mr. Turnbull is very particular about what kind of trash we set out."

"Say, where is he, anyway? Making more deliveries?" I chuckled. "I haven't seen much of that old boy since Coon Ebers died and left behind that pretty widow of his." I looked down at the Fisk boys. "I know what I'll do with them. I'll drag them outside. Maybe the coyotes will haul 'em off."

Kate giggled again. I loved it when she laughed, bubbling over in cascades of splashing guilelessness. But it was no good this time, for I knew I had to tell her about Chicago.

Kate's smile became a look of concern. "What is it, Ty? You're sure Jenny's all right?"

I looked at her. "She's fine, Kate," I said. "Just fine. But over the next few weeks you can bet she's going to need someone around to help her through it.

"I can't imagine," Kate said, pinching her lips, thinking, as she always thought about others, and then brightening. "Maybe I could take some time off—a week, maybe two. I've been working here two years, and I've never asked Mr. Turnbull for time off. I could go out to the ranch—maybe stay there and help your mama around the house. You know, cook meals and such."

"No, that's not it," I said.

"What's not it? Is there more? Tyler, you're hiding something from me, aren't you? There's something else."

I couldn't hide anything from Kate. Never could. I looked into her hazel eyes, falsely bright in the artificial light and not showing the beauty of her real highlights, and searched for the right words. The Cole Porter song "My Heart Belongs to Daddy" was playing now, but that didn't help any. "Well, there is something . . ." I said, glancing away and wondering just then who had played the records on the Wurlitzer.

A clatter of hooves outside interrupted our conversation, and I suddenly remembered Nate.

I looked out the door. The glow was gone out of the sunset, and everything was drenched now in the blood red light of the advancing storm front, cold and mean and suddenly scary.

And then a chestnut horse with white socks flashed by the door, and, through the storefront window, beyond the two forever happy cutouts, I saw a dark shape with a mane of black hair, flying off the horse and running toward Nate Fisk.

"Oh, no," I thought aloud.

"What is it?" Kate asked.

"Sammy!"

29

Nate was bent away from the truck when I saw him. His hands were still tied behind his back, holding him fast to the door handle, and the twilight showed him clearly in silhouette against the splash of the solitary streetlamp, now lighted, and the deep bluing red of the sky beyond.

Sammy Two Feathers was driving his fists into his face and stomach. Nate was groaning, his head hanging, and Sammy was giving him a terrible beating.

"Sammy!" I shouted over the wind.

Kate came up beside me and looked out the door. "What is it?"

"Stay here!" I said, running out of the drugstore into the sudden cold. "Don't, Sammy!"

The winds were fierce and untoward and blowing every which way, howling like Furies past my face and ears and pushing me off course. And as I ran toward the truck, head and body inclined to the wind, I saw the horses trotting loose-reined up and down the street, whickering and crow-hopping and panicked in their sudden thrilling freedom, and everything looking reckless and gone to the devil.

"Sammy!" I shouted.

Whether or not he heard me, or whether he simply didn't care, the Crow boy drove another fist into Nate's stomach, and Nate bent over it with a groan.

Then I saw the flash of silver along the quick arcing of a deadly crescent, and I knew that Sammy had pulled out his long-bladed knife.

"Sammy, don't!" I yelled, running up to him. "Sammy!"

He turned on me, his mass of black hair lying flat on the wind, and I could see the murder in his eyes, glinting like two fiery red coals. He yanked Nate's head up by his hair and lay the edge of the blade against his throat. "Stay away from me, rancher boy," Sammy threatened, "or so help me, I'll cut him."

I could see he meant it.

Nate stared at me, his eyes pleading, and it was the first time in my life I had ever seen such fear in someone's eyes—someone who knew he was going to die.

"Take it easy, Sammy," I said, holding up my hands, pleading with him now as I stepped cautiously forward. "Come on, Sammy. This won't solve any problems."

"He hurt Jenny," Sammy said, not looking at me. He was looking into Nate's face with vengeful eyes.

Nate blinked at him, cold terror tearing at his features.

"I know he hurt Jenny," I said. "He's gonna pay for that, but this isn't the way."

"He is scum. He does not deserve to live."

"I don't expect any of us do," I said. "But this will go hard on you."

"I don't care."

"Think of your mama, Sammy," I said. "Think of your mama. She needs you. You've got a good job now. Papa's gonna keep you on at the ranch. You got a chance to turn it around. Won't do anybody or your mama any good, you getting thrown in jail."

The point of the blade hesitated, flashed, then, with a darting flick of the edge, the piggin' string was cut. Nate slumped forward to the ground, knees first, just catching his fall with his hands. Then Sammy, quick as a flash, flew upon him and straddled his back. He took hold of Nate's hair, pulling back on his head, then he slipped the knife around to his forehead and cut off a hank of hair, leaving a neatly shorn patch of white scalp, and he let the head drop forward.

Sammy jumped off Nate's back and thrust the shock of hair against the blood red sky, screaming a Crow war cry.

Nate foundered on the ground, his shoulders hunched, and his eyes blinking down at the hard pack between his hands.

Just then I heard an echoing roar approaching us rapidly from the direction of the grange hall. Both Sammy and I turned as a truck sped into view, following the long curve of road past the drugstore and heading east out of town on the road leading to the Fisk ranch. It was Ned Dilbert, I could see, bent over the wheel, his eyes glaring with mischief. A few moments later three more trucks rumbled into view, clearly with a singular purpose, and then the drivers were slowing down behind the runaway horses, who were kicking and crossing the street, back and forth.

The men glanced over at the three of us in the vacant lot, and seeing Sammy with his knife and the form of Nate Fisk on his knees, they pulled over against the far curb, perhaps thirty yards west of our position.

There were several men in each truck bed, many of them holding rifles and shotguns, every one of their faces turned in our direction and their eyes glinting with grim wonder.

Sammy turned and glared at me. He grinned with a triumphant flash of teeth and, shaking the thatch of hair, said, "This is good coup! Plenty good coup!" He spat contemptuously at Nate. Then with a laughing bark he raced across the vacant lot that separated the drugstore from the hardware, through the heavy dark trees lining the perimeter, and away into the shadowy labyrinth of the alleys.

"That you, Tyler Hochreiter?" a man called from across the street, the wind carrying well his voice.

"It's me," I returned, having to shout into the face of it.

"Everything all right?"

"Sure. Everything's fine."

"Who was that buck run off?"

"It was Sammy, one of our hands."

A man in one of the truck beds stood up and pointed in my direction. "Say! Ain't that one of them Fisk boys on the ground?"

"Why sure!" one of them yelled. "It's the youngest one!"

That caused an immediate stir.

Two more trucks rattled alongside the others and stopped, their engines idling and popping, and then Ned Dilbert came back, passing by us in the opposite direction, curving away, then getting out of his truck and asking what had caused the holdup. The men in the cabs conferred briefly with one another, ignoring Ned, looking occasionally over at Nate and me.

Just then the horses came galloping back down the street, crossing in front of the men, no longer crow-hopping and whickering and the wildness gone out of their eyes. They trotted over to me, I patted Ginger on the neck, then the two of them moved briskly off toward the line of trees across the lot, reins dragging, and began to graze amid the long grasses there.

Then everyone climbed out of the trucks, all of them standing in a dark line across the street beyond the reach of the solitary streetlight, as many as fifty men, wearing mackinaw shirts and scotch caps and holding rifles and shotguns. And for a moment there was just a low murmuring through their midst that the chilling wind would lift and then quell. I could see their eyes glimmering in the scant light, across the way at Nate. The fear that I had seen earlier on their faces at the grange had been eclipsed by something new.

The wind died down, but the chill remained, the temperature dropping by the minute it seemed, and a shiver scurried over my limbs. *Might snow any second,* I thought, glancing quickly at the black snarl of clouds overhead. I turned the collar up on my jacket, wishing I'd thought of a sweater.

The men swung their heads as Big Bob Baker emerged from one of the latter two trucks.

"That you, Tyler?" he called.

I could see his breath in the cold air. "It's me, Bob. How're you fellas? Cold, ain't it?"

"That one of the Fisk boys?" Big Bob asked, his bulk dominating the dark line of men.

I looked down at Nate, and he looked pathetic. He was wearing a pitiful expression, and, as the streetlight shone on his long black hair and neatly shorn scalp, the hate suddenly went out of me.

"Everything's fine, Bob!"

A low angry murmur rifled through the menacing silhouettes. There was a rattling of metal.

Big Bob started diagonally across the street, and the men followed him, the line pouring into a double file behind him, then stepping onto the sidewalk. Some of the men continued east along the street until they were perpendicular to Nate and me, then cut toward us, while others spread out over the vacant lot and angled toward us in a kind of pincer movement.

"Best you get inside, Tyler!" one of the men called out to me. "Don't want you getting hurt."

"Shut up!" Big Bob said to him. Big Bob was in the fulcrum of the pincers, coming straight at me.

"Everything's all right, Bob," I said, stepping in front of Nate. "Ain't no call for anything."

And then Kate stepped quickly out of the store onto the sidewalk, and a moment later Booster and Arly showed themselves in the doorway, rubbing their heads. I don't think either one of them even saw her, distracted as they were by their sore heads.

Arly looked pale and sickly in the light shining out from the store, and I don't think he saw anything thing at all. I'd hit him pretty hard, I could see. He was listing to one side, and he looked as if he might vomit.

Booster looked mean as ever; however, the shine was clearly off it. He glanced over at the line of men approaching from across the vacant lot, and I heard him grunt, grunt as if he were noting some fixture on the wall he didn't care for. For all I knew, he might have thought the men were coming into the store to buy Coca Colas.

Booster poked the new dent out of his hat, slapped it against his leg, then slapped it back on his head and looked in my direction. Seeing me, his face narrowed into a scowl.

"Hochreiter!" he shouted.

Big Bob saw the Fisk boys and stopped. "Some of you boys fetch them two," he ordered, and immediately a half dozen men ran over to them with ropes.

There was a scuffle, some punches thrown, but Booster and Arly were no match and were quickly subdued. Booster was cursing a blue streak until someone rapped him on the mouth. Then he got a confused look in his eyes as though it was beginning to dawn on him that maybe the men weren't there to buy Cokes.

Nate climbed unsteadily to his feet and groaned. He felt the bald place on his head, rubbing his fingers over it, and glanced over at the store. Fear jumped into his face again when he saw the men pulling his brothers along.

"Art—Harry—get a rope on that other'n there," Big Bob ordered.

Art Nicholson and Harry Beale separated from the line and took hold of Nate's arms, and I watched helplessly as they tied his hands behind his back. Nate gave no struggle.

"That's got him," Harry said, finishing a knot.

"What do you have to say for yourself now, young fella?" Art Nicholson, a normally soft-spoken man, added, sounding tough and out of character. "You ain't so cocksure of yourself now, are you?"

Nate said nothing.

Art gave him a little cuff beside his head, then got a satisfied look on his face as if he had accomplished something.

"What are you going to do?" I asked Big Bob.

"Yeah, what're we gonna do with these boys?" somebody asked.

The men, closing around the Fisk boys in two or three ranging groups, began to nod their heads and grunt maledictions to one another, as though seeing the Fisks tied had loosed some pent bravado. They looked around at one another and grinned. And then the grins melted into expressions of bewilderment. No one appeared to have the vaguest idea what to do with their prizes. Everyone turned and blinked at Big Bob.

Big Bob looked at me, but it was no longer Big Bob looking at me, not Big Bob the fiddle player with a fine tenor voice looking at me. It was someone whose pleasant, easygoing disposition and features had become something dark and inscrutable, the fear in his eyes having grown over his face into a violent mask.

Booster, past the initial shock of things apparently, glared at me. "Huh!" he grunted contemptuously. "Just you remember, Hochreiter," he snarled, "you and me ain't finished our business yet. I don't know how you got that lucky punch in without me seein' it, but I'll guarantee you it won't happen again."

I just shook my head.

"You're just a rotten coward like the rest of these yellow bellies." Booster laughed at them. Then he began to hurl insults at those around him. "Nothin' but a bunch of losers."

There was an immediate shift in the mood, like a sharp bit of wind going over a smoldering fire.

"Booster," I said. "Haven't you got the sense to keep your mouth shut?"

He turned his hateful eyes on me, struggled a moment to break free of the men holding him, then snarled, "You just wait till my pa shows up with the law, Hochreiter. You won't be so high and mighty." He sneered at those around him, bobbing his head and chortling. "You and the rest of these yellow skunks'll come crawlin' to Pa once your papers get called in. We'll see who laughs then."

The smoldering coals fluttered into a roaring flame.

"What are we waitin' for?" someone shouted angrily. "There's some fine-looking trees yonder," he suggested, pointing across the lot.

Several of the men's eyes suddenly burned bright with murder.

"Yeah, why not?"

"That's the idea!"

"Let's do it! Who's got some rope?"

"Somebody make up three nooses!"

"I'll get 'em," Ned Dilbert barked.

It was as though a little spark had gotten over the break into a forest of old timber, the wind carrying it, then touching off the dry tinder here and there to rage out of control. Those men along the periphery who were as yet uncommitted to anything but a good row, gaped at one another with astonishment, until they too, in twos and threes, were caught up and overwhelmed by the blaze.

Even I felt the heat of it licking at me, sucking me into it. I got scared, seeing it go through the ranks so fast and unchecked. "You can't do this, Bob," I tried to reason with him.

For a moment Big Bob's face seemed confused. Then it went taut.

I felt Kate's hands on my arm. She was trembling. "What are they going to do, Tyler?"

"Why, we're gonna lynch these boys, missy." One of the men holding Booster laughed. He slapped Booster on the back. "Hear that, smart mouth?"

Booster's head perked. He chuckled uncertainly. "Naw!"

"Yeah! Hang 'em."

"That's the idea! What do you say?"

"Let's hang 'em."

Nate looked at me and then at his brother. "Booster!" he called out. "Where's Pa, Booster?"

The other man holding Booster snickered. "Yeah, you tell us where your pa is, boy. We could make a clean sweep of this."

Booster was quiet now, his eyes ranging over the men with a startling revelation.

"You can't do this, Bob," I said. "It's murder."

"It's self-defense," somebody called out.

"That's right!"

"It's them or us!"

"You bet! Hang 'em!"

"Who's got the ropes?"

"Comin'!" Ned Dilbert squealed, running toward us.

"Hey, wait a minute!" Booster yelled, kicking his legs and butting his head at the men holding him. "You ain't gonna hang me. You ain't!" He began cursing and fighting something fierce, until someone tapped the side of his head with a rifle butt, and he slumped over.

"I'm going to call the sheriff!" Kate cried.

"You tell your girlie to keep it to herself, boy, or we'll find a rope for you too!"

I looked into the boil of silhouettes. "That you, Ned? Ned Dilbert?" I said, clenching my fists. "You just come on over here and try to put a rope on me."

Big Bob looked over his shoulder and said, "I told you to shut up, Ned. You just shut up, hear? Or we'll throw a rope on you."

Ned spat at the ground, then grinned maliciously at everyone.

"Bob, you're not serious about this, are you?" I said. "You're just trying to scare 'em a little, aren't you?"

No response.

"We're talking about a lynching here, Bob—a lynching!"

No response. Big Bob was looking across the lot at the dark line of trees.

"Bob, you've got to do something! This is murder!"

Big Bob started away.

"I'm going to call the sheriff," Kate said to me. She pushed her way through the men, then ran inside the store.

I saw Enos Stubbins in the crowd. "Enos! Are you in this too? Can't you do something?"

Enos just looked at me and chuckled. "It's something, ain't it?" Then he spat an arc of tobacco juice at his feet.

"Come on!" someone said, sensing the moment ripe. "Let's get to it!"

"Yeah! Let's get to it!"

There was a loud shout of angry voices, a bolstering kind of comradery that deadens the mind, and then the men led Booster and Arly and Nate away.

Booster revived some and dug his heels into the ground. "You ain't gonna hang me!" he shouted, twisting and swinging his head. "Ain't none of you yellow cowards gonna hang me!"

Arly was still too dazed to comprehend the moment, and he went along without too much trouble.

Nate was quiet. He kept looking over at Booster as though he was going to pull some trick out of his sleeve, and then he would look at me, his eyes staring with disbelief.

I walked alongside Big Bob, pleading with him, but his face was grim and set in a kind of trance. And I felt as though the world had suddenly come apart at the seams.

30

Reaching the trees at the far perimeter of the vacant lot, the men threw their ropes over the thick limb of a big elm, and the dangling nooses swung dark for several seconds against the red band of light that clung to the hills in the west. Someone thought to wrangle our two horses to make the hanging a more efficient one, but they were off grazing somewhere, out of reach along the ravine in the cool grasses, and so it was agreed upon to just hoist the boys up with several men to a rope.

The three boys were positioned beneath the nooses.

Booster was in the middle, struggling with his bonds and trying to keep the men from getting the rope over his head. He wagged his head and made a terrific fuss, but it was no use. The men, even though working with unpracticed dexterity, had the noose secured around his neck in little time; and as two men held his arms, several others stepped back to draw the rope taut.

Booster gave a little cry as the rope pulled at his throat, and he stood up on his toes as though to grasp a final drowning breath. When he realized that they had not yet hanged him, he caught himself, glanced menacingly around, and unleashed a string of profanities.

Arly was to his right. His shoulders hung loosely from his big frame, and his knees were slightly bent. He looked up calmly as the noose was lowered over his head, then blinked curiously at it—even nodded at one of the men, as though the man were fitting him for a new hat. I'd hit him harder than I intended, I thought, staring at him.

And Nate was to Booster's left, his shoulders back and arched against the horror, and his eyes jerked suddenly as the knot slid taut against his neck. He looked at it like a snared rabbit and began to cry, "Boos? Ain't you gonna do something, Boos?"

Booster ignored him and glared darkly at the crowd. "My pa'll have your heads for this," he threatened no one in particular. "I swear he'll have every last one of your sorry heads on a platter."

"I'd use my wind a little more constructively if I was in your shoes, boy," one of the men holding him said. "You may want to entreat the Almighty."

Booster snarled at him. "Well, you ain't in my shoes, you yellow coward, so shut up."

I wanted to tell him to shut up.

One of the men behind him chortled. "It's going to be a pleasurable sight seein' you dance over the pit of hell, sonny."

Nate looked over at me with those rabbit eyes, and I had to look away.

I suddenly felt sick to my stomach. I just stood staring at everyone—at my neighbors, my friends, most of whom I had known since childhood. I couldn't believe they were about to hang the Fisk boys.

I glanced reflectively across the vacant lot, windblown and dark now except for the solitary streetlamp in front of the drugstore, fifty yards away. It looked lonely in its little circle of light. A dog barked somewhere in the distance and complemented the loneliness. I sighed, feeling helpless and lost, feeling something dark and leathery flapping up from my sick stomach into my throat. I took a deep breath and blew out a wintry cloud of despair. And the dog complained against the sudden chill in the air.

Just then I could hear the familiar rattle of our truck approaching, the signature miss of the fourth cylinder and the stutter of the front left wheel bearing. I turned and saw the headlights sweeping around the curve, saw the pickup slowing, backfiring, and then the lights passing over the men in the field to light them briefly before falling away to the road. I could see Papa behind the wheel, the truck slowing further as he looked out the window at the crowd. Billy was in the middle, craning his head around Papa, and it looked like Jim Skeller on the other side of him.

The pickup pulled into the lot next to the Fisk truck, then rumbled back toward us, kicking up gravel and dust and the wind spreading the dust over the jiggling cones of light. And then the headlamps swung over the ground and shone on the crowd, and those caught in its sudden glare seemed unearthly apparitions rising, and they shielded their faces with their arms and looked away.

The truck ground to a stop. For just a moment, as the dust billowed over the lights, it seemed yellow smoke was spuming out of the earth as though it were on fire, and I was reminded of a passage from Dante's *Inferno* that described a scene in hell.

Then, seeing Papa's face through the smoke, seeing the hard, sure, masculine lines of it taking shape as the dust swirled away on a lick of wind, I felt the dark thing mount off my throat and flap into the air.

"You've gotta stop this, Pa," I said, running over to him. "They're going to hang the Fisk boys. All three of them!"

Papa said nothing, looking past me as he stepped out of the truck. He threw a quick, fierce look at the three Fisk boys, then strode over to Big Bob.

Billy climbed out and leaned his rifle against the seat next to the .45- 70. He looked past me at the men holding the ropes behind Arly, Booster, and Nate, and he blew out a long, low whistle. "Didn't think it'd come to this," he said. He shook his head. "Shoot! All three of 'em!"

"Where's Pa in this?" I asked him.

"I don't think it much matters anymore."

"It matters."

I looked over at Papa, and he was arguing with Big Bob. Jim Skeller was there now, and the men grouped around Papa and Big Bob were staring wildly at them, to see which way it would go.

Papa could argue the stripes off a skunk, but this was an animal of a different stripe. These were his friends, men he had known for years, ranching men, not killers; men who respected Papa, who stood in awe of the gift that burned in his breast. But something had changed, some pinprick had opened a rift in the heavenlies to expose a corner of devils, and the devils whispered wickedness into each man's soul.

"I hate this as much as you do, Bob," Papa said sternly. "You know I do. But this ain't right, and you know it. Hang the Fisk boys? Come on, Bob. What in the world has come over you?"

"It's out of my hands, Hank," Big Bob said, not looking at him. His face was set in that grotesque mask. "You know I never put in for a lynching."

Papa grunted, disgusted with him, I could see. "Well, you put in now, Bob."

Someone from the crowd shouted, "You were with us at the grange, Hank—full of fire and brimstone, as I recall. What happened?"

"Yeah, what happened?" another added. "The sight of a little rope give you cold feet, Hank?"

Papa glared at the man, and he shrank from the glare. Then Papa turned to the others and spoke with the authority of a general.

"Listen, men, you do this thing, and the law will be on you like white on rice. This ain't the way."

"Tell us the way, Hank," one said, without respect. "You want us to sit down and have a chat with him. Maybe we could meet with him after church Sunday."

Several laughed, without humor.

"Is that what you think we should do, Hank?"

"No, I don't," Papa said. I could see him fighting back the anger.

"Then what, Hank?" another man asked. "Do you think for a minute he's gonna listen to one word we say? You heard him today. You saw how he called in the federal marshal to back up his little game. He's declared war on us, Hank. He's declared war on our wives and children—on everything we hold dear. Well, I say we got to strike back. Ain't that right, fellas?"

"That's right," several agreed.

"Tell it, Hal."

"And hanging his three boys is going to stop that?" Papa countered. "Fisk won't have just one federal marshal doing his work, he'll have the entire state militia down on us."

"It don't matter," Hal continued. "We can't survive if we don't do anything. This way, at least we'll make Fisk hurt too."

"That's right, Hal!"

"Hit him where he may feel it," Hal added. "Assuming that a snake has feelings." His eyes narrowed on the Fisk boys. "Starve our children—well, we'll just see about that."

"There's other ways of making a man hurt without lynching his sons," Papa argued.

"Yeah? Tell us, Hank. Tell how we're gonna do that."

"Yeah, Hank. Let's hear your bright ideas."

Papa's face suddenly burned with anger. He shook his fist at the men. "First thing you can do is stop acting like a bunch of fool babies and start acting like men." Then he threw his hands on his hips and laughed contemptuously. "What am I saying? There ain't a man among you, as I can see."

"Ain't no call for that, Hank. No call at all."

"Shut up, Ned, and let him talk!" Wade Wanamacher said sharply. "One minute one way or t'other ain't gonna make no never mind."

The argument went back and forth for several minutes, heatedly, sometimes Papa gaining the upper hand, sometimes someone bringing up a point that swung it the other way. The thing that mattered though, as I could see it, was that they were talking, and the Fisk brothers, foul as they were, were still breathing. Papa always said if you talk a thing long enough you'll wear it out. Maybe that's what he was trying to do—wear it out until no one gave a hoot.

Then the wind blew and with it a change. Something changed in the faces of these once friendly, hard-working men. There had been some shift in the dynamics, some aberration in the collective soul. Everyone was shaking his head now, and I knew it was over.

Papa had lost.

The men rallied with a shout and pushed past him, and Papa just stared at the ground, his fedora pushed back, rubbing the back of his rugged neck with his right hand. He had failed. *Papa had failed.* It dawned on me in that moment that my father was not a superman, not a general in command of a proud and devoted division that would brave the fiery rifles for him, nor the soul-tender with his finger on the pulse of the land. The pulse had skipped a beat, and he had missed it. It dawned on me now in that terrible light that he was just another man who often couldn't fix things that were broken.

I glanced into the cab of our truck, saw Papa's rifle leaning against the seat next to Billy's, the Winchester Model '95, the model Teddy Roosevelt was so fond of, and I knew what I had to do.

I grabbed the rifle, chambered a round, then fired a shot over the crowd toward the distant bluffs.

Everyone turned, and for several stunned moments there wasn't a sound but the echoing report on the wind. And then even the wind tucked into the hills, and there was only silence.

"It's over!" I said, chambering another round, then leveling the muzzle at Big Bob's chest. "Tell 'em it's over, Bob, or so help me I'll shoot you dead."

Big Bob looked at me, amazed, then he looked at the rifle in my hands. Everyone else was looking at me too.

"Put that rifle down!" I heard Papa yell.

"No, Pa. Can't do it. I can't allow a lynching." I felt his eyes glaring at me. *Glare all you want,* I thought.

"Take it easy, Tyler," Wade Wanamacher said. "Let's talk this thing through."

I grunted. "Talk it through? No, Wade, your kind of talking only leads to the end of a rope. Time for talking's over. Tell 'em, Bob. Tell the men it's over. Tell everyone to go home."

260

There were a tense several moments. Scores of menacing eyes glimmered out from the huddles of dark silhouettes, a single thought burning through them. I felt a thick pulsing swell in my throat and realized that it was my heart; I hoped that I wouldn't faint. *O God, what am I doing?*

Thoughts rushed me, mocked me, flew about my head, screaming at me to put the rifle down and have done with this foolishness. *It's out of your hands, fool*, I thought. *Papa has failed, fool, has stumbled over the gift and shown himself mortal. What can you do?* But I knew, sighting along the rifle, that I had stepped over some invisible line from which I could not retreat—not and walk away with any sense of manhood or dignity.

Have mercy, Father. A prayer winged off my soul. *Have mercy on this fool of fools.*

The tension mounted and drew taut over the desperate scene, until I thought the air might shatter.

And then Art Haroldson stepped forward. "Tyler's right," he said, the toughness all gone out of his face. "It's over. What in the world are we doing here? Have we become savages, men? Have we? I ask you. What's become of us? What—" The words caught in his throat. Then he raised a hand to his face and began to weep.

Several men looked down at the ground. Others fidgeted embarrassedly, nudging the dirt with their boots or straightening their caps. Others, still, angled their heads and loosed their accumulated lipfuls. A collective shudder went through the crowd of dark men as the tension was released into the atmosphere.

Then Big Bob seemed to break out of a deep sleep. He coughed. His head bobbled as he looked into the faces of the men around him, his eyes sparking as though seeing them for the first time.

There was a long silence. No one said a word, looking at him, then looking at me with astonished eyes.

I lowered Papa's rifle.

It was over.

Someone took the .45- 70 from my hand. It was Papa, and he nodded his head at me.

"Ain't we gonna hang 'em?" Ned Dilbert said, breaking the silence.

His question melted on the wind. Art Haroldson turned and walked away, shaking his head. Two or three others followed. And then the whole of it began to break apart, the men leaving in quiet wonder with their heads bent in doleful attitudes. And the devils skulked sullenly away.

Ned Dilbert watched the crowd dispersing. "You mean we ain't gonna hang 'em?"

Big Bob looked at the little man. "Go home, Ned." He wiped his face with a handkerchief, then put it back in his coat pocket. He looked sad and tired as he turned and walked away.

The wind ripped down the street, blowing bits of paper and debris and dirt, the dirt stinging like tiny needles against my cheeks. The temperature had dropped considerably, and everything was dark overhead, except for that thin red band of color stretching over the mountains in the west like a long streamer of fire. I wiped my nose and wished again that I had remembered my sweater.

And then it began to snow. I could see the flakes, small at first and driving on the wind, then growing fat and fluffy as cornflakes, twinkling bright against the sky, floating down as the wind tucked in gentle swirls, and then going dark against the distant aureole of the streetlight. It seemed strange it's snowing in August, but in Stillwater County it snows in August sometimes, and when it does you can bet on a hard winter.

A couple of the men began to cut Arly's wrists free, and then Booster's. Booster was strangely quiet now, staring at me from beneath the dark shelf of his brow with a look of profound bewilderment. Who knows what he was thinking?

I looked over the hood of our truck and saw Kate exiting the drugstore and running toward us. She was yelling something, though I couldn't hear over the wind. Some of the men were gathered around Papa, the fear returning to their eyes as they asked him what they might do about Josiah. I watched him for a moment, seeing him in a new light and feeling the dark thing gone.

And then a movement caught the tail of my eye. Turning to it I saw Ned Dilbert step out of a disintegrating knot of men into the glare of the headlamps, black against the glare, holding his rifle, with his hands flexing on the stock and pistol grip. His face was impassive, like a face of dead stone, but I could see that something murderous had come over his eyes. I knew in that instant, looking at Ned as he started forward, levering a round into the chamber, that he was going to shoot Nate Fisk.

"No!" I shouted, running, holding Ned just inside my field of view. And beyond him, halfway across the lot, I could see Kate still running toward me and yelling something I couldn't understand.

And as I reached Nate I swung around and saw the rifle coming up on line with my chest, in slow motion it seemed, with everything in slow motion it seemed: my hands going up, Kate running toward me, shouting, and Papa turning with a hand outstretched, his eyes glaring wide; and a blur of man shapes turning on a gasp of wind, and then seeing the squinting red eye and the jerk of Ned Dilbert's shoulder and the long, bright tongue of orange licking out at me from the muzzle . . .

There was an interlude of silence—it seemed an eternity—during which the sum of my life and its purpose stood in sharp relief against the brightness of my mindscape. It was a terrible revelation. For I knew—beyond question I knew—that God was on His holy throne, sitting in unapproachable light as He dispensed justice and mercy, the goats gathered on His left and the sheep on His right.

In which fold am I, Father? I wondered in that flash of time. But I knew the answer. Yes, I knew. "Our God is a consuming fire," and the thought of it shook my frame to the core.

And then I felt a mule-kicking jolt of fire rip through me and hurl me across a vast void of weightlessness. And as I fell, forever falling along a long, dark tunnel toward a pinpoint of light, a crack of thunder sounded over me like the Voice of God, ballooning out to envelop me. *I will teach you mercy,* the Voice sounded, reminding me of His goodness. *I will teach you mercy,* sounded the refrain, and then the thunder rang off, with Kate's voice echoing clearly back to me through the peals:

"Tyler, don't! O God, no, my Tyler!"

And then the tunnel closed over her pretty face, and a flutter of snow froze on the air a moment before everything went black.

31

A graying light penetrated some black and dreamy mist. A single monotonous note hummed low over the mist. There was a dripping noise as well, somewhere off to the right, the drops sounding as though fallen from a great height.

Shapes gathered in the mist—vague, watery shapes that crowded oppressively close in the graying light. Definition was added to the shapes in degrees, and the humming and the dripping noises were added to the shapes, and the whole of it seemed, upon first waking glance, a vast and watery tomb.

The high-pitched wail of a baby—or what sounded like a baby—sounded as though from a great distance, all hollow and eerie, and it contributed an unearthly ambience to this shadowy place that encompassed me.

The image of Lucifer flashed in my mind, that elusive, tawny streak of color. Then out of the mist a single red eye came slowly, stalkingly, as though the big cat were creeping toward me out of the fog, advancing silently, peering intently at me, then settling with his tail flicking snakelike.

And beyond this image the dripping continued, falling . . . splashing . . . falling . . . splashing . . . torturing . . . and the humming noise droning without end . . . and from somewhere in the murky haze there was suddenly uttered what seemed a low and menacing growl.

Where am I? I wondered, feeling a prickling of fear pass through my limbs. *What happened?*

And then I remembered the squinting little red eye of Ned Dilbert glowering hatefully over the barrel of the rifle and the lapping tongue of fire stabbing out at me. A clap of pressure sounded somewhere in my chest, and I groaned out of reflex.

I've been shot. I remembered. *Am I dead?* The thought startled me. *Where am I, if I'm dead? Is this heaven? Is this—*

My heart began to race as I blinked in wonder against the black wall of fluid space. Then as my eyes began to adjust to the darkness, I saw a thin rubber tube extending vertically from my right forearm, leading up to a small dark shape—a bottle shape, I could tell—and the bottle suspended from some complicated apparatus of metal. I considered the thing for a moment, wondering what it could be.

And then I noticed the distinctive smells of ether and alcohol pervading the air, the sterile medicinal smells that usually accompany our first and last breaths in life, and a wave of relief passed warmly over me. *Hospital! That's it! I'm in the hospital. In a room . . . in a bed. I must be alive!*

Invigorated by this revelation, I glanced above me to my right, and there, looming suddenly out of the dark wall, was a machine of some kind, possessing a single, glowing red light. The machine made a humming noise, and the glowing red light, devoid of mind and feeling, seemed to be staring at me.

Beneath the machine was a sink. I could tell it was a sink, because I heard the monotonous clapping of water droplets as they were launched rhythmically from the lip of its faucet to plummet and spatter against the enamel basin. Relief was added to relief, as I recognized these at once to be the instruments of my mind's torture.

And then I heard the growl again, the elusive, menacing rattle of the predator. *Is that you, Lucifer?* I wondered, the thought entering my mind as I shifted my eyes across the nigritude of the room. Nothing. No big cat waiting atop some promontory of darkness and gathering to pounce.

I turned my head to the left, to the source of the graying light, and winced when excruciating pain radiated from a point five inches down and six inches to the left of my chin. An involuntary groan escaped my lips, for it felt as though something had leaped upon my chest and was clawing into my ribs. *O Jesus!*

I took several shallow breaths, allowing the pain to subside, and it ebbed away in petulant, nagging shudders. Then opening my eyes, I beheld a lighter shape—a window, I saw, beyond the black precipice of what had to be my bed—with a dark and bent shape in front of the window. *Papa.* The dark and bent shape was Papa.

I stared at him for a while, blinking several times to clear my eyes. I wasn't sure if he was awake, for he was sitting with his head lowered onto his chest in some brooding attitude. And then I heard him snore, and the snore trailed off with a growling rattle. *Ahh! There you are!*

Papa stirred in his chair, his head rising with a jerk and then lowering to settle on his chest, quieting, then his body settling into

265

that brooding slump of repose. After a few moments his breathing thickened, then rattled from some deep place in his throat, deep and catlike but no longer stalking and fearsome.

I watched him sleeping for several minutes and listened to the comforting purr. Suddenly I remembered him talking to Big Bob Baker and to the men, seeing the violence in their eyes, and then remembering the downcast look of Papa's face when he had finally lost it and the men were rushing past him to hang the Fisk boys. *I loved you in that moment, Papa, first loved you wholly and truly without the fear, and wishing then to hold onto that love and never have to let it go.* Then I remembered how everything had gone to fertilizer at the last, seeing the rifle coming up and nothing to do but run; *and, running, thinking how desperately I wanted to tell you that I loved you, Papa, and that I was going to stay on the ranch and that everything was going to be all right, but knowing as I looked into the hateful little eyes of Ned Dilbert that it was over and lost.*

I felt the kick of it again in my chest, and I let it subside, breathing it away slowly. Then I let go a melancholy sigh. I let those thoughts hang in the air, revisited them in whole and then in part, thought them through until they were worn out, and at some point I wondered what became of the Fisk brothers. There was nothing in that well, so I gave it up. And then, suddenly, threading through the void, through the alcohol and the ether smells in the room like a lingering breath on the air, came the ambushing scent of wild strawberries, and my thoughts were given over to a pleasant reverie.

Presently I heard the muffled approach of footsteps, echoing down some corridor and slowing to a stop outside the room. A door opened somewhere to my right, showing a vertical shard of light on the opposite wall, and then a shadow cut into the light, followed by footsteps across the linoleum—a woman, by the sound of the tread.

"Kate? Is that you?"

The woman laughed quietly. "It's grand to see you're back with the living," she said, feeling my wrist, then laying the cool palm of her hand against my forehead. "You gave us quite a start, lad. Quite a start, indeed."

"Mrs. McGlenister?"

"Saints! but ye sound disappointed." She turned and threw the light switch.

I winced from the sudden glare. It took a moment for the light to separate the room into color, to push the once dark and oppressive shapes away into their corners. I blinked up at her.

Emily McGlenister was a short, heavyset Irish woman in her mid-fifties, with fiery red hair and twinkling green eyes. And the eyes, intelligent and full of mischief, were set in round, happy red cheeks that bunched up like apples when she laughed, which was often.

In truth, she reminded me of a rather large elf, a jolly elf lady dressed in white dress, cap, stockings, and shoes, who had helped Doc Turner deliver every one of us Hochreiter kids into the world and subsequently tended to our myriad infirmities. There wasn't a single inch of our growing bodies that she hadn't poked, prodded, pinched, or pierced, and at a certain time in my metamorphosing chronicle of existence I remember growing profoundly embarrassed in her presence.

"Uh . . . no, I'm not disappointed."

She chuckled wryly. "Am I still your sweetheart, lad?" she said in a thick Irish brogue. "Your one and only true love?"

I felt my face flush. "Uh . . . sure, Mrs. McGlenister. Always and forever."

"Good. We shan't let dear Kate Morgan in on our little secret, shall we?" She smiled. "Here—open wide."

I obeyed without question, and she stuck a thermometer in my mouth. It tasted of alcohol and burned the swollen corner of my lip.

"Under the tongue now—there!" She stood back and looked at me with an appraising eye, her green eyes twinkling over some profound thought. "'Tis a grand lassie that Kate," she said, smiling. "Aye! Anyone would think she had the eyes for you the way she hovered and fretted about last night."

I nodded my head stupidly and mumbled something akin to "I know" through the thermometer, but it made no earthly sense.

The large elf woman laughed, shaking her head and the rest of her, then she checked the bottle of blood suspended over my right arm. "You're a very lucky boy," she said, jiggling the bottle, then fiddling with a small clamp.

I mumbled an affirmative "Mm-mmm."

"How do you feel?"

I mumbled a not so affirmative "Mm-mmm."

Mrs. McGlenister laughed. "Daft question, wouldn't ye say?"

Suddenly the baby wailed a lusty cry, and I followed the sound to the door with my eyes.

"Mrs. Ruiz," the nurse said, reading my question. "Eight pound five ounce bouncing bambino. That makes number eight." Her eyes twinkled, then she threw her head back and roared. "That old bessie throws another one, and Hector Ruiz will have enough to start his own baseball team!"

I tried to smile and almost lost the thermometer. I just caught it with my teeth.

"Here, now, let's see what manner of fire the devil's touched you with," Mrs. McGlenister said. She took the thermometer, angled her head as she rolled it in the light, slowing as the mercury came into view. She frowned.

"What's the verdict?" I asked.

"Just shy of a hundred."

"That's not so bad, is it?"

"It's a little up from last night," she said, shaking the mercury down, then laying the thermometer on the little stand next to the bed.

I didn't remember her taking my temperature, and I didn't want to ask her about it.

Mrs. McGlenister walked around to the other side of the bed and pulled the sheet off my chest. "Let me just have a look-see," she said.

I looked down to see what she was doing and saw a little blood spot showing through the white bandages.

"Never you mind," she scolded, lifting my chin.

And then I felt the dig of the heels in my shoulder and groaned.

"We'll see if we can't get you something for that," she said.

And then I remembered Papa. I looked over at him, and he was awake, sitting ramrod straight in the chair now with both hands on his knees, his brown fedora on his right knee, looking out of place and uncomfortable in the gray light that framed him. He looked the very picture of Bapa Otto, with his pale blue eyes staring at me across the bed, except that Papa's hair was sticking out every which way from his hat, and he had no rifle in his hand.

"Hello, Papa."

He nodded curtly. "Mornin', Tyler." His eyes darted from the bottle of blood, to the long thin tube, to my eyes. Then he stared at me for several long moments. "How're you doin', son?"

"All right," I said, then, adjusting my position, stifled a groan.

Papa looked at Mrs. McGlenister. "Em?"

"He's just fine, Henry," she said. Then she frowned, adding, "But *you* look awful."

Papa stiffened in his chair.

She walked over to Papa and raised the shade behind him. The morning light streamed into the room, and I could see through the frosted panes of the window that it was a bright and cold day and that it had snowed heavily during the night. The hills in the distance were covered, and I could see snow on the rooftops of the buildings in the town, and I saw it caked on the limbs of the trees and caked on the windowsill, and it made fluffy crescents against the panes.

"You been here all night?" Mrs. McGlenister asked Papa, pausing to regard his face in the light.

But Papa didn't answer her. He just stared at the spot of blood on my chest as though he hadn't heard her, looking austere and distant and seeming more like Bapa Otto than I'd ever noticed before.

"May I have a glass of water?" I asked Mrs. McGlenister, suddenly very thirsty.

"Water? Sure, laddie. I don't see that the old man would have any objections to that," she said, heading toward the sink against the right wall.

"And what 'old man' would you be referring to, Emily?" Doc Turner said as he walked heavily into the room.

The jolly elf lady didn't bat an eye as she brushed past him to the sink. "You, you old fossil." She smiled, winking around him at me. "You don't get yourself some sleep, I'll be tending to you next."

"I'll sleep next year."

She grunted.

Doc Turner looked at me with a resigned expression. "See what I have to put up with around here, Tyler? The troops are in open rebellion." His eyes were red-rimmed, his white hair tousled, and he looked tired to the bone. His stethoscope was draped around his neck and lying against the front of his white scrubs, and he was holding a large manila envelope in his hand. He looked across the bed at Papa and nodded his head. "Henry."

Papa nodded back. Then he glanced around the room and began to drum his fingers on his knees.

"Your mama will be pleased to hear you're awake," Doc Turner said.

"Where is she?"

"She and your brothers are out in the waiting room. I told them to hold off for a minute while I checked on you."

"Who's home with Jenny?"

Doc Turner smiled tiredly. "Don't you worry about your sister," he said. "She's in good hands." He pulled a chair from against the far wall, adjusted it next to the bed, and, laying the manila envelope at the foot of the bed, he sat down. He lifted his glasses and rubbed his eyes, pinching them together several times, then he fitted the stethoscope to his ears and pressed the cold end of the thing against my chest. He listened carefully to my heart and then to my lungs. The area to the left side of my chest was tender to his touch, and I winced involuntarily.

I glanced over at Papa, feeling embarrassed. His eyes were rapt, and then he settled back into his chair and glanced anxiously about the room, like some pauper suddenly finding himself awaiting the audience of the king.

"You took his temp?" the doctor asked the nurse.

"Ninety-nine point five," Mrs. McGlenister said clinically. "Could be a little infection started."

"Too soon," Doc Turner said. "Take a deep breath, son—let it out easy."

I did, and it smarted something fierce.

The doctor listened around. "Again, easy. Again. That's it." He unhooked the stethoscope and folded it around his neck. "Change his dressings in about an hour or so," he said to Mrs. McGlenister.

"Yes, Doctor." She handed me the glass of water. "Shall I give him something for his pain?"

"I'm all right," I said quickly.

"Just the same," the doctor said, writing something on the clipboard at the foot of my bed, "give him a quarter grain of morphine—see if that does it. Oh, and check to see if we have any more A-positive in the refrigerator."

Mrs. McGlenister clicked her heels, the way the German people do in those newsreels. "Yes, Doctor."

"None of that now," Doc Turner said, looking suddenly weary again.

Mrs. McGlenister winked at me, took my glass, then went out.

"How is he, Walt?" Papa said, having waited patiently to ask, I could tell. I detected a slight tremor in his voice.

Doc Turner regarded him for a moment. "His lungs are clear, Henry—heart sounds fine. We got most of the bone fragments out, but we'll want to keep him here for a few days to keep an eye on things, of course."

"Bone fragments?"

"From where the bullet grazed his ribs."

"Yes, of course," Papa said quietly as his eyes wandered to the spot of blood on my shoulder.

Doc Turner patted me on my legs. "Would you like to see?"

"See?"

The doctor chuckled as he stood up. He removed a wide x-ray film from the manila envelope, went over to a view box on the wall adjacent to the bed, and fixed the film against the glass. As he flicked a small switch the glass lighted, and I could see the shadowy outline of my skeleton, light against the murky haze of my fleshy parts.

I stared at it. It gave me an eerie feeling seeing my insides like that, but I was intrigued just the same and continued to stare.

I had seen x-rays of people's feet once in a drugstore in Billings. They had an x-ray machine there—clearly a novelty item to attract business—that you could put a dime in and it would take pictures of your skeleton. I never had a spare dime, or if I had I wouldn't have wasted it on pictures of my feet, but there were plenty of kids lined up to try it.

"The bullet deflected off two of your ribs," the doctor said, pointing to a wicked dark line on the film that meant nothing to me. "See this here—and here. These are the bone fragments. Nasty little things. Got most of them though. Then the bullet exited between your left scapula and clavicle. I don't know how you managed that, Tyler, unless you had your arm extended." He shook his head in amazement. "You're a very lucky boy." Then he added with a measure of disgust, "Not too many places a bullet can pass without tearing everything to hamburger."

I gaped incredulously at the doctor. "You mean the bullet passed *through* me?"

"That's right," he said. "Can't see it on the x-ray, but it went through you clean as a whistle."

"Then—"

"Once the bullet passed through you," he said, voicing my fears, "it struck Nate Fisk in the chest and lodged about an inch from his heart."

Suddenly I felt the blood leave my head. My mind glanced about in a bit of stupor as I looked up at him. "Is he—is he dead?"

"No, Tyler, he's alive," Doc Turner said. "I was able to extract the bullet and get him stabilized." He smiled at me, then turned off the light on the view box and returned the x-ray to the envelope. "It'll be touch and go for a while, but he's alive, thank God." He paused for a moment of reflection. "Thank God. Had you not stepped in front of him and deflected it, well—"

The doctor broke out of his thoughts and walked tiredly over to the bed. "No point in discussing the what-might-have-beens in the world, is there?" he said. "He's in the good Lord's hands now, and that's enough. I would say that His angels were working overtime last night with you two boys."

"Yes," I agreed, still reeling from the news.

"Thought you might like to have this," he said, fishing something out of his coat pocket. He handed it to me.

I gazed queerly at the misshapen bullet in my hand. *Just a little thing, really, a bullet,* I thought. *Not much to it at all.*

"Make a necklace or something with it," the doctor said, smiling wanly. He shook his head. "It was a foolish thing you did, Tyler," he said. "Brave . . . but foolish."

I made no response.

Doc Turner tousled my hair and turned to leave. "I'll go fetch your mama. She'll be wondering."

"Give me a minute, Walt," Papa said. He rose awkwardly to his feet, holding his hat with both hands. "Just a minute."

The doctor looked at Papa from the doorway. He glanced at me, then back at Papa. "All right, Henry."

Then he left, and I heard his heavy footsteps receding down the corridor.

Feeling Papa's eyes on me, I turned and saw that he was looking strangely at me.

He nodded his head and said, "Son . . ." He seemed to choke on the word, then he looked abruptly out the window, and the wintry morning light just caught a glistening of tears in his eyes.

32

Papa grunted disgustedly as he wiped his eyes. "Must've caught a piece of grit in the air."

I glanced away from him, feeling uncomfortable.

He turned his back to me and peered out at the wintry townscape, which from my vantage looked a replica of one of those Courier and Ives greeting cards—everything all bright and happy-looking, with here and there smears of bluish smoke curling from the chimneys of houses and shops, and bustling along the walks and streets were people wrapped in their winter coats with the flaps of their scotch caps pulled down over their ears against the chill morning air.

As he gazed out upon that happy scene, Papa's thick fingers edged around the brim of his hat as though they were imprinting his thoughts in the worn brown felt, then they went quiet, and he just stared out the window a long time.

I stared at his back, wondering what he was thinking, waiting for him to say something. But he didn't. He seemed content to observe the world's passing in a brooding silence.

So I looked up at the ceiling, looked at the level of blood in the bottle, then across the room at nothing, and then returned to his back. He hadn't moved. It was as though he had become integral to the picturesque scene framing him, a contrasting shape within the painting, dark against a field of white, lending to it negative space and depth.

"Looks like this one'll stick for a while," he said, rousing from some reverie and speaking in a voice I didn't recognize.

His voice startled me. "What?" I looked past him at the snow-capped roofs, receding gently, sloping away to the big trees lining the Yellowstone, and to the bridge going across it, and then beyond to the white hills, everything stark and brittle-looking against a wall of dark slate. "Yes, looks like it."

He shook his head. "This is something, ain't it?" he said, breathing in the scene like a greedy god. "I surely do love this time of year!

Good thing we got the hay up when we did, huh? Who'd of thought this?"

I wanted to say, "You did, Papa. You thought this. You decreed it." But instead I said, "It's something, all right."

He glanced quickly over his shoulder. "How're you feeling?"

"Swell."

"You're sure."

"Yes," I lied. My shoulder was hurting pretty bad. I was feeling a bit nauseous too.

"Emily will be along in a minute or so for the pain."

"Really, Pa, I'm fine."

"The doctor says you need it," Papa said, sliding momentarily back into the voice I recognized. "He knows what's best."

I said nothing. I didn't know what to say, so I just looked at him, feeling a desperate isolation beginning to close over me. It felt as though I had gotten caught on an elevator with a stranger, the doors closing, closed, with no place to go, with nothing in common with the stranger but an acute awareness of his presence and the compulsion to watch the arrow counting down the floors. Papa felt it too, I'm sure. The tension. The arrow marking an interminable descent.

His eyes looked suddenly lost on his face as he glanced about the room. He cleared his throat and slapped his leg lightly with his hat. "Nice room they put you in," he said. "Got your own sink and every-thing." He nudged the bedpan under the bed with the toe of his boot, and it made a hollow tin grating sound. "Got the latest in plumbing too, I see," he added, forcing a smile.

I started to laugh but was cut off by a stab of pain to my shoul-der. "What they do to Ned Dilbert?" I said, stifling a groan.

"You mean after Big Bob Baker beat the stuffing out of him?" He grunted sardonically. "Sheriff Bonner's got him locked up down at the jail, the little fool."

I had nothing to add to this, so as quickly as the squall of conver-sation had picked up it died, and a silence clapped over the room. I compressed my lips against the thickening vault of isolation.

Papa worked his thoughts around the rim of his hat during the interlude, then he looked at the swelling on my lip, and I could see remorse cloud over his face and a thought struggling to emerge from beneath the cloud. It was as though there were a pitched battle being waged there, and I remembered Sammy's words about the two lions.

Which one is he feeding now? I wondered.

"You hungry?" he asked, breaking the silence. "Want me to get you something?"

"No. Not just yet, thanks. Maybe in a little while." I was still feeling a bit queasy.

"I can call for some toast or something," he pressed. "They got a small cafeteria here, you know. Coffee? Doughnuts? Anything?"

"No, Pa. Really, I'm fine."

"You're sure?"

"Really."

And again the conversation sputtered to a halt. Again, a silent, desperate interlude.

Papa's eyes crept around it to the spot of blood on my shoulder. "They say that God looks after fools and Irishmen," he said. Then he grinned. "If that's true, then I expect the bullet hit your German half."

I smiled. "I've always considered my right side to be my German half."

Papa chuckled. "Then your Mick side had better learn to duck, 'cause whoever made up that saying is a bald-faced liar."

"Or a fool," I added.

We both laughed for a moment. Real laughter. It felt good.

"Well, it's something you'll be able to tell your children about," Papa said. "Worst I ever got was a load of number seven shot in my thighs."

"You never told me you'd been shot."

"Nothing much to tell," Papa said. A light came up into his eyes and spread over his face like a door opening. "Happened when I was about Billy's age—maybe a year younger. Me and your Uncle Freddy were duck hunting up on Mystic Lake, and there were some pintails out in the middle. I waded out as far as I could—up to my knees—but them ducks were too far out, and they knew it. Freddy was on the other side, and I signaled him to give 'em a scare so I could shoot 'em on the wing." Papa shook his head and chuckled. "Know what that fool uncle of yours did?"

I didn't have a clue.

"That fool leveled his gun in my direction and let fly. I saw the pattern hit the water about fifteen feet in front of me, and then—whammo!—it clipped me just above the knees," he said, raking his hand over his legs. He laughed. "Felt like someone laid a switch across my thighs. Them pellets stung like blazes, let me tell you."

I was amazed. "They penetrate your skin?"

"No. Freddy was too far away to do any real damage." He smiled. "Made a mess of little red spots, though."

"What'd you do to Uncle Freddy?"

"I liked to tear his head off, but what can you do with an idiot dog? You'd just wear your arm out whipping it." Papa laughed again. "He was something, Freddy was—crazy as a loon. Never would've amounted to much as a rancher, though your Bapa Honus did everything in his power to make him one."

Then a shade passed over his face. His eyes grew distant and sullen. "The next year, he and a bunch of other fools went charging off to the war in France," he continued. "They climbed aboard the train in their shiny uniforms, all glory-eyed and bursting with pride—the band playing 'The Stars and Stripes Forever,' and everybody waving flags at them like they'd already won the war."

Papa shook his head in disgust. "Every one of them boys got cut to pieces in one of those idiot trench charges, and that was that." He glanced out the window, took a deep breath, and blew it out dolefully. "Freddy and his friends were buried on some hill in a town in France I can't even pronounce. No band playin' for 'em that time. Nobody waving flags." He grunted. "Your Bapa Honus loved that boy, loved him more than life itself. He was never quite the same after that. The spirit in him just broke and withered away."

I waited a moment for Papa to say something else, but he didn't. "You never told me that about Uncle Freddy."

"Hadn't thought of it until just now."

"I would've liked to known him."

"Yeah," Papa said. "He may have made a lousy rancher, but he sure was a hoot. But I've said enough," he added. "I've yakked more than a truckload of old biddies."

Just then I heard several people walking down the hall toward my room, heard them walking past the door, speaking Spanish fast and excitedly, then continuing on down the hall with their happy chatter. A door opened, and I could hear the Ruiz baby wailing full throttle—he had in his voice the makings of a fine catcher, I thought —and added to his cries were several "Oohs" and "Ahhs" that needed no translation. And then the door was closed, and everything went quiet.

Papa and I looked at each other for a moment, in which his face evinced mild bewilderment, both of us waiting for the Muse of dialogue to descend and deliver us from the awful silence. Something was

276

descending between us, I could feel, looking at the quiet, losing struggle on his face.

Papa wheeled about and began to pace beside the bed, as he did in front of the tractor and other things beyond his ability to fix. "Words were never my strong suit, Tyler," he said clumsily, pausing to look out the window, then turning and making for the sink. "I expect you know that by now."

I smiled at him.

"It's what a man does, not what he says, that matters," he was quick to add. "My pa used to always tell me that. He was a fine man, your Bapa. A fine man."

I agreed.

Papa paced slowly, deliberately, working it out through his feet. "You're the oldest, Tyler. I made all my mistakes on you. I don't expect you'll understand this until you've had kids of your own."

I nodded my head.

He noticed the dripping faucet and turned the handles. The dripping continued. "Last night, as I watched you sleeping, Tyler," he said, frowning at the faucet, then turning, "I got to thinking about the day when you were born. It was so clear in my mind, it was like it happened yesterday."

He drew up at the end of my bed. A smile played with the corners of his mouth. "I remember looking down at you," he said, the smile lingering, "lying in your mother's arms with your face all blotchy and wrinkly and your little eyes squinting up at me, and I remember thinking, *A son! I've got me a son!* Didn't matter that you looked like something the dogs fished out of the creek—I had a son to carry on my name. Someone to go huntin' and fishin' with—to go on rides with, just you and me, talking about the hay, or this cow or that, like a father should with his son. Someone to help me work the ranch—to build something together that would last for generations."

He sighed wistfully upon the scene. "It was a grand day—" Papa broke off to clear his throat, as though he had something stuck there.

I looked away from him and gazed wonderingly at my hands folded over my stomach.

"Yes, yes . . ." he mused, and he resumed his pacing, occasionally glancing over at me to make a point. "When you were a boy and got sick or something, I knew what to do to make you better. When you got out of line, I knew what to do to get you in line. But as you grew older, something changed between us. It was like a gorge had opened up, with you on one side and me on the other, and I couldn't get over to you. I tried—the Lord knows I tried—but I didn't know how to reach you."

"There's something I want to tell you, Pa," I said.

"Let me finish," he said, cutting me off with those pale as August blue eyes of his. "I wanted you to be a rancher 'cause ranching's what I know. It's *all* I know. We'd have a common ground. But the only thing I knew to give you, you had no use for. You were always reading in them books." He looked at me sharply and grunted. "I resented them books, Tyler. I resented them taking you."

He shook his head ruefully. "Last night as I carried you to the truck, thinking I was going to lose you, I said a prayer. Now the Lord and I aren't always on the best of terms, but I knew He was listening—if not for me, then for your mama."

I felt a hot wash of tears brimming over my eyes. "Papa—"

"You and me are different, Ty," he interjected, "different as cattle to horses. But one ain't better than the other, just different."

"You had Billy, Pa."

"I wanted you."

He paused by the window, waited a moment, reflecting. "A man without a dream is a fool," he went on. "But a man who has a dream and doesn't do everything in his power to make it happen—stand or fall—is either a bigger fool or a coward. And I ain't got use for either of 'em. I don't expect the Lord does either. A man has to make his own footprints."

I stared at him dumbfounded, as the meaning of his words began to sink into my thick skull.

"You following me?"

I nodded.

"Good. Then that's that." He smiled at me. "There's no point in fixing something if it ain't broke, is there?"

"No, I suppose not." But that wasn't it, was it? There was more. I could sense it—sense something bright and new, perhaps dangerous—lurking along the periphery of our conversation, waiting to leap.

Ours eyes met for a blink of time, and in that fleeting moment a little light of understanding whirled between us.

Papa reached his hand to me. "Tyler—"

"Yes, Papa?"

I could see the words on his face, the dangerous thing rushing to leap, then pulling up short, as though uncertain of the terrain. Papa's hand wavered on the air a moment, then lowered and settled to his side. And then it was gone. With his lips drawn tightly over his teeth, he slapped his brown fedora back on his head and stood glaring resolutely out the window.

I just saw you, Papa, I thought as I watched him retreat behind some proud and invisible bulwark. *Really saw you.* I'd just caught a glimpse of the elusive soul winging across that transient glimmer, unfettered and wild, before disappearing in a tawny flash. In that moment I felt an enormous surge of love for him, greater than I knew I possessed.

"I love you, Papa," I blurted, before I could call the words back.

He looked at me with a start. His eyes blinked with astonishment as the world, in that glimmer of time, changed upon his face. "Yes . . . well . . . you too, son," he said with a little embarrassed grin. Then his eyes began to glisten, and he looked back out the window.

I shook my head, smiling at his back.

The door opened then, and Mama, Billy, and Trout filed reverently into the room as though to view a corpse. For a moment we all looked at one another a little self-consciously. No one said a word. It was one of those occasions when, for that moment of time, no one knows quite how to behave.

Trout edged to the foot of the bed and blinked wonderingly at me. It seemed I had acquired some mythical stature in his eyes.

Mama looked inquiringly at Papa. Papa nodded his head and fidgeted with his belt loops.

Then Billy broke the awkwardness and laughed. "Look who's the hero now," he said, thrusting a finger at me. "Why, they'll be naming streets after you, Ty. Maybe even a baby or two."

Down the hall, Baby Ruiz suddenly let out a real paint-peeler, as though to affirm the idea.

Billy looked down at the blood spot on my shoulder and shook his head. "If that weren't the craziest thing I ever saw," he added, chuckling. "I sure hope they teach you some sense in that college of yours."

"You hush," Mama scolded him. She bent over me and smiled and lightly touched my cheek with the tips of her fingers. She was overwhelmed with emotion, I could see, for as she smoothed her cool, healing fingers over my cheeks, big silvery tears began to stream from her eyes. "Praise be! Praise be!" she repeated over and again.

"I didn't go to the grange, Mama."

"I know, son. I know."

And looking up into her eyes I knew what she was thinking. *You were right, Mama,* I thought. *You were right.*

279

"How is Jenny?"

Mama nodded and continued smoothing her hand over my cheek. "Kate's with her now." She smiled. Then seeing the look of disappointment wash over my face, she added, "She was here earlier, helping Mrs. McGlenister tend to you. She'll come soon."

Trout, still in awe, edged closer. Then his eyes widened on the bullet sitting on the stand next to my bed. "Keen! Is that the bullet that shot you?"

"The very one."

His eyes fastened on the little lump of lead and brass as though it were a kind of mystic talisman. "Wow! Ain't you lucky!"

"You know there's no such thing as luck, Joseph," Mama corrected him.

"What do you mean?" Trout said, undaunted. "Lookit this keen bullet he's got. Can I take it to school next week and show everybody, Ty? Why, I bet there ain't nobody there ever seen a bullet that's been in two people before!"

"That's enough, Joseph," Mama said.

Holding the bullet to the light, the boy wrinkled his nose. "Hey! How come there ain't any blood on it?"

"*Isn't,*" Mama corrected.

"Huh?"

Mama let it alone.

"Can I take it to school, Tyler?"

"Sure, why not?"

Trout let out a hoot.

And then a marvelous thing happened. It seemed as though the ceiling had suddenly parted to allow a boon of mirth to descend flutteringly upon our bosoms. For several minutes we all laughed, suddenly and unexpectedly—Billy leading the charge with several jokes, shooting one after the other in rapid fire. Papa laughed at the jokes, and Mama laughed, in spite of the off-color nature of some of them, tears spurting from her eyes. And watching them I laughed as well and, feeling the bite of pain in my shoulder and not caring, shrugged it off and laughed the louder.

Aping Billy's success, Trout made bestial noises. He made goofy faces, and everyone ignored him, and suddenly that too was funny. Then suddenly everything was funny. Baby Ruiz wailing down the hall was funny. Trout's faces were funny. The bedpan was funny. Even the bullet was funny (you had to be there). And Billy, like a skilled collie, herded the laughter to a field of hilarious abandon.

Then, once the laughter reached some indescribable zenith, it collapsed achingly in upon itself and rolled down and away in happy tumbles, every one of us wiping his eyes and chuckling in sated wonder. It seemed the laughing fit had cleansed some harbored darkness from our souls.

Every so often Mama would look at Papa in the smoothing aftermath, pick up a few stray giggles like a little girl collecting butterflies, then smile down at me. She'd put her cool hand against my cheek and say, "Praise be! Praise be!" Then there came a knock on the door.

We all turned to look, wondering, still smiling as Josiah Fisk stuck his head inside the room. I heard a tiny rush of wind, Mama's hand stifling it at her mouth.

33

May I have a word with you, Henry," Josiah asked. It wasn't a question, though; it was rhetorical, a statement of intent.

No one said a word in the stunned silence that followed. The happy mood pervading the room turned instantly dark and threatening as everyone blinked fiercely at the intruder.

"I'm busy right now," Papa grunted. "I'll see you later."

"I won't be a minute," Josiah retorted. And not waiting for an objection, he stepped into the room. His eyes going quickly from face to face, he paused to remove his white beaver Stetson and smile civilly at Mama. Then, when he found Papa's unyielding glare, the two men stared at one another for several moments, like two old male wolves suddenly come upon the other. I thought the ceiling was going to close in over us, the tension was so tight in the small room.

Josiah glanced awkwardly at Mama and the boys, making his intentions clear.

Papa continued to glare, the Hochreiter deadliness crawling over his face, hunching the shoulders and thrusting the head forward ever so slightly in the animal wariness I had learned to fear. He looked as mean as I've ever seen him look.

Mama, quick to perceive, put her arms out and gestured to Billy and Trout. "Come along, boys," she said, casting a furtive glance at Josiah Fisk. "What say we go have some breakfast in the cafeteria?"

Josiah nodded curtly at her. "Beulah."

Mama forced a smile.

"I ain't hungry," Trout whined. "I want to stay here. There may be some more shootin'."

Mama took hold of his ear and bridled him to her will.

"*Ouch!* Hey—*ouch*, Mama!"

"You mind me, young man," she scolded, then ushered him out of the room. Their voices trailed down the hall.

Billy paused at the door. "Want me to stay, Pa?" he asked, glowering at Josiah.

"No," Papa said abruptly, both his hands slowly coiling and uncoiling at his side. "We won't be a minute."

Billy cast a menacing look back into the room before closing the door behind him.

"You had something to say?" Papa demanded.

Josiah returned his stare, his back arched proudly. He seemed somehow less imposing in the well-lighted room, less a ghoul of the night, but there was an aura of danger that clung about him, like that of a rattlesnake sunning itself across your path.

"We've known each other for a long time, Henry," the rancher said. "We haven't always seen eye to eye on things."

Papa said nothing.

I could almost hear the buzz of thoughts going back and forth between them.

"I've always thought well of you," Josiah went on. "Even respected you, though your methods were different than mine."

Papa's eyes narrowed on the man. "I expect there's a point to this," he said.

Josiah regarded his face a moment and chuckled. "You never were long on social amenities, were you, Henry?"

"I ain't feeling too sociable right now, Josiah. If you've come in here to just pass the morning, I'd prefer the company of my wife and boys."

Josiah shook his head and grunted. Then he looked down at me, ignoring Papa. He gazed at my face for several seconds, then his eyes strayed to the spot of blood on my shoulder before returning to my face. His eyes narrowed.

"Hello, son."

I nodded. His eyes were a menacing glimmer of gray blue beneath the heavy beetling brows, I noticed. Until now I'd thought them black, and I realized that I'd never been this close to the man before. I glanced quickly at Papa.

He was staring intently at Josiah Fisk—the dominant wolf watching the other dominant wolf appraising his cub, a low growl rattling in his throat.

"I heard what you did to my boys," Josiah said. Then he grunted amusedly. "I just want you to know that they deserved whatever whoopin' they got from you. Booster said you got a mighty quick left hook. Never saw it coming, he said. Said it kicked like a mule."

Then the man's face seemed to shade over with a menacing thought. "They're gonna fetch plenty more when I get home," he sneered. "You can bet on it. Neither one of them boys are worth the powder to blow 'em to the devil."

He cleared his throat and seemed to collect himself. A spark of sentiment glinted in the corners of his thick, leathery mouth.

"But Nate—well, he's his mama's favorite, isn't he? Him being the baby and all. She wouldn't take it too well if he got himself hanged or shot to death."

Then a change came over his demeanor. He looked suddenly haggard and wan, his shoulders slumping forward as if the effort to hold them erect was abruptly irrelevant. His hands hung, forgotten, at his sides, the fingers taut and bony as they clutched the brim of his hat. And then I noticed that his dark woolen coat and trousers were rumpled as though having been slept in.

"Doc Turner says he's going to live," he said, the truculence going out of his eyes as he gazed thoughtfully at his hat. He blew out a sigh. "Said if the bullet had struck an inch to the left, then it would have penetrated his heart, and—"

He clutched his face suddenly and wrung it several times with his hand. He looked up at the ceiling, shook his head remorsefully, and cursed. He cursed again, then he looked down at me, his eyes glistening, and gently patted my right shoulder with the tips of his fingers. "I'm much obliged to you, son," he said with a gravelly voice. "Much obliged."

I just nodded my head and smiled. "Thank God."

"Yes, thank God." Josiah returned my smile, then looked over at Papa.

A change had come over Papa too, it seemed. His arms hung loosely at his sides now, and his thumbs crept curiously to his pockets. The wariness, however, lingered in his eyes.

"I heard about your daughter, Henry," Josiah said sadly. He peered into the crown of his hat, as though there were words in there he might borrow. "I'm sorry to hear about that, real sorry. She's a good girl. I hope she'll be all right."

"No, she's not going to be all right," Papa said with an edge. "She's going to have your son's baby. That's something won't never be all right."

Josiah pulled out a handkerchief and blew his nose. "Yes, I know," he said. "Walter told me this morning. I swear I don't understand this generation of young'uns."

Papa waited, then the color rose into his neck and ears. "That's it?" he snarled. "That's all you got to say?"

Josiah folded the handkerchief back into his coat pocket. "What do you want me to say, Henry?" he said calmly. "That I failed my son? That you failed your daughter? A lot of failure will follow me to the grave, and when I stand before almighty God I'll take my due." He grunted contemptuously. "I expect you will too. We're both sons of the devil, Henry—done our fair share of crimes against the soul. Got 'em plenty black by now, so don't act so high and mighty. That may work for you and the preacher on Sundays, but not with me it don't. I ain't got the stomach for it."

Papa reeled a bit, I could see, from Josiah's words. His body seemed to stage a revolution. The color leaped from his neck to his face. His glare was as sharp as case-hardened steel. For a moment I thought he might leap across the bed at the man, but whatever fight was in him just withered, like yesterday with Billy. His eyes lowered to the floor.

Josiah put on his Stetson and turned to leave, then he halted by the door. "Oh, there's just one more thing, Henry."

He reached into his vest pocket and pulled out a sheaf of papers. Then he tore it in two. "The beef contract," he said, tossing the papers into the trash receptacle beside the bed. "Wasn't much of a deal, it turns out. I imagine we can work things out, Henry, don't you? No point in starting a range war."

Papa looked up at the man, astonished. "No, I don't see any profit in it."

Josiah turned, and, when he had closed the door quietly behind him, Papa sat down on the edge of the bed and stared out the window, his head bending to some unseen weight.

I looked at him for a while, gazed upon the rugged profile of a man, my father, who for the better part of my life had stood larger than life—like an Olympian god at times—against a backdrop of lesser men, those who were the clay-footed mortals, the once faint and timorous shadows who had for so many years groveled at his feet. But "how are the mighty fallen," to tread upon the earth of fallen men.

I love you, Papa.

And outside the framing light, a gentle snow began to fall.

34

The months that followed redefined in me the nature of the natural order. The turning of the seasons meant nothing to me now. The sun and the moon were irrelevant orbs in the sky as dividers of night from day, the latter being separated now by increments of intense study and exhaustion. I had become an initiate of a sacred order, where the watchful eye no longer gazed upon the stars in their courses for inspiration or to guide one's industry, but turned instead from these to adore a more glorious luminary.

Knowledge.

During those months away from home, I had come to believe that the universe and its mysteries lay hidden in dusty wooden halls, filled with old books, only to be revealed by the lofty intonations of men with translucent skin, men whose bodies seemed adjunct appendages to their huge brains, who reigned like despots over a society of pie-eyed sponges.

College was everything I had imagined it to be. For three wondrous months I ambled over the campus in a perpetual awe of red brick and ivy. It was a hallowed place, where the trichotomy of mind and body and soul were sanctioned and nourished. Indeed, I had chanced upon a cloister for the scholar, a haunt for kindred spirits, and a highway for the beggars of truth and understanding, several of whom met religiously every Friday and Saturday night in a little dive called Freddy's on the South Shore to discuss theology, American literature, and the war in Europe, over flat sodas and greasy hamburgers.

I had found my place in the sun.

But it was Christmas break now, time to go home and enjoy the holidays, to put the toil of books aside, to rest from the dizzying pursuit of the Holy Grail. I smiled in wistful reverie, then took a deep breath and blew out a sigh. The window of the Pullman car fogged, then gradually cleared, revealing the great and marvelous touch of God's fingers.

The horizon, now a broken array of tabled buttes and hills, dark and powerful against the lowering sky, fell slowly behind me to extend—forever, it seemed—across a vast and rolling prairie newly blanketed in snow. The thin gray line of dawn was just creeping in beneath the dark clouds in the east. I could see it now and then, off to my right, as the train bent north, the heralding light suffusing the distant brow with a blush of magenta, then spreading a ruddy ruggedness out over the rising shoulders of Montana. Fierce northerly winds drove over the rushing bleak surfaces, leaving great billowing drifts and myriad points of grain poking through the snow, giving the terrain the appearance of a massive, unshaven face.

Small gray towns and gray ranches sprang up like seeming afterthoughts over the barren whiteness, showing the speed of the train as they rushed by. They were encircled by ranks of dark, leafless trees, rattling buttresses against the shrilling winds that evoked in me a terrific loneliness. Woolly cattle and horses stood in motionless huddles along snow-mounded fences and windbreaks of shrubs and old broken buildings, their breath showing briefly in trailing white clouds.

The train pulled into Billings. Only Laurel and Park City remained, and then on to Columbus. An hour to go maybe. Some people disembarked, others climbed aboard and found seats in front of and behind me. Then the train pulled out of the station.

The clackety-clack of the steel wheels clapped a rhythmic cadence . . . *da-dun, da-dun* . . . *da-dun, da-dun* . . . and quickly lulled me into a doze, and I laid my head against the window. It was cold, too cold, and I pulled away and adjusted my body to a more comfortable position.

I felt a tinge of old pain in my shoulder, remembered leaving home with my left arm in a sling and everyone at the station sending me off: Papa standing there with his hands in his pockets, his hat cocked to one side, a smile on his face; Mama's arms folded across her chest, dabbing the corners of her eyes with a handkerchief; Billy and Trout trading punches; Kate blowing kisses up at me and reminding me to write as she followed my window to the edge of the platform. In time the color faded from their faces, and I was left with only vague hues of sepia. I was too tired to remember anything more—my brain hurt, it was so packed with knowledge—so I let their faces go with a happy sigh and tried to get some sleep.

Failing at this, I opened the first of two letters and reread it in the pre-dawn light for the hundredth time.

Dear Tyler,

How are you doing? We're all fine here at the ranch. Jenny's doing well. I know you've been asking about her. She reads your letters on the porch swing for hours on end and prays for you at supper. The Fisk boy's been over to the house once since he got out of the hospital. It didn't go well. Jenny doesn't want to see him, so Sammy ran him off. Just as well. I don't trust that boy. Sammy spends much of his time doting on her like a puppy. I think he likes her. He's a good hand. The tractor's never run better. Wait till you see the new barn. We got it up right before the big snows hit. Nils is proud.

Billy got the imperial three weeks back. It was a good hunt. Wish you could've been there. Billy's a fine shot with that bolt-action of his, took the elk on the move. A fine shot. Mama thinks we need to have the rifle surgically removed from his hands. Floyd Ackerman did a great job with the head. Wait till you see it.

Izzy and his dogs got onto Old Lucifer, but he gave them the slip again. That old lion is a sly one. Izzy swore up a storm, a real doozy of a storm. It snowed for two solid weeks afterward.

I looked out the window and smiled, watched the Yellowstone River curl into view in the distance, a dark gray streak dully mirroring the now tarnished gray overcast as it undulated through the terrain. Then it rushed alongside the tracks and dogged us for a while, flickering through stands of big cottonwoods, birches, and aspens before it fell glinting away behind some low wind-scorched hills. I glanced down at the letter and picked up where I left off.

Hope everything is going well for you up there at school, son. We hear you're on the Dean's List. Is that good or bad? Mama says it's good. Charley says it's good too, but Enos says it's like getting called on the carpet by your commanding officer. I swear, those two will argue before the throne of God.

By the way, did you call on Phil Hazlett at the stockyards like I asked you to? Beef prices are going up because of this stupid war in Europe. Billy says we're going to get into it sooner or later. He's even talked about enlisting in the Air Corps. Got a sudden interest in defying the laws of gravity. I'd appreciate it if you'd talk to him when you get home.

Got to go. Mama's hollering at me from the kitchen. I think one of the pigs got into the house. It'll make a nice Christmas dinner, you can bet.

Love, Papa

P.S. Kate tells me to send you her love every time I see her. She's a peach.

The second letter had arrived the next day. However, the post-mark showed that it had been mailed two weeks after the first one. I opened it, glanced at the salutation that read "Dear Tyler . . . Some bad news . . ." then I folded the letter and held onto it as I gazed out the window. Everything went misty for a moment, and I wiped my eyes. *Some bad news.* Always with the good comes a little bad, it seems. The proverbial fly in the ointment.

I stared out at nothing for a long time, then watched as the breaking sun knifed quickly over the snowy plain to strike along the purpled buttes in the north, then, moments later, cutting them in half with shards of golden light.

"Penny for your thoughts?" a voice said.

Startled, I looked up, and there was a woman standing in the aisle smiling down at me. She must have just boarded at Billings because I hadn't noticed her before. I smiled politely and started to turn away, thinking she had spoken to someone else.

"Beautiful, isn't it?"

"Beautiful?"

"The countryside, of course."

I looked back out the window. "Uh . . . yeah. It sure is." I shrugged embarrassedly. "I'm sorry, my mind was in another world."

"I can see," the woman said. She stifled a yawn. "Thought I might give my legs a stretch. Hate being cooped up, don't you?"

"Yeah," I agreed, just to agree.

Then the woman, instead of giving her legs a stretch, leaned against the seat in front of me and gazed outside.

Well, all right, I thought, *the conversation's over.* I smiled at her politely, then glanced out the window, hoping she'd take the hint. She didn't. She continued to stare outside as if I weren't even there. I was suddenly in one of those awkward "now what?" situations. I thought I might excuse myself to the rest room.

It was then that I noticed something familiar about her face. I studied her more carefully out of the corner of my eye, but I couldn't put my finger on it. She looked to be in her late thirties, early forties, but I could never tell with women. Her features were a bit hard, particularly around the eyes (which were dark brown) and at the corners of her mouth, which was a no-nonsense, businesslike affair that dominated the square lines of her jaw. She had long, mousy blonde hair, worn in the current bangs and curls fashion, that helped to soften the lines of her face. She was certainly well dressed and pleasant-looking —one might even say attractive.

289

What is it about her face? I thought, perusing it, drawn into those dark brown eyes that were strangely haunting. *I've seen her before.*

"I just love the dawn, don't you?" she said finally. "The world's so new and fresh—with the breath of God on everything." She shook her head with a sigh. "Every day's a promise of new life and hope, my daddy used to tell me when I was a little girl. 'A gift just waitin' for His children to open.'"

"He sounds like a wise man."

She smiled at me. "You come all the way from Chicago?"

"That's right."

"Chicago's a fine town," she said. "Lots of things to do and see in Chicago." She glanced at the letter in my hand. "From your girl-friend? Saw you readin' it."

I put the letter into my pocket. "No, from home."

"Where's home?" Then she caught herself and chuckled. "I don't mean to pry, you understand. Just making conversation."

"That's fine," I said, resigned to the fact that she was determined to talk my ear off. "I'm from Columbus."

"Is that right? It's a small world. So am I. Just picked up the girls in Billings last night, and we're headed back."

"The girls?"

"Hazel and Suzy there," she said, gesturing down the car.

I looked back, purely a reflexive action, but the only girls I saw were sitting two rows back, across the aisle, and looked to be in their twenties. The one on the aisle was heavyset, but she had a pretty face, which she was tending to in a small mirror. The other one looked foreign, perhaps Oriental. I nodded at them. The heavyset one glanced at me quickly, then looked back in her mirror and touched a curl into place at her temple. The Oriental girl stared impassively at her hands.

I looked up at the woman, and she read the confusion on my face.

"Aw, don't mind them two," she said, waving them off. "They ain't much on personality until you get to know 'em. They've just fallen on hard times. Billings is a rough town."

I nodded, even more confused.

"I run a boarding house for young women outside Columbus," the woman continued, "so I thought I'd let them stay with me for a while—you know, till they can get a new start." She pulled out a pack of Chesterfields from her coat pocket, tamped the end of a cigarette against her thumbnail, then put it in her mouth. She felt in the pocket for matches. Not finding them, she cursed under her breath.

Suddenly it hit me where I'd seen her. *The lady in the Columbus train station, three and a half months ago.*

She looked imploringly at me.

"Sorry, don't smoke," I said, shrugging.

A man and a woman were seated across the aisle from me, the woman sleeping, the man reading a newspaper in the gray light that filtered in through the window. He glanced up from the paper at the woman talking with me; and when he had taken note of her face, his eyes went wide, then he quickly retreated behind his paper.

The woman found her matches in her breast pocket, lit her cigarette, and blew a cloud of smoke at the ceiling of the Pullman, shaking the match. "By the way, my name is Abigail Spenser," she said, tossing the match to the floor and stretching out her hand.

I took it politely and gave it a shake. She certainly was an affable soul. "Pleased to meet you."

She picked some bits of tobacco off the end of her tongue. "My friends just call me Miss Abbey," she said with a big smile. "I don't believe I caught your name?"

Now *my* eyes went wide. "Miss Abbey—"

"Don't tell me we got the same name." She chuckled.

Suddenly I felt a strange prickling sensation in my ears—"No . . . uh . . . my name's Hochreiter—Tyler Hochreiter"—wishing I could retreat behind something.

"Hochreiter . . . Hochreiter . . ." she mused, wriggling her nose as she tried to place the name. At length she said, "No, doesn't ring a bell."

Thank God.

"Don't expect you've been by the house, then?" she asked, taking a drag.

I gulped. "House?" I flushed. "Uh . . . no, ma'am."

"'Course you ain't." She giggled. "What takes you so far from home, a handsome fellow like yourself?"

I felt myself flush beet red. "Er . . . college."

"College?"

"Chicago Divinity School. I'm studying to be a minister," I was quick to add.

Her face went blank. She seemed taken aback. "Really? A minister. Ain't that somethin'?" she said, studying me. "So you're a minister."

"Not yet. I'm still in school."

She stared at me until I had to avert my eyes.

"My father was a minister, you know."

"How about that."

"A fine one too. Dyed-in-the-wool Southern Baptist. Made sure I made the confession when I turned six, then gave me a good dunkin' in the nearest crick." She whistled, trailing a ribbon of smoke through the air with her hand. "I'm goin' to glory!"

She chuckled, then shook her head in fond reverie. "Yes, sir, when I was a little girl he used to tell me a Bible story every night before I went to bed." Then she broke it off with a shrug. She wouldn't look at me right away. "He was a fine minister, all right," she said, blowing out a sigh. "God rest his soul."

"He—he passed away?" I asked a little awkwardly. "I'm sorry—"

"It's all right," she said with another shrug. "He died a few years back." Then her expression changed to a scowl of contempt. "Got stabbed to death by a drunken Indian, down in Lodge Grass."

That hooked me. "Lodge Grass?"

"Yeah, crummy little town on the Crow reservation. You heard of it?"

"Yes, I've heard of it." *It certainly is a small world,* I mused, wondering if it was Sammy Two Feather's father who had killed him.

She looked out the window and smoked her cigarette.

"You got family or anything?" I asked.

The woman blew a wreath of smoke into the air, then glanced at me through it with her haunting brown eyes. "Yeah, I got family. The state's got my mama up in Warm Springs—gave her a padded cell. She went crazy after my daddy died—started walking around town, grabbin' folks by their lapels and telling them she was Eleanor Roosevelt." She grunted. "And Jimmy—that was my little brother—thought he'd join up with the merchant marines and see the world. His ship got torpedoed by a German U-boat last July—went down somewhere in the North Atlantic." She chuckled sardonically. "Life's a peach, ain't it?"

I had nothing to say. They didn't teach me how to handle anything like this in Bible college.

She finished smoking her cigarette, then she stubbed it out on the floor with her shoe. And then the dark look passed from her eyes as suddenly as it had arrived. She tilted her head and looked at me as though I were a puppy. "A minister, huh? Ain't that somethin'?"

"Not for a few years." I shrugged, wishing I could just crawl into a hole.

The woman brightened. Then whatever it was she let pass, I could see. She lowered her eyes and studied her fingers a little while, as they worked the frayed ends of the seat covering in front of me. She chuckled. "I was just thinking that maybe you might—" She broke off.

"What?"

"I thought you might come by the house sometime and preach us a sermon."

"P-preach you—" I had to clear my throat. "Preach you a sermon?"

"Just say a few words maybe—nothin' elaborate or anything," she said, smoothing the frayed ends down with her hand. "I'm sure the girls would appreciate it, bein' it's Christmas and all." She looked at me out of the corners of her eyes. "We don't get out to church much."

"Uh . . ." I felt that strange prickling in my ears again. "I . . . uh . . ."

I saw the disappointment cross her face as clearly as a drawn shade.

"That's all right," she said, chuckling, trying to hide it, I thought. "I understand. I'm truly pleased to have made your acquaintance, though, Tyler Hochreiter. I'm sure you'll make a fine minister some day. Just you stay out of trouble—stay away from them Indian reservations." She smiled and turned to leave.

I caught her hand as she started past me. "Wait—Miss Abbey!" I said earnestly, then quietly, "Wait . . . please."

She glanced down at her hand.

I let it go. "It's not what you think," I said, fumbling for the words. "It's . . ."

"It doesn't matter." She smiled. "Don't trouble yourself. Really. I was being presumptuous." She chuckled again. "It's a flaw in my character."

"That's not it at all," I said, frustrated. "It's just that I'm not qualified to preach. I haven't studied sermon prep yet—not until my junior year."

She looked at me for a moment, then she threw her head back and laughed.

The man across the aisle peered over his paper at us.

"What's so funny?" I asked.

"Shoot, if that's all that's troubling you—" Miss Abbey continued to laugh "—who'd give a hoot? Why, half the girls at the place don't even speak English and wouldn't know a sermon from a horse auction. And the other half . . ." She paused, allowing her laughter to subside. Then she looked intently into my eyes. "The other half wouldn't care how well you preached. Just you bein' there would mean a lot to them. Ain't nobody gonna find fault." She smiled big. "'Sides it'd give you some practice."

I considered her words. "I'd likely be pretty awful."

"Probably."

I grinned at her. "It *would* give me some practice, wouldn't it?"

"Then you'll come?"

Looking into her face I could see the ghosts of pain, of anger, of shame, darting in and out from behind the smiling edges of her eyes, pulling at the corners of her mouth. I regarded her face a moment, felt the weight of her pain, and I thought my heart might break in two.

"I'd like to," I said, meaning it. "If you'll have me, I'd like to come very much."

She reached a tentative hand toward my face, then pulled it back and folded it in the other. "Thank you." She smiled. Then her eyes suddenly suffused with tears, and she shook her head. "A minister. Won't that be special for Christmas? I'll bet your mama's proud."

We arranged the date that I should come, then Abigail Spenser, minister's daughter, house madam, walked back to her seat opposite the other two girls, sat down, and gazed out the window.

For the longest time I sat in a daze, feeling a mixture of numbness and excitement.

I glanced out at the Yellowstone. Its broad back gleamed in the sun as it writhed sluggishly alongside the tracks like a reptile late for its winter sleep. And the rushing-by trees, flickering past the windows at regular intervals, gave the effect of a crude kinetoscope at work. But I saw none of its show, for in my mind I had begun to compose a sermon. It would be a simple one, one without eloquence or freight of books—a story, really.

I paused, suddenly reminded of Sy. "It is good to let your stories out," the aged Crow once said to me, his keen wet eyes glistening in the starlight, for "they are too heavy if you keep them inside."

I chuckled quietly, allowing my thoughts to drift along the stony banks of the Stillwater. *Yes, they are heavy,* I mused. *Too heavy.* And so, thinking what I might say to a house full of . . . well . . . prostitutes, I loosed the weight of a story downstream on a little chip of wood, one that told of a baby Boy who, many years ago, had come from heaven to walk among sinners and to teach them the way of mercy.

"*Ichik, Ichik,* it is good story," I heard Sy's voice echoing through my mind.

"Yes, it is," I agreed.

35

The train whistled to a stop alongside the station platform. It heaved and huffed like a monstrous steel beast, with great blasts of steam hissing furiously through its grating teeth.

"All aboard for Big Timber, Livingston, and Bozeman," the conductor cried. And a charge of excitement raced through me as I made for the door.

Every town has its own smell, a signature fragrance that identifies it from every other town—just as every woman possesses her own unique scent. As I stepped off the train, I took a deep breath of Columbus, my home. It smelled good and clean and invigorated my travel-weary bones. Home, sweet home, as they say.

Then glancing quickly about the small gathering of people who were stepping off and on the train, I saw Billy waiting for me by the station house. He was alone.

"Hey, Tyler!" He laughed. "If you don't look a sorry sight!"

"Yeah, good to see you too, Billy."

"Here, let me help you with one of them bags," he said, reaching for the smaller one. "Hey! What do you got in here—bricks?"

"Books."

"Books? Ain't you tired of studyin'?"

"Where's the family?" I asked, looking up and down the platform. I suddenly felt let down.

"At the house," Billy said, leading the way toward the truck. "Mama's fixing you a big supper. Papa was on the phone with Jim Skeller when I left."

"Any trouble?"

"No. Some rancher out of Meteetsee wants to sell him a string of stock horses."

I gave the station one last look. "You seen Kate?"

"No. Should I have?" he asked with a wry smile.

"She said she'd meet me at the station," I said, ignoring him.

Miss Abbey and the two girls walked past us. "Don't forget our little date," she said, smiling brightly.

I returned her smile. "Next Saturday night—seven o'clock."

"It'll be wonderful!"

"I just hope you won't be disappointed."

"You'll do just fine."

Billy stared incredulously as the three women walked away and descended the platform. I thought his jaw might hit the floorboards. "What—" He looked at me, blinked, then back at them, blinked some more, then looked back at me. "Why, that's—"

I grinned, cutting him off. "You're going to hurt yourself, wagging your head like that."

"Huh?"

I chuckled. "You wouldn't understand." Then I stepped off the platform.

"I guess not," Billy said, scratching his head. "Hey!" he called after me. "What do they teach you in that Bible college anyway?"

We waited until the train pulled away from the station, crossed the street to where the pickup was parked, then threw the bags in the back.

Billy looked at me across the bed; I could see it in his eyes. "I guess you heard?"

"Yeah. Papa wrote me."

"His heart just gave out, Doc Turner said. No other reason than old age."

"Wish I could've made it home for the service."

"Everybody was there," Billy said. "Half the Crow nation showed up wearing war bonnets and beads. Everybody singing and chanting, beating drums and such. It was something. Gave old Sy a proper send-off."

"That's good."

"It was kind of sad, though," he said. "Nobody knew what year he was born to put on the stone. Not even Jimbo."

"Papa said you and Jimbo found him by the river?"

"Yeah, a little place downstream where there's a break in the river. Found him on one of them little islands, dressed to the nines in his buckskins and headdress. He was sitting with his back against a big willow, staring out across the river at the hills. Strangest thing you ever saw."

"Big Medicine," I said.

Billy looked at me, surprised. "Yeah, that's the place. That's what Jimbo called it too. How'd you know? You been there?"

"Yes, I've been there. Sy took me from time to time."

"He did? He never took me."

I looked at him and smiled. "I guess you didn't need to go."

We climbed into the truck, Billy pressed the starter and put it in gear.

Sycamore Stands Tall has fallen, I thought as we drove away from the station. Then I thought of the words Sy had once told me were spoken to the departing Crow soul—the *ira'axe.* "You are gone, do not turn back, we wish to you farewell."

I gazed out the window, thinking of him standing outside the stables, wavering slowly in the wind, waiting for the great blue heron to come and take his soul away. *I will miss you, my friend,* I thought, glancing up at the sun poking through the overcast. *Farewell.*

I told Billy to stop off at Johansson's. There was something there that I needed to collect. We drove up, and the little bell sounded at the gas pump. A moment later Took galloped out of the store, wearing a red, black, and orange mackinaw jacket and a fleece-lined cap with a bent bill and one of the flaps standing away from his ear.

"Hey, Billy," he said, grabbing hold of the window. "Want me to fill 'er up?"

"No, thanks, Took," Billy said. "Tyler's just here to pick something up."

The boy looked past Billy's face at me and stared for a few moments.

"Hey, Took," I grinned. "Remember me?"

Took frowned at me, then loped back into the store.

"I guess not." I shrugged. "No need for you to come in. I won't be a minute."

"Sure enough." Billy pinched a lipful of snuff between his lower teeth and gum, then picked up an aviator magazine and began to leaf through the pages, until he found a section showing aerial photographs from the Battle of Britain. "Papa wants me to talk to you about that," I said. "Thinks you're nuts with your sudden interest in flying."

Billy laughed. "I expect he would. Pa doesn't understand anything that either don't make hay or eat it."

"Well, if he asks, tell him I talked to you."

"What do you think, Ty? You think I'm nuts too?"

I grinned. "You know better'n to ask me that."

"Yeah, well, you can think I'm nuts all you want, but like it or not, we're gonna get into this thing over in Europe before too long, and when we do I don't fancy dragging my tail around in some mud hole like Uncle Freddy did."

"You're still nuts."

"Ah, go on."

I shook my head and climbed out.

The war was all anyone was talking about these days it seemed: Hitler, Mussolini, the imperialist Japanese army ravaging China. How might the violent aggression of madmen, thousands of miles away, affect the simple way of life here along the foothills of the Beartooths? To most of the ranchers, who cared only for the price of beef, the size of the trout in the Stillwater, and the elk on the mountains, Europe was as far away as Pluto.

I gave pause to Billy's dark prophecy. Would we be in it before long? American boys fighting and dying on faraway soil? If so, what part would I play? If any. I didn't want to think about it now. It was Christmas.

Charley and Enos looked up from their game of checkers as I entered the store. Nils had the place fixed up nice and Christmasy. Decorations everywhere and a little tree in the window. It made me feel good and warm inside.

"Well, if it isn't Tyler Hochreiter," Charley whistled. "Back from college already. Bet your head's just full of the smarts now."

"It smarts all right." I chuckled. "Don't think I can cram anything more in it."

Enos slung a dollop of tobacco juice into the can at his feet. "They take you off that list you was on?" he wondered. "What you do, anyway? Get into a scrap with them lightning fists of yours I hear tell about?" Enos chortled.

Charley shot the little man a scowl. "Ignore him, Tyler," he said. "It's good to see you." Then he narrowed his eyes on Enos. "Any more outta you, and I'll stuff you in that spittoon of yours. Now make your move."

"I just did."

"Where?"

Enos pointed at his checker with an impish grin. "There."

Charley studied the little wooden piece with a bewildered look on his face, and then he began to pull on his lower lip. Suddenly his eyes went wide. "Wait a minute! You can't move there. Your piece was over here," he said, picking up the checker and slapping it where it had been. Suddenly a light went on in his head. He glared at Enos. "You're trying to cheat me!"

Enos smiled broadly. "And getting away with it for over twenty years." He looked at me and winked big.

Charley was incensed and shook his big fist in Enos's face. "Why, I ought to break your scrawny little neck."

"Come on, Charley," Enos said, putting up his hands in a conciliatory gesture. "Here—" He quickly reset the board. "I'll let you win one now."

A low growl rattled in Charley's throat.

"All right, all right! I'll let you win two, then."

Leaving those two to their business, I looked over at Stu Dunnegan, who until now had been buried behind headlines that read: "British Launch Counteroffensive in Egypt."

He glanced over the edge of the newspaper and nodded at me. "Good to see you, son," he said, his eyes straying to the rebellion of hair that had gathered over my ears.

"Good to be back," I said. "Home, sweet home."

Stu chuckled as he returned to his paper.

Just then Nils came out of the storeroom, followed by Took, who was pointing at me. "Well, who haff we here?" Nils beamed.

"Hey, Nils." I walked over to the counter and shook his hand. "I hear you built us quite a barn."

"Hoo! Hoo! Hoo! You ain't never seen such a barn!" the big Swede boomed. "Just let me tell you about that barn." Which he proceeded to do over the next several minutes.

While he talked, I listened politely, but at the same time my eyes ferreted surreptitiously about the knives and fishing reels, over the flies and around the handguns, then on into the wristwatches and jewelry. *Where was it?* I wondered. Panic seized my chest. *Somebody's bought it already.* My heart sank.

And then I saw it, a tiny glimmer of light partially obscured by the box of a silver brooch, peeking out of a burgundy box. I stared at it for a moment, until a big thumb and forefinger took hold of the box and removed it from the case.

"This what you're looking for?" Nils smiled, holding it before me.

"Yes," I said, a little embarrassed.

Nils set a black velvet mat on the glass counter, then removed the thin gold ring from the small box and set it in the center of the black mat. The diamond, clutched by tiny gold prongs, seemed smaller than I remembered it. I scrunched my nose at it and raised an eyebrow.

"That's a full quarter of a carat." Nils beamed proudly.

"A quarter carat, huh? Is that big?"

"Is that big?" Nils grunted at such a thought. "Why, you could build a barn on that stone!"

And then as I continued to gaze upon the diamond, a marvelous thing happened. Suddenly the little stone seemed to come alive and pull the very light from the room, harnessing its magical properties, then beginning to glow like a chip off some asteroid that was hurling a fiery blaze across the jet of night.

I gaped at it in awe. My fingertips brushed tentatively over the texture of the velvet.

"Can I pick it up?"

"Sure," Nils said. "Give it a spin, as they say in Detroit." He chuckled at his American humor.

I held the ring before my eyes and twirled it back and forth, gazed dumbstruck as radiant beams of color shot out through its tiny facets, and flickered in a reach of light. "She sure is a beaut!" I admitted.

Took leaned around his father and watched the tiny jewel blaze at my fingertips. His pale blue eyes widened behind their thick lenses. He chuckled as his trembling fingers reached out to touch it, and I saw a shiver of excitement go through him.

"How much?" I asked Nils.

"That little dandy? Hmm, let me see." He picked up the velvet box and looked at the bottom. A broad smile stretched across his face. "It's only forty-five dollars."

"Forty-five—" The glow snuffed out of the ring as quickly as if the tiny chip of light had plunged into a black ocean. "Yes, it's very nice," I said, placing it back in the velvet box.

Nils frowned. "Wait a minute," he said, lowering his spectacles off his forehead. He lifted the small box and reread the price on the bottom. "Hoo! Hoo! Did I say forty-five dollars? I meant to say fifteen."

I brightened. "Fifteen! Really? Let me see!"

Nils snatched the box away before I could read the price. "What? You don't believe me?"

"Uh . . . sure I believe you."

"You got fifteen dollars?"

"Yes, yes, I got fifteen dollars," I said. "I think—" I dug out a crumpled wad of bills from my pocket and placed it on the counter. A nickel and two pennies rolled over the surface, and I quickly flattened them with my palm and raked them to one side. Then I extricated the bills from the wad and made a stack of ones and fives. I made a careful count, laying the bills neatly in front of Nils. ". . . Thirteen, fourteen, fifteen—"

"Good, good!" Nils cried, gathering them up.

"Wait, I got one more."

"No, no," the big Swede said, waving off my last dollar. "You keep it and take your girl out on the town tonight."

Stu Dunnegan looked up from his paper and shook his head.

Just then the little bell rang over the door. Suddenly my heart leaped in my breast, for I knew who it was—instinctively I knew. I turned, and there she was, all bright and radiant in a pretty coat and dress I hadn't seen before, looking more beautiful than I had ever seen her look, with the morning sun showing the reds and golds through her thick auburn hair like a fiery coronet, and she was wearing a smile that could melt winter.

"It's Tuesday," Kate said, smiling at me with those pretty hazel eyes, and her white teeth flashing. "I have the day off."

"S-so you have," I stuttered. A lump swelled in my throat the size of a baseball, as a faint scent of wild strawberries drifted in on the morning breeze and curled about my face.

And when Kate stepped toward me, smiling as the little bell rang off behind her, I was reminded once again that the storm had passed, that it had gone through me with its fury, done its worst, only to trail a faint rumbling of thunder in its wake, the thunder echoing back off the bluffs along the Stillwater a single word. Mercy . . . mercy . . . *mercy* . . .